Disinheritance

MARY KINGSWOOD

SUTORS PUBLISHING

Published by Sutors Publishing

V2

ISBN: 978-1-912167-56-2 (paperback)

Cover design by: Shayne Rutherford of Darkmoon Graphics

Author's note:

this book is written using historic British terminology, so *saloon* instead of *salon*, *chaperon* instead of *chaperone* and so on. I follow Jane Austen's example and refer to a group of sisters as the Miss Wintertons.

Contents

About the series

One man with a secret. A family torn apart by the consequences.

Walter Atherton, Viscount Birtwell, has drifted through his charmed life without a care in the world. As the eldest son and heir to an earl, he has never had to make his way in the world. His days are filled with pleasure, and to set the seal on it, he will shortly be married to a vastly wealthy heiress. His future is set fair for happiness. But the brutal murder of the family chaplain reveals a dreadful secret, and Walter finds his whole future upended. What on earth is he to do now?

Miss Winifred Strong fell in love with Walter years ago - how could she resist his careless charm? But the daughter of a mere baronet is no fitting wife for a future earl. When the disaster strikes and Walter is suddenly cast down in society's eyes, Winnie allows herself just a sliver of hope. Surely now her old friend will turn to her for comfort... and love? Or must she remain a spinster forever? But a trip to London brings her an unexpected way out of her dilemma — if she has the courage to take it.

This is a complete story with a happy ever after. A traditional Regency romance, drawing room rather than bedroom. Book 1 of a 6 book series.

Isn't that what-his-name? Occasionally characters from an earlier series pop up, or are mentioned. Lady Esther Franklyn's father, the Duke of Camberley, approved the marriage of his daughter, the Lady Grace Bucknell, to George Skelton, the Earl of Brackenwood's heir, in *The Governess.* Lady Esther's brother, the Marquess of Ramsey, had a tumultuous romance in *The Betrothed*. Lady Harbottle, in *The Widow*, and the Duchess of Orrisdale, in *The Duke,* were also Bucknells before their marriages.

About the series*:*

Book 0: The Chaplain: a man adrift, dreaming of a home *(a novella, free to mailing list subscribers).*

Book 1: Disinheritance: a man freed, looking for a new purpose in life

Book 2: Determination: a man pursued, forced to outwit his adversary

Book 3: Anger: a woman alone, trying to choose a different path in life

Book 4: Secrecy: a woman neglected, scheming to secure her own happiness

Book 5: Loyalty: a man of dreams, torn between the past and the future

Book 6: Ambition: a woman thwarted, unswervingly set on making a brilliant debut in society

Want to be the first to hear about new releases? Sign up for my mailing list at https://marykingswood.co.uk.

Principal Characters

The Atherton family of Corland Castle, North Riding of Yorkshire:

Charles, 11th Earl of Rennington (55)

Caroline, Countess of Rennington (50)

Their children:

Walter, Viscount Birtwell (29)

Mr Eustace Atherton (27), living on his own estate nearby, Welwood-on-the-Hill

Josie (Josephine), Lady Woodridge (26), married to Viscount Woodridge; they have two sons

Izzy (Isabel), Lady Farramont (24); married to Ian, Viscount Farramont (35); they have two daughters

Mr Kent Atherton (22)

Lady Olivia Atherton (18)

The earl's blind sister: Lady Alice Nicholson (48)

Her husband, the earl's chaplain: Mr Arthur Nicholson (55)

Their daughter, Miss Tess (Teresa) Nicholson (20)

The George Atherton family of Westwick Heights, North Riding of Yorkshire:

The earl's younger brother: Mr George Atherton (50)

Mrs Atherton (Jane, 45)

Their children:

Mr Bertram Atherton (25)

Mr Lucas Atherton (23)

Miss Julia Atherton (20)

Miss Emily Atherton (18)

Miss Penelope Atherton (16)

Master Philip Atherton (6)

The Strong Family of Birchall House, North Riding of Yorkshire:

Sir Hubert Strong, bt (53)

Kitty, Lady Strong

Their children:

Miss Winifred Strong (24)

Hebe (22); married to Mr William Plaister of Pickering

Their daughter: Prudence (1)

Mabel (19) married to Mr Charles Danby of Knaresborough

Miss Lily Strong (17)

Master Harris Strong (15)

Master Lionel Strong (12)

Mr Alfred Strong (48) unmarried

Aunt Minna (46) married to Mr John Wilton of York, with many children

Aunt Sofia (42) married to Mr Edmund Blackwood of Westminster, London; 1 son

The Franklyn Family of Highwood Place, North Riding of Yorkshire:

Mr Charles Franklyn (46)

Lady Esther Franklyn (33), daughter of the Duke of Camberley

His daughter from his first marriage:

Miss Beatrice Franklyn (21)

Their children:

Master Henry Franklyn (7)

Master Charles Franklyn (3)

The Murder Investigators:

Captain Michael Edgerton (37), formerly of the East India Company Army

Mrs Edgerton (Luce, née Willerton-Forbes, 30)

Mr Pettigrew Willerton-Forbes (38), a lawyer

Mr James Neate, a lawyer masquerading as a footman

Mr Alexander Grant Saxby (Sandy, 25), now known as Mr Alexander

Miss Peach, a former governess

1: Murder In The Night

CORLAND CASTLE: JUNE

The screams echoed through the castle. Walter, Viscount Birtwell, dragged himself reluctantly from sleep, at first puzzled, then scrambling in alarm from his bed. Instantly he tripped over something, cursing roundly. Where was he, anyway? Then he remembered — the principal guest room.

It was already light enough to see, although not yet full light. Perhaps close to four o'clock. Still the screams continued, high, piercing, terrified. What on earth was happening?

Without waiting to light a candle, he hauled open the heavy wooden door and stumbled out into the corridor above the stairs. Dark, but not impossible to see. One hand against the wall to guide him, he half ran towards the screams, tripping only once over a chair, and avoiding just in time a heavy marble-topped table.

Aunt Alice's room... that was where the noise was. The door was closed, but there was no doubting that the screams emanated from behind it. In the distance, he heard voices approaching from the other direction... his father, he thought, and his brother, Kent. A light flickered far away down the corridor. Unlike Walter, they had waited to light a candle.

The screams stopped. Without hesitation, Walter pushed open the door and went inside.

What he saw within chilled his very bones. In the middle of the room, Aunt Alice stood in her nightshift, liberally drenched with blood. In one hand, she held an axe, blood still dripping from it. And on the vast canopied bed which dominated the room, a mound of torn sheets and blankets, and more blood — so much blood! A few feathers from a ripped pillow floated here and there. And from beneath the blood-drenched mound of bedding, one arm dangled, motionless.

Uncle Arthur. And he was dead, very dead.

"Who is it?" Aunt Alice's voice was high with alarm. Her eyes were turned towards Walter, but she could not see him, having been blind since a childhood illness.

"It is I, Aunt Alice."

"Walter! What has happened here, Walter? What has happened to Arthur? Is this blood?"

She held up one red hand.

"It is blood. Where did the axe come from, Aunt?"

"Axe? Is that what it is? I tripped over it on the floor. What has *happened*, Walter? I could not hear him breathing, but when I leaned over to listen... when I touched him... Is Arthur...?" Her voice broke on a sob.

Walter took two quick steps into the room, so that he could see the bed more clearly, but he had to avert his eyes hastily. It was too horrible for words.

"He is dead, Aunt."

She uttered an unearthly wail, dropping the axe and falling to her knees, with a high, "No! No! No!" of despair.

Behind Walter, his father arrived with Kent. The Earl of Rennington was fifty-five, already stout and wheezing slightly now from the exertion of running. Walter's youngest brother, Kent, was twenty-two, with his mother's slender frame and dark eyes, wide now with the excitement of a night-time alarm.

"What is going on? A nightmare?" he hissed at Walter, grinning, but Walter merely stood aside to let them through. The sight would soon wipe that grin from Kent's face.

Then he saw his sister and cousin following them into the room, with a gaggle of servants rushing up behind them.

"No!" Walter cried, jumping forward to block the girls' way. "Out, both of you. At once! Go back to your room and stay there."

They would have bridled at this cavalier treatment, but he pushed them roughly back through the door and closed it behind him, muffling the shocked exclamations of the men as they saw the devastation within.

"Go!" he said sternly, and waited until they had ambled, grumbling, down the passageway.

Leaving several footmen on guard outside the door to prevent anyone else from entering, Walter went back inside. Aunt Alice had not moved, but at least she was silent now, as tears cascaded down her cheeks. Kent was patting her shoulder awkwardly.

"Ah, Walter," his father said, with obvious relief. "The girls..."

"I have sent them back to their room and told them to stay there."

"Good. They should not see this. But what can have happened here? This is quite dreadful!"

"It is not for us to determine what happened, Father. This is a matter for the magistrate."

"Ah, of course. Strong will know what to do. We must send for Sir Hubert at once."

"The most urgent matter is Aunt Alice," Walter said firmly. "Kent, pray get her out of this room... to her sitting room, perhaps, and send for her maid. And someone must go to the village for Little."

"Yes, yes, the apothecary," his father said, distractedly. When Aunt Alice had been led away, unresisting, by Kent, Lord Rennington turned to his son and heir. "This is very bad, Walter. How could someone break in and *murder* Nicholson in his bed like this? He was an inoffensive man, I should have thought — the chaplain, too. A man of God. Who would want to kill him?"

Walter hesitated, then said firmly, "Father, when I first arrived here, Aunt Alice was standing beside her husband's dead body, that axe in her hand and, as you saw, coated in her husband's blood. You do not think that—?"

"Alice? *Alice* murder her husband? Nonsense, boy. She adored him, and she would never hurt a fly. Besides, how could a blind woman wield an axe? No, it was an intruder. It must have been. I hope I know my sister well enough to say with absolute conviction that she did not murder her husband."

"I only report what I saw. It will be for Sir Hubert to determine the truth of it."

His father's face brightened. "Yes, Strong will unravel this mystery. He is very dependable. We must send for him at once."

***

Sir Hubert Strong was only two years younger than Lord Rennington, but in somewhat better condition. He brought with him his younger brother, Alfred Strong, a genial man who held a government office. He had also brought the coroner, a physician called Ashbridge, from Helmsley.

The three men pored over the body, gradually lifting away the remnants of the bedding to examine the wounds more fully.

Walter could not bear to look. He, Kent and their father huddled in a corner of the room, looking at the window, their feet, the clock on the mantelpiece — anything but the desolate remains of Arthur Nicholson, aged fifty-five, ordained clergyman and chaplain to the earl and his family at Corland Castle. Nicholson had lived at the castle for thirty years, and had become a member of the family when he married the earl's sister, Lady Alice Atherton. He was generally well liked, had no vices, kept no low company, had no known enemies. It was incomprehensible that anyone would want to murder him, and especially in such a violent way.

Eventually, the magistrate and coroner had finished their examination of the body and they all withdrew to the earl's study to discuss their findings. Walter explained all that he had seen, and Sir Hubert immediately denounced the idea as impossible.

"Lady Alice murder Nicholson? Absolutely not," he said robustly. "Undoubtedly, she found the axe on the floor, just as she said."

"I like the idea as little as you, Sir Hubert," Walter said. "I only tell you what I saw."

"And that is very proper of you, Lord Birtwell," Alfred Strong said. "However, we are all too close to the persons involved to judge impartially what might have happened here. I think this is a job for outsiders."

"Not Bow Street Runners!" the earl said, in horrified tones.

"No, no! Nothing so public," Alfred Strong said. "There is a man who has some experience of such matters, very discreet, who might be able to help us. He has a group of people who devote themselves to such cases. Do you remember the Hartlepool Hatpin Murder?"

"I do!" Kent said. "A brilliant piece of deduction. Edge… something."

"Captain Edgerton," Alfred Strong said. "Now known as Edgerton, Alexander and Associates. Very well known amongst my friends in town. May I make enquiries as to whether he would be willing to assist us?"

"Please do," the earl said wearily. "If he is discreet. It is the least we can do for poor Nicholson. By all means, send for this captain, and let us see if he can work out what happened here."

"Excellent," said Ashbridge. "I know of him by reputation, and he is a stickler for detail. To be sure to meet his exacting standards, I shall review the body once more, and make a thorough analysis of all the wounds, with diagrams and measurements. Everything must be analysed and recorded."

He went off happily, spending the rest of the day at the castle, measuring and making notes.

Late in the afternoon, Walter's other brother, Eustace, arrived. Eustace was the younger by two years at twenty-seven, but he had had the good fortune to inherit a modest estate from a neighbour who had taken a liking to him, and now had his independence. Walter's inheritance would be far greater, and include the earldom, but still he envied his brother his freedom.

Walter, Kent and their father were huddled in the earl's study when Eustace walked in.

"Eustace? Were we expecting you?" the earl said distractedly.

"No... no, I was just passing." His gaze passed from one to the other, puzzled. "The servants are all of a twitter... has something happened?"

"The most damnable thing," the earl said. "Nicholson has been murdered in his bed."

"*Nicholson?*"

"It is unaccountable, is it not?" Walter said. "Who under the sun would want to murder Nicholson?"

But Eustace was speechless. The four of them sat round the brandy decanter, sunk in gloom and despondency, with only the faint hope that a captain from Hartlepool might be able to help.

***

Miss Winifred Strong was watching from her bedroom window for her father and Uncle Alfred to return to Birchall House. As soon as she saw their horses plodding wearily up the drive, she ran lightly down the stairs and had the front door open even before Maynard got there.

"Well, Papa? Who is it? Who has died?"

Sir Hubert gave a little smile. "The chaplain. Nicholson."

Mr Nicholson! Thank God it was not... anyone else. She was very sorry for it, naturally, and desperately sad for poor Lady Alice, for whatever would she do without her husband? But at least another person was quite safe.

"Mr Nicholson... oh. Then... a sudden illness? An apoplexy? His heart? Although he seemed fit enough."

"Would that it were so simple. Come into my book room, Winnie. And you, Alfred. You need a drink... at least, I do, and I'm sure you must.

Such a sight as we have seen! No, Maynard, we can see to ourselves. Tell Lady Strong that we are returned, will you?"

"What will you have, Papa?" Winnie said, crossing to the table where the decanters stood ready.

"Brandy. A large one, and the same for your uncle."

Winnie's eyebrows rose, but she swiftly poured the drinks and handed them round.

"What a day!" Sir Hubert said, downing half his glass in one gulp. "Winnie, I shall tell you all, because there will be no possibility of keeping it quiet, but you must not make idle chatter of it. Not that you are at all an idle chatterer, but you know what I mean. No talking about it in front of the servants, and if anyone calls on your mother, do not mention it unless they do."

"Papa, this is serious indeed. You are alarming me! What on earth happened to poor Mr Nicholson?"

"He was murdered in the middle of the night by a man with an axe."

Whatever Winnie's fears had conjured up, this was far, far worse. She sat down suddenly on the nearest chair, her head spinning. *Murdered!* And with an axe!

"But who would do such a thing? And why? And will he murder anyone else?"

Uncle Alfred said calmly, "Well! That is a possibility we had not considered. We should have, of course. What is your opinion, Hubert?"

Sir Hubert frowned. "It seems unlikely to me. The axe was left behind, after all, and whoever wielded it has disappeared."

"Yet such a frenzied attack is surely the work of a deranged mind," Uncle Alfred said.

"All the more likely, then, that his lust for blood has been sated for the moment," Sir Hubert said. "One such murder is fantastic enough, without anticipating a whole series of such events. Until we know the reason for this murder, we cannot speculate on whether there will be a repetition. So long as all the doors are locked at night, the residents of Corland Castle should be safe enough."

"That did not protect them last night," Uncle Alfred said in subdued tones.

Silently, Winnie refilled the glasses, and as her mother came in just then with her younger sister Lily and was told what had happened, more interesting elements of the discussion had to be left to another time. At that moment, Winnie wished with all her heart that she had been born a boy, for then she would have lingered over the port with the gentlemen after dinner, and heard all the details that she craved.

However, when dinner came and went, she had not been in the drawing room with Mama and Lily for long when Maynard came in.

"Beg pardon, my lady, but the master wishes to know if you can spare Miss Strong for a few minutes. He'd like to see her in the dining room."

"Oh... of course, for I have Miss Lily to bear me company. Run along, Winnie."

With eager steps, Winnie ran along. It was not that she had any ghoulish interest in poor Mr Nicholson's terrible death, for she had heard all she wanted to about that. Rather, she had a great interest in the earl's family, with whose estate their own more modest park abutted, so that the two sets of children had grown up together. When Walter, Eustace and Josie, the three eldest of the earl's offspring, had roamed free, they had as often as not found their way to the boundary with Birchall House, while Winnie, Hebe and Mabel were as much on Corland ground as their own. And both sets had regarded the Strongs' tree house, so close to the boundary that branches reached across it, as common territory.

And what Winnie wanted to hear more than anything just then was how Walter was taking the news that the chaplain had been murdered. Walter… all her thoughts at that moment were with Walter, as they so often were. Not that she could ever tell anyone that. It was her Great Big Secret, never to be spoken of. Only Mama knew of it, and she had promised never to tell.

Papa and Uncle Alfred still sat at the dining table, a glass of port apiece, the decanter unstoppered. They rose as she entered.

"Ah, Winnie, there you are. Come and sit down, my dear," her father said, holding the chair next to his own for her. "Would you like a glass of wine?"

"I should like to try the port, if I may," she said, and the two men laughed. Uncle Alfred poured a small amount into a glass for her, and she sipped it cautiously. It was rather pleasant, strong but not fierce, as brandy was.

"Now, Winnie," her father said as he resumed his seat, "your uncle reminds me how useful you have been to him in the matter of taking notes and writing them up in a fair hand, and so we thought to ask if you would do the same for us in this affair at the castle."

"Of course, Papa, if I can. What would you wish me to do?"

"Nothing unseemly or distasteful to you, I assure you, merely to help us to arrange— No, let me explain properly. Normally, as magistrate, I would investigate any crime within my area, but in this case… so brutal a murder, and knowing the family intimately, as I do… as we all do, it is impossible for me to be entirely impartial."

"I am sure you would not let your friendship with the earl influence your duty, Papa."

"Certainly I would do my best not to, but it cannot but intrude. My every feeling rejects the notion that any member of the family could conceivably be responsible for such a heinous crime, yet the possibility must be considered. Therefore, your uncle has recommended calling upon the services of a man with some experience in dealing with such events."

"Murder? There are men who are experienced in the matter of murder?"

"In solving them, yes, and other mysteries, too," Uncle Alfred said. "Lord Rennington has written to secure the services of this man and his colleagues, but it may be some time before he can arrive, assuming he is even able to accept the commission."

"Exactly," Sir Hubert said. "Meanwhile, I must do what I can to record everything of importance in the matter before he arrives, before memories fade or evidence is destroyed."

"Like the footprints in the flowerbed when someone broke into Highwood Place?"

"Exactly so! It will be a huge undertaking, but your uncle has agreed to help me. Will you assist us, Winnie? Be our taker of notes, and point out to us the obvious details we might have missed?"

"I should be delighted to do whatever I can, if it will help the family at the castle."

"There! I knew you would! You are a good, sensible girl, Winnie. We shall set out at eight tomorrow, so breakfast early and wear your riding habit."

2: Edgerton, Alexander And Associates

Captain Michael Edgerton dismounted in front of the White Horse Inn at Birchall. He extracted his sword and attached it to his belt before handing his mount to the ostler who ambled out to attend to him.

The common room was quiet, with just a couple of elderly farmers playing cribbage in a corner. At a table in the window, he saw the head of golden hair he was looking for, and crossed the room to join his friend, Alexander Saxby.

"Well, Sandy."

"Well, Captain. Pleasant ride?"

"Very dull. Not a drop of rain, a light breeze and no hint of trouble."

Sandy laughed. "Aye, that sounds dull. Never mind, ye'll find all the trouble yer heart desires up at the castle."

Michael rubbed his hands together in delight. "Excellent." Waving over the potboy, he ordered ale and a bowl of stew and sat down opposite the Scotsman. "Now, tell me everything, Sandy."

"It's not much yet, only what the earl's told me and taproom gossip." Sandy pulled out a notebook. "Corland Castle, home to the 11th Earl of Rennington. The murdered man is Arthur Nicholson, aged fifty-five. The chaplain. Discovered by his wife, the Lady Alice, sister to the earl, at four in the morning. She was covered in blood and holding an axe. Her husband was on the bed, killed by an axe."

"Ah. Tell me she found the axe on the floor, or this would be far too simple. Besides, I should hate to see an earl's sister hang."

"She says she did. Also, she is blind... has been blind since childhood. Very distressed. Her screaming woke the household."

"Four in the morning... almost light, then."

Sandy nodded. "The earl called in the magistrate, a neighbour, Sir Hubert Strong and the coroner, Mr Ashbridge. Sir Hubert's brother, Mr Alfred Strong, recommended us."

"What about the chaplain... any enemies? Of course not. Chaplains are mild-mannered scholarly sorts, not given to ungentlemanly behaviour. Any thoughts on who it might be? Did the earl give you any clues? Or the taproom gossip?"

"It's universally agreed to be an intruder who wandered in, picked up an axe from the display in the great hall — the walls are covered with them, ye'll love it — went up the stairs to the chaplain's room and laid into him."

"And left without being seen, I suppose. No helpful trail of bloody footsteps?"

"No blood beyond the carpet in the bedroom. I've identified the doors where an intruder might enter the castle, but he'd have to know where they were, and have a key."

"Not impossible, but... improbable, shall we say. Much more likely to be someone inside the castle."

"Aye, I'd say so. The magistrate's compiling a complete list of everyone who was there on that night for us. The earl's made a room available for us to use for interviews and suchlike, and we can stay there if we want to. I've taken a room here for now, but the castle would be a deal more comfortable."

"Oh, yes. Better food, better wine, and we shall be on the spot."

"Will they invite ye to dine with them? That would be useful."

"I hope they will once I have Mrs Edgerton with me." Michael grinned. "She will be here the day after tomorrow, if there are no delays on the road. I have suggested that her arrival should be impressive, and that she mention her cousin the earl at every opportunity. That should get us to his lordship's table. What about you, Sandy? I know you prefer to masquerade as Mr Alexander, the plain Scotsman, but this is one occasion when your connection to Lord Saxby might be useful to us."

"Aye, ye can mention Cam if ye like. We dinnae want them thinking we're all upstart nobodies like you."

He grinned, and Michael laughed easily. "No, it would never do if they thought you were nothing but a bank clerk."

"But I'm not a bank clerk, not anymore," Sandy said with dignity, shaking his golden head at Michael. "I'm cousin to a baron, and a gentleman — or near enough. And Neate? Is he to be yer valet this time?"

Michael sighed. "That works with Willerton-Forbes. He looks as if he needs a valet, but no one looks at me and wonders how my man gets my boots to shine." He held up one foot, the boot liberally encased in mud and dust.

"No, they look at ye and wonder why ye carry a sword everywhere."

"One never knows when one might need it," he said with a grin.

"Have ye ever needed it?"

"That is not the point. It is all very well for a great tall fellow like you, Sandy Saxby, but when one is less than impressive in stature, one is inclined to be overlooked or dismissed as unimportant. I prefer people to take me seriously. Ah, my sustenance. Thank you, my good man."

Tossing a coin to the potboy, he tucked in with relish, and all conversation was at an end until his appetite was sated.

There was no point in further delay, so they collected their mounts and made their way the short distance to the small village of Corland, and thence to Corland Castle.

Michael laughed when he saw it. "Luce will feel quite at home here. It is every bit as authentic a castle as her old home, although a shade more imposing, I grant you. These earls, they do like to pretend they live in an ancient monument, but with all the modern conveniences of bell pulls and cooking ranges. We need not fear to suffer too many privations if we stay here."

"There was a real castle here once, all stone flags and draughts," Sandy said. "Very medieval."

"Naturally there was, for how else were the marauding Scots to be kept in their place?"

"The English built them to huddle in, being too cowardly to face the Scots," said the Scotsman with a grin.

Michael grinned back, but refused to rise to the bait. "There is a wide bridge to the entrance. Is that a moat beneath it?"

"Only a pretend one. It's dry, being access to the basement, but it looks good from here, I'll grant ye."

They rode slowly round the perimeter of the grounds by way of reconnoitre. Corland Castle was indeed an imposing building, a solidly square edifice of two stories in height, with a large circular tower at each corner. Two bridges crossed the void for the basement, one at the end of the carriage drive leading to the front door, and the other connecting a back door to a small terrace and the pleasure grounds beyond.

"No vines or trees that would allow admittance to the upper windows," Michael murmured. "The drainpipes... maybe in broad daylight, but not at night, and that's a nasty overhang beneath the upper windows. Not easy. I shall check the windows, but I believe an intruder would have to come in through one of those doors, or else by way of the basement. Well, shall we go in?"

Since the question was rhetorical, he did not wait for an answer, wheeling his horse about and riding up to the front door. Grooms emerged immediately from somewhere below the bridge. Michael dismounted, strapped on his sword again, without which he felt naked, and strode across the bridge. He had no need to ring or knock, for the door opened as he approached and the butler and a footman emerged.

"Welcome to Corland Castle, Captain," the butler said, before he could speak. "I am Simpson, the butler, and this is Wellum, the under-butler. His lordship is expecting you." He eyed the sword warily. "Do you wish to leave your weapon here, sir?"

"Thank you, but I prefer to keep it with me."

"Very good, sir. Please follow me."

He led the way out of the entrance hall into a rather fine library, and then to a door set in the furthest corner. With a smart rat-a-tat-tat, he opened it and marched in.

"Captain Edgerton and Mr Alexander, my lord."

Then, with a deep bow, he withdrew. Michael found himself in a small room, completely round, one of the corner towers. It was fitted out with a small desk in front of one of the two long windows, and a grouping of chairs cosily arranged round the fireplace, filled at this season with a painted screen. The earl was a man of not yet sixty, but showing the signs of an over-indulged life, who greeted them affably.

"Ah, come in, come in. Erm... the sword... are you expecting trouble, Captain?"

"I like to be prepared for all eventualities. My card, my lord. You are acquainted with my colleague, of course."

"Yes, yes, Mr Alexander."

"He likes to be known as such, but his proper name is Alexander Saxby, cousin to Lord Saxby of Maeswood Hall, in Shropshire. My wife will arrive soon. She is cousin to the Earl of Morpeth."

"Ah, yes, Morpeth... I have met him. And you are an army man, Captain?"

"East India Company Army, my lord."

"Well, you would have seen action enough out there. And now you investigate murders. Thank goodness you are here, and so speedily, too. I cannot sufficiently express my gratitude. Poor Arthur! He was my brother-in-law, you know. My poor sister's husband. Not that he and I were terribly close, but... well, he was part of the family. Thirty years he has been here. Arrived fresh from his ordination to play chaplain for a while, until a proper living came up, but then he married Alice and never left. This is a desperate business, and no knowing whether the fellow responsible might come back and murder us all in our beds. Until he is under lock and key, we are none of us safe, and hardly able to get a wink of sleep. And who can it be, that is what has us all at sea — we have not the least idea. Even the magistrate, Sir Hubert Strong, can make nothing of it. Do sit down. Will you take a glass of something, gentlemen? Madeira? Claret?"

"Thank you, but no. If you permit, my lord, I should like to see the deceased."

"Ah, well now, that would be difficult, since we buried him yesterday. This hot weather, you know... but Ashbridge took very detailed notes. The coroner, that is."

"I look forward to seeing them. May I see the place where the incident took place?"

"Well... it is the Lady Alice's bedchamber, and she is still in residence, so to speak."

"The poor lady is blind," Sandy put in, "so it's awkward for her to move to new quarters."

"Of course," Michael murmured, but he thought the lady must have nerves of steel to return immediately to the scene of her husband's slaughter.

"Ashbridge and Sir Hubert permitted us to... erm, tidy up, so she was able to return that same night. My sister could not see the... erm, the deceased, so she has no image in her mind. Those of us who saw him... well, I need not describe it to you, Captain. A soldier like yourself... you must have seen plenty of gruesome sights, but it turned my stomach, I can tell you."

"I am sure," Michael said neutrally. "No matter, I can see the room another day. But may I ask... it was the gentleman's wife who discovered the body, I understand?"

"My sister, Alice, yes. Nicholson's wife."

"And was covered in his blood and holding the axe which was presumed to have killed him?"

"Now, just what are you suggesting, Edgerton? That *my sister* slaughtered her own husband? Utter nonsense! She merely stepped on the axe handle and picked it up, and then, not hearing any sound from her husband, touched the body. She is blind, so—"

"Yes, yes, I understand, my lord, but I have to ask. How did she happen to discover the murder at that point? Did she hear it happen? Was she perhaps asleep in the room, heard something, rose to investigate? Or in an adjoining room, perhaps?"

"How should I know their personal arrangements?" the earl said testily.

"Of course. The Lady Alice's screams woke the household, I understand. Who was the first to arrive?"

"My eldest son, Viscount Birtwell. I arrived just behind him with my youngest son, Kent."

"My lord, is it possible that the murderer was still in the room? If, say, the Lady Alice heard it happen, came to investigate, and the murderer hid — behind the curtains, perhaps?"

The earl paled. "You mean... the villain might have been there... when we arrived?"

"Is it possible? Was there an opportunity for him to slip away? Was the room left unattended at any point?"

"Slip away... unattended... well now, let me think. We were all concerned with Alice, of course, so... but no, Birtwell had footmen stationed outside the door. To keep the girls out, mainly, but no one could have slipped out undetected."

"Excellent," Michael said. "My lord, what are your instructions for us? Do we have a free hand to enquire within the castle and surrounding villages? Or even further afield, if information leads us in a different direction?"

"Surely there is no need to upend the entire North Riding, Captain? The solution to this problem must be within the castle, one supposes? I cannot see the necessity to look beyond it."

Michael bowed. "Then you have some idea already who might have done this dreadful deed? Someone within the castle?"

The earl blinked at him. "Not the least idea, Captain. Nicholson had not an enemy in the world."

"No enemies? But perhaps someone would benefit by his death?"

"Benefit? His daughter, I suppose. He has left his fortune to her, but Tess is only a girl... not yet one and twenty. You can hardly suppose... no, it must have been a passing intruder."

"Then how am I to discover his identity if I can ask no questions beyond the castle?"

The earl frowned, puzzling over this conundrum. "I suppose," he said slowly, "you may enquire further if you have a good reason. If some evidence points to a person beyond these walls. But until then, I prefer you to focus your efforts on the castle itself. It is disruptive enough to have a murder here, without ruffling the feathers of all our neighbours, too. You must be discreet, Captain, that is imperative."

"It shall be as you wish, my lord. I believe you have a room set aside for us to use as we work?"

"Yes, yes. Let me ring for Simpson. He will show you the way. So glad you are here, Captain, and your colleague, too. You are very welcome to stay here, naturally. Erm, do you wish to dine with us?"

"That is entirely a matter for you and Lady Rennington to decide, my lord," he said smoothly.

The earl gave a nervous little smile, clearly not sure whether a former captain of the East India Company Army was a fit person to dine at an earl's table, but Simpson appeared just then, and Michael and Sandy bowed themselves out of the earl's presence, and followed the butler in silence.

***

Winnie jumped when someone knocked at the door of the old nursery. Simpson entered and bowed.

"Captain Edgerton and Mr Alexander, sir."

"Thank you, Simpson," Sir Hubert said.

Captain Edgerton was not in uniform, but there was no mistaking the military bearing in his manner, nor the businesslike sword he wore. He bowed with a flourish, and after passing his eyes briefly over Sir Hubert and Uncle Alfred, they lingered on Winnie.

The golden-haired Mr Alexander stepped forward. "Sir Hubert, Mr Strong, Miss Strong, may I present Captain Michael Edgerton, formerly of the East India Company Army and Tattersall's, and now of Edgerton, Alexander and Associates? Captain, this is Sir Hubert Strong, the magistrate here and a neighbour, his brother, who lives with him, Mr Alfred Strong, and his daughter, Miss Winifred Strong."

Winnie curtsied, as the captain bowed again to each of them in turn.

"A lady here?" he murmured, with a pleasant smile. "Do you have an interest in this matter, Miss Strong?"

"My daughter has some skill with the pen, so she has been helping us by taking notes," Sir Hubert said. "Hers is the plan of the castle pinned to the wall over there."

The captain turned towards it. "Ah, how very useful. And these names written on the various rooms?"

"They show where all the castle residents were at the time Mr Nicholson's body was discovered," Winnie said. "Or where they were supposed to be, anyway."

The captain chuckled. "An astute observation. Just the three floors?"

"There are a few attic rooms, where the footmen sleep. I have listed them at the side here. Access is by this spiral stair. The original plan, from which I copied this, is framed and hung on the library wall, and the original architect's drawings are in the library, too, in case you need to know where all the chimney flues lead."

"Unless anyone discovered a quantity of soot where it should not be, we can probably eliminate the flues," he said, but he was impressed by her attention to detail. "And there are just these two doors at ground level, by the bridges?"

"Yes," Winnie said. "They are locked and bolted from the inside at eleven every night by Simpson and Wellum, unless the family are still out, or there are guests for dinner, neither of which was the case on the night in question. On the lower level, there are four doors, here, here, here, and here. This one leads directly to the wine cellar, opened only when the vintner delivers, and locked and barred within otherwise. The kitchen door, here, is locked and bolted whenever the kitchen shuts down for the night. This one is the nearest door to the stables, and is locked whenever the outdoor servants retire for the night. It is not bolted, however, because the footmen on their days off and sometimes the young gentlemen of the family stay in the village until quite late and come back in that way."

"They would have to have a key, of course."

"Yes. Several keys are kept on a hook in the butler's pantry, and anyone could take one. The fourth door is the one the gardeners use, or the gentlemen who come in from shooting with muddy boots. It is directly by one set of service stairs for convenience, and it is supposed to be locked and bolted at nightfall, but no one knows whether it was locked on the night in question. Over there on the chalkboard is a list of all the castle residents on the night in question. I have only talked to the servants, but they generally know what is going on."

"How thorough!" the captain said. "Miss Strong, if ever you want a more adventurous life, I should engage you in the twinkling of an eye for my little band of associates."

Winnie laughed out loud at that, and bobbed him a curtsy. "I thank you for the compliment, sir, but I am not looking for adventure. I like order, that is all. My mama says that if I am asked what day of the week it is, I should have to make a list before I could answer."

"Your ability with lists is beyond compare," the captain said.

"Who *are* your associates, Captain?" she said. "Apart from Mr Alexander. No ladies, I presume."

"Ah, now there you would be wrong, for my wife is one of my merry band, and there is also a lawyer by the name of Willerton-Forbes, who is not adventurous at all, but has a similar liking for order as yourself. He deals only with legal matters, however, so he will not be joining us on this particular adventure."

"But your wife will? I look forward to meeting her. When will she be here?"

"The day after tomorrow, all being well," he said, and his smile changed from a slightly roguish one to something altogether softer. "Forty-eight hours," he added, with what sounded suspiciously like a sigh.

3: Breaking In

"That one, I think," Captain Michael Edgerton said thoughtfully, gazing up at one of the ornate drainpipes that adorned the exterior of Corland Castle. "No clutter around the bottom, and that window up there looks like it might be readily prised open."

"Ye must be mad," Sandy said with a grin. "I'll scrape ye off the ground if ye come to grief."

"Nonsense," Michael said briskly. "Nothing to it. I have climbed far worse, I assure you."

Two or three of the grooms paused their sweeping to watch, and Michael thought he saw the glint of coins changing hands. That was fine by him. They could bet on him all they liked, but unless the murderer lived within the castle, he must have broken in somehow and nipping up a drainpipe was as easy as winking to a man used to climbing.

And it was indeed as easy as winking. Up he went, leaving the kitchen level behind and then past the ground floor. Looking down, he saw quite a crowd gazing up at him, as half the servants abandoned their chores to watch the entertainment. He gave them a flourishing wave, which raised a small cheer, then turned back to the pipe.

He had paused, considering the best way past the overhang that divided the two principal floors when there was an ominous creaking sound. He froze, listening. For a moment, there was silence. Then, with majestic slowness and a great showering of masonry dust, the whole top of the pipe was ripped away from the wall, leaving Michael dangling one-handed in mid-air.

Down below, screams and running feet and general pandemonium broke out. Michael pondered his options. He was too far from the wall to reach it, even if he could find sufficient hand holds. If he tried to slide down the pipe, it might break off altogether and hurl him to the ground. Below him was only hard-pressed earth, without a single bush to break his fall. A broken neck would be the worst outcome, he supposed. An arm or leg — that was probably the best he could hope for.

He hung, motionless. Below him, men were scurrying round. And the women, too. They had found a large sheet and were opening it out directly below him to catch him if he fell. It was only thin — a tablecloth, perhaps — so it was unlikely to break his fall completely, but it was better than nothing. But now ladders were appearing, and being fitted together. Would it reach? It would not... but wait, another one appeared, was fitted on. It reached! Gently, inch by inch, the men below manoeuvred the ladder into position beside him. He stretched a hand, grasped it, held it tight... one foot transferred... then the other... he was safe! Swiftly, he descended to the ground to be engulfed by the crowd, who were laughing, relieved but teasing him about his misadventure.

"I believe I owe you all a round of drinks," he said to a general cheer of approbation.

The butler appeared at the kitchen door, his face stern. "Whatever is going on? What is this, a holiday?"

"Cap'n Edgerton's been breakin' in to t'castle," one of the grooms yelled.

"Not breakin' in, exactly," someone else said. "More like breakin' t'water pipe."

"Yes, I am afraid this is all my fault," Michael said, as he dusted himself off. "I had better go and make my apologies to his lordship for damaging his castle."

"Still, that was useful," Sandy said. "At least ye know that no one got in that way."

***

Walter woke suddenly, heart pounding. What had happened? Something had woken him, some sound. Not screams this time, thank God! But what was it?

The dogs. Distant barking, far below in the basement where they slept. Someone breaking in! The murderer had returned.

He threw on a robe, and this time stopped to light a candle. Then he opened the drawer of his bedside cabinet and took out the loaded pistol that he now kept handy, just in case.

Outside on the landing, all was quiet. Perhaps no one else had heard anything yet. He crept down the stairs to the half landing, where a display of armoury gleamed dully in the flickering candlelight. On either side, his grandmother's monstrous Chinese urns, almost as tall as Walter, stood silent guard.

Down again to the great hall, the array of swords and pikes and maces on the walls like a ghostly army. Then down the service stairs to the basement, the barking becoming louder with every step. He could hear voices now, at least two distinct voices, in amongst the cacophony of canine displeasure. The scullery... that was where the disturbance was.

Walter burst in, to find a man in rough clothing crouched on a table, an island of safety in a sea of angry dogs, while the kitchen boy, eyes wide with fear, his hand shaking so hard he was in danger of snuffing out his candle, ineffectually tried to call the dogs to order. Seeing Walter, the dogs instantly quieted and ambled over to be stroked and petted.

Pointing the gun directly at the stranger, Walter said, "I hope you have a good explanation ready for the magistrate, fellow. Or perhaps I should just shoot you at once. Came back for another go, did you?"

Astonishingly, the man smiled, revealing a set of teeth that gleamed in the candlelight. "Captain Michael Edgerton at your service, sir. Engaged by Lord Rennington to investigate the murder of Mr Nicholson."

"Really," Walter said disbelievingly, the gun not wavering in the slightest.

"Really. To whom do I have the pleasure of speaking?"

"I am Birtwell."

"Then I beg your pardon for disturbing your slumber, my lord."

"What are you doing in the scullery in the middle of the night, Captain? If you *are* a captain, that is. Royal Navy or mercantile?"

The teeth gleamed even more. "East India Company Army, my lord. Retired. Tattersall's for a while, but now of Edgerton, Alexander and Associates, investigators of murders and other wickedness. As part of my investigation, I was discovering how easy it would be to break into the castle at night. The dogs are a very effective deterrent, however, and a man with a gun even more so. You look as if you know how to use it, too."

"I am accounted a good shot," Walter said, not taking his eyes off the fellow's face.

The door was pushed open wider and Walter's father emerged from the darkness, candlestick in hand. "What the devil—? Oh, Edgerton, it is you. What are you doing on that table?"

"Avoiding the dogs, my lord. I am very glad you are here to vouch for me to Lord Birtwell, who is defending his home with admirable determination."

"Well, it serves you right for creeping about in the middle of the night. Foolish thing to do, disrupting the household. If you want anything, just ring for it, like anyone else. I am going back to bed."

And he stomped off again, his candle disappearing into the night.

"He is always cross when his sleep is disrupted," Walter said.

Carefully setting his gun down on a high shelf, he lit some more candles, then shooed the dogs back to the kitchen where they habitually slept.

"Matt, go back to bed," he said to the kitchen boy. "I can deal with this. Captain, you may get down now and explain to me what is going on. My father may be satisfied with the idea that you were looking for a bit of bread and cheese in the middle of the night, but I would like the full story. Did you really break in?"

"Indeed I did," the captain said, hopping agilely from the table. "I need to understand just how this murder could have been committed. I tried the drainpipe, without success."

Walter chuckled. "I heard about that."

"Yes, well, not my finest hour. So I looked for some other way in. My inspection of the basement revealed a loose catch on the window here. Look... easy to pry open from the outside with a pocket knife."

"Would one of the doors not be the easiest way in?"

"Certainly, if one has a key and it is not bolted on the inside, but that seems to be unpredictable. Whereas this window can be opened on any day of the week."

"You have now proved satisfactorily that no one could have got in that way, not with the dogs around, anyway."

"Ah, not quite, my lord," the captain said with a smile. "No *stranger* could have got in, certainly, but someone who was known to the dogs — that would be a different matter."

"So the murderer was not a stranger," Walter said thoughtfully.

"Possibly. I have one more point of access to try. Would you be good enough to wait for me just inside the garden door, my lord?"

"It should be locked and bolted."

The captain grinned. "So it should. Nevertheless, I should like to try it."

Walter laughed, and agreed to it. The captain nimbly jumped onto the draining board, pushed open the window and hopped through. By the time Walter had crossed the kitchen and reached the garden door, it was already opening as the captain walked in.

"Unlocked, and the bolt is broken," he said, then paused, waiting. "No dogs here? Ah, now I hear them coming, but there are service stairs just a few steps away. If I were to run..."

"So *anyone* could have walked in that night?"

"It would seem so," the captain said, as the dogs poured into the passageway, tongues lolling.

Walter knelt to soothe them. "Hmm. So he might come back?"

"That is always possible. I am pleased to observe that you keep a loaded pistol to hand at night, my lord, but it might be wise to change the locks on all the external doors and to fix that broken window latch. And remind the servants to keep these doors locked and bolted at night."

"I shall send for Tom Shapman first thing tomorrow," Walter said. "And now perhaps we can go to bed."

***

Tom Shapman turned out to be surprisingly young, not a day over twenty-five, a tall, well-built man with the sort of good looks which would set the local girls sighing. He changed all the external locks, fixed a broken bolt on the garden door, and then set about repairing the broken window latch, as Michael watched.

"Is this how he got in — the fellow that did for poor Mr Nicholson?" Shapman said, as he crouched on the scullery draining board to unscrew the window latch.

"It is possible," Michael said cautiously.

"The doors would've been locked, I suppose, but anyone might have had a key," Shapman said. "Happen there were several sets made."

"Possibly. You did not fit the original locks, then?"

"Not me, sir. They were likely done when the castle was built, judging by the style of them. I've only been here four years. Changed a couple of locks in that time — the silver store, when Mr Simpson lost his key, and a desk drawer for his lordship. Mostly I do windows, or fix warped doors."

"Do you live in the village here, Mr Shapman?"

"Not Corland. Down at Birchall, four, five miles from here. That's where me family live."

"All locksmiths, are they?"

Shapman laughed. "Pa's the sexton at the church. Me brothers are farm labourers, mainly, but I apprenticed as a carpenter, since old Will Barker were the only one in the village and getting on a bit. He does furniture, so I do mainly doors and windows, so as not to tread on his toes, like. I like doors. It's precision work, just like a cabinet, but not fancy. No one wants fancy doors."

"Just so long as they open and close, eh?"

"Aye, that's it. It's all in the hanging and the balance."

"So what are they saying at Birchall village about this murder?"

Shapman paused in his work, looking sideways at Michael. "You want the gossip, do you?"

"Certainly!" Michael said with a grin. "His lordship has confined my questioning only to those who are within the castle, and since you *are* within the castle...?"

The carpenter chuckled. "Sorry to disappoint, sir, but I don't have much to tell. Everyone's very shocked, of course, but no one knows owt about it. Like who did it, or why."

"No one saw any mysterious strangers passing through that day? No one saying darkly over their ale, *'Ah well, he had it coming, because of...'* well, some secret or other?"

Shapman shook his head. "Never knew any harm of the man, meself, and never heard of any from anyone else."

"So he had no enemies?"

"Not that I know of. There — that's the window done." He jumped down, uncurling a height that Michael could only envy. "If there's nothing else, sir, I've a listing barn door to see to."

Michael sighed. "Of course. Thank you for fixing the window and locks, Mr Shapman. I shall sleep easier knowing no stranger can break in here."

***

Mrs Michael Edgerton arrived in some style, in a post chaise and four with two outriders, her lady's maid, her own personal footman, and an elderly lady with twinkling eyes and a delighted smile on her face. The elderly lady was rather shabby, but Michael was amused to see that his wife had decided to be the lady of fashion for this visit. He wondered just how much her very fetching bonnet had cost.

"My companion, Miss Peach," she said grandly, gesturing towards the elderly lady as she swept past Simpson and Wellum into the entrance hall, and spun round to take in all the room's features. "Oh yes, very like Hurtsmere Castle. My uncle, the Earl of Morpeth's principal seat," she added to the bemused housekeeper. "A trifle larger, perhaps. I am afraid I have brought rather a quantity of luggage, but it is so difficult when one is in town for the season, is it not? One sees so many delicious confections that one positively must have."

Michael suppressed a smile, knowing perfectly well that Luce never went near London if she could avoid it, and had moreover come directly from Westmorland. The housekeeper bobbed a curtsy, and requested her to *'please step this way, ma'am,'* which Luce graciously agreed to do. Michael trailed along behind her, enjoying the spectacle.

As soon as the housekeeper had left them alone in their room, taking the still smiling Miss Peach with her, Luce turned to Michael and said in a theatrical whisper, "Well? Did I do it right?"

"You did it perfectly, although I am not sure how you became so stylish overnight. I know precisely what clothes you had in Westmorland. Where did the lady's maid come from?"

"An agency in Harrogate."

"And the old biddy?"

"Not an old biddy, Michael. Miss Peach is my former governess, who retired some years ago to assist her married sister to run a small tea garden in Harrogate. She has been bored to flinders, I assure you, and is delighted to become a companion for a little while. She is blessed with insatiable curiosity, so she will be very useful to us. As for my stylish wardrobe, the sister knows a friend who sells the cast-off clothing of fashionable ladies, so I was able to become excessively fashionable in a couple of hours. They do not all fit me very well, but Peachy is adept with a needle, as am I, so we shall do splendidly. How is it going, Michael?"

"Slowly. One cannot just jump in with an earl's family and start asking pointed questions. We shall get on better now you are here, however, for we shall certainly be asked to dine with the family, and then we can get a better look at them. You must keep an eye on the ladies for me, you know."

"I shall try, but they will say nothing in front of me. That is one of the advantages of Peachy — we shall retire to a corner of the drawing room with our stitchery, you see, and sooner or later they will forget we are there. Peachy also likes a hot drink at bedtime, so is inclined to wander below stairs for the purpose. We are very optimistic that the servants will be usefully mellow at that time. Did you like my personal footman?"

"James Neate, you mean? Oh, yes. That is clever. He will mingle below stairs, and with any luck he will be asked to serve at table."

"Who have you talked to so far?" she said, as she removed the very fetching bonnet with a sigh, idly stroking the feathers that adorned it.

"Only the earl, and he was... not precisely unhelpful, but very unwilling to embroil himself in the details of the affair. He wants the murderer found and the whole business tidied up as soon as may be."

"That is understandable."

"Oh, yes, and I shall be very happy to oblige him, if I can, but I have a feeling things are going to get messy. However, he has given me *carte blanche* to talk to anyone and everyone in the castle, and the magistrate is being very accommodating. His daughter is a terrific help, and the coroner has left me an exceptionally detailed description of the body, which is very useful since the fellow has been buried already."

"You have not talked to the widow yet, then?"

"No, nor the daughter."

"Oh, there is a daughter, is there?"

"Teresa — Tess, just twenty, who is seemingly set to become a very wealthy woman, but only if she marries a gentleman. Those are the terms of her father's will, apparently. A bit of a surprise, by all accounts."

"That he left her a fortune on such terms, or that he had a fortune at all?" Luce said, eyebrows raised. "In my experience, chaplains tend not to be wealthy men."

"You, my dear, are a very perceptive woman. That is indeed an intriguing question."

"So, is the daughter a suspect?"

"Everyone is a suspect at this point... well, perhaps not the earl himself, or his lady. If either of them had a problem with Nicholson, they could simply dismiss him. And the Dowager Countess is bedridden, so she is out, too. But anyone else, including Nicholson's daughter, although so far as anyone knows, she was unaware of the fortune that might be hers. The principal suspect at this point, regrettably, is the grieving widow, who was discovered standing over her husband's body with blood dripping from the axe in her hand," he said grimly.

"Oh dear," Luce said.

4: A Prowl Around The Castle

With the arrival of Captain Edgerton, Winnie's father decreed she should travel to Corland Castle in the carriage thenceforth.

"It was all very well when it was just us and all very informal, but to be honest, Winnie, I expected Captain Edgerton to want you out of the way from now on. However, it seems your orderly methods made quite an impression, and if you are to be involved with the investigation as it proceeds, and moving about the castle and so on and so forth, you will find a day gown more convenient than your riding habit. The captain asked especially if you could wear a white gown today... do you know why?"

"No, but I am sure he has a good reason," she said calmly. "Not that I have worn white for years, but I can borrow one of Lily's."

"You look so pretty in white," her father said wistfully. "I do like to see a young lady in white."

That made Winnie smile. "So sentimental, Papa! But you know how I attract dirt. Brown is the most suitable colour for someone like me — the colour of mud."

When they arrived at the castle, well before the usual hour for the family to be up and about, they found the energetic Captain Edgerton already ensconced in the room which had been made over to him for his investigation. He and Mr Alexander were busily rearranging furniture.

"It seems we can use both this room and the tower room beyond," the captain said, "so we are going to keep the tower room as an inner office, with all our notes and your plan of the castle, Miss Strong. Then we can use this outer room for interviews."

Winnie wandered through to the tower room, where her plan of the castle had already been nailed to the wall, and the chalkboard list stood beside the empty fireplace. A small desk and a couple of chairs sat haphazardly about.

The captain followed her through. "Do you approve, Miss Strong?"

"It is not for me to approve or disapprove your dispositions, Captain. It is just a little odd to see the nursery put to such use."

"Ah... the nursery, was it? It was not marked as such on your plan."

"It is a very long time since it fulfilled that purpose. This tower room was the night nursery for the babies, and the outer room was the day nursery, and latterly the schoolroom. I used to come here myself, sometimes. Lady Rennington very graciously allowed us to share the various masters she engaged for Josie, Izzy and Olivia. Italian, dancing, drawing... I attended all of those, but not the regular lessons. They had a very high-class governess, but we had only Mama and Papa."

"Then you probably did better than they did," he said.

"Oh no. They are all fearsomely accomplished, and married very well. At least, Josie and Izzy did, and Olivia will when she makes her appearance in town. She was wild to go this year, but Lady Rennington thought the Dowager Countess would expire in the middle of it, so it was put back a year. The whole family stayed at home this spring."

"But her ladyship has not... erm, expired as yet?"

Winnie chuckled. "No, although she is very frail, and keeps to her bedchamber now. There is every expectation she will have expired before the start of next season. Six months before, ideally, so that everyone will be conveniently out of black gloves."

"Miss Strong, even though you may not be *fearsomely accomplished*, as you phrase it, you have qualities that any man of sense would value more highly, I assure you."

"Well, though I say so myself, I make an excellent gooseberry jam," she said gravely, "and my apple tart is regarded as the finest in the parish."

He chuckled, and said, "You see? A sense of humour is far better than fearsome accomplishments. Miss Strong, it is still too early for the family to be up and about, so this would be a good time for me to prowl round the castle and get my bearings. Would you be so good as to show me around, since you seem to know the place very well? Not the basement, for the servants will be scurrying about down there, and I should not like to get in the way, but the principal apartments."

"I cannot show you all the tower rooms," she said. "Lord Rennington's study is his private sanctum, and I have never been inside it. The Dowager Countess has one of the two off the gallery, and the other is the armoury and contains the most dangerous weaponry, so it is kept locked."

"I shall get Simpson to unlock it for me later."

With her father and uncle trailing behind, they descended to the great hall, and thence to the library, dining room, drawing room, parlour, music room and long gallery. Several of the rooms featured suits of armour, arranged with appropriate weaponry, but it was impossible to tell if any of them had once featured an axe. The captain then returned to the great hall, spending a considerable time minutely examining the various pikes, muskets, swords and axes displayed on the walls there. There were no gaps to indicate a missing axe, however, and the Strongs could tell him nothing about them, so eventually he led the way back to the nursery.

The captain had ordered breakfast to be served there, and although Winnie had already eaten, she was not averse to a little more tea and toast, while Sir Hubert and Uncle Albert tucked in with relish.

As she sipped her tea, Captain Edgerton said, "I am trying to fix the earl's family in my mind, but it is a little confusing. There are five children, is that correct?"

"Lord and Lady Rennington have six children, three sons and three daughters. Walter is twenty-nine, and Eustace is twenty-seven, both unmarried. Josie is twenty-six and Izzy is twenty-four, both married. They are Lady Woodridge and Lady Farramont now. Kent is twenty-two and Olivia is eighteen. Unmarried."

"And waiting for Grandmama to expire. Yes, I see. Eustace is the one I was missing. I knew of the two married daughters, and I met the other three at dinner last night."

"Yes, you would not have seen Eustace. He inherited an estate from a neighbour, about twelve miles from here, so he no longer lives at the castle."

When all had eaten their fill, the captain said, "Shall we walk around the upper floor? And perhaps I might examine the room where Mr Nicholson was found? If the Lady Alice permits, of course."

From the nursery, in one direction all the rooms were unused, kept as guest chambers, so they set off in the other direction, past one empty room and then to the room usually occupied by Walter. Now, however, the door stood open, and it was busy with men with brushes, smelling strongly of paint.

"Redecorating," the captain murmured. "I wonder when this was started."

An enquiry elicited the information that work had begun before Mr Nicholson's demise.

"I have misled you, Captain," Winnie said, frowning. "I marked Walter on the plan as being in this room, but he must have been in one of the guest rooms. No wonder he was the first to reach Lady Alice."

"No matter," the captain said easily. "This is why I like to walk around, to see for myself. Shall we move on? Now this corner is where Lord and Lady Rennington have their apartments, and this one is Mr Kent Atherton. Then an empty room?"

"That was where Josie and Izzy slept before they married."

"Ah. The Lady Josephine and the Lady Isabella?"

"Isabel. Then Tess and Olivia. The Lady Olivia and Miss Teresa Nicholson. And this... this is the suite occupied by Lady Alice and..."

"The late Mr Arthur Nicholson," the captain put in smoothly. "Miss Strong, may I prevail upon you to discover if her ladyship is within, and when it may be convenient for us to examine the bedroom? I do not need to see her ladyship at present, but I must see the place where the death occurred."

"Of course."

Winnie knocked quietly on the door, then pushed it open. As she hesitated on the threshold, a head popped out from behind an open wardrobe door, the frown immediately replaced by a smile. Winnie recognised Malling, Lady Alice's maid.

"Ah, Miss Strong. Come to pay your respects, have you? She'll be right glad to see you."

"How is your mistress, Malling?"

The maid pulled a rueful face. "Very low, madam, very low indeed. They were as close as two people could well be, and her ladyship depended on Mr Nicholson for so much. Come in, and I'll tell her you're here."

She ushered Winnie into the room, dominated by a vast canopied bed, before disappearing through a far door to the adjoining tower room. Winnie averted her eyes from the bed with a shudder. This, surely, was where the dreadful event had taken place. Yet there was nothing to indicate it. Everything was clean, the rug beside the bed spotless, the floorboards surrounding it polished to a high shine. The bed itself looked ready to receive its occupant. It was oddly disconcerting.

Malling was back in moments, and showed Winnie through into the tower room beyond. Winnie had expected a dressing room, but in fact it was arranged as a cosy sitting room, the round walls giving the space an unusual intimacy. Lady Alice and Lady Rennington sat side by side on a sofa, both in unrelieved black, holding hands.

"Miss Strong, my lady," Malling said.

"Winnie! How kind of you to call," Lady Alice said, holding out one hand in roughly the direction of the door, her eyes gazing unseeingly in the same direction.

"Lady Alice. Lady Rennington." Winnie made her curtsy, then crossed the short space between them to take Lady Alice's hand, and kneel at her feet. "Oh, Lady Alice, I am so very sorry. This is so—"

"Thank you, but say nothing about it," Lady Alice said quickly. "I cannot yet speak of it. Pray tell me of yourself, your family. How do you all go on? Your uncle is home for the summer, is he not?"

For a few minutes, therefore, they talked of Birchall House and the Strong family, before Winnie said gently, "Lady Alice, Captain Edgerton would very much like to see... the bedchamber. Should you mind that? He would not come in here."

"He does not wish to talk to me? For I cannot, at least, not yet. It is all too raw." Her voice trailed away into nothing.

Winnie was still holding her hand, so she stroked it gently. "No, no, nothing like that. He only wants to look at the place where... well, to look. He means only to help, and would do nothing you dislike."

"Let him look where he will if it helps to bring Arthur's murderer to justice," she said, more robustly. "The perpetrator cannot be allowed to get away with such a dreadful crime."

"No, indeed," Winnie said. "Thank you, my lady."

Rising to her feet, she curtsied respectfully and left the two ladies to their grief, summoning the gentlemen into the bedroom. Malling was still in the bedroom, folding undergarments, but the captain sent her away.

Never having been involved in a murder before, Winnie had no idea what to expect. If she had thought about it, she might have supposed that examining the room would be a swift affair, a quick look at the position of the bed, and not much more. The room was immaculate and surely there was nothing to be gleaned from it? But the captain prowled about, back and forth, this way and that, at first just looking, but then examining the furnishings in greater detail. He paced out distances, opened and closed the window, looked into the closets and even crawled under the bed. Then he asked Winnie to make a sketch of the room, showing every item of furniture, with the pacings recorded.

"Good. Sandy, will you ask Lord Birtwell to attend us here, if convenient?"

Winnie's stomach gave a little flip. Lord Birtwell... Walter. She would see him, then, an unexpected gift.

When Mr Alexander had left, the captain turned to Winnie. "Have you been in this room before today?"

"No, sir, never. Occasionally, I slept in one of the guest rooms when I was here for a ball, and I have been in Josie's room often, but most of the family rooms I have never seen."

"So you cannot tell me if anything is out of place or has changed?"

"Oh, I can answer that very easily. Everything would be exactly as it always was. Because Lady Alice cannot see her surroundings, she requires everything to be kept in the same position and not moved about. That is true of the public rooms, too. I would be prepared to swear that nothing has changed, but Malling would confirm it."

"The maid? I will ask her later. Ah, here is Lord Birtwell."

Again, that little flip of the stomach as he strode in, quite at his ease, looking around the room and taking in the presence of Sir Hubert and Uncle Alfred. Then he saw Winnie and smiled that warm, lazy smile that always tied her in knots inside.

"Well, well, well, Mouse! What are you doing here?" he said, carelessly flicking her cheek with one finger.

Before she could respond, Captain Edgerton said smoothly, "Miss Strong is helping me with my enquiries, my lord."

"Is that appropriate?" His eyebrows lifted. "How can a *lady* be of help to you in such a gruesome business?"

"In the same way as Sir Hubert and Mr Alfred Strong, my lord, by knowing Corland Castle and its inhabitants well, while being herself an outsider and therefore above suspicion."

Walter's eyes narrowed at the words *'above suspicion'*, but he said only, "If any lady can help, it would be Miss Strong. She is the most sensible female I know."

Winnie stored the compliment away with a little burst of pleasure. To be thought sensible was not much, but a great deal better than nothing. As he moved further into the room, she had the opportunity to feast on the sight of him, so tall, so perfectly proportioned for a man, so very desirable. But he was not for her, she knew that.

He had always been kind to her, including her in every childish game as they grew up, even when his brother Eustace would have kept her out. So many times he had been kind to her! Once, when he and Eustace had ridden over to see them, when they left, Winnie had run after them down the drive. Seeing her following, Eustace had only laughed and ridden off at a rapid pace, but Walter had stopped, dismounted, and walked beside her all the way to the gates. How could she not love him? But he was the heir to an earldom, and would never look so low as a baronet's daughter.

Captain Edgerton had not taken his eyes off Walter, either. "My lord, I believe you were the first person to reach this room when the incident occurred. Could I ask you to describe to me, if you would be so good, where you were when you first became aware of something occurring, what you heard, and what you then did?"

"I was asleep in bed, of course, when—"

"And your room is...?"

"Oh... the principal guest room, since my own room is undergoing renovation. My mother always redecorates two or three rooms each spring.

I am currently in the south-western tower... from here, to the right and past the stairs."

"Thank you, my lord. Pray continue. You were asleep in bed and...?"

"I heard screaming, so naturally I came to investigate and found..." He glanced at Winnie. "You know what I found, Edgerton."

"Did you pause to don a robe? Light a candle?"

"No, it sounded too urgent. It was almost dawn, so there was already a little light... not much in the passageway, but a little. I wore only my night shirt. Do you really need so much detail, Captain?"

"It helps me to visualise the situation, my lord," he said smoothly. "So you left your room and came down the passageway in some haste, and then...?"

"I came into the room and—"

"The door... was it open or closed?"

He frowned, thinking. "Closed, I think. Yes, I am sure, for the screams grew louder as soon as I opened the door. I went in and saw Nicholson on the bed, and Aunt Alice standing beside it, the axe in her hand. There was... blood everywhere."

Again he glanced at Winnie, and she nodded encouragingly.

"Was there a light burning? A candle or lamp? Was the fire lit?"

"Nothing of that nature, only a little light filtering past the curtains at the windows. It was dim, but I could see a little."

"Any hint of candle smoke in the air?"

He frowned, considering. "I recall nothing of that nature."

"Very good. What was it you noticed first, my lord?"

He paused to consider. "Aunt Alice. She wore only a nightgown, her hair plaited as if she had just risen from her bed. Then I noticed the bed... the torn blankets, the feathers from a shredded pillow, that sort of thing. It was clearly Nicholson. I could not see his head, but one of his arms dangled from beneath the covers — what was left of them. But it was Aunt Alice I noticed the most. Even in the dim light, I could see that there was blood all over her, and a great pool of it on the rug beside the bed, dripping from Uncle Arthur's arm. Is this... the sort of detail you want, Captain?" His voice was low, uncomfortable.

"This is excellent detail, my lord. The feathers from the pillow... were they in the air or settled?"

He frowned, pondering. "Some in the air, I think. Most were settled... no, I am not sure. Is it important?"

"It is difficult to say at this stage what is important and what is not, my lord. Pray continue."

"Aunt Alice stopped screaming when she heard me come in. She said, *'Who is there?'*, or something of the sort and I told her who I was. She wanted to know what had happened, if Nicholson was dead and I could see that he was, so I told her that. Then the others arrived... the girls... Olivia and Tess, so I chased them out before they could see the dreadful scene, and stopped anyone else from entering the room. My father took charge after that, and we sent for Sir Hubert, the magistrate."

"Ah, Mr Alexander," Captain Edgerton said, as the Scotsman came into the room. "Have you brought it? Excellent. My lord, Mr Alexander is carrying the axe which was found on that fateful night. Could you tell me if you recognise it? Is it from the castle?"

Walter glanced at it, but shook his head almost immediately. "The great hall is full of old weapons like this, but I know nothing of them. Eustace would know... my brother. He has made a study of our collection, although there are no gaps on the walls where an axe such as this might have hung. We looked that first day. I should think the murderer brought it with him, do you not agree?"

"It is possible," the captain said equably.

He then spent some time arranging Mr Alexander on the bed in the exact position in which Mr Nicholson had been discovered, according to Walter's memory of events. So it was no surprise when he then turned to Winnie, and she understood why he had asked her to wear a white dress, so similar to a nightgown.

"Perhaps, Miss Strong, I could trouble you to stand here on the rug, where the Lady Alice stood? Thank you... about there, Lord Birtwell?"

"A little closer... a step this way. Turn slightly to the right. There."

"Excellent. Would you take the axe, Miss Strong?"

"No, other hand," Walter said. "Aunt Alice held it in her left hand. Just dangling."

"Is the Lady Alice left-handed or right-handed?"

"Oh, right-handed. She uses her fan in her right hand. She said she just trod on the axe handle and—"

"I will ask her ladyship about it when I interview her," the captain said.

Winnie shifted the axe to her left hand. "It is surprisingly light," she said. "It looks as if it would be heavy, but it is not very. See, I can lift it easily."

She raised it above her head and swung it in a sharp chopping motion, whereupon the captain leapt forward and whisked it from her hand.

"Careful, careful! It is very sharp, Miss Strong. But it satisfies me on one point, that a lady could wield this axe without difficulty."

"A lady?" Walter said sharply. "Then you are seriously thinking... you propose that Aunt Alice murdered her own husband? I confess, I wondered myself after finding her here covered in blood, but she is blind, after all. How could she do it? And she is the daughter of an earl, may I remind you."

"Rank is no bar to wickedness, my lord," Captain Edgerton said, looking him steadily in the eye.

"In general, yes, but in the particular... Aunt Alice would not hurt so much as a fly. Anyone who knows her would tell you as much."

"Which is precisely why I have been engaged to investigate this murder," the captain said calmly. "Knowing none of you, I can therefore make no assumptions. In fact, I *must not* make assumptions. I did so on my last commission, and two innocent men almost died because of it, so I no longer say of *anyone* that he or she could not possibly have done the deed. The Lady Alice Nicholson was discovered beside the freshly murdered body of her husband, covered in his blood and with the axe which almost certainly killed him in her hand, so she must be at the very top of my list of potential murderers. No one will be more pleased than I to prove her innocence, I assure you, but at the moment, that proof evades me."

5: The Man On The Stairs

Captain Michael Edgerton sat in the old nursery facing Sandy across the scarred table that served as their interview desk.

"Who is next, Sandy?" Michael said.

"It should be Mr Eustace Atherton, the middle son, but he's away somewhere, and he doesnae even live here."

"He has gone to Doncaster, a long-standing engagement, but one wonders why he thought it appropriate to abandon his family with a murderer on the loose. He knows about the weapons, too, so he might have told us where the axe came from. There are suits of armour all over the place, have you noticed? And all sporting a suitably ferocious pike or sword or mace — or axe. Well, skip Mr Eustace for now."

"Mr Kent Atherton, Captain. Who will smile and tell us he knows nothing, saw nothing and the chaplain was a saint."

Michael chuckled. "True, but it has to be done. Ring the bell, will you, and let us see what Mr Kent has to say."

"If he can be found and hasnae gone off shooting pheasant."

Michael winced. "In June, Sandy? Hardly."

"I cannae get my head round the proper seasons for shooting things. In Canongate, we thought ourselves lucky to have meat on the table at all."

Mr Kent Atherton arrived within five minutes, looking inappropriately excited. "At last! I thought you would never get to me. How are you getting on, Captain? Found the murderer yet, have you?"

"It is early days, sir," Michael said.

Kent was a slender, dark-haired man of twenty-two, not above average height, with a cheerful countenance featuring a perpetual smile. Despite the seriousness of the subject, he chuckled. "He got in through the scullery window, it would seem. But Shapman has fixed it, and changed all the locks, so he will not be coming back, will he? A pity, for I should very much like to see you defend us from attack with that businesslike sword, Captain. Seen some action, has it?"

"The night of the murder, sir..."

"Ah, straight to the point," Kent said with another chuckle.

"You were asleep in this room on the plan... is that correct?"

"It is."

"Please describe what happened, sir, and what you did. Be as precise as you can."

"I heard Aunt Alice screaming fit to burst. Just screaming and screaming, continuously. I put on some clothes... a nightgown and robe, and lit a candle, then stuck my head out of the door to see if I could see what was going on."

"You did not rush towards the screams?"

"Not at first. I thought most likely it was a fire, so I was expecting smoke... maybe flames. But there was nothing like that. Then Father's door opened, he saw me and we set off to Aunt Alice's room. She was still screaming... the whole house must have been awake by this time. Someone was coming up the main stairs, and we saw Walter... Lord Birtwell go into Aunt Alice's room ahead of us. You know what we found there. It was... horrible." For the first time, the smile slipped. "I cannot bear to think of it. Please do not ask me to describe it."

"We have a full description from the coroner's report, sir. There is no need for you to say any more about it. However, there is just one point on which I would like your opinion. There were feathers strewn about from a torn pillow. Were they all settled on the bed or were any floating in the air?"

"You want to know how recent the murder was, of course. There were some still floating in the air, but Aunt Alice may have disturbed them. She was covered in blood, so she must have touched Uncle Arthur."

"Thank you, sir. What happened after that?"

"The girls appeared... my sister Olivia and my cousin Tess. Walter pushed them out of the room and set footmen to guard the door. There were several footmen who had come down from the attics."

"So apart from the footmen from the attics, and various members of the family from the bedroom floor, who else was there?"

"No one."

"Then who came up the stairs?"

Kent frowned. "How odd. No one would come up the main stairs, would they? The servants in the basement would come up the service stairs, but none of them were there, anyway."

"Tell me precisely what you saw of this person, Mr Atherton."

"It was while we were on the balcony above the great hall... just here." He pointed to the map. "There is a clear view over the main stairs from there, and the skylight admitted a little light. Enough to see someone on the stairs, anyway. Naturally, I assumed it was someone responding to the screams, as we were, but now I wonder—"

"Yes?" Michael said gently. "What do you wonder, Mr Atherton?"

"Whether what I saw was someone going *down* the stairs, not up. Someone running *away* from the screams, not towards them. Is it possible, Captain, that I saw the murderer leaving the scene?"

"It is possible," Michael said gravely. "Was it a man or a woman?"

Kent exhaled slowly. "I cannot say! If only I had taken more notice at the time."

Later, when he had gone, Sandy said, "At least ye can eliminate a few people from suspicion now, Captain. If the murderer was running down the main stairs, it couldnae have been anyone from the earl's family — or Lady Alice."

Michael thought about that. "Only if he is telling the truth."

***

Captain Edgerton's questioning proceeded slowly, working in strict rank order, having started with Lord Rennington himself, to end eventually with the kitchen boy and the youngest apprentice gardener. Sir Hubert and his brother were cordially invited to attend if they wished, but Sir Hubert declared himself happy to hand over responsibility for the investigation to the captain.

"I am not ashamed to admit that this is outside my experience," he said cheerfully. "You seem to know what you are about, Edgerton."

Winnie was a little downcast at this, for what could be more exciting than to help investigate a murder? She never minded working with her father on his correspondence or the accounts, and Uncle Alfred's government work had its moments of interest, but most of it was dull labour indeed, whereas Captain Edgerton was engaged in an enterprise of the utmost moment. And of course, being at the castle meant the chance of an occasional glimpse of Walter.

"I should still value your advice from time to time, Sir Hubert," the captain said.

"Of course, of course. Why not come for dinner now and then? I am seldom from home, and my brother Alfred is here all summer now. He works at the Treasury in London, but we enjoy his company when Parliament is not in session. We may talk about your findings over the port, if you wish."

"That would be most agreeable. But perhaps I might borrow Miss Strong for a while longer, if you and Lady Strong can spare her? I should like someone with an eye for detail to sort through the papers in the late Mr Nicholson's room. Mrs Edgerton has already made a start, but there are drawers and boxes full of letters and bills going back decades. Miss Strong is ideally suited to assist with such a task."

Winnie's spirits lifted instantly. "I should love to help," she said at once, before her father had a chance to object.

"Naturally, anything we can do to assist your endeavours, Edgerton," her father said, but he frowned, all the same.

"You have concerns, Sir Hubert?" the captain said.

"What your wife does is her own affair... married lady, you see. But Winnie... well, I should not normally wish her to sort through a gentleman's letters."

"Even when the gentleman is a man of God? Unless you have any reason to think there might be anything amongst Nicholson's letters that a gently brought up young lady should not see?"

Sir Hubert's face cleared. "No, of course not. I never heard any rumours of that nature, and if there had been anything unbecoming of a clergyman, certainly it would have been noised abroad. There are no secrets in a household like this."

Captain Edgerton nodded sagely, and Winnie was given the leave she sought. It was not that she expected to see Walter at all, for she would be hidden away in Mr Nicholson's room, and Walter would be elsewhere, if he were even in the castle at all, but there was a comfort in being in his home, at least, and knowing that perhaps he was not very far away from her.

Mrs Edgerton was something of a surprise, being an elegant, willowy creature at least half a head taller than her husband.

"Thank goodness you are here, Miss Strong," she said, her eyes smiling at Winnie as she opened the door to her. "I started this task with my companion's aid, but Miss Peach has not the methodical nature necessary, and constantly became distracted by Mr Nicholson's letters from his family. All the domestic trivia! Endlessly fascinating to a spinster of a certain age, no doubt, but not at all to the purpose. Come in, do, and see what we have to deal with."

Winnie surveyed the room with a sinking heart. Mr Nicholson's room, which was next door to Lady Alice's suite, was not large, no doubt being designed originally as a dressing room, but there were no wardrobes or wash stands, nor the bed that often sat in a married man's dressing room. Instead, there was a desk, a smaller writing table and two walls fitted out with bookcases, and cupboards beneath. The cupboards were filled with drawers, and the drawers were filled with papers.

"I have made a start on the desk drawers, where I felt the most important papers should be, but then I discovered all these." Mrs Edgerton waved a hand towards the cupboards. "Frankly, I find it somewhat daunting. I do not think he ever threw anything away."

"Goodness," Winnie said, opening a drawer or two at random, and leafing through the papers. "Old bills, letters... this one is thirty years old. Are we looking for anything in particular?"

"Anything relating to legal or financial matters. His will left his fortune to his daughter, but no one seems to know what this fortune might be, or where it is hidden."

"There is no money here?"

"Almost a thousand pounds in coins and notes in the safe."

Winnie's eyebrows rose. "So much? Papa never keeps more than two hundred at home."

"Sensible man, but I understand there was a certain amount of gambling for high stakes went on here. Mr Nicholson was often successful. Could you make a start on these drawers while I work through the desk?"

"Of course. I shall make three piles — personal letters, bills and anything legal or financial."

"Ah, my husband was right," Mrs Edgerton said. "You have an orderly mind, Miss Strong."

For a while, they worked in silence, Mrs Edgerton at the desk and Winnie sitting on the floor, happily sorting into neat piles. After a while, as the piles grew unwieldy, she found string and bundled them up with a neat label on each, *'Letters from Andover, 1777-1785'* or *'Tailors' bills, 1790-1800'*.

But then she came to an oddity.

"Ma'am? I am not sure what to do with this letter. It is from the Bishop of Winchester, relating to Mr Nicholson's ordination. Should I start a new pile, or just put it with the Hampshire correspondence?"

"Is it merely a form letter of congratulations?"

"No, it predates his ordination. It seems to suggest he tried to be ordained previously. *'I wonder, sir, if you have reconsidered your desire to be ordained, since I have not heard from you in the two years since our last meeting at Christmastide? I remain willing to accept you into the church as a priest, but if you have found an alternative path in life, then I wish you well.'*"

"May I see it?" Quickly, she scanned it. "Well, it is official enough that my husband will want to see it. He is interested in Mr Nicholson's early life as well as his more recent doings. Miss Strong, you are clearly familiar with your father's affairs, so would you give me your opinion of these accounts? There are some entries I cannot quite make out. For a clergyman, Mr Nicholson wrote a very poor hand sometimes."

***

Captain Michael Edgerton had interviewed all the members of the Atherton family who had been at the castle on the night of the chaplain's murder and had reached the upper servants. After the butler and housekeeper, he called a halt for the evening, as Sandy clenched and unclenched his writing hand, stiff and aching from a day of taking notes.

"Not to worry, Sandy," Michael said cheerfully. "By the time we get to the housemaids and footmen, there will be nothing to write." He affected a broad Yorkshire accent. *"Oh, no sir, never saw or 'eard a thing, sir. I were fast asleep in my bed all night, sir. Could 'ave knocked me down with a feather when I 'eard what 'ad 'appened."*

Sandy laughed. "So why do ye bother asking?"

"I want them to look me in the eye as they say it. If they cannot, I shall know they are lying. Ah, Luce!" It was the oddest thing how after six years of marriage, his heart still flip-flopped when his wife walked into a room. "Had a good day, my dear?"

"No. You give me the dullest tasks, Michael. However, I like Miss Strong. She is a sensible, useful girl who gets on with the work without fuss. She has devised a system for sorting everything into piles, and then tying them into bundles. You will have no trouble laying your hand on Mr Nicholson's hatter's bills for the year 1803, should you ever need them. Here is your mail for today. This one is local."

"From Lady Strong, inviting us to dinner. We have a choice of dates. Tomorrow if we want to eat en famille, or the day after if we should care to dine with some of the neighbours — the Franklyns. Do you know anything of them?"

"The daughter is betrothed to Lord Birtwell."

"Ah, so she is the future Countess of Rennington? Then I should certainly like to meet her. Sandy, you are invited too, if you care to come."

"Why not? It will make a change from this place. Have ye finished with me, Captain?"

"Yes, off you go and change for dinner. Leave your notes. I shall lock them away in the tower room."

When Sandy had gone, Michael smiled at his wife and patted his knee invitingly. Laughing, she draped herself on his lap, and allowed herself to be thoroughly kissed.

"I am sorry Nicholson's papers are so dull," he said when they eventually surfaced. "However, it must be done. There could be a letter hidden in those piles of hatter's bills that would show us exactly why Nicholson was killed."

"That reminds me," she said, stretching to reach her reticule without falling off his lap. "Miss Strong found this. She gave it to me because she could not work out how to file it, but it puzzles me for other reasons entirely."

Michael read the letter carefully. "It puzzles you because it took him two attempts to be ordained?"

"No." She flipped it over to show the direction. "It was sent to him here. The bishop wrote to his family home, but they forwarded it to Mr Nicholson here. So he must have come here *before* his ordination."

"No, I believe... I am tolerably certain he was already ordained. Can you reach Sandy's notebook?" Another stretch brought it within reach. "Let me see... it was the earl who told us the story... where was it? Ah, here it is. *'Father met N at an inn... snowed up... got on well... brought him back to be chaplain.'* Now, here is the crucial point. *'Father brought the...'* What does this say? Oh, special licence. He had got it in town and was bringing it with him. *'Thought could not be married because of snow, but N newly ordained, able to marry us. Very convenient.'* The earl thought it a wonderful story, Nicholson arriving with his father and able to marry them, despite the snow, because it is quite a distance to the church at Birchall, and the parson was elderly. The whole of the bride's family had gathered for the occasion, seemingly, and Nicholson saved the day. But he must have been ordained— Oh, but the bishop says *'as a priest'*. Perhaps he was already ordained as a deacon. He could have married them as a deacon. Only the Holy Sacrament is reserved for priests."

"Yes, that must be it," she said, "although... the bishop seemed to think he might have given up the idea of being a clergyman altogether."

"Hmm, *'an alternative path in life.'* I think I might write to Pettigrew. He would enjoy a little visit to Winchester, I am sure, to find out precisely when Nicholson was ordained, and as what. And meanwhile, I shall confirm when the earl was married."

"You can ask him at dinner," Luce said.

"No, no, no! Independent verification, my dear. There is bound to be a copy of Debrett's somewhere in the library."

"I know where the family Bible is kept," she said. "It was the first thing Peachy looked for."

"Even better! What a treasure you are!"

"Are you going to kiss me again?" she said hopefully.

"Later, wife, later. Show me this family Bible first."

6: An Invitation To Birchall House

Walter unfolded the letter again. An invitation to dine at Birchall House with the Strongs was not a rare event, but this was a little different. *'I know you will not be entertaining at Corland until this ghastly business is behind you, so I am sure you will be happy to spend an evening with Miss Franklyn.'* He was always pleased to see his future wife, of course, but Lady Strong's kindness only underlined his own neglect. Bea had been home from town for two weeks now, and he had not even seen her. They had exchanged notes when she first returned, but then there had been the Nicholson business. Even so, that did not preclude him riding over to call upon Bea, and finding out how she had enjoyed her season, but somehow he had not managed to do so.

After writing to accept the invitation, he had dashed off a note to Bea to say how much he looked forward to seeing her again and hearing all her news. Now, as he sat in the carriage, he wondered, only half in jest, whether he would even recognise his betrothed after so long. It was more than three months since she had left Yorkshire to enjoy herself in town, and their letters had been sporadic, to say the least.

The carriage felt rather crowded, for although Mrs Edgerton's odd companion, Miss Peach, had been left behind, there were still four of them to be conveyed, and the Scotsman and Walter himself being both tall and broad shouldered, they bumped each other constantly as the carriage bounced over the rutted road to Birchall. Walter had to hold tight to the strap, wishing he had thought to order the Atherton travelling carriage, which was better suited to these country roads.

"You are betrothed to Miss Franklyn, I understand, Lord Birtwell," Mrs Edgerton said, as he straightened himself after a particularly bad jolt.

"I have that honour."

"Is your engagement of long standing?"

"Almost a year now."

"And now Mr Nicholson's tragedy may delay the marriage even further. You would not wish to show any disrespect to your uncle by marriage. I do hope you will not have to wait too long for your wedding day. Long engagements can be so trying, I feel. Once an understanding is reached, then one wants to get on with it."

Walter was spared the necessity of answering by Captain Edgerton. "With the heir to an earldom, the settlements will undoubtedly be complex."

"Oh no, that was all arranged months ago," Walter said airily. "Miss Franklyn did not wish to be married before the season, that is all. She desired to have sufficient time to buy her clothes."

"Ah, the wedding clothes, of course," Mrs Edgerton murmured. "How very sensible of her."

What Bea had in fact desired was for them to be married during the season in the congratulatory glow of the entire Beau Monde, but the Dowager Countess's illness had put paid to that idea. The whole family dared not leave home as they awaited her final hours, and whenever it happened, Walter would be in mourning for some time. Even before that, there was Nicholson's demise, and there must be a period of mourning for the poor fellow. Perhaps Walter would not be leg-shackled before Christmas. A few more months of freedom yet from petticoat rule.

When they arrived at Birchall House, with Sir Hubert and Lady Strong on the steps to greet them, Captain Edgerton sprang out of the carriage first to assist his wife to alight, then Walter politely ushered the Scotsman out. As he stepped down onto the drive, he could not help smiling at the sight of Birchall House, gently glowing in the late afternoon sun. It was not an imposing edifice, like Corland, nor particularly distinguished by architectural merit or great age. It was a pleasant family house, and Walter always felt as if it were as much his own home as Corland.

He had spent almost as much time here as he grew up, as he and Eustace and Josie devised their childish games with Winnie, Hebe and Mabel. Such fun they had had! Even when he was away at Eton for months at a time, his first action on returning was to run the mile or so to the boundary with Birchall, and climb up to the tree house there. It was the refuge for all the children from both families, and where they were always looked for first when they were summoned for something or other. He had hardly been to the tree house this year, just once or twice when he was particularly miserable to be stuck at home and not enjoying his last months as a free man. Often he found Winnie there, rocking gently on one of the swings, a book on her lap. She always teased him out of the doldrums. Good old Mouse! A true friend to him, always.

He made his greetings to Sir Hubert and Lady Strong and followed them into the house.

"Maynard, how are you?"

"Very well, my lord. Thank you kindly for asking," the butler said, smiling paternally at him, as he took his hat and gloves. "Miss Franklyn is already in the drawing room, my lord."

"Ah, very good, very good."

He strolled after the others, pausing to make a minute adjustment to his cravat in the mirror as he passed it, and so was the last into the room.

"Viscount Birtwell, my lady," Maynard intoned, even though Walter had already seen Lady Strong as he arrived. But he understood the reason in his first glance around the room, for Lady Esther Franklyn was sitting beside Bea, and that put everyone on their mettle. Even so experienced a butler as Maynard adhered more rigidly to correct protocol when the daughter of a duke was in the house.

Winnie scurried into the room behind him, laden with a tray of sweetmeats. "Well, Mouse," Walter said, flicking her cheek affectionately. "Escaped from your murder enquiries for a while, have you?"

"Good evening, Walter. Miss Franklyn is over by the window, with Lady Esther."

And away she went, always busy about some business or other, as if she had never heard of the existence of servants. He smiled at her retreating back, her hair as brown and glossy as a mouse, one strand somehow always escaping the hairpins and falling across her cheek. He would have liked to whisk the tray from her hands and sit her down for a comfortable chat, but she was busy, as usual, and duty called him to his betrothed and her stepmother.

Across the room, the two women were watching his arrival, Lady Esther Franklyn with well-bred dignity, Bea smiling and waving, her abundant black curls bouncing. There was no danger of missing her in a room full of people, not with hair like that. How could he ever have thought he might not recognise her?

With a nod here and a quick word there, he made his way across the room, and executed his bow. "Lady Esther, what an unexpected pleasure. Am I to understand that His Grace's health has improved?"

"My father is a great deal better, I thank you, Lord Birtwell. In fact, he was well on the way to recovery by the time I reached Marshfields, as I suspected would be the case. My family is generally blessed with excellent health. I am pleased to be able to return home so swiftly. And how is the Dowager Lady Rennington?"

"Very frail," Walter said. "She barely knows her own family now."

"That is a great tragedy when it happens," Lady Esther said. "She is much in my prayers, Lord Birtwell."

"As His Grace is in mine," Walter said smoothly. Then, feeling that his duty had been done by his future mother-in-law, he sat down beside Bea. "Well, Bea, how was town this year? Did you miss me?"

"Oh yes, of course. There were any number of occasions when an extra gentleman would have been most welcome. Vauxhall's was quite dreadful. They let anybody in, without the least discrimination, but happily Lord Firstock was able to accompany us, and kept the riff-raff away. He was quite my saviour this season, most attentive and very put out to discover that I was already betrothed."

"Was he so?" Walter said, not much interested in Lord Firstock. "He was never much in the petticoat line before, but I suppose even a nodcock like him can do the pretty if he must. Did you see anything of Chalfont or Hickson? Or Dunstable? I expected to read the announcement in the *Gazette*, but not a word."

"Oh... I cannot recall all your friends, Walter. They all look the same to me. Besides, we were much engaged with the Bucknells this year. Dear Charity has quite taken me under her wing... the Marchioness of Ramsey, you know. We met almost every day, at least until the duke was taken ill, and everyone rushed off to Marshfields, and Papa and I had to come home, for I could not stay without Mama."

"Hmm... I suppose I shall have to write to Dunstable to find out what is going on. Did you never see him, even at Almack's? He would have been there, squiring about that young lady of his."

"I have told you, I cannot tell one of your friends from another. You should have been there yourself, if you care so much about them. And if you *had* come, we could have been married already and I should not have needed to leave town so early. As a married woman, I should not have needed Mama to chaperon me."

"You know why I could not come, Bea, not with Grandmother so ill. I could not be dancing and enjoying myself while she is quietly fading from this world. We shall be married some time or other."

"Yes, but when?"

"Not for a few weeks, at any event. There will have to be a decent mourning period for Nicholson, but we can have the banns called after that."

"You would go into mourning for the chaplain?" she said, her blue eyes widening.

"He was my aunt's husband, so yes, of course."

"And then the Dowager will die, and who knows when you will leave off the black crêpe? Mama has had a better idea — we could be married from Marshfields, far away from all this tragedy."

"Marshfields! What business have we there? The duke is no relation of yours."

"He is my stepmother's father, so he is certainly a relation... of a sort, and he is most amenable to the idea. He has always had a fondness for me, you know, and when word reached Mama of the trouble over the chaplain, she saw at once that we could not be married from home, not with a *murder* in the background. There is no chapel at Marshfields, but they have the ballroom — we could have a wedding ball! Would that not be fun? Mama has managed it all for us — her cousin will arrange the special licence, and her uncle the bishop will officiate."

"Lady Esther is too kind, but I think we will not trouble all these people," he said tersely. "I am in mourning for my uncle, Bea, and cannot contemplate a wedding at this time. Excuse me, I must make my greeting to your father."

And so saying, he rose and removed himself and the fiery ball of rage inside him to a safer distance, before there was an explosion.

***

Winnie moved about the room, doing her duty as the eldest daughter of the house, ensuring that the guests were mingling and that everyone who wanted had a drink and something to nibble, for dinner was late, as usual. Dinner was always late when there were guests, for Mrs Mann was getting old and easily grew flustered.

She saw the quarrel, however, if that was what it was. Yes, definitely a quarrel. She had known Walter all her life and could interpret every nuance of his face, and Bea was not a person to whom the word *'nuance'* could ever be applied. Every inner emotion was writ large across her features. So they had fallen out about something, although she could not tell what. But it was not her concern. All couples had their disagreements, and whatever the cause of this one, it would not stop them marrying and therefore was of no moment.

Dinner, when it eventually arrived, was amusing, in part because of Walter's efforts to ignore Bea and hers not to be ignored, but also because Winnie was seated next to Captain Edgerton, who regaled the table with improbable but highly entertaining stories from his years in India. From time to time, he turned to her and enquired in a low voice about the other guests, and especially the Franklyns.

"Mr Franklyn?" he murmured.

"Unexpectedly came into a fortune ten years ago, married Lady Esther shortly thereafter," she responded in the same low tone. "They moved here five years ago, and have two small sons."

"Lady Esther?"

"Second daughter of the Duke of Camberley."

"About thirty?"

"Thirty-four."

"So Miss Franklyn is her stepdaughter. Her mother must have been a striking woman."

The mass of black curls, of course. But Winnie could only say, "I have no idea. There is no portrait on display at Highwood Place."

"No, I suppose there would not be, with a second wife in residence. Did Lady Esther marry him for his money?"

"What an impertinent question, Captain! What would you say if I asked you such a thing?"

"I would answer at once that I only married my wife for her fortune and her rank as a baron's daughter." He smiled, his teeth gleaming in the candlelight, but he threw a glance that was far from indifferent towards his wife where she sat further down the table.

"Yes, I am sure you did," Winnie said, unable to suppress her own smile. "Do you never stop asking questions?"

"Sometimes, but only while I work out what the next question should be. People are fascinating."

"Indeed they are, Captain." And not the least fascinating was the captain himself.

"You must talk to a great many people as you go about here and there, Miss Strong," the captain said. "What are they saying about the murder? Who do the villagers think might be responsible?"

"You have kept me rather busy lately, Captain," Winnie said with a smile. "I have not been in the village much at all since poor Mr Nicholson's demise."

"Nevertheless, I am sure you have heard some talk."

"Oh, there are plenty of wild ideas. The simple-minded lad from the mill. The widow who talks to her chickens but not to her neighbours. The potter's youngest boy, who is always in some sort of trouble. The Franklyns' butler who waters the wine. The new chambermaid at the inn, who has wicked eyes, whatever that may be. Or the usual favourites — the Romanies or the tinker or the charcoal man or the smugglers from Scarborough way or the half-pay soldiers wandering the countryside."

"Do any of those strike you as plausible, Miss Strong?"

She gave a wry laugh. "Not one. For one thing, they would have to get to the castle from the village. Then they would have to know how to break in, where to find the axe, and where the chaplain was sleeping. That is before one even gets to the question of *why* the potter's boy or poor Mrs Wilde or the smugglers, for heaven's sake, should bear a grudge against him in the first place."

"That is indeed the key to the mystery," the captain said slowly. "He seems to have been a well-liked man, yet someone disliked him enough to kill him. If you hear anything to the point, will you let me know, Miss Strong?"

"Of course. We all want the murderer caught."

When the ladies withdrew, Winnie made a point of sitting beside Mrs Edgerton. "Your husband tells me he only married you for your fortune and rank, but I do not believe him."

Mrs Edgerton laughed. "He tells everyone that. It amuses him to say so, but he had more money than I did, in fact, and he was not exactly nobody. He is the son of a gentleman, despite his odd career. Besides, my father was only a baron for a few weeks, and before that he was merely a lowly government official."

"Do you not mind the captain saying such things?"

"No. He will tell me all about his conversation with you later, you see, so it is not as if he is insulting me behind my back."

"Well, if you do not mind it... but I should not like it myself. I like my father's way, for he talks about the grey times before he knew my mother, and the brightness of the years since. He tells the whole world how much he loves her."

"And that is admirable, Miss Strong, but not all men can express their feelings so openly. Michael is one such, but it does not mean he feels nothing. When we first met, he climbed the ivy to my window on the third floor every night just to leave a little love token on my pillow — a single rose, a heart-shaped stone, a poem..." She sighed. "It was *so* romantic, and he said not a word, so I had no idea who it was, not for a long time. He still does silly things of that nature, so I know how strong his affection is. Love is not in words, it is in actions. A man shows his love by what he does, not by what he says."

"That is very wise," Winnie said, but secretly she still preferred a man who could express his love in words, too. Privately, perhaps, for not everyone was as besotted as her father, or as open-hearted, but there had to be a declaration of love. And that made her look at Bea, and wonder how Walter expressed his love for her. Not in his actions, that much was certain, for he had never treated her any differently, from the time she had moved to the North Riding five years ago to the time when they were betrothed. But perhaps he was ardent when they were alone together.

That thought was too dispiriting for words. She could bear him marrying Bea if it were merely a pragmatic matter — the heir to an earldom marrying a rich and well-connected young lady. At least Winnie could still be his friend. But if he were deeply in love with Bea, then there would be no room for Winnie in Walter's life at all, and that would bring her unbearable grief.

But it appeared her friendship was still necessary to him, for as she took him his tea, he whispered to her, "The tree house tomorrow?"

She nodded, her heart beating quicker in anticipation. The tree house! He was going to confide in her again — at last!

7: A Bit Of A Rogue

Winnie's day was busy from breakfast until late at night, for there was always something to do in a house with five adults and two lively boys in it. Theirs was not the sort of grand establishment where the ladies sat about on chaises longues with embroidery frames all day, while servants glided about in silent efficiency. The kitchen lurched from one crisis to the next, the linen cupboard was in a perpetual state of near disaster, and Mrs Penfold and Mrs Mann, the housekeeper and cook, had maintained a state of mutual hostility for as long as anyone could remember.

Lady Strong escaped from the battlefield into her beloved garden as often as she could, capable of forgetting time altogether while there was a trowel in her hand. Thus the management of the house, in so far as such a thing was possible, had fallen to Winnie since she had first let down her skirts and put up her hair. Order was as natural to her as breathing, and although the servants still affectionately disregarded her instructions more often than not, remembering her as the grubby child she had once been, she kept the household accounts and the still room, her particular domain, in pristine order.

Before breakfast, however, her time was her own, and she often went out for a walk, to clear her head in preparation for the day to come, mulling over all the tasks to be accomplished and arranging them into the most efficient order. Today, there was no mulling, for her day was already planned. After breakfast, she would go to Corland and continue organising Mr Nicholson's long life into neat bundles, bound with string and labelled appropriately. Her thoughts this morning were bent in an entirely different direction, her feet speeding eagerly along the path through Mama's flowerbeds and then into the woods that fringed their modest estate. Deep in the trees, she came to her favourite place in all the world, the clearing where stood the ancient oak tree. High in its branches sat the old tree house, and beneath the sturdiest limb hung two swings.

He was there! Walter lolled on one swing, idly pushing himself back and forth with one foot. He looked up at her, smiling, and her heart was lost all over again. If only she could be indifferent to him, to see him as nothing more than her old childhood friend. It was so difficult to pretend she cared nothing for him, to express only pleasure at his betrothal to Bea Franklyn. Sometimes, when they did not meet for some time, the intensity faded a little and she could pretend to herself that she was putting him behind her. But then she would see him again, just as handsome and smart and carelessly affectionate towards her, and her heart would explode into tiny pieces all over again.

"Well, Mouse, there you are! Late as usual... or am I early?"

"We are both early, I think," she said, taking the other swing. "I have not heard the church clock yet."

"I must have walked faster than I thought," he said. "Anger, I suppose. I am still in a rage with Bea."

"Walter, you should not talk to me about Miss Franklyn."

"No, no, not about *her*, but about what she is proposing. She wants us to marry at Marshfields, if you please, with a ball beforehand and a special licence and a bishop and all the duke's family looking on, no doubt. What is this obsession with special licences, Mouse? I remember all that fuss with Izzy, insisting on marrying in the chapel at Corland, and even Josie talked about it, although good sense prevailed in the end. *You* would not want all that to-do, would you?"

"Oh no. The banns and Mr Dewar at St Timothy's would do for me." But her spirits sank a little. Would she ever marry? Not Walter, for she could hardly expect such good fortune, but someone... a kind gentleman who would provide her with her own little house and a cluster of children to dote on. How wonderful that would be!

"Exactly, and for me, too. Drag a couple of yokels out of the tap room to act as witnesses, and there you are — all done."

She shook her head at him. "Surely you would want your family about you on such an important occasion?"

"Well... I suppose so," he conceded graciously. "But women make such a *fuss* about things. Even Josie got into a spin about it, and there were the most enormous number of parties and dinners to celebrate the thing. And now Olivia is going the same way, determined to be married in her first season, and has the whole thing planned out. And as for Bea — I cannot understand her at all, Winnie. She is a mystery to me. If only she were as sensible as you, eh? You are so quick-witted and rational, and if you were ever to marry, you would be just as sensible about that. You would never come up with crazy ideas, like this business of marrying at Marshfields.

But that is Bea in a nutshell — always some new scheme to drive a man demented."

Winnie had to bite her tongue to stop herself from crying out, *'Then why are you marrying her?'*

He sighed, and went on without waiting for her to say anything. "I suppose she will have her way in the end. She always does!" He chuckled. "It saves me the bother of thinking about it, and it is her wedding, after all, so it might as well be what she wants. Anything to keep her happy. But even if it should be at Marshfields, I should want a decent interval to mourn poor Mr Nicholson. You would want to mourn an uncle, would you not?"

"Oh yes! I am very fond of all my aunts and uncles."

"I was not exactly fond of Nicholson, but I am very fond indeed of Aunt Alice, and I should not like to do anything that would be disrespectful at such a time. What do you think would be an appropriate mourning period for an uncle by marriage?"

"Your mother would be the best adviser, Walter."

"I shall ask her, of course, but what do *you* think? Three months? Six? Longer?"

"My own opinion would be at least three, since he lived at Corland with you, but you must be guided by your mama."

"Three months. *At least* three months," he said happily. "Yes, that is my opinion exactly."

***

"We seem to be at *point non plus,*" Michael said gloomily. "No one has seen or heard anything useful, and we cannot even find out where the wretched axe came from. If it was within the castle, no one admits to knowing where. All we have learnt is that anyone could have walked into the basement, for the door nearest the stables was never bolted and the bolts on the garden door were broken. Supposedly both doors were locked, but the keys were readily available, and the lock is easily picked. Neate did it in no time at all. There is also the scullery window with the broken latch. The dogs would deter a stranger, but barely stir for anyone known to them. So none of that helps."

"Was there nothing in his letters that raised concern?" Sandy said. "No hint of blackmail? No deep, dark secret?"

"Nothing that might cause anyone to kill the fellow," Michael said with a sigh, passing round a decanter of sherry to the five investigators assembled in the old nursery. "James, is there nothing rumoured below stairs?"

James Neate shrugged. "He is described as a bit of a flirt, but flirting is hardly a murdering affair."

"No, or half the men in England would be dead by now," Michael said. "And in Scotland, too, if Sandy is typical of his race, but that, too, has brought us nothing of interest. One would think that kitchen maids would tattle more freely when exposed to so much Caledonian charm. And Luce, surely you and Miss Peach between you could have managed to eavesdrop to better effect. The earl's skin complaints and Mr Eustace's preference for silk sheets are not exactly pertinent to our enquiries."

"Oh, but so *interesting*, Captain," Miss Peach said, beaming. "Silk sheets! Imagine the expense! And I discovered that whole business with the mutton bones."

The former governess was a nondescript sort of woman, but Michael had to admit she was enthusiastic. A little too enthusiastic, perhaps.

"Peachy, we are not concerned with kitchen thievery," Luce said. "We did our best, Michael, but as we expected, the whole castle has closed ranks against us. They look us straight in the eye and tell us that Mr Nicholson was a blameless chaplain who was devoted to his wife, had no vices and no one can think of a reason why he might have been murdered. I have to say, their shock seems genuine to me."

"Yes, no one said, *'Ah, he was a bit of a rogue, but we never thought anyone disliked him enough to murder him.'* A bit of a rogue would be a good starting point."

"I think he *was* a bit of a rogue," Sandy said. "He was said to be lucky with the cards, but a man cannae have the luck with him always, unless he's making his own some of the time, it seems tae me."

"And flirting with the maids in his own home may suggest something more when he is away from home," Neate said.

"He was seldom away from home, though," Michael said with a frown. "York occasionally, for shopping or church business. Trips to Pickering once or twice a month. He belonged to a political society there."

"A chaplain, attending a political society?" Luce said. "That could have been an excuse, to cover up something nefarious."

"No, he actually attended the meetings," Michael said glumly. "Sir Hubert knows one of the members and made enquiries. They keep attendance records, and Nicholson was often called upon to make the speech of thanks to the speaker. He dined with several of the group beforehand, then stayed at a cheap lodging house overnight, returning the next morning. He used to go with the 10th Earl, but since his death he continues to go alone, and the only part of that which tickles my suspicious nature is the cheap lodging house. To go from the splendour of Corland Castle to a room in a less than salubrious part of town seems unlikely, somehow."

"The footmen say he was tight-fisted, Michael," Neate said. "He never laid out his own blunt if he could help it. Any sign of Mr Eustace?"

"He is still with friends at Doncaster or some such place," Michael said. "His father has written to request he return, for no one else knows anything about the weapons, and nothing appears to be missing, so where did that axe come from? And I have still not exchanged a single word with the widow. One does not like to intrude on so much grief, but she is still the most likely murderer." He sighed. "So we are in exactly the same position as when we arrived. All this diligent work, and we are not an inch further forward."

"I cannot believe that Lady Alice murdered her husband," Luce said. "Why on earth would she?"

"That I cannot begin to guess until I talk to her," Michael said. "One of the usual reasons — love, hate, money, jealousy, revenge. Who knows? What I should like to know is why, if it was her, she chose to use an axe."

"Now that's easier tae explain," Sandy said. "How else can she do it, without eyes tae see? She cannae shoot him, can she? Nor stab him, for that needs precision. She cannae arrange an accident. She cannae poison him. So she waits until he is fast asleep in bed and she knows precisely where he is, and then lays into him with an axe. He wouldnae know a thing about it."

"Then she screams and pretends she just found him like that," Neate said. "It does make a queer kind of sense, Michael."

"Or perhaps she truly did just find him like that," Luce said. "She hears something, wakes up, gets out of bed, walks round to his side of the bed, trips over the axe, picks it up, realises it is covered in blood and screams."

"No, no, no," Sandy said. "If she woke while her husband was being attacked in her own bed, she'd have screamed then, and I cannae believe she slept through it all and only woke up after it was all over. Did they share a bed anyway? These aristocratic couples rarely do."

"This is why we need to talk to her," Michael said tersely. "If she has a good explanation—"

There was a knock on the door and a footman poked a head round. "Gen'leman to see you, Cap'ain, sir. A Mr Wilton-Forth."

Michael laughed. "Willerton-Forbes. Send him in, do."

But the man who crept into the old nursery behind the footman was not the self-assured Mr Willerton-Forbes Michael had left behind in London some months ago. He was as fashionably dressed as usual, and no one would ever suspect that he was a lawyer, but all his customary insouciance was gone. He wore the most woebegone expression he had ever seen.

"Pettigrew? Whatever is the matter? And what are you doing here anyway? Surely a letter would have done?"

Willerton-Forbes glumly shook his head, accepted the glass of sherry Sandy pushed into his hand, downed it in one and held it out to be refilled.

"Ah." Michael steered his friend into a chair, and waited.

"It is dreadful, Michael," Willerton-Forbes said. "When you wrote, telling me of the letter from the Bishop of Winchester, I imagined it would be a routine matter of checking the dates. A day of travel, an hour or two in the bishop's office, a day home, or perhaps even home the same day. But it was not so simple."

"He was not ordained when he came here," Michael said, filled with foreboding.

"I can find no evidence that he was *ever* ordained. You understand the import of that, I am sure."

"The earl's marriage is not valid. Well!" Michael exhaled slowly. "I wanted to discover that Nicholson was a bit of a rogue but this is more — far more — than I had bargained for. What a devil of a coil."

"Exactly. The Earl of Rennington is not, and has never been, married, his children are all illegitimate, his heir cannot now inherit and how on earth are we to tell him?"

***

The earl graciously agreed to receive Michael and Willerton-Forbes in his study the following morning, where Michael introduced Pettigrew.

"Mr Pettigrew Willerton-Forbes, my lord, a distinguished lawyer from Markham, Willerton-Forbes and Browning. Also the youngest son of the Earl of Morpeth."

"Hmm. Willerton-Forbes? Any relation to Sir Rathbone?"

"He is my uncle, my lord."

The earl's brow cleared. "I know him well. Not sure why you need a lawyer in this business, Edgerton, but I am sure you know best. How are your enquiries proceeding? Have you tracked down the culprit yet?" he said, beaming at them, for all the world as if they were investigating the theft of a loaf of bread, and not a brutal murder.

"Not yet, my lord," Michael said. "We proceed slowly at present while we await interviews with the Lady Alice Nicholson and Mr Eustace Atherton."

"So I understand. I am sure they will oblige you soon. Eustace has been informed, and as for poor Alice — well, one cannot rush these matters. Take as much time as you need, Captain, for you and your charming wife are a welcome addition to our little gathering. You take us out of ourselves at this distressing time. But you have found something of which you wish to inform me?"

He smiled at them benignly, and Michael quaked inside. No one could doubt his courage, he hoped, but he had a thousand times sooner face an oncoming army with a sword in his hand than tell a belted earl that his entire life was based on a lie. But it could not be shirked, and he had agreed with Pettigrew that he would start the tale.

"It is another matter entirely, my lord. Amongst the late Mr Nicholson's papers, we found this letter from the Bishop of Winchester."

He handed it over, and watched as the earl read it, saw him notice the date and frown, watched him turn the letter over and read the direction.

"I do not understand," he said slowly. "This letter is dated two years *after* Nicholson was ordained."

"Quite so," Michael said. "The discrepancy was odd enough to attract my attention, so I wrote to Mr Willerton-Forbes and asked him to make enquiries."

"I went to Winchester," Willerton-Forbes said, "and there I discovered that Mr Nicholson had indeed presented himself for ordination two years before the letter was sent, and had in fact been accepted. However, it appears there was... an incident."

"An incident? What sort of incident?" the earl barked.

"An incident with a scullery maid," Willerton-Forbes said with distaste. "In the dean's house. The bishop felt, not unreasonably, that such behaviour was incompatible with the standing of an ordained clergyman. That, in point of fact, an ordinand who spends the night before his ordination in activities expressly forbidden by the church might not be in a suitably pious frame of mind for the service of ordination."

"Good Lord!" the earl said, with some feeling. "Then... he was not ordained at all?"

"Not at Winchester, certainly," Willerton-Forbes said. "The records there have a list of those ordained, and Nicholson's name is on it, but with the word *'Deferred'* written beside it. In fact, his name was sent off to the newspapers as one of those ordained, so no doubt his family believe him to be so, but he was not, not then. And not two weeks later, he was here, officiating at your marriage, Lord Rennington."

The earl had not had more than the usual half-hearted education expected of gentlemen of his age, but even he understood the consequences.

"But if he was not an ordained clergyman... our marriage is not valid!"

"That is so," Willerton-Forbes said. "The countess is not your wife, and your children—"

"Are illegitimate," the earl said, with such finality that a heavy silence descended on the room. He walked about the room, the letter still in his hand, while Michael and Willerton-Forbes waited. "But is it certain?" he said finally.

"I cannot be entirely certain, no," Willerton-Forbes said. "There is always room for mistakes and misunderstandings, shall we say, and the records at Winchester — the word *'Deferred'* — that could easily be a mistake. The notice was in the newspapers after all, the bishop of that time is long dead, the clerks and clerics at Winchester now know nothing of the matter. But I found one very elderly, but perfectly lucid, clerk who was there at the time and remembers the occasion well. He is quite certain that Nicholson was *not* ordained at that time."

"Hmpf. And what is to be done about it? Can it be set right?"

"For Lady Rennington, the difficulty may be remedied. You may remarry at any time, my lord. But for the children... in England, illegitimacy is a stain which can never be removed."

"In England? Then could we remove it elsewhere?"

"My lord, you could move to Scotland, marry Lady Rennington there and the children would be legitimate... in Scotland. Since your title and estates are in England, that will not avail you."

"Then Birtwell loses everything? And there is nothing to be done about it? Dear God!" He rubbed a hand tiredly across his face. "But Nicholson!" he cried, waving the letter angrily. "Why would he do such a thing? Why pretend to be ordained?"

"Shame, I should imagine, my lord," Michael said. "To go off to be ordained, everyone expecting it and then be turned away at the last moment because of a thoughtless piece of folly... he would very likely be too ashamed to speak up. He arrived here, he was believed to be ordained, and at once he was asked to officiate at a wedding. He would not have wished to admit to lying."

"I remember now, he was reluctant to do it," the earl said. "He had to be talked into it. I suppose he thought we would never find out, and he was almost right. If he had not been murdered and his papers examined, we would not have known, even now. Foolish man, to leave such a mess behind him! But he was always that way — never taking the difficult decisions. He was always going to do things, but somehow, if it interfered with his comfort, it never got done. The only person he cared about above himself was Alice — he was the most attentive husband a woman could ever want. They were always together. Poor Alice!"

For a few moments, he was silent, sunk in reverie, and Michael and Willerton-Forbes waited patiently for him to come to himself again. When he did, he pulled chairs forward for them. "Edgerton, bring that tray over to the desk will you? Yes, that one with the decanter and glasses, and pour us all a large measure. I feel the need to fortify myself, for what on earth am I to do? What *can* I do?"

"If I may suggest, my lord..." Willerton-Forbes said tentatively. The earl waved him to continue. "As I see it, you have three options. The first option is to do nothing at all. We do not *know* for certain that Mr Nicholson was not ordained, and no one has challenged the status of your marriage, so you could simply continue as if nothing has happened."

"But when Birtwell comes to inherit... *can* he inherit?"

"That is the question. If he knows nothing of this matter, then once you have laid down the burdens of this earth, your eldest son will apply to the Privileges Committee for the right to assume your title. At that point—"

"They will discover the difficulty."

"They might. They might not think to question the status of your chaplain, in which case all is well. But if they do, the claim might very well be rejected, throwing the family into turmoil at an already difficult time. If Lord Birtwell is married by this point—"

"Lord, yes!" the earl said. "He is betrothed to Miss Franklyn, and they will be married very soon. He will have children of his own — a son, expecting to inherit in his turn. No, I cannot do nothing. What is the second option, Mr Willerton-Forbes?"

"To tell those most affected, but to keep it as a private matter. Then, when the time comes, Lord Birtwell stands aside and permits a claim from the next in line. Who is the next heir, my lord, after your own sons?"

"My brother, George. He has several sons, so the succession is safe, at any rate. But this matter cannot honourably be kept private. Miss Franklyn, at the very least, must be told of the change in Birtwell's fortunes, and then there is Olivia — how could she go off to town next year to find a husband, when she is illegitimate? Oh, and there is Izzy! My second daughter, who was married in the chapel here by Nicholson five years ago. Her marriage is invalid too, and her daughters are illegitimate. She and Farramont will need to marry legally before there is a son. Dear God, what a mess! But what is the third option? To make our disaster public, I suppose."

"To face up to the full consequences, yes," Willerton-Forbes said gently. "My suggestion is that you take yourself at once to York, and talk to the Archbishop. I assume you know him well?"

"Well enough, yes."

"Lay the whole before him, and he will advise you. It may be that he will find some way to declare your marriage valid after all, or if not, he will institute enquiries through the official channels to determine once and for all whether Mr Nicholson was ordained. Then you will know."

"Then we will know," the earl repeated grimly. "Say nothing of this to anyone yet, gentlemen, until it is quite certain. It is perhaps fortunate for Nicholson that he is already dead, for I could cheerfully strangle him with my bare hands at this moment. I do not normally hold with violence, but for him I could make an exception. I wonder what other secrets he held... I shall send Alice to you this morning, Captain Edgerton. She has hidden behind her grief for too long. We need to know who killed that man."

"And *why*, my lord," Michael said softly. "Because until we know that, we cannot know whether you or anyone else of your family may still be at risk."

8: An Interview With Lady Alice

The Lady Alice Nicholson was brought to the old nursery by Lady Rennington, who twittered unhappily. "I am not sure what you said to my husband this morning, Captain, to send him haring off to York, and now he is insisting that poor, grieving Alice answer all your questions, when she is very far from well enough."

"Do not be concerned, Caroline," Lady Alice said, her voice softly melodious. "This must be done eventually, and I want to do everything I can to help the captain to catch Arthur's killer."

"I shall stay with you, to support you through the ordeal."

"No. Please go. In fact, I should like everyone to leave, excepting only the captain himself."

"Alice, I do not think—"

"Go, Caroline."

Having seen her sister-in-law settled on a chair in front of the table that served as a desk, Lady Rennington did, indeed, go, and Sandy likewise. Lady Alice sat very upright in her chair, her hands neatly folded in her lap. Even at forty-eight, she was a beautiful woman, her golden hair showing no sign of grey.

"We are alone, Lady Alice," Michael said. "There is no one in the adjoining tower room, and both doors are closed. You may speak privily to me, whatever you wish to say. I usually have Mr Alexander with me to take notes, but since he is not here, will it disturb you if I make a few notes myself?"

"Not at all."

"Would you like a glass of wine? Or shall I send for tea?"

"I want nothing, Captain. I should like to get this over with. I assume you wish to know how I came to be standing beside my dead husband covered in his blood?"

"Eventually, yes, but first I should like to know more about Mr Nicholson. I have heard a great deal about him, but it is all outer features. I know, for instance, that he was handsome and affable, very agreeable company and an excellent card player. Never put himself forward in an unbecoming way, but always willing to be helpful. All of which sketches a very pretty picture of a well-liked man, but does not tell me much of his character, of his inner thoughts and private moments. That is where you can be of inestimable value, my lady, and more than is usual in a wife, for you would not be distracted by a handsome face or a ready smile. You saw him in other ways, and that is what I should like to hear today. Might we start at the very beginning — with the first occasion on which you met Mr Nicholson?"

She smiled, the memory clearly a pleasant one. "Arthur arrived with my father a few days before Christmas. He had just been ordained, and had met Papa on the way north. They were snowed in for some days at an inn, and found that they got on well, so Papa brought Arthur with him to be our chaplain. Papa had been gone for some time, so we were all gathered in the entrance hall to meet him, and there was Arthur. He made me a full bow, which few bother to do."

"You could tell that?"

"Oh, yes. I cannot see, Captain, but my other senses are acute. I can distinguish the difference between a respectful bow and something more perfunctory. Arthur was always very respectful towards me, and he *noticed* me. He saw me in a way that no one else at Corland truly did. We used to meet often... I thought accidentally, but he used to loiter wherever he thought I might be. I took my exercise in the gallery every day, and he was often there, sitting with a book. I could detect that peculiar smell that books have — the leather and a certain mustiness from the paper and glue. I asked him one day what he was reading and he described it, and read me short passages. And so we fell into the habit of meeting there. He would read aloud, and then we would discuss the subject matter. He had the most beautiful voice... smooth and mesmerising. I could listen to him for ever. Sometimes a new topic would arise from our discussions or he would simply bring books that he thought would interest me, and not just the dull histories that my governess had thought suitable. Arthur would read all manner of books to me, and the newspapers, too. I had never realised before how I had thirsted for such knowledge."

"I can see how an attachment would form under such circumstances," Michael said.

"Oh yes! We were very drawn to each other, right from the start." For the first time, her voice wavered, but she took a deep breath and continued. "He understood, better than anyone else, that I had been living only half a life until that point. I went nowhere, did nothing, had no friends. I hated to be dependent on others, so I stayed on familiar ground. But he had rope guides put around the garden so that I could walk there unaided, and he got me riding again — that was wonderful! We roamed the moors day after day in the summer, talking, always talking. We never tired of talking to each other." Another long pause, her breathing ragged. "Of course we fell in love. It was Arthur who put the idea into Papa's head that I might marry one day. No one had ever thought it possible, you see. *'How can she marry when she cannot even display herself in the dance?'* Mama said once. But Arthur thought everything was possible. Once Papa got the idea in his head, he tried to make a match with a baron, but happily that fell through. Arthur and I married and have been blissfully happy ever since that day. I know many wives say such things, Captain, but in our case it was true. We were everything to each other, spending many hours each day together. I used to have a footman with me at all times, to be sure I came to no harm, to prepare my food at table and so on, and a secretary to read and write my letters, but Arthur took on all of those duties. I cannot imagine how I shall go on without him."

Again she paused to steady her breathing, and Michael sat scratching away with the pen to give her time to recover her composure. After a while, when she seemed calmer, he said, "You have just one child — a daughter?"

"Yes, Tess. Teresa, but we have always called her Tess. She is twenty years of age now. You have not talked to her yet, I believe."

"Not without your permission, Lady Alice, but I must do so eventually. I shall ask the same question I ask everyone, to which I receive the same answer — no one can think of a single reason why anyone should want to murder Mr Nicholson. But perhaps you can, Lady Alice?"

"No, indeed. Arthur was a good man. He had no enemies, no vices, no secret life beyond the castle. It is a complete mystery to me."

"Did he ever talk to you about his life before he came here? His family, for instance? His ordination? His friends?"

But she shook her head decisively. "Never. He always said that when he married me, the old life was gone, and he had been reborn... that was the exact word he used. Nothing before that meant anything to him. His sisters wrote to him often at first, but gradually the letters dwindled. None of his family ever came here and he never went south again. In fact, he hardly left the castle, except for an occasional night in York or Pickering."

"He belonged to a political society in Pickering, I understand."

"Yes. That was my father's influence. They were the greatest of friends, always, despite the difference in ages. Arthur was never close to my brother Charles, even though they are the same age. But Charles is not the man our father was. Papa loved company and good conversation and cards. He and Arthur used to sit up for hours after the rest of the household had gone to bed, playing piquet, drinking brandy and talking about this and that — masculine interests. Politics, I suppose. Poor Arthur was greatly grieved when Papa died."

Michael dutifully wrote it all down, but all his instincts rebelled at such a glowing portrait of the dead man. No one, it seemed, had a bad word to say against Mr Arthur Nicholson, and to his wife, he was a positive saint. And yet, buried deep in his past was a dreadful secret — that he had never been ordained, and by allowing the earl's family to believe that he was, he had thrown them into the most appalling situation. Not such a saint at all, then. Michael decided it was time to push his widow a little harder.

"It surprises me a little, Lady Alice," he said smoothly, "that such a happy marriage as yours did not produce more children."

"Yet you have none yourself, after several years of marriage, Captain Edgerton," she said coldly. "Does that make yours an *un*happy marriage?"

Now *that* was more like it! A prickly response at last. Interesting, too, that she knew anything of his own marriage, when she had been sequestered in her room for weeks. "Not at all, my lady. We have never been blessed, as sometimes happens."

"Blessed... yes." Her face changed, a shadow passing across it. "A child is a great blessing indeed. Captain Edgerton, the precise state of affairs between man and wife is customarily a private matter, but in this case it bears on the question of why I came across my husband's body in the middle of the night. I shall therefore explain the circumstances to you. When we first married, I assumed... we both assumed that I would conceive immediately. Nothing happened. For month after month, and year after year, nothing happened, while Caroline... Lady Rennington... produced healthy babies in the wink of an eye. We were subjected to a great deal of advice. Herbs to aid conception, hot baths, cold baths, long walks, long rests, spicy food, bland food. I tried everything. But then... a miracle. A child was conceived... we hardly dared to hope, and I was dreadfully ill the whole time. When she wanted to be born after only seven months, we prepared ourselves for a terrible loss. But the miracle held, for she was born *alive!* She was so tiny, and frail — we were terrified to hold her. But she lived long enough to be baptised, she began to grow, to thrive... and she lives still, our little Tess. But it had been so difficult for me, and Arthur felt it would be best not to tempt providence. He did not want to lose me, he said, and so we decided... to be chaste."

Michael nodded, the pen flying across the paper. "So you slept in separate rooms?"

"Not at first. Arthur was a man of honour, so it did not seem to be necessary. But..." She sighed. "So many nights he stayed up with Papa playing piquet and then he would come to bed full of brandy and... well, sometimes he forgot our agreement. So after that, I had a bed made up in my sitting room each night. If he would be likely to reach his bed late and well refreshed with brandy, I would retire to my own room. I told everyone that I suffered from headaches, but I do not want to tell even so small a lie to you. But I never slept well alone. Often I would wake in the small hours alone and desperate to be near him. Can you understand that, Captain?"

"Very easily, ma'am. It is why my wife chooses to travel about with me, despite the privations, rather than staying comfortably at home. One of the reasons anyway."

"One of the reasons? But perhaps I should not enquire."

He laughed. "Nothing private, I assure you. My work has its risks, you see, and Mrs Edgerton would rather be on hand if I am to be shot or fall off a roof — or a drainpipe! But loneliness is a powerful driver, too, for both of us. We are never quite at ease when we are apart."

"Precisely so! I am not at ease sleeping apart from my husband, so if I wake in the night in my little bed in the sitting room, why then I creep through to the bedroom and if he is there and fast asleep, I climb into bed beside him. Then we have the great joy of waking together. These separations are... *were* such a trial to us both. We looked forward eagerly to the day, surely not far off now, when it would not be necessary."

"And so that morning you woke in your sitting room, you went through to the bedroom and—?"

Her breathing grew ragged again. "I knew at once something was wrong. I cannot tell you how or why, I just knew. So I went round to Arthur's side of the bed but my foot touched... something. I did not know what, only that it should not be there. Everything in the rooms I use is kept the same, always, with nothing out of place that might trip me. It means I can walk about confidently. But now there was something on the floor. I picked it up... it was wooden, like a pole, but heavy... the axe, I know now. I realised then that something terrible had occurred. I listened for Arthur's breathing, but there was nothing... no sound at all. I leaned over him to hear... perhaps he was just deeply asleep... the covers were torn and there was sticky stuff... his blood. I... I cannot remember much else. I screamed, people came... I cannot remember. Charles was there... he took charge. It was... it still is a nightmare. How could my life change so abruptly, so *horribly*. Who would do such a thing? And why with an axe? It seems... unnecessarily primitive. You will find this man, will you not, Captain Edgerton?"

"I will do my very best, Lady Alice."

But as he wrote it all down, his overriding thought was that while it was perfectly plausible, it was also very glib. Certainly it could have happened exactly as she said, but equally, she could have planned the entire business, and she seemed entirely too calm for a new widow who loved her husband as much as she claimed.

***

Michael lost no time in summoning Tess Nicholson to the old nursery. She was a slight, dark creature, not a conventional beauty but with a strange ethereal prettiness of her own. She eyed Michael and Sandy warily. Luce was there too, as chaperon, sitting quietly in a corner with some needlework, but Tess ignored her, even though they had dined at the same table several times.

"Miss Nicholson, you will be aware that I am talking to everyone at Corland Castle to try to find out precisely what happened the night your father died, and who might have killed him."

"What happened is easy," she said. "Someone broke in, found an axe and went to Papa's room, then crept out again. A castle full of people and not a single person saw or heard anything, until Mama started screaming. And he could come back at any time."

"Perhaps," Michael said neutrally. "Can you think of anyone who might want your father dead?"

"No, no one at all. He got on well with everyone."

The sainted chaplain again. "Did he get on well with you?"

A slight air of puzzlement. "Yes, of course."

"Did he have plans for your marriage?"

Her eyes narrowed. "My... my *marriage?*"

"I am thinking of his will, Miss Nicholson. That seems to imply—"

"Oh yes, the *will!* He leaves me his fortune, but only if I marry a gentleman! The presumption! As if I cannot choose for myself."

"I suppose his intention was to protect you from fortune hunters, Miss Nicholson," Michael said. Anger! That was something to work with! "How much is his fortune, do you know?"

Instantly, she was wary again. "I have no idea. It cannot be very great, can it? As a chaplain, his income could not have been large."

"Perhaps he inherited something from his father?"

"No, I believe not."

"Did he have investments? Money in the bank? We found only a thousand pounds in his safe, apart from your mother's jewellery."

"A thousand... then that is mine, is it not?"

Michael smiled. "Eventually, no doubt, but there are procedures to be gone through first. It is best to leave it to the lawyers."

"But Uncle Charles is the executor of the will, so he has the power to release money to me," she said with a quick smile. "I shall ask him, I think."

"Since you are not yet one and twenty, there will be trustees to manage your fortune on your behalf," Michael said.

Her eyes flashed again. "Only until I marry, Captain Edgerton. Then my fortune will be mine."

"No, it will be your husband's, and only if he is a gentleman."

With an exclamation of disgust, she rose and would have left the room, but Luce reached the door before her. "Miss Nicholson, I am sure you wish to catch your father's murderer as much as anyone... or more, perhaps. Will you not stay a little longer, and help us learn something of your father? Everyone agrees he was a good man, yet someone slaughtered him in his bed. *Please* help us to find out why... and who it could have been?"

Tess's eyes slid from Luce to Michael to Sandy, assessing them. Then she said calmly to Luce, "I am very sorry my father died, and in such unspeakable circumstances, too. However, I cannot forgive him for leaving me money conditionally. What sort of man does that to his only daughter? What sort of father distrusts his daughter so much that he cannot allow her a free choice of husband?"

"One who loves you, and wants the very best for you," Luce said at once. "Parents' choices are often incomprehensible to their children, and it is only with hindsight that one understands the reasoning behind them. If your fortune is very great, then you will be besieged with men of ambition hoping to line their own pockets. Your father would have protected you from such men while he was alive, and he tries to achieve the same end now that he is dead. There are a great many gentlemen in the world, you know, so it is not a very restrictive condition. You are bound to find one who suits you well. Do not be angry with your father. He had your happiness at heart when he wrote that will."

"No, he did not," Tess said icily. "He was being vindictive and mean, and I hate him for it. Good day to you."

And she was gone, leaving Michael oddly elated. At last, a sign that the sainted Mr Nicholson was not quite so perfect as all that, and was thoroughly disliked by at least one person. "Sandy, add her name to the list of suspicious persons."

"Michael, she is angry because of the *will*," Luce said. "She knew nothing of that before her father's death."

"So she says," he said darkly.

9: About Axes

Lady Alice's maid confirmed that the sofa in Lady Alice's sitting room was always made up into a bed each evening, but not always slept in.

"Her ladyship suffered from the headache sometimes, sir, and then she liked to be alone and quiet until it passed off."

"And did she have the headache on the night Mr Nicholson died?" Michael said.

"I cannot say, sir. Perhaps. She never complained, so it was hard to tell."

"And was her bed slept in that night?"

"Yes, sir, it was."

"Has she paid or pressured you to say this?"

For a moment, her mouth worked but seemed incapable of speech. When she found her tongue, her indignation waxed long and loud, involving the grave of her dead mother, the Holy Bible and God as her witness. If it was all an act, it was certainly one worthy of Drury Lane.

After the maid had left, Sandy sighed. "Well, that's nae very helpful. It doesnae advance our case against Lady Alice one jot."

"It is as we suspected," Michael said. "She could have murdered him in cold blood, planning it with meticulous attention to detail, or it could be precisely as she describes — she came through and discovered him thus. And we cannot prove it one way or the other, and unless we can find a reason why she might have wanted to kill him, we cannot accuse her."

There was one piece of good luck, however, for the mysterious Mr Eustace Atherton finally made himself known to Michael. He was very different from his father and oldest brother, who were both imposingly built, mostly with muscle in Lord Birtwell's case, although Lord Rennington was running rather to fat. Eustace was more like the youngest brother, Kent, both men being lean and dark haired. Eustace was of a restless nature, pacing about the old nursery, slapping his gloves against his thigh, picking up loose items idly then tossing them down again.

"Well, Captain, whatever did you say to my father to send him off to York in such haste, eh?" was the first thing he said.

"I am sure his lordship will inform you when he has anything to impart, sir," Michael said.

"Oh, very discreet. Your London lawyer went with him, I hear."

"You are well informed, Mr Atherton."

"I know everything that goes on in this place, Captain. I may live twelve miles away, but this is still my home."

"Is it? But you do not live here, Mr Atherton. You were not here on the night Mr Nicholson was murdered... were you?"

"No, no. I was at home, tucked up in bed with— Well, never mind with whom. Let us merely say that I did not awaken the next morning until gone ten o'clock." He grinned lasciviously. "It had been a tiring night."

Michael eyed him with distaste, but chose not to pursue the point. "If you know everything that goes on here, sir, perhaps you can tell us who murdered Mr Nicholson, for we are quite at a loss to account for it. He seems to be a perfect saint, with not an enemy in the world."

Eustace gave a crack of laughter. "A saint? Not him! You should not listen to Aunt Alice, for she will certainly give you a false impression. He was all for what he could get, you know. He only married Aunt Alice to guarantee his place here... or so my grandmother says. She has never much liked him. He cheats at cards, too, and no one likes a cheat. I think he was feathering his own nest, for when Grandfather died, there was nothing like as much money as there should have been. I would have looked into it, but Father is too easy-going. He never likes to make a fuss. I persuaded him to appoint a proper land steward when he inherited, so Nicholson could not defraud him any further. Grandfather left Nicholson a house in his will — did you know that? Pickering, seemingly. It is leased out — a charitable case, Nicholson said, but I dare say he was making money from it."

Michael eyed him thoughtfully. Was this a truer picture of Nicholson, or merely the jaundiced eye of a cynical man? "Perhaps he was not quite a saint, for which of us is?" Michael said. "Nevertheless, there does not seem anything in all this to justify murder."

"Justify? No, for who would want to murder the *chaplain?*" Eustace said slowly. "Father, maybe, when he gets on his high horse, or Izzy, definitely, when she gets in one of her frenzies, but not the *chaplain.* It sounds like the work of a madman, to me."

"You think someone broke into the castle and crept up the stairs, wandered into a bedroom at random and attacked a man sleeping peacefully?" Michael said mildly. "And then crept away just as quietly?"

"You do not think so?"

"It seems a trifle implausible. Does it not seem so to you?"

"But how else to account for it?" Eustace said, hurling himself into a chair impatiently. "You are not saying that someone inside the castle did it, are you? One of the servants, loyal to us for years and years, suddenly takes umbrage at one of the chaplain's sermons? Or — Good God, are you suggesting it was one of us? One of the *family?*"

"If it were, who would your suspicion fall on?" Michael said, watching him carefully.

"What a question! Not any of the ladies, obviously. An axe, for heaven's sake! As for the men... no, I cannot think of anyone... not really. I mean, Walter has a temper on him, sometimes, but... no, he would not. I am sure he would not. Of course, Walter is very close to Aunt Alice, so if he saw some imagined insult... but no, I cannot think it of him. Not Father, certainly, and Kent is too sweet-natured for violence of any sort. I suppose Farramont would be the only one whose character I cannot vouch for. He is secretive, that one."

"Farramont? *Lord* Farramont? The Lady Isabel's husband?" Michael said in astonishment. "But he was not even here!"

"Who told you that? Yes, he was here that night. He was hunting for Izzy, of course, but although she *had* been here, she had already left. Typical of her. Farramont arrived during dinner, ate in his room and left at first light, so I suppose his presence was barely noticed."

Sandy's pen flew over the paper, writing down this new information. Michael felt a sudden surge of fury. After talking to every single person who lived in the castle, from the earl down to the kitchen boy, not one had mentioned the presence of Lord Farramont on the fatal night. It had been left to the one person who did not even live there to tell them of it.

Eustace was equally informative about the axe when it was shown to him, his thin face lighting up with boyish enthusiasm.

"Was this what was used? How strange! I thought it would have been one of the medieval ones from the great hall, but this is relatively modern, a boarding axe, such as the Royal Navy use. This comes from my own collection at Welwood-on-the-hill."

"Then how did it get here?" Michael said sharply.

"I brought it, of course. I am not allowed to interfere with the displays on the walls, except now and then, when everything is taken down for spring cleaning or Mother is redecorating, but there are other possibilities — the suits of armour that decorate odd corners, for instance. I rearrange them and their weaponry on a regular basis. This one was part of the grouping on the half-landing on the stairs between the great hall and this floor."

"There are three suits of armour there, with swords," Michael said. "One has a pike as well, and one a mace."

"And the third had this axe. The murderer must have gone up those stairs and taken up the axe as he did so. I should have noticed its loss at once if I had ever come that way, but I always use the service stairs. Shall I show you where the axe was positioned?"

Michael followed him out onto the landing, and round to the stairs. Halfway down, a large niche in the wall, flanked by giant urns, held the three suits of armour, and it was easy to see where the axe would have fitted into the display.

"Ah, the belt is broken," Eustace said. "The axe was tucked into the belt, like so, but the murderer must have wrenched it away from its position so forcefully that it broke the belt. But that was where I put it."

"So anyone could have taken it," Michael said, with a sigh. "And how was it that none of the servants recognised it? Someone must have dusted the display, after all, but I suppose they do not pay much attention. When was the axe placed here?"

"Oh... perhaps a week or so before the murder. Maybe ten days. That was when I last rearranged the display. I change them about every few months, for my own amusement — no one else cares. They are due for another change quite soon."

"Please do not rearrange anything!" Michael said sharply. "At least, not until we have the murderer safely in custody."

"Oh, of course. I can give you the provenance of all the items on display. The pike and two of the swords are from the armoury here, and the rest are my own."

"That is a fine broadsword," Michael said, running his fingers appreciatively over the hilt. "May I?"

"Of course. A man who carries his own sword at all times is clearly a connoisseur."

Carefully, Michael drew the sword from its holder, admiring the delicate metalwork of the hilt and the sturdy blade. "Ah, Hounslow made, I see. Civil War?"

"Very likely. Now this one... well, what do you think?"

"French? Much more recent, of course."

"1745. Have you seen the Russian one in the armoury?"

"With the bird's head pommel? Yes! A fine piece."

And somehow, by wandering around the great hall and then to the armoury, two hours drifted by in the pleasurable discussion of swords. Eustace was quite willing to fetch anything from the walls that Michael wanted to try out, which turned out to be a great many of them. He had seldom been so well entertained within the confines of Corland Castle before.

"You like him, I think," Sandy said, as they locked away their notes later that day.

"He is very knowledgeable," Michael said with a shrug.

"Is he a suspect? He was twelve miles away when Nicholson was murdered, tucked up in his bed with a female, which would be easy enough to verify. He did not even wake until close to ten o'clock. Or so he says."

"For a moment there you had me worried, Sandy," Michael said with a grin. "*Everyone* is to be held in suspicion, at least until we have independent verification of their whereabouts. And there is something distasteful in a man who points a finger at his own brother."

"He said he was sure it couldnae be him," Sandy said.

"Nevertheless, he has raised the suspicion in our minds. Lord Birtwell was the first person to reach the deceased — perhaps he was already up and about, eh? But Mr Eustace told us about Farramont, which no one else saw fit to mention, so we must be grateful for that little gem."

"Aye, that's true enough. Tis an odd thing, though, that he knows everything that goes on in a house that's not his own."

"The servants' gossip, I expect," Michael said with a shrug. "Very useful for us, though. We can use Mr Eustace as an extra pair of eyes and ears. He has invited me to view his collection of weapons at Welwood-on-the-hill, so I shall take the opportunity to see what more gems he might have for us. And if I can borrow a carriage, I can take Neate as my groom and he can snoop around the stables, and see what he can find out."

***

Michael stood on the main stairs, gazing at the armour display. The axe had been tied roughly into the position it would have occupied before the belt had been broken. On either side of him, the housekeeper and the housemaid responsible for the stairs both shook their heads.

"I never saw it there, and that's a fact," the housekeeper said firmly.

"I don't *remember* no axe," the housemaid said, dubiously. "But if Mr Eustace says it were there—"

"I expect he's misremembering," the housekeeper said. "Most likely it was somewhere else altogether. These things are scattered all over the house, so how he can remember where one is in particular beats me."

Michael nodded as if in agreement. To the maid, he said, "You clean the stairs every morning, is that right?"

"Aye, sir."

"But early, before it is light, perhaps? Too dark to see anything clearly."

"No, sir, sun's well up at this time o' year. There's plenty o' light on the stairs from the glass roof."

"And do you dust the armour display every day? Or every couple of days?"

The maid slid her eyes warily towards the housekeeper. "Oh, every day, sir, without fail."

"Hmpf," the housekeeper said, frowning. "*That* would be a miracle, Milly Thompson. I know how you skimp on the bits you think no one notices."

"I don't like cleaning all those sharp things," Milly said. "Not after Dolly Ithwaite was almost skewered by one of those great, tall things."

"A spear?" Michael said.

"I remember that," the housekeeper said. "It wasn't tied on properly and came crashing down. I gave Mr Eustace a piece of my mind, so I did, putting my girls at risk like that. But I never saw that axe just there, and that's the truth, sir."

"Well, it *might* have been there," Milly said. "I don't remember it, but it might have been, I suppose. I don't always notice what I'm dusting."

"That's because your head's in the clouds, my girl," the housekeeper said. "If that's all, sir, we've got work to do."

"One more question, if you would be so good. Lord Farramont — did he stay here the night Mr Nicholson was murdered?"

"No, sir, definitely not."

"But he did stay the night recently?"

"Oh yes, sir. One of his flying visits, for Lady Farramont had already left. But it weren't that night."

"Was it before or after the murder?" Michael persevered. Goodness, this was hard work!

"Before. Definitely before, but I couldn't rightly say what night. He never went on the board, since he'd missed dinner."

"The board?"

"Guests go on the board in the kitchen, so everyone knows how many for meals and what rooms they're in, but his lordship arrived late, had a tray in his room, then left before breakfast. I keep a record of the board, but he were never on it. Can we go now?"

"Of course. Thank you for all your help."

But it was not much help at all, in fact.

Nor was the head groom much better.

"Lord Farramont? No, he weren't here that night, sir. I think it were the night before... but I can't be sure. But it weren't *that* night, because we all heard the screams from poor Lady Alice and it weren't even light then, not properly. His lordship wanted to be off at first light, so we'd have been just getting his lordship's carriage ready for him when the screaming started, and we weren't. We were all in our beds, you see, sir. So whatever night it was, it weren't *that* night."

"Well, that's nae use," Sandy said disconsolately, when they returned to the nursery. "What are we to do now?"

"We add Lord Farramont to our list of suspects," Michael said. "Until we know for sure that he was not here... but then he could have left and returned later, for all we know. And Mr Eustace, too. We only have his word for it that he was tucked up in bed with his lady-bird. And Miss Tess Nicholson and her mother."

"The list is getting longer," Sandy said.

"And we still have no conceivable reason why any of them would have wanted to kill the chaplain."

"Is it possible it's to do with this ordination business?" Sandy said. "Someone got wind of it and took revenge? The heir, maybe? He's likely tae lose everything."

"But how would he have known? It is hardly likely that Nicholson himself would have told anyone. We only found out by chance, from that one letter. If Miss Strong had not spotted it, or Luce had not realised the significance of it, no one would know to this day."

"Blackmail, perhaps? The chaplain tells the heir he knows something that will lose him the inheritance unless he pays up."

"Hmm, interesting," Michael said. "I like the idea of blackmail very much. It could be how he has managed to accrue this fortune he has left to his daughter, yet it is also an activity likely to get a man murdered. According to Eustace, his brother has a temper *and* he was the first on the scene. He could have killed the chaplain, nipped back to his own room to rid himself of his bloodstained garments and reappeared when the screaming started. Add Lord Birtwell to the list, Sandy."

10: A Summons From The Earl

The message was brief, but unequivocal. "The earl sends word that you are to attend him at a quarter before noon in the study, my lord," Rashleigh said, as he woke Walter at a disagreeably early hour.

Walter groaned. "Now what is afoot? Whatever have I done this time?" His mind ran quickly over his activities of the last few days, but could recall no transgression.

"I couldn't say, my lord. All I can tell you is that the rest of the family is summoned at twelve, but you are to present yourself a quarter of an hour earlier."

That raised a prickle of alarm. He was to see his father first? Then it *was* something he had done wrong. But what could be serious enough for the whole family to hear? Even that business with Maria had been dealt with privately. "The rest of the family? Everyone?"

"Everyone, my lord. Lady Rennington, the Lady Alice and Miss Nicholson, Mr Eustace, Mr Kent and the Lady Olivia."

"That truly is everybody."

"And also Mr George, Mrs George and Mr Bertram."

"Even the Westwick family. Then it must be about Nicholson. They must know who killed him." But why was he summoned first?

"Perhaps, my lord. It is clearly a serious matter, so I took the liberty of waking you in good time to dress. You will wish to honour your father by arriving on time and looking your best."

Walter was indifferent to looking his best, whether it honoured his father or not, but he would certainly not want to be late, so he submitted to Rashleigh's ministrations with a good grace. He knew how long it took him to dress in the morning and it was as well not to rush the business.

He arrived in the library some ten minutes ahead of the appointed time, to find the study door wide open and his father, pocket watch in hand, awaiting him.

"I beg your pardon, Father, am I late?"

"No, no, not at all. You are early, in fact, but that is all to the good. The more time we have before the others get here, the better. Come inside."

If the unusual nature of the summons had not alarmed him, his father's breathless, almost nervous, manner would have done it. "Whatever has happened?" Walter said. "It must be something dreadful, I am sure. I have never seen you so agitated."

His father drew him inside and closed the door. "Dreadful, indeed. I can barely speak of it, but it must be done. It cannot be shirked." But immediately he lapsed into silence again.

"Is it to do with Nicholson's death?"

"No... well, yes, in a way... but not precisely so." He passed a hand across his brow. "Dear Lord, I am making no sense at all. Pour me a glass of something, will you, Birtwell... Walter."

That was the moment Walter knew he was in serious trouble, for his father never called him by his Christian name unless he was excessively upset with him. Ever since Grandfather had died, Walter had been *'Birtwell'* to everyone in his family. Only a few of his oldest friends still called him Walter. But he poured claret for his father, and another glass for himself, for he was sure to need it, and waited.

"It is Nicholson's fault, that is the problem," the earl said, then paused to fortify himself, downing half the claret at a single swallow. "You see—" He stopped again, then drained the glass, set it down and laced his fingers together. Then he went on in a low, trembling voice. "Nicholson was not ordained, therefore my marriage is invalid, therefore you... all of you are illegitimate."

Walter could not catch his breath. He felt as if he had been pushed off a cliff and now he was falling, falling and who could tell when he would hit the ground? *Illegitimate?* Then—

"I cannot inherit."

"No, and there is nothing that can be done about it. Dear God, if only there were! If only this could all be set right, but it cannot! I have been to the Archbishop at York, and he has been checking for me, to see if Nicholson had been ordained anywhere else, but an express arrived late last night confirming that he has never been ordained. I thought... hoped, perhaps, that he had remedied the situation later, so that Izzy's marriage might be safe, but—"

"Izzy! Nicholson married her, too."

"Precisely. Not Josie, luckily, for that would have been dreadful if those two little boys had been disinherited as well, but Izzy's daughters — well, it is not so bad for girls. A pretty girl with a good dowry will always be able to marry well... or well enough, anyway. But you! I cannot tell you how much it grieves me."

"So if I cannot inherit... none of us, not Eustace or Kent, either, then... Uncle George?" Walter's voice sounded distant to his ears, as if he were under water.

The earl nodded. "He is my heir presumptive now, and then Bertram after him, and of course virtually everything is entailed. At least Eustace has his own estate and a very pretty little independence, but I do not know what is to become of Kent, truly I do not."

"And Olivia. What of her season next year?"

"That is not to be thought of now, but she is young, still. She will find a husband in her own time. Birtwell... Walter... Miss Franklyn must be told about this change of circumstances. She will be disappointed, naturally, for I think she looked forward to being Lady Birtwell and later Lady Rennington, but it need not prevent the marriage. Her fortune is sufficient to enable you to live as a gentleman, and naturally I shall continue your allowance while you are getting settled. Langley Villa is not entailed, so you will still have that. I shall make it over to you entirely, so there is no uncertainty. You may marry as soon as you please. It is the one consolation I have, that you will not have to look for employment, or live under my roof for evermore. You will be very comfortable, I believe."

"Do you think I should cry off?"

"And break Miss Franklyn's heart? No, indeed. She is not marrying you for the title, Walter, not a fine, handsome young man like you, and anyone can see how strongly attached to you she is. She followed you about like a puppy for years."

"Franklyn may cut up rough."

"He is a sensible man, so he will not stand in the way of his daughter's happiness. He always thought Miss Franklyn was marrying above her station, you know, allying herself with the Athertons. He was only an attorney before his sudden acquisition of wealth. Your situation would have been difficult if you had not already found the woman of your heart, but as it is... you will do well enough, Walter. A happy marriage can compensate for any number of worldly disappointments."

Walter made no quibble over *'the woman of your heart'*, for his feelings towards Bea were not something he wished to discuss openly, even if he understood them himself. Fortunately, the clock struck twelve, and his father opened the door to admit the crowd gathered outside. There was a bustle of finding enough chairs for the ladies and settling them, while the men stood uneasily behind them. Probably there had never been so many people squashed into that small room before.

It was clear from his mother's white face that she was already aware of the disaster which had befallen them. The others displayed varying degrees of anxiety, for this was an unusual enough event to cause alarm even in the most sanguine breast. Only Kent, always the most happy-go-lucky of the family, was cheerful and even excited by the unexpected summons.

"No Eustace, I see," he said, chuckling. "I suppose he has lost his way on the ride over here."

"It is barely twelve miles, and he makes the journey often enough that he can scarcely lose his way," Olivia said. "How silly you are, Kent."

"Eustace has no sense of direction," Kent said, grinning. "He can lose his way in his own house."

"Hush, children," Mother said. "Do not be squabbling at such a time. Charles, must we wait for him? Can we not just get this over with?"

And that, more than anything else, underscored the dramatic nature of the meeting, such that even Kent and Olivia subsided. Father would not start without Eustace, however, so they waited until, a full twenty minutes after the designated hour, Eustace strolled in.

"Well, whatever happened here?" he said, looking at the long faces. "Has someone else died?"

"How can we know?" Olivia said. "We have been waiting for you to arrive. Why are you always late, Eustace?"

"He is here now," the earl said tersely. "It is immaterial whether he is early or late, for the situation will not change, no matter how long we wait."

"For heaven's sake, Papa! Tell us what has happened," Olivia cried.

And in the same meagre handful of words he had employed with Walter, the earl turned his whole family's life upside down. Walter stood to one side of the fireplace, watching their faces as they came to understand the consequences. Bewilderment, disbelief, anger, shock — all of those. But most of all, fear. That he recognised, for he felt it himself. What would their lives be like now? There was not one of them in that room who would be unaffected by it. Aunt Alice's hands flew to her mouth, tears sparkling on her lashes. Olivia cried out, "No, no, no!" in a strange, high voice. Eustace swayed as if he might faint. Even Uncle George and Bertram, who stood to gain the most from the change, paled and exchanged unhappy looks, while Aunt Jane, the future countess, burst into tears. Only Kent laughed and said, "Well! That is not what I expected, not at all," seeming not displeased.

They went round and about it, asking the same questions as Walter, receiving the same uncompromising answers. No, there was nothing to be done. Yes, Walter — indeed, all the boys — were disinherited. No, Josie was not affected. Yes, Izzy was in the same situation. They went around and about, but eventually their questions trickled away.

"I suppose you will have to give up Miss Franklyn, Walter," Eustace said, into the lengthening silence.

"There is no need to consider such a drastic step," the earl said.

"But Walter has nothing to offer a wife now," Eustace said. "No title, no money of his own, so—"

"What does that matter, when they have a mutual affection strong enough to sustain them through every adversity?" the earl said sharply. "They will have enough to live on, that is the important consideration."

"From *her* fortune," Eustace said. "I should be ashamed to live on my wife's money, and not bring anything to the marriage myself."

Uncle George laughed. "I have been living on my wife's money for decades, Eustace. Two people should not be forced apart merely because of a disparity in wealth. It is not as if Walter set out, penniless, to secure Miss Franklyn's fortune. He won her heart fairly, when the advantage of the match was all on her side. Why should he give her up now, when the balance has shifted somewhat? He is still the same man she fell in love with, after all."

Eustace subsided, but he looked at Walter thoughtfully, as if he doubted his uncle's pronouncement. Walter could not in all conscience argue the point. Physically, he was indeed the same man as before, but his position in society was markedly different. He had gone in a moment from being a viscount with great rank and wealth awaiting him, his future mapped out in its entirety, to being an outcast — an illegitimate son with no future at all.

Even his name had been taken from him. He no longer knew who he was.

***

Walter went straight to the stables and waited while his horse was saddled. His groom Herbert, like all the servants, was aware of something momentous occurring, and asked a few questions, in a roundabout sort of way, but Walter was not minded to enlighten him. He would find out soon enough, for such events could not be kept from the servants, and thus from the world. It was why he must ride at once to Highwood Place to tell Bea that she was not to be a countess after all.

The hard gallop over the moors did a great deal to clear his head. However bad his situation, there was nothing at all to be done about it, so there was no point in railing against fate. By the time he slowed for the descent, the windows of Highwood glinting below him in the afternoon sun, he was much more philosophical. He would settle matters with Bea, perhaps set a date for the wedding, he might even tamely agree to be married at Marshfields, if she wished it. Their future together would alleviate the pain of losing his inheritance. There would be children and a comfortable life, even without the title. He would not be shunned because of this misfortune which was not his fault... was not the fault of anyone living. And there was no longer the heavy burden of rank and duty and obligation to weigh him down. That thought was unexpectedly freeing.

The Franklyns' butler greeted him with a knowing smile. "Good day, my lord. Miss Franklyn will be delighted to see you. The ladies are on the terrace at present."

"I should like to see Mr Franklyn first," Walter said.

"Very good, my lord. If you would care to wait in the library, I will fetch him to you."

My lord... that would have to stop. “Tell him that Mr Atherton is here to see him.”

“Very good, my lord,” he said imperturbably.

Walter prowled restlessly around the library until the door opened and Franklyn entered. He was something over forty but aging well, still a fine figure with abundant dark hair. He had been a successful attorney for many years, marrying his partner’s daughter and then raising Bea alone after his wife’s death. When he unexpectedly came into great wealth, however, he reinvented himself as a stylish gentleman, swept a duke’s daughter into marriage, and bought Highwood Place for her to preside over his table when she was not mingling with her grand relations. Walter thought himself tolerably well dressed, but Franklyn always put him in the shade.

“Ah... Lord Birtwell! I thought Hobbs said... but no matter. Bea will be very glad to see you, I am sure. But you have something you wish to say to me?”

“Not Lord Birtwell,” Walter blurted. Now that it had come to the point, he was unsure how to explain his situation. His father’s example was before him, however, so, seeing the puzzlement on Franklyn’s face, he went on hastily, “My parents were married by Nicholson, our chaplain, but it turns out he was never ordained. So...”

“The marriage is invalid?” Franklyn said. “Then you are—”

“A bastard. Yes. I cannot inherit the title or father’s estates.”

Silently, Franklyn moved to a console where decanters and glasses stood, poured something and pushed a glass into Walter’s hand. “And you have come, very properly, to tell me of it... and to tell Bea that she will not be a countess after all. You are an honourable man, Birtwell. No... I beg your pardon, not Birtwell. Mr Atherton. I understand now why you told Hobbs to announce you thus. But this will make no difference to your marriage? The house your father promised you—?"

"He will honour that agreement, and the increased allowance, too."

"He is a good man, your father. And for my part, I see no reason to object to the match. You will have Bea's fortune, and I can do something extra for you. I shall not be depriving my other children if I give you another ten thousand... twenty thousand, shall we say. Then you would have sixty thousand in total, as well as the house and your father's allowance. We shall have to adjust the settlements accordingly, but that is the work of a moment. I cannot compensate you for the income that would have been yours as earl, but I can make sure you can live as a gentleman."

"You are very generous, sir. I cannot tell you how much I appreciate your understanding."

"No, no, say nothing about it. Bea is all I have of my dear Eloise now, and I would not wish her to be made unhappy by this change in circumstances. So who now stands to inherit? Your uncle, of course. What a shock for him! I well know how even the best of fortune can upset one's life."

Walter let him rattle on, not attending. So his future was settled. He would live in that tiny house in the village, himself and Bea and a growing number of children, and no expectation now of ever leaving it for the castle. Perhaps that was unfair — Langley Villa was not exactly a rustic cottage. It had been the Dowager Countess's home until she grew too frail and removed to the castle, and it was more than adequate for one elderly lady. But a large family? Even though they would be barely a mile from the castle and would still have access to the park, it would feel very cramped. There would be no escaping—

Escaping what? That was an odd thought. What did he wish to escape?

But Franklyn's musings required at least a small part of his brain and prevented him from considering the point seriously. Then Bea and her mother arrived, and Walter was forced to adopt his respectful demeanour. Lady Esther always had that effect on him. She was never less than meticulously polite, but centuries of aristocratic breeding gave her a degree of hauteur that always made him feel like an unworthy supplicant in her august presence.

"Lady Esther," he murmured, bowing over the hand she graciously held out to him.

Bea got a quick nod, but then she never curtsied to him, so she could hardly expect any greater courtesy. Today, she slipped one arm through his, smiling up at him. "Why did you not join us on the terrace, Walter, instead of calling us into the stuffy library? There is a most refreshing breeze outside."

"There is some information to impart to you, Bea," her father said.

She noted his sombre tone, and looked puzzled.

"Atherton?" Franklyn said. Even Lady Esther displayed a delicate wrinkling of her highbrow at this form of address.

Walter looked helplessly back at Franklyn, who nodded slightly, and proceeded to give the ladies a summary of the salient points. It was more gently phrased than Walter would have managed, and also more comprehensive.

"So he will not be an earl?" Bea said eventually.

"No, but that need not affect your plans," her father said. "Lord Rennington and I are of one mind on that, and you need not worry about money, Bea. Your settlement will not be any the worse for this change in Mr Atherton's circumstances."

"What about the castle? He will have that, surely?"

"It is entailed, Bea," Walter said. "Almost everything is entailed. Not Langley Villa, fortunately, so we shall still have a place to live."

"But you are still your father's eldest son. He cannot cut you out completely."

"Lord Rennington has no choice, my dear," Franklyn said. "When property is entailed, then, like the title, it can only go to the eldest *legitimate* son."

"So... Eustace gets it?"

"He is illegitimate, too," Walter said. "We are all illegitimate, Bea. Father has *no* legitimate children, no heirs. We are all disinherited. The title and estates will go to Father's younger brother, Uncle George."

"And then Bertram," she said, with a look almost of triumph. "Very well, I shall marry Bertram instead."

"Bea!" her father said, shocked. "Surely you cannot... there is no need... were you only ever interested in Walter for his title, then?"

"Oh no, for he is much better looking than Bertram, but I should very much like to be a countess, Papa. I certainly will not marry a man who is not even a proper son and cannot inherit. I have forty thousand pounds, after all, so I am entitled to marry into the peerage, or at least a baronet. Even Sir Hubert's wife is Lady Strong, and I want to be a proper lady, too. If Walter cannot do that for me, then I will not marry him. May I go now?"

With a flick of his head, Franklyn dismissed her, and she bounced out of the room, quite unperturbed.

11: Changes

Walter was too stunned to move or even to speak, but Franklyn turned to his wife, sitting composedly watching him, her expression serene.

"This is your doing, madam, I must suppose, filling her head with grandiose ideas so that she forgets her true station. *'Entitled to marry into the peerage'*, indeed. What nonsense!"

"All I have done, Mr Franklyn," Lady Esther said placidly, "is to introduce her into a society superior to any she might have known before. It is inevitable that, with such examples before her, she will lift her eyes a little higher in her search for a husband. Why should she not marry into the nobility?"

"Because her father was an attorney and her fortune came from iron foundries, that is why. I put no rub in the way of her union with Mr Atherton, but only because I thought it was a love match. I never thought her *entitled* to marry so high. Well, I shall write a note to Mr Bertram

Atherton to warn him that Bea is setting her cap at him, and that he should not fall for her wiles."

Lady Esther actually laughed. "Her wiles, Mr Franklyn? Heavens, you make her sound like a veritable harpy. She is merely a girl looking for the one match above all others that will make her happy, and she has wisely realised that her comfort will best be assured by marrying as high as she can manage. If Mr *Walter* Atherton had no objection to your former profession and the source of Beatrice's fortune, then I am sure Mr *Bertram* Atherton will have none."

And with that she rose, and swept gracefully out of the room.

Walter and Franklyn gazed at each other in utter bemusement, before Walter abruptly burst into laughter. "Women!" he said with feeling.

Franklyn gave a wry smile. "I am excessively relieved you see some amusement in this situation, my lord... I mean, Atherton. I cannot apologise enough for my daughter. To think that she pursued you so relentlessly for... what, four years? And all the time, the only thing she cared about was your title."

"No, no," Walter demurred. "I am *much* better looking than Bertram."

Franklyn laughed outright at that, although he shook his head, too. "It was very wrong of her to say such a thing. Do you know, when I married my wife, one of the advantages of the match, as I saw it, was that she would instil a little conduct in Bea, and teach her to behave in a truly ladylike manner. Not that Bea was ever precisely unladylike, but her thinking was not always correct. But this... this is appalling!"

"Bea has every right to end our engagement if she wishes," Walter said mildly. "I do not blame her for that. She betrothed herself to the heir to wealth and title, and to find herself about to marry a bastard with no expectations whatsoever... I cannot blame her for severing the connection."

"I confess, it made me uneasy to think of you living as a gentleman on Bea's fortune and bringing very little to the marriage. The world frowns on such unions, so if I had not believed her heart to be engaged, I should have turned you away myself. No, it is not her decision that I deplore, but the manner of it, Atherton! She could have let you down gently… change of circumstances, uncertain future, something of that nature."

"But is it not better to find out the nature of her attachment to me before the marriage, rather than afterwards? I thank God that this terrible situation was revealed before we were irrevocably bound to each other. Never has the saying *'for better or for worse'* had greater resonance."

"True enough," Franklyn said. "But if you are not to live like a gentleman on Bea's fortune, what will you do? You will not want to be a burden on your father's estate for ever, so will you seek a career, or perhaps become a fortune hunter in good earnest? I have to say, you have looks and charm enough for the enterprise."

"I have no idea. I knew nothing of this until…" he glanced at the clock. "Less than three hours ago, and I have been thinking only of Bea since then. Fortune hunting holds no appeal, and I cannot imagine any career for which I would be fitted. I am too old now for the army or navy or the law, and I cannot feel I am suited for the church. I do not wish to become a grocer."

Franklyn laughed. "No, indeed! But you need not stoop so low. You are very well suited, I should think, to become a steward at one of the great estates of the north. Your father's, possibly, but if not, he must know all the other principal landowners of Yorkshire. Or if you have an interest in the other side of land management, the buying and selling and exchange of contracts, I know three or four well-established partnerships of attorneys who would be very happy to offer an accelerated apprenticeship to a man of your calibre. There is good money to be made, for those with an eye for detail and of known character. Your family's reputation would ensure your success. But there is no need to rush into anything. You must take the time to adjust to your altered situation. Whatever you do, be assured that I shall always stand your friend."

Walter said all that was proper, and took his leave, but as he rode home, he was surprisingly light-hearted. He was now free of an engagement that he had drifted into without much thought, and Bea's rejection had no power to hurt him.

***

Sir Hubert Strong received a note at breakfast one morning.

"From Corland," he said, with a smile, as he broke the seal. "Rennington will be getting up some scheme or other, I dare say. Fishing, perhaps, or— Good God!"

"Sir Hubert!" said his lady, in shocked tones.

"I beg your pardon, but this—! It is—! I can barely make it out. It *cannot* be true. No, I must have misunderstood. Winnie, dear, read it out loud, for it concerns... well, you will see."

"Very well, Papa."

Winnie took the paper from his trembling hands and smoothed it out.

"My very good friend, I write with the most extraordinary news which has cast us into the greatest anguish. All our lives are overturned and will never again be as they were. I tell you this so that—'"

"Oh, whatever has happened?" Lily cried. "They are dead! They are all dead!"

Winnie glanced up. "Not all, Lily, or Lord Rennington would not be able to write to us. May I read on?"

Lily held her handkerchief to her mouth, in preparation for the gruesome details, but Mama said placidly, "Yes, do, Winnie."

"'I tell you this so that you will understand the truth and will not therefore have to suffer the rumours that will no doubt swill about. Here is the plain story — Mr Nicholson, our chaplain until his demise, was not ordained when he first came to us. He was not therefore authorised to conduct marriages, and thus—'" She hesitated, and then resolutely ploughed on. " *'Thus my marriage to my dear Caroline is void, and all our children are now illegitimate. George is now my legal heir, and Bertram after him. I have talked to the Archbishop of York, but nothing can be done about it. Isabel is also a concern, since Nicholson married her, too. Josephine is safe, for she was married in town and Nicholson had no part in that. Miss Franklyn has been informed, and the result is that Walter's betrothal is at an end...'"* Her voice wobbled only for a moment, before she continued with greater firmness. *"'...and what is to become of him and the younger children I cannot say. You will understand that we cannot presently receive company, even from such good friends as yourselves, so pray do not be offended. We do not wish for condolences, and we cannot imagine that anyone has any practical advice to offer us in our extraordinary situation. When we are a little more settled, we will open our doors to callers again. There is only one thing you may do for us now, and that is to remember us in your prayers. Rennington.'"*

She laid the letter down on the table. How strange it was — a letter just like the many hundreds of other letters from Lord Rennington to Papa over the years, all of them to arrange some pleasurable event or other. A cricket match, or an archery competition. Fishing, shooting or hunting, as the season permitted. A long ride over the moors, if no other entertainment offered itself. He was not a man who liked to idle away the hours at home, and although he had slowed down in recent years as his liking for good food inhibited his more energetic pursuits, he still liked to be outdoors, and preferably with amenable company.

And then *this* letter, the words telling of the most incredible turn of events. Mr Nicholson not ordained at all! The earl's marriage void! The children all illegitimate! And Walter's betrothal ended...

Lily's exclamations of horror and the more measured voices of Mama, Papa and Uncle Alfred would run on for some time, Winnie knew.

"I have eaten enough, Mama. May I go now? I want to get on with the jam before the next batch of fruit arrives."

"Of course, dear," her mother said vaguely, before turning back to the discussion.

Winnie had been busy in the still room for no more than half an hour before her mother crept in.

"Winnie..."

"Yes, Mama?" Although she knew perfectly well what she was about to say.

"Winnie dear, you are a good, sensible girl, and you will not become... *carried away* by this news, I am sure. Walter may no longer be betrothed to Bea Franklyn, but that does not mean he is... available."

"I know, Mama."

"His circumstances are very different now, with no money of his own and no expectation, as well as the taint of illegitimacy."

"*That* does not affect anything. I hope we would not turn away from him on that account."

"We must as Christians sincerely pity him, and keep him and all his family in our prayers, certainly, but we must be aware that he is not even a gentleman any longer, and his future is most uncertain. He may have to look about him for a career, and even if he can establish himself in some way, he will move in a very different level of society. We may see him in the same old way, but he will not necessarily view us as he did before, do you see?"

"Of course, Mama. Besides, he has never noticed me before, so why should he notice me now?"

"I knew you would understand. Nothing has changed, not really."

"No, Mama."

But it was not true. *Everything* had changed.

***

Michael kept discreetly out of the way for a day or two after the shattering announcement. It would not do to tread on the toes of the earl's family, so abnormally sensitive at the moment. But the disruption brought opportunity, too, and most specifically the regular visits from the earl's new heir, his brother Mr George Atherton, and his son, who were bidden to learn about the estates which would eventually be theirs. He asked Simpson to request a meeting. However, it was not Mr George Atherton who appeared, but his son, a pleasant-looking man of twenty-five.

"Simpson said you would like to talk to my father," he said. "He and my mother have gone to see the Dowager, but he sent me instead, to see if I might be of service to you. Bertram Atherton."

Michael made him a low bow. "Thank you, sir. I am very much obliged to you. His lordship has insisted we confine our enquiries to the castle only, so I must take every opportunity of consulting with passing visitors. May

I present to you my wife, cousin to the Earl of Morpeth, and my esteemed Scottish colleague, Mr Alexander."

"Mrs Edgerton. Alexander." Mr Bertram bowed politely, eyeing them with interest. Michael guessed that he and his friends had been the subject of much gossip in the neighbourhood.

Michael offered him a chair and poured Madeira, while Mr Bertram gazed warily at the axe resting on a sideboard.

"What did you wish to ask, Captain?" he said.

"You live at Westwick Heights, is that so?" Michael said, and Bertram nodded. "That is at Birchall village, I understand, some four or five miles from here."

"That is so."

"I have been told that no one from Westwick Heights was at the castle on the night that Mr Nicholson was murdered. Is that correct?"

"To the best of my knowledge. I cannot vouch for every last one of the servants, but no one from the family was here and none of the servants ought to have been here. We rarely stay at the castle, since we live so close."

"And you did not dine here?"

"No. I recall we had guests that evening — the Cathcarts, and Miss Parish." Sandy's pen scratched away. "Are you writing down every word I say?"

Sandy looked up and grinned disarmingly.

"I cannae write as fast as ye speak, so no. Every other word, maybe."

Bertram chuckled. "I suppose you have to keep notes of everything. I shall try to speak more slowly."

"Thank ye kindly," the Scotsman said, dipping his pen into the ink again and holding it in readiness above the paper.

"Did you know Mr Nicholson well, Mr Atherton?" Michael said.

"As well as anyone else, I suppose. He was Aunt Alice's husband, and he has been here for my entire life, but I cannot say that I took much notice of him."

"Did you like him?"

An awkward question to answer. "One does not like to speak ill of the dead..." Bertram began hesitantly.

"Oh, please do," Michael said testily. "I am so tired of hearing about the sainted chaplain, for it cannot be denied that someone thought ill enough of him to take an axe to the poor man. So if you know of anything, anything at all, that might suggest a reason for that, I should be very glad to hear it."

Bertram nodded. "He had an eye for the ladies, that much is certain. Whether he ever did anything about it I cannot tell you, but when the port was circulating after dinner, he would comment on various women who had caught his eye. Some quite lascivious comments, sometimes. Then he would always say, *'How fortunate that I am a happily married man,'* and everyone would laugh, but it made me uncomfortable, all the same. Although I suppose that is better than Eustace, who boasts about his innumerable conquests."

"Did Nicholson cheat at cards?"

"An interesting question," Bertram said. "I never caught him at it, but I did wonder. He and the late earl used to play piquet at night after everyone had gone to bed, and poor Grandfather always seemed to lose at those sessions, and quite large amounts, sometimes. He made a joke of it, saying that he should stick to playing during daylight hours for he had better luck, and Nicholson would just smile and say nothing. I dare say he plied him with brandy, for Grandfather liked a glass or three while he played, so maybe there was nothing more to it than that. In other company, sometimes there were complaints that Nicholson made mistakes in adding up the scores, and always in his favour, but I never saw anything like that myself."

"Do you know anything about this house that the late earl left to Mr Nicholson?"

"Not a thing, except that no one even knew about the house until Grandfather's will was read. Well, the lawyers did, but no one in the family. My father thought it odd, for it was only a modest property and rented out, but he could find out nothing about it. Nicholson would only say that it is a charitable case."

"A retired servant, perhaps?"

"Then why not say so? If that were all, he could say, *'Oh, it is only old Phillipson who was gamekeeper over at High Broughton,'* could he not? I know Father thought it was a bit havey-cavey. Have you been to see it?"

"Not officially," Michael said, with a sudden grin. "We are restricted to the castle at present, but if a colleague should happen to go to Pickering for... oh, to buy a new comb, say, and should happen to desire a walk around the town to stretch his legs, he might just happen to pass by a certain house."

Bertram laughed. "But it cannot be relevant to the man's murder, can it?"

"Until I know everything there is to know about the house, it is impossible to say," Michael said with a sigh. "I know you have weightier matters on your mind just now, Mr Atherton, but perhaps when you have a moment to spare for the matter, you might consider whether there is anything else you might be able to tell us which would be helpful. You and your father are, so to speak, somewhat detached from the castle, and may therefore have a wider perspective on Mr Nicholson."

"Certainly, and I do not regard the upheaval in the succession as being necessarily weightier than the question of murder, Captain. Our lives have been shaken up a great deal, it is true, but Mr Nicholson is dead and in the most violent way. Anything I can do to assist you shall be done, I assure you, and I am sure I speak for all my family when I say so."

"You are very good," Michael said. "You are looking into his lordship's financial holdings, I understand, Mr Atherton. I wonder if you have come across anything relating to Mr Nicholson's affairs. We have found very little amongst his own papers. He kept every tradesman's bill and personal letter since the day he arrived here, but nothing of money or property or business of any sort. Yet there is a fortune for his daughter, somewhere."

"We heard about that. He never seemed wealthy enough to leave a fortune behind him."

"So he describes it in his will. Some minor bequests, provision for his wife according to the settlement, and then *'the remainder of my fortune to my daughter, Teresa Nicholson, on the sole condition that she marries a gentleman, and if she should not, or remains unmarried at the age of thirty, to be given to Pembroke College, Oxford, to found a Fellowship on whatever terms may be deemed appropriate.'*"

"Yes, it is very peculiar," Bertram said thoughtfully.

"Indeed." Michael grinned again. "Perhaps, sir, you might be so obliging as to keep the idea in mind and let me know of anything you hear which would bear on the matter? Or anything in the earl's financial affairs that strikes you as… odd, shall we say."

"You think Nicholson might have been feathering his own nest?"

"If he had amassed a fortune, then it had to have come from somewhere, for he certainly never became rich on a chaplain's stipend," he said darkly.

Bertram nodded and left the old nursery with a thoughtful expression.

12: The Means For Murder

Captain Michael Edgerton leaned back in his chair. "Well, Luce? What did you make of Mr Bertram Atherton?"

His wife smiled as she gathered up the used wine glasses. "He seems an inoffensive young man."

"Yes, but they all seem inoffensive," Michael said. "Everyone is affable, the chaplain was a saint and no one has a bad word to say about him, yet someone chopped him up with an axe."

"Michael, please!" Luce protested. "I do not need to be reminded of the gruesome nature of the murder."

"But that is what makes the matter so intriguing," Michael said. "If you were to murder someone, Luce, how would you do it, do you think?"

"Oh, poison. A few drops of something unpleasant in the brandy decanter... or that flask of whisky Sandy keeps in his pocket, if he were to be my target. A final drink before bed, and... poof. How about you? A duel?"

"No, no, no. The idea is to kill someone without being detected, and not have to flee the country at once. Poison is quite ingenious, because you could arrange to be far away at the time, and it might even be passed off as a natural death. My own choice would be to shoot my target. I would wait until there was a big party out with guns and by picking the moment, no one would notice a thing. The birds would fly up, there would be a volley of shots and my man would be found flat on his back, stone dead. Poof. Sandy? How would you kill a man?"

"Drowning," the Scotsman said. "A rock to the back of the head, hold him under water, and then let the body float downstream. Ye'd never know he didn't just fall in."

"Remind me to keep on the right side of both of you," Michael said soberly. "But that is the point — none of us would consider breaking into a building full of people at dead of night, going up two flights of stairs, picking up an axe that just happened to be left lying around on the way and then slaughtering a man sleeping in his bed. One could be discovered at any moment. It is just not practical."

"Yet it happened," Luce said softly.

"Precisely. But why? Why kill the chaplain at all, but if you must do it, why kill him in that reckless way? It makes no sense."

"Unless the murderer had no other choice," Sandy said. "If ye cannae shoot or drown or poison a man, but ye know exactly where he'll be... and ye have a legitimate reason to be in his room..."

"You mean his wife, I suppose," Michael said. "The adoring wife who was so devoted to her husband, yet was discovered beside his bed covered in his blood and with an axe in her hand. The *blind* wife, who cannot shoot or stab or use poison against him. Yet I dislike that idea. It is possible, but not probable, in my view."

"Then who else?" Luce said. "Anyone in the castle could have done it just as easily, but why such a violent method, especially with the difficulty of disposing of blood-stained clothing? As you discovered, Michael."

Michael chuckled. "Yes, I thought it would be easy enough — wear an old shirt to do the deed, roll it into a ball and hide it somewhere, then stuff it into the kitchen fire when no one is looking."

"Which smothered the fire and nearly got the kitchen boy turned off without a reference, until you confessed that it was your doing," she said, smiling at him.

"And it was difficult enough to get to the fire without being spotted," he said. "I had to try it, just to see how easy it would be."

"Only to find that it is not easy at all," Luce said. "And that is precisely my point, there are far easier ways to kill the chaplain. Anyone who lived in the castle could simply put rat poison in the decanter of brandy he kept for his own use in his study. A gentleman with access to a gun could hide behind a bush as he rode on the moors. It had to be someone who had no other option — an outsider who crept into the castle and picked up the axe as a handy weapon."

Michael sighed. "You are right, of course. I am also inclined to think that Nicholson was not blackmailing the heir regarding the disinheritance. He seemed to be genuinely shocked by the revelation — they all did. So let us begin again. Lady Alice remains our principal suspect, purely because she was discovered beside the body. But who else? Someone from outside the castle, but who? One of the labourers in Corland village? How likely is that? And beyond the handful of cottages here, it is miles to the next habitation — four miles to Birchall, and fully twelve to Mr Eustace's house at Welwood-on-the-hill."

"With a fast horse—" Sandy began.

"From Birchall, one would not even need to ride," Luce said. "The road takes a wide sweep, but there is a good, clear path, no more than a mile, or a mile and a quarter, from the castle, cutting across Sir Hubert Strong's estate. Was there a full moon that night?"

Michael calculated. "Near enough. A path... interesting."

"Peachy discovered it. She is an indefatigable walker, and is not content to confine herself to the gardens, as I am. It was very tiresome when she was my governess, I assure you, but happily I no longer have to tramp miles every day."

"Where is Miss Peach, by the way? I have not seen her for days."

"She has been ingratiating herself with Mrs Dewar and the Miss Dewars at the Birchall rectory. The ladies have any number of good works in hand for the parish involving sewing or knitting and suchlike. Peachy sits and sews and listens to all the gossip. She is insatiably curious, you know, and she finds that trading a very little bit of castle gossip — nothing too secret, naturally — elicits a great deal of village gossip. She has discovered that Mr Nicholson was not particularly well liked at Birchall, but she has not yet found out why."

"Ah! Interesting," Michael said. "And if the village is only a mile or so on foot from the castle... who lives at Birchall? Apart from Mr George Atherton and his family."

"Sir Hubert Strong is the principal inhabitant, at Birchall House, which is the nearest residence to the castle. Westwick Heights, where the Athertons live, is further away, up the hill on the western side. Then there are the Franklyns at Highwood Place, but that is some three miles outside the village, out on the moors. There is the rectory and any number of shops and tradesmen of one sort or another."

Michael fetched the map, and unrolled it. Silence fell in the old nursery, as they all pored over it.

***

Winnie enjoyed summer, when the days were enlivened by a round of family visits. The first to arrive was her father's sister, Aunt Minna, whose York home had seen Winnie's first tentative steps into a larger society when she was seventeen. It was Aunt Minna who had chaperoned her at the York assemblies and hosted the evening parties for eligible suitors. Nothing had come of those two modest seasons, but Winnie retained a great fondness for her aunt and her large, rambunctious family.

On this visit, Aunt Minna and Uncle John had brought only their three eldest children, but since they were of an age with Winnie's sister and two young brothers, there was a vast amount of juvenile silliness prevailing. The adults were too absorbed in discussing the shocking news from Corland Castle to curb their behaviour, so the noise soon rose to an unbearable level.

Winnie sat silently a little apart, too old for childish games, and having nothing to add to the conversation. The tumult in her heart was too great for rational speech. Walter was free! She cared little for the reasons for it, whether he had honourably stood aside now that his prospects were gone, or whether Bea had jilted him just when he most needed her staunch support. All that mattered was that he was free, he would not marry Bea and therefore he was at liberty to choose elsewhere.

Not that he was likely to choose Winnie, of course, she understood that. He had surely had every opportunity to offer for her, had he ever wanted to, but he had never seen her in the light of a wife, and perhaps he never would. But the odds had improved from zero to something greater than zero. Possibly infinitesimally small, but still greater than zero.

The excitement prevailing meant that no one noticed that dinner was half an hour late. When eventually they drifted through, Winnie found herself in an island of good sense, between her father and Uncle John, the latter a quiet, rather studious man, who left his lively wife to manage their ramshackle household in York while he buried himself in his library.

The two men talked of Walter and what he might do with himself now, and Winnie was content to listen quietly. If Walter himself could not be present, the next best thing was to hear him talked of. Uncle Alfred was willing to help find him a government post, but as that would take him away to London and far from Winnie, she could not like the idea.

After dinner, the men lingered over their port, but Lady Strong diverted the young ladies away from frivolity by opening the instrument, settling Lily at her harp, the cousins at the pianoforte and allowing them to expend their energies in song and music.

"Was I ever as silly as those three?" Winnie whispered to her mother, when Aunt Watson was called upon to adjudicate a dispute between the young cousins over the music.

"No, dear, you were always my good, sensible girl," her mother said with a wan smile, leaving Winnie unsure whether she meant it as a compliment or not.

The boys and Uncle John at last joined the ladies, but Uncle John came over to Winnie. "Your father asks you to join him in the dining room. There is someone here from the castle — a captain."

It was indeed Captain Edgerton, who made Winnie a flourishing bow, then held the chair for her as she sat. Her father pushed a glass of port towards her.

"How are they all at Corland, Captain?" Winnie said.

"Very shocked, naturally. How could it be otherwise? The ladies weeping, the men grim-faced... it is a dreadful business. Miss Strong..." He hesitated, then seemed to gird his loins. "Miss Strong, you may or may not be aware that it was the letter you found that started us down the road to this outcome."

"The letter I found?" she said, startled. "Which letter was that?"

"The one from the Bishop of Winchester."

"Oh. *Oh!* That was how it was all discovered?"

"It was. We have not told anyone that the letter was found by you, and I suggest you do not mention it to anyone. You did not understand the significance of it, after all."

"No, I merely wondered how to file it. But if I had not found it, Mrs Edgerton would have done so. It would have been found, one way or another."

"Precisely," the captain said, smiling at her. "So it is irrelevant who it was."

"And they would resent me if they knew it was my doing, is that it?"

"They might. I would not wish there to be any rift between you and the Athertons on that account."

"Thank you, Captain. That is very thoughtful of you. But tell me, how goes your investigation? Is there much progress?"

"As I have been telling your father and uncle, I am no further forward at Corland. I thought I had had a breakthrough in discovering that Lord Farramont had stayed at the castle on the fateful night, but apart from Mr

Eustace, no one recalls the precise day. The grooms rose before dawn to prepare his carriage for departure at first light, but they have no idea which day that was. It hardly matters, though, for his lordship's man slept in the same room on account of the early start, and it seems unlikely that a man would rise from his bed, step over his valet, go off and murder someone with an axe and then quietly go back to bed."

"Unless the valet was helping him in some way," Winnie said.

"An accomplice?" The captain frowned. "Possibly. Valets can be excessively loyal to their employer. I shall try to talk to Lord Farramont, but he is not high on my list at present. I am still trying to find a reason why anyone would wish to kill the fellow at all."

"And with an axe, too," Winnie said with a shudder. "It is a particularly gruesome method to choose. But I cannot imagine Lord Farramont would kill Mr Nicholson. He seems too quiet a man to rise to violence."

"But the same may be said of everyone," the captain said. "Except... Miss Strong, I am told you know Mr Walter Atherton better than almost anyone else. Would you say he is prone to outbursts of temper?"

"Walter? Heavens, no! A more easy-going man would be hard to find. Although... he dismissed a groom once who neglected a horse of his."

The captain gave a bark of laughter. "Entirely understandable! I would do as much myself. But no duels or tavern brawls? No fisticuffs with his brothers?"

"Not that I ever heard. He and Eustace were very close as boys. Not so much now, since Eustace no longer lives at the castle. As for Kent, no one could quarrel with him, for he never gets angry about anything."

"Hmm. This is the trouble, you see, Miss Strong. Every little hint of something amiss trickles into the sand and turns out to be nothing. We have exhausted the possibilities at Corland, and I do not have permission from the earl to extend my enquiries to Birchall."

"I do not think that would help you, Captain. Many of the villagers here owe their livelihoods to Corland in one way or another, so they will not speak out against the family."

"That your father has already told me. Yet there must be someone, somewhere who knows something germane. After all, someone crept through Corland Castle at dead of night carrying an axe and that person must have been driven by powerful emotions. Sooner or later we will find some trace of that."

13: A Morning Walk

Winnie woke the next morning to steady drizzle. It was not enough to deter her from her morning walk, although her heavy cloak soon made her clammy and hot. She walked quickly through her mother's gardens, a riot of colour at this season, the heavy blooms bowed over and dripping from the rain. These walks had been more pleasurable with her sisters. The three of them, Winnie, Hebe and Mabel, had walked out every morning without fail, unless the rain was torrential or snow was falling. It was their greatest pleasure, to be away from adult eyes, chattering about their own affairs. Very often they would end up at the tree house, and one or other of the Athertons would be there, and there would be teasing and laughter, until someone checked a watch. Then they had to run back to the house to avoid being late for breakfast.

Now the Athertons seldom came, Hebe and Mabel were married and gone away, and Lily had never been a great walker. Only Winnie was left to her solitary walks, to wonder where the years went. How had those carefree children turned into serious adults? How was it that she was still here, still taking her walks, still unmarried at twenty-four, when her younger sisters were settled already, their nurseries filling, their lives contented? When the autumn came, she would be off to Knaresborough to support Mabel through her first confinement, and after Christmas it would be Pickering for Hebe's second. Already she was falling into her rôle of spinster aunt.

Not that she minded that. If she could not have children of her own, then helping with her nephews and nieces would fill the void inside her that so longed for motherhood. Children were such a joy, and she could imagine no greater pleasure than raising them. Her own, if she could, but if not, then those of her sisters and brothers. They would keep her busy and stop her fretting for a life that could not be hers.

Yet she could have married, once. She could have had her own house, and two or three children of her own by now. The offer had been made, but she had turned him away. At the time she still had hopes of Walter, still believed that one magical day he would look at her and see her, truly *see* her, for the first time, and then he would want her the way she wanted him. But that was six years ago, and a year later Bea Franklyn had arrived and set her cap at Walter with unshakeable determination, and he, foolish man, had fallen into her trap. Not quickly, it had to be said, for it took her four years to ensnare him, but inexorably. When Bea set her sights on an object, she never gave up.

Normally, such dreary thoughts would dampen Winnie's spirits as even the rain could not. But today, nothing could cast her down, for Walter was free! And even if he never discovered all the love stored up for him in Winnie's heart, she was not yet a confirmed spinster, for she had the example of Aunt Sofia before her, who had married only three years ago at the age of thirty-nine, and was blissfully happy. Twenty-four was not the end of all hope, after all.

She came under the trees of the home wood at last, and although she was dripped on, the canopy kept off the worst of the rain. She was able to throw back her cloak and free herself from its constrictions. That was better! Laughing a little, she lifted her face towards the trees, feeling the little splashes on her face, delighting in even so small a pleasure. There was so much enjoyment to be had, even from a simple walk on her own, so she was smiling and humming a little tune as she rounded the bend to the tree house.

He was there, sitting on one of the swings, idly pushing himself with his foot. Her heart did its usual acrobatics, and a little shiver of delight brought her deliciously awake after her reverie. But he looked so woebegone, his head drooping, that her spirits instantly plummeted. Poor Walter, who had lost everything, even his future wife.

"Walter? Oh, Walter!" Heedless of the mud, she knelt on the wet ground before him. "I am so, so sorry. If only there were something I could do or say that would help, but if you want to talk, I am happy to listen."

"Thank you, Mouse. You are very good, but I do not wish to talk about it."

"No, of course not. How is everyone at the castle?"

He gave a wry laugh. "Why do you think I needed to escape? Olivia is hysterical because she is not to have her come-out next year after all, Kent is planning to become an engineer of some sort, if you can believe it, and Tess has vanished altogether. Oh, and Mother says she will not marry Father. He is to find himself some slip of a girl straight from the schoolroom, she says, to breed more sons. Legitimate ones, this time."

"No!" Winnie cried. "Surely he would not... would he?"

"I have no idea. Everything else at Corland is insane just now, so why not? I hardly know my own family. Mouse, why on earth are you kneeling in all this mud? You will be filthy."

"It is of no consequence with clothes as old as these," she said, but she scrambled to her feet and took the other swing. "Was it awful, telling Miss Franklyn?"

"It was, rather, but do you know what was the worst of it? The wretched butler calling me *'my lord'*. I told him to announce me as plain *'Mr Atherton'*, and he did it, too, but then he just kept going with the *'my lord'*. I have been Birtwell for ten years, Winnie, and even my family called me that, and now... now I hardly know who I am any more. Where did Lord Birtwell vanish to, and who is this Mr Walter Atherton? I have lost everything, even my own name."

"You are still *Walter*," she said gently. "You are the same man, are you not? You have not lost your good character, your honour, your understanding. You have a quick mind, when you choose to use it. You have strength and good health and the proper number of limbs. And you have a family surrounding you who all love you. You have friends who care for you. What does it matter what label is attached to you? No one who truly cares about you is the least bit concerned with what name you declare yourself to the world. The viscountcy was only a courtesy title anyway, not a real one. For legal purposes, you have never been anything other than plain Mr Walter Atherton, as you call it."

He laughed suddenly, his whole face lightening, so that her breath caught. He should not be so handsome! It was unfair to poor spinsters like her.

"Ah, you always find some way to make me feel better... my wise little Mouse."

Immediately she recognised the fallacy of her argument. How could she say that names were of no consequence, when she hated with a passion that he called her *'Mouse'*. Such a derogatory name, for mice were the lowest of the low, rodents of little account, insignificant little creatures. Small and brown and nondescript, just like her. Not radiant and fiery and sparkling, like Bea Franklyn. But years of hiding her feelings enabled her to summon a smile at the compliment.

"So what will you do now?" she said, trying to sound nonchalant, but her feet twitched in her anxiety, setting the swing moving. "Will you have to... go away?"

"Oh... no. I should not think so. Father has said he will continue to support me. Where should I go, anyway? I have no home but Corland. But I shall have to find some employment, I suppose. Support myself, eventually. Be independent, although I have no idea what I might do."

"There are any number of things you could do."

"Like what?" he said suspiciously.

"We are in need of a new groom. Twenty pounds a year, board and lodging found. Oh, and livery provided."

He laughed. "A groom. Really, Mouse?"

"Well, you are very good with horses, Walter. Or if that does not appeal, Mr Phipps at the home farm is always looking for hard-working young men as labourers. It is only twelve pounds a year, but Mrs Phipps is an excellent cook, and her hams are the best in the North Riding. She has several comely daughters, too, any one of whom would make you an excellent wife."

"A farm labourer! And this is the opinion you have of my prospects, is it? That I should become a farm labourer and marry a farmer's daughter.

Father thinks I should enter the church. He has several livings at his disposal. Can you see me making sermons?"

"No. Although you would be very good at it, if you were to do so."

"Do you truly think that? You must think me a cod's head if you do. I am not at all devout, Winnie."

She smiled and shook her head, pushing the swing a little harder. Despite the rain, it was sultry today and even so slight a breeze was welcome. "It is not at all necessary to be devout. All that is required is to be in church at certain times and days, and to speak in suitably ringing tones from the pulpit, and you could do that perfectly well. You are an excellent speaker, when you turn your mind into the proper channels. Most of the time, you are too lazy to do much thinking."

He gave a shout of laughter. "Mouse, you know me all too well. Preaching sounds far too much like hard work. Mr Franklyn suggested I become a land steward, or if that does not appeal, he can arrange for me to be apprenticed to an attorney."

He pulled a face, making Winnie laugh. "There are worse jobs. What about the government? Uncle Alfred can help you there. He was talking about it only last night. That might suit you." Although it would not suit her at all. She held her breath awaiting his answer.

"Perhaps. At least I would feel I have not strayed too far from my original path in life. When one has been raised from birth to expect a seat in the Lords and the right to help shape the kingdom, it would be unbearably distressing to settle for life as a country attorney. Now, Eustace thinks I should find myself an heiress. Prance around town for a few weeks and then marry some wealthy merchant's buck-toothed daughter and live in comfort for the rest of my life. I confess there is a certain appeal to the idea."

"Must she be buck-toothed?" Winnie said. "Do wealthy merchants not have pretty daughters now and then?"

"No, never. It is an invariable rule. Look at Bea, if you want proof."

"Bea is not buck-toothed!" Winnie cried, scandalised. "That is a horrid thing to say, Walter, especially since you were about to marry her."

"Not precisely buck-toothed, but she is not *pretty*, is she? All that bouncy hair and pert manner... and she is positively ugly when she says she will not have me now, but will marry Bertram instead."

Winnie's jaw dropped. "She did not! That makes her seem so... so..." Her foot shot out, stopping the swing so abruptly that she nearly slid off the seat.

"Avaricious? Selfish? Mercenary? Grasping? Hateful? Despicable? Greedy? Rapacious? Yes, all of those."

"Then it was her! I wondered, you see, if you had chosen to step aside now that your prospects had changed, which would have been very honourable and just what one would expect of you, but she *jilted* you! And all because you are illegitimate."

"No, it is because I am not going to be an earl, and therefore cannot make her a countess. But Bertram can, so she has decided she will marry him instead."

"But he is nothing like you! You could not be more different! To throw you over for *Bertram* — it is unaccountable. Oh, poor Bertram! Does he know yet?"

"Franklyn sent a note across straight away, to warn him. But I think you need not worry about him. He is a much stronger character than he appears. As for me, I want no more heiresses, for not only are they buck-toothed — or have too much hair and pert manners — but they want nothing to do with a penniless bastard like me. So it will have to be one of Mrs Phipp's comely daughters after all."

14: A Guest

Winnie was aware that Uncle Alfred had been very much engaged at Corland, talking to Walter about a possible government post. Even so, it was a complete shock to return to Birchall House one afternoon, weary and muddy from a visit to a sick farmer's wife, to find a pile of boxes in the hall labelled *'Viscount Birtwell'*.

"Viscount Birtwell!" she exclaimed.

"We've been instructed to refer to the gentleman as *'Mr Atherton'*, Miss Winnie," Maynard said.

"Oh yes, very proper, but what are his boxes doing here?" A sudden flutter of excitement. "Is he staying here?"

"He is, madam. Mr Alfred has taken the young gentleman under his wing, so to speak. They are all in the drawing room."

Winnie was hot, windswept and dusty from tramping across the fields, but the burning desire to see Walter overcame any instinct to make herself presentable, so she marched straight into the drawing room. The room was full, the children rolling on the floor in some unfathomable game of their own, the women sitting about decorously with teacups, while the men stood beside the open window, drinking Madeira, Walter amongst them... and there as usual were the internal butterflies that made her feel awkward and stupid.

With an effort, she forced herself to her usual cheerfulness. She spoke loudly, to be heard above the hubbub of the children. "Walter! What a pleasant surprise."

He turned, he saw her, he smiled... and her heart turned over in the most violent way.

The room quietened suddenly, and Mama set down her tea cup with a distinct rattle. "Really, Winnie, have you no manners? Look at you, coming in here in all your dirt."

"I thought it a courtesy to our guest to—"

"Time enough for that when you are respectable."

"Yes, Mama. I beg your pardon. I shall go and change at once."

She curtsied with dignity and left the room, but no matter what Mama said, it *was* a courtesy to greet a guest at once. Besides, she was not so very disreputable and not at all muddy. Still, she must do as she was bid.

By the time she had summoned Martha, had changed into her newest gown, and had washed and tidied herself, almost an hour had passed, and by then no one was in the drawing room but Mama.

"Where is everyone?" Winnie said.

"Minna is in the nursery with the children, Lily has gone up to change for dinner already, and I cannot tell you where the men have gone."

"How long is Walter staying?"

"A few days... I hardly know, for it was all very sudden," she said fretfully. "Your uncle went off to the castle as usual this morning, and came home with Walter and his boxes this afternoon, and not a bit of notice to me, none at all. Still, I make no objection, even though I cannot like it, for we must do what we can for the poor boy. Ah, there is the dressing bell now."

So saying, she sailed majestically out of the room, leaving Winnie mystified. She had never made the least objection to unexpected visitors before, and Walter was unlikely to be a difficult guest, so it was hard to see a reason for her fit of pique. Winnie straightened a few cushions, closed open books and tidied away the journals, then settled down with the newspaper. Lily would have Martha's services first to change for dinner, so there was no point in rushing.

She had not been there two minutes when the door opened and Walter came in, creating the familiar flutters in her stomach. Did it never end, this foolish delight in his company? Ah, but he looked so splendid, so tall and manly, his clothes so well-fitted to his admirable form. And he really should not smile at her that way, not if she were ever to recover her sanity where he was concerned.

"There you are, Mouse!" he said in pleased tones. "I wondered where you had got to."

"I had to change my gown."

"I know, but you have been gone ages. Is this not fun? In all the times I have visited this house, I have never yet stayed here, except that one time when it snowed, do you remember? Probably not, for I was only seven or eight, so you were just a baby then. It was too bad a storm to walk or to take the horses out, so I stayed in a little attic room, and your father and uncle walked home with me the next morning. Are you pleased to see me, Mouse?"

"Of course, but why are you staying? Has something dreadful happened?"

"Not yet, but it is about to. Izzy is coming home."

"Oh dear!"

"Quite so. She wrote Mother a dreadful letter, ranting over no less than ten pages, if you please, and not even franked, for Farramont was away somewhere. Eustace is holed up at Welwood, no doubt with the doors and windows barred. Aunt Alice still keeps her room, where Malling will defend her. Even Mother has bolted, gone to Aunt Myrtle at Harfield." An anxious frown crossed his face, making him look like a boy again. "I hope she comes back soon. The place is horrid without her. As for the others, nothing ruffles Kent, not even Izzy, and Olivia is cut from the same cloth, but I could not stand her frenzies, not just at the moment, not when we are all rubbed raw as it is. So your uncle very kindly invited me to stay until Izzy subsides or Farramont arrives to take her away or she is locked up in an asylum, whichever comes first."

Winnie giggled. "Really, Walter! Izzy is... a bit excitable, let us say, but she is not as bad as all that."

"You did not see the letter."

"Poor Lord Rennington, left to deal with it on his own, and not even Lady Rennington to share his trouble. I confess to a little surprise that she would leave the earl just now."

"That is to persuade him to marry someone younger," Walter said. "I thought she only said that in the heat of the moment, but she is very set on it, seemingly, so she has gone — leaving the stage for the next act, as she puts it. But I wish she had not *abandoned* us."

"Your poor father! How dreadful for him!"

"He is very shocked, naturally, but it is hardly dreadful for him. What, to be forced to marry some pretty young creature? There are plenty of men who would envy him that. Uncle George is all for it, too. He has no wish at all to inherit, and Aunt Jane has wept pretty well constantly since she heard the news. She says that her soul is at Westwick, and even if George inherits, she will not live at Corland. She will live in the Dower House, she says, and be perfectly content there. Westwick will go to Lucas now, I suppose."

"So much upheaval," Winnie said thoughtfully. "No one is unaffected, but you have had the worst of it, Walter. You have lost so much."

"Yet the odd thing is that what I most resent is not being Viscount Birtwell anymore. The earldom, the castle, all Father's estates... that is just a burden, frankly. But I did like being a lord — even if only by courtesy, as you so helpfully reminded me."

"I should have thought you would be more distressed by the breaking of your engagement, Walter," she said sharply. "For all you joked about Miss Franklyn's curls, you must have had some fondness for her, or you would not have planned to marry her, and now that happy future together is not to be. That, surely, is of greater significance to your life than a mere title."

"A mere title... really, Mouse, what a thing to say! That *mere title* gave me my place in the world. I knew who I was and what I was required to do. That certainty is all gone. But as for Bea... shall I tell you a secret?" He looked all round the room, although they were quite alone, and then whispered, "I am rather relieved it is all off with Bea." Then, in his normal voice, he went on, "There! Are you shocked?"

"Yes, I am. You should not say such things, even to me. It is disloyal to Miss Franklyn, Walter."

"Well, I would never say them to anyone but you. To everyone else, I look sorrowful and say that, naturally, I am heartbroken but I completely understand Miss Franklyn's decision. Oh Lord, is that the time! I shall have to scramble into my evening togs. I shall see you again at dinner, Mouse."

And with that he was gone, leaving Winnie bemused and not altogether in charity with him, running away and leaving his father to face Izzy's wrath alone, and then so disrespectful to Bea! It was not right, not right at all. But she supposed he must be devastated by the dramatic change in his circumstances, and so concealed his pain behind a flippant manner. He had always been so, even as a child.

Martha had laid out one of her reliable old evening gowns, but Winnie instructed her to look out her newest one. She allowed the maid to do as she pleased with her hair. She had not Bea Franklyn's striking locks, nor did her hair obligingly curl without excessive effort, but there was an abundance of it, with a fine, healthy shine, and Martha had grown quite skilful in arranging it. Winnie felt, therefore, that she looked well as she descended to the drawing room.

The room was crowded, full of noisy, chattering people, the young ones in excitable groups, the men's voices booming, and Aunt Minna shrieking with laughter, while the younger children, not yet tidied away to the nursery, raced around squealing.

Winnie winced, but then she noticed Walter across the room on one of the window seats, his head down, his face drawn with misery and her heart went out to him. He put such a good face on it, joking his way through his troubles, but he was cast down, there was no doubt about it.

Before she could follow her instincts and go to him, Uncle Alfred saw her and drew her into the room. She found herself in a corner with only her parents and her uncle.

"I am glad you are here, Winnie, for I have had a letter from London, from your Uncle Edmund."

Uncle Edmund was the handsome young man who had swept Aunt Sofia off her feet just three years ago, when she was thirty-nine. She had seemed destined to remain unwed, spending her time helping Uncle Alfred with his Treasury work, but now she had her own house and a baby, a beacon of hope for ageing spinsters everywhere.

Winnie was puzzled, for although Uncle Edmund worked with Uncle Alfred at the Treasury, she could not see that he would have anything to say that might concern her.

"He writes that there is a small situation brewing at the Treasury, and he would like my assistance. Since I shall have to go to town to deal with it, I thought it would be a good opportunity to introduce Walter into my circle. I can show him what I do, and he can see if such work might interest him."

"So you and Walter will be going off to London?" Oh. So she was not to have Walter around for very long. Her spirits sank instantly.

"Yes, if his father agrees. The change of scene will do him good, rather than brooding on his situation."

"Oh yes! Something active to do — that is an excellent idea," Winnie said.

"Then we are all of one mind on the subject," her father said, his eyes twinkling. "Everyone needs a change of scene from time to time, do you not agree, Winnie?"

"Certainly I do. Especially when Walter's home is so unsettled at the moment, it will do him a great deal of good to travel, and leave his troubles behind for a while."

"What about you, Winnie?" her uncle said. "Should you like a change of scene?"

There was something in her father's manner and his beaming smile that aroused all her suspicions. Could he be asking her the question she thought? Was it merely a general enquiry or... something else? But she could not make presumptions, so she answered circumspectly.

"I am not dissatisfied with my present situation, but it is always refreshing to visit a new place... or simply a different place."

The men laughed and exchanged glances, but Mama frowned, becoming apprehensive.

"Perhaps you could come with us, Winnie," Uncle Alfred said. "You are so helpful with writing notes and letters, and making lists. We should be very glad of your assistance, and it would be a little holiday for you, too. Would you like that?"

"Oh, I should like it of all things!" Winnie said without hesitation.

"Go to London?" Mama said sharply. "Why would you want to?"

"I should *love* to see Aunt Sofia again, and Baby John and their new home, because descriptions in letters, no matter how detailed, do not convey what a place is truly like. And the sights, Mama! St Paul's and the Bank of England and Hyde Park and the Tower and... oh, so many places! And the theatres and musical performances... are the theatres still open?"

"Many of them, yes," Uncle Alfred said.

"Oh please, may I go, Mama? Papa?"

"I have no objection," her father said quickly.

"But *London!*" Mama said, in shocked tones. "I understand why you might want to see Sofia again, Winnie, for you were always close, but she will come here... sooner or later, she is bound to. And as for the rest, we have churches and theatres and sights enough in York to satisfy you, if sights are what you crave. You might go there with Minna and John when they go home, you know."

Winnie's face fell. "I have been to York many times, Mama, so nothing there is new to me. I should very much like to go to London, but only if you can spare me. I should not wish to go away if I am needed here."

Her father's smile broadened. "I think perhaps she might be spared for a short visit, eh, Kitty? You have Lily for company, after all."

"But London!" Mama said again. "It is all dissipation and frivolity! Balls and routs and gambling and nothing but selfish enjoyment."

Uncle Alfred shook his head. "You need not be concerned about that, Kitty. Sofia and Edmund live sober, respectable lives, not in the least dissipated. Besides, at this season, almost everyone of consequence has left town to pursue their frivolities in Brighton or Bath or their country estates. Absolutely nothing of a frivolous nature will occur, you may be sure."

"Church... what about church?"

"Sofia and Edmund attend St Margaret's every Sunday, and occasionally the Abbey." Gently, he went on, "You must know that Sofia would not let any harm come to Winnie. Two or three weeks in London will not turn her head, you may be sure, and it will do her a world of good. I can employ her to take notes for me, which she does so well and so accurately, and Sofia will see that she has a little gentle amusement while she is in town. Really, Kitty, even you cannot suggest that a visit to St Paul's Cathedral is frivolous."

"No, no. Perfectly unexceptionable. But what about chaperonage? It is a journey of several days."

"She will take Martha, I suggest," Sir Hubert said. "She has plenty of sense, and will share Winnie's chamber when they stay at an inn, and in London, Sofia will be her chaperon."

"Sofia never steps out without Percival, Kitty," Uncle Alfred said. "The footman, if you remember. He is a great, tall fellow, who amuses himself now and then by a little prize fighting, which he usually wins. And if we venture out at night, Winnie will have three gentlemen to protect her. She will be perfectly safe, you may be sure."

"You seem to have an answer for every possible concern," Mama said grudgingly. "Very well, you may go off and enjoy yourself, Winnie."

"Thank you, Mama," Winnie said demurely, but inside her heart was so full she felt she would burst. She would go to London! With Walter! She could scarcely believe her luck.

15: Journey To London

The evening passed off much as usual, Winnie supposed. The young female cousins giggled and whispered together. Their male counterparts insulted each other loudly and ate enormous amounts of food. The adults talked about the events of the day in well-modulated voices, interspersed with reproving comments to the children. Only two people were largely silent, both Walter and Winnie frequently lost in their own thoughts, although for entirely different reasons.

Winnie could not begin to imagine how Walter must be feeling. She wondered how she would feel, to discover that she were suddenly illegitimate, but it could not be the same. She had no great title and vast estates to lose, no high position in society from which to plummet, no engagement to be broken. She would not lose very much at all, for her parents would hardly throw her out, so she would go on exactly as always. Whereas for

Walter, every facet of his life would now be different. But he was very capable, when he set his mind to it, so he would forge a new path for himself.

At the end of the evening, the four men settled down to whist and brandy, and much as Winnie wished she could stay, Mama's "Shall we retire, ladies?" was spoken in a tone which admitted of only one possible response. So Winnie went to her room, clutching the newspaper under her arm, to read while she waited for Martha. But it was not Martha who knocked on her door a few minutes later.

"May I come in?"

"Of course, Mama. Have I done something wrong? If you do not wish me to go to London—"

"No, dear, no, it is not that. Well, not solely that."

"I should not wish to do anything you dislike, or to cause you any anxiety on my account. I am quite ready to give it up if—"

"No. Your father has approved it, and I am satisfied that you will be well looked after. You are a good girl, Winnie. You work hard, you are obedient and dutiful, and you deserve a little pleasure in your life. But I do have a concern regarding London, all the same. Or rather, regarding Walter."

"Mama, you need not worry about that. I have no expectations there, and in fact, I am quite at odds with him today. He does not always think as he ought."

"That is true. I like him well enough, but he has not always the proper degree of... of rectitude," she said with distaste, startling Winnie into silence. "But it is not his behaviour of which I must speak, or yours either, for I trust you without reservation on that score. But Winnie, I *fear* for you. On this journey to London, you and Walter will be very much thrown together. Several days on the road then two, perhaps three, weeks in town, and however strong your resolve, the heart can be a great deceiver. It would be very easy, in such constant proximity, to come by degrees to think that he feels more for you than is the case. Dearest, I do not want you to be disappointed, and so you must not allow your hopes to be raised."

"Mama—"

"No, let me finish, dear. I am going to tell you something now that I have never told you before because... well, you did *not* need to hear such things. But now I think it best you know. When you came home after your second season in York, after you refused Mr Seymour and explained to me why you had done so... it seemed to me that we might look about us for a match closer to home, and nowhere is closer than Corland, is it?"

Winnie sat up straighter. "You tried to arrange a match for me... with *Walter?*"

"Naturally, I did not tell anyone of your *tendre* for Walter, but it seemed like such an obvious thing to do," her mother said, with a slight lift of one shoulder. "Such close neighbours, and the two of you had been friends for years. It is not as if you were wildly ineligible, after all, as the daughter of a baronet, and five thousand is not a trivial dowry. Perhaps your father could have done something more for you, if it had come off. And the earl was not unresponsive at first."

At first? Winnie trembled all over — she had come so close to achieving her heart's desire, yet had known nothing of it!

"He thought Walter was too young to marry, that was the only sticking point initially. He would think about it, he said. But then, a few months later, when your father raised the matter with him again, it was a different story. It was out of the question, he said, because you were not a fit person to marry into his family. Your propriety was in question."

"What? But what have I ever done wrong that would preclude me marrying an Atherton... or anyone?"

"That he did not say, or nothing specific, anyway. But you see, Winnie, this is what comes of barging into drawing rooms without so much as removing your bonnet. I was quite ashamed of you this afternoon, and as for courtesy towards a guest, that is best achieved by presenting yourself in your best light."

"Mama, do you seriously mean to suggest that Lord Rennington rejected me as a possible bride—" A bride! For an instant, her self-command almost deserted her. "—a possible *match* for Walter because I sometimes look a bit dishevelled and dirty?"

"It is more than that, Winnie. You are not and never have been ladylike, and anyone marrying into an earl's family has to be a lady at all times, to grace the dignity of her position."

Winnie laughed suddenly. "Did you not hear Bea Franklyn talking about her great friend Charity? A lady who spills things and bumps into things and trips over things and says whatever stray thought wanders into her head, and she is married to a marquess and will be a duchess one day. It sounds like a put-off, to me. Lord Rennington obviously thought he could do better for Walter than the mere daughter of a baronet."

"With Bea Franklyn?" her mother said, raising her eyebrows. "The way she set her cap at Walter was not at all ladylike."

"Aunt Sofia said she was a devious, scheming little minx, as I recall."

"Hush, child! You must not repeat such things. But even though that is all off, I want to be sure you understand that Walter is not for you. Even if this trip to London seems to be bringing you closer together, his father will not countenance the match."

"I understand, Mama. I will be sensible."

"Good girl."

And finally Mama left, Martha came in and readied Winnie for bed, and then left her alone. But Winnie did not get into bed. Instead, she sat on the window seat, allowing the cool evening to waft in through the open window. And she smiled.

It made no difference how many times her mother tried to tell her that nothing had changed, that Walter was still out of reach, that the earl would not approve. Walter was not the heir to an earldom any longer, he was not even the earl's son in any legal way. He was no one, a man without family or profession or fortune, and he was of age. He could marry where he chose... or where someone chose him.

So if they should happen to be thrown together and he should happen to fall in love, there was nothing at all to prevent them from marrying.

If he should fall in love. That was the stumbling block, just as it always had been.

***

JULY

The earl's middle daughter, Izzy, blew into Corland Castle like a summer storm, and blew out again just as swiftly, following her mama to relations in County Durham. Shortly behind her, the much calmer person of her husband arrived.

Lord Farramont was a solemn-faced man of thirty-five, an imposing figure topped by hair that might be described as sandy by a kindly observer.

The less kind would call it flame red. Michael lost no time in requesting an interview with him, and less than an hour after his carriage had rolled into the yard, the viscount appeared at the old nursery.

"I understand from Simpson that you wish to see me, Captain," he said, his countenance unsmiling. "Here I am, although I cannot imagine that I can help you with your enquiries. I was not here when Nicholson was murdered."

"I am very glad to have that confirmed, my lord," Michael said. "A glass of wine? Or—?"

"Nothing, thank you. I can certainly confirm it. Is that all?"

"But you did spend a night here, I believe? You arrived late, shared a room with your valet to facilitate an early start and then departed at first light. That is so, is it not?"

"It is. But that has nothing to do with Nicholson."

"Do you recall the precise date of that visit, my lord? The servants are not at all certain, and there was a suggestion that it might have been the very night of the murder, in which case—"

"I might have wielded the axe myself?"

"Did you?"

"No, Captain, I did not. As I have already said, I was not here that night."

"Then which night was it? If you can remember."

The viscount reached into a pocket and produced a notebook, thumbing over the pages. "The first week of June, was it not? I was here the night before Nicholson's demise. Here it is. See for yourself."

He slid the notebook across the table. The pages were filled with small, neat writing, each date underlined and then the activities of the day recorded. *'Arr CC 9.10pm. I gone. D in room.'* And for the next day was written,

'Dep CC 5.10am. Ch 3T Thirsk 9-10.15am. Ch KH D'ton 2.20-3.5pm. Arr QH D'ham 6.20pm.' In the margin were the costs associated with each stage of the journey. Michael could only admire such methodical attention to detail.

Michael wrote it all down, having travelled the Great North Road often enough to interpret the inn names. He had a friend in Durham who could surreptitiously check that Lord Farramont had, in fact, stayed at the Queen's Head. And if he had been in Durham on the night of the murder, he was far enough away not to be under any suspicion.

"Thank you, my lord. That confirms that you could not have… ah, wielded the axe. Can you think of anyone who might have done?"

"I cannot."

"Thank you, my lord."

He rose, bowed and allowed Lord Farramont to leave, without so much as the twitch of lip or eyebrow to suggest that he was anything other than an automaton. Mr Eustace had called him secretive, but Michael would have said it was more an unhealthy degree of reserve. But then the aristocracy could be like that, buttoned up as tight as a drum with the lower orders. Perhaps the viscount was a paragon of open-hearted delight with his own kind.

There was only one moment when Michael glimpsed something gentler beneath the surface. At dinner that night, when the ladies had withdrawn, the earl turned to Lord Farramont.

"You will follow Izzy to Harfield, I suppose."

"If that is where she has gone."

"She *said* she would go there, for her mother is there, but one never knows with Izzy."

"Wherever she is, I will find her," Farramont said, his expression softening momentarily.

"Of course you will! And you will remarry and all will be well."

"I have a special licence," Farramont said.

The earl's face crumpled. "Exactly! I wish—! Farramont, if you go to Harfield and see my wife, will you... will you tell her that I should be very happy to have her home again. *Very* happy."

"I will tell her that, sir," Farramont said quietly. "I shall tell her those exact words."

There was clear sympathy in his eyes, which Michael entirely understood, for both of them had lost their wives to Nicholson's duplicity, and neither knew quite what the future would bring.

***

Winnie could not wait to begin the journey to London. She armed herself with road maps of the route, a guide book describing the great houses, monuments and scenic features they would pass along the way, and a blank journal to record her impressions of the sights. On the day of departure, she was dressed, packed and ready to depart shortly after dawn, and paced impatiently about the hall until the others appeared.

They left Birchall House in grey dampness, Uncle Alfred's carriage for Winnie, Uncle Alfred and Walter, and Lady Strong's for the two valets and Martha, almost as excited as Winnie. As soon as they reached Helmsley, Lady Strong's carriage was sent back to Birchall, a hired post-chaise was acquired and Sir Hubert's steady coach horses were swapped for two teams of four, with postilions. Thus equipped, they rattled along the toll road at a steady pace, onwards and southwards, the weather miraculously clearing as they progressed.

Winnie savoured every moment. After York, each town or village or hill or mile post was new to her, every vista worthy of comment, every inn meal to be recorded meticulously in her journal. She carried it in her reticule at all times, bringing it out for additional descriptions whenever there was sufficient lack of motion to permit it.

"What do you find to write in that little book of yours, Mouse?" Walter said.

"Everything!" she said, with a sigh of pure pleasure. "I shall probably never make such a journey again in my life, so I want a record of every detail, no matter how trivial, so that I can read it in years to come and remember."

Walter only laughed. She did not mind a bit. He could laugh at her all he liked, for quite apart from the obvious pleasures of the journey were her secret delights, all of which involved Walter. Sometimes he sat facing her, with his back to the horses, so she could gaze on his handsome countenance every time she looked in that direction. Even more delightful were the times when he sat beside her, his well-muscled thigh only inches from her own more modestly proportioned leg, his shoulder rubbing against hers. Sometimes, he would bend forwards to read the guidebook that lay on her lap, and she would find his head almost touching hers. If she had raised her hand, she could run her fingers through his unruly hair. Such exquisite pleasures were not recorded in her journal, but were seared onto her brain. If her hopes were not realised, they would warm her in the dark years ahead when she would be an affirmed spinster, flitting from house to house to assist with her nephews and nieces.

After four days on the road, so well arranged by Uncle Alfred that no setback occurred and all was comfort and ease, the travellers finally arrived in the Metropolis, weary and aching from inactivity, but, in Winnie's case at least, thrilled with everything she saw. The two men amused themselves by competing to spot the most trivial detail of the streets, from pie sellers to hackney carriages to crossing sweepers.

"I have seen crossing sweepers before, you know," she said gently.

"Certainly you have, but not *London* crossing sweepers," Walter said, grinning. "Be sure to note it well, so that you may write an accurate description in your journal."

In no time they had passed the last toll gate and were amidst the chaotic bustle of the main thoroughfares. On either side could be glimpsed smaller streets where warehouses and craft yards and shops jostled higgledy-piggledy with narrow houses, and children ran barefoot between the carts and standing horses. Soon after passing Smithfield they began to see some of the great edifices of the city — the Old Bailey and Newgate Prison, the Guildhall and the Admiralty, and finally the awe-inspiring twin monuments of Westminster Hall and Westminster Abbey. And everywhere, on side streets or nestling amongst houses or sometimes in the middle of the street, churches attesting to the piety of the population. At last they turned aside onto a fine residential street, round a corner and then another, before drawing up in front of a tall, narrow house, squeezed into a row of wider properties.

"Welcome to our humble abode," Uncle Alfred murmured.

The door opened and there was Aunt Sofia beaming at them, arms spread wide. Winnie scrambled out of the carriage, ignoring the hand Walter offered, and ran straight into her aunt's arms. Aunt Sofia was a small, well-rounded person, with black hair tucked neatly under her cap and a face already showing the lines of frequent laughter. She hugged Winnie fiercely, then held her at arm's length.

"You are too thin, child. Working yourself to the bone, as usual, I suppose. We shall have to feed you up a little. Ah, but it is so good to see you, Winnie. Now, here is my husband Edmund, and that great tall fellow manhandling your boxes is our indispensable Percival."

Edmund Blackwood was a fine, handsome man with a mane of blond hair, and a decided twinkle in his eye. Winnie decided at once that she would like him enormously. She had been sure she would, for anyone who fell in love with Aunt Sofia was clearly a man of excellent taste, but now that she could see him, she was quite sure of it. The indispensable Percival, a large Negro footman, she was less certain about, for he was intimidatingly tall, a good head taller even than Walter, but he smiled as he passed her by, a large box balanced on one shoulder as if it weighed nothing, and she decided she liked him, too.

Tucking Winnie's arm into her own, her aunt turned to Walter. "You poor boy! Such a great many trials for your family. How are they bearing up?"

"Tolerably well, Mrs Blackwood."

"We must see if we cannot cheer you up just a little while you are here. But come inside, all of you, come along. Oh, Martha! How lovely to see you again, dear. No, no, leave the luggage, the men will deal with it. Mrs Benning will show you everything. Come along, Winnie. I cannot wait to show you your room."

"No, no, no! Baby first, Aunt."

Her aunt's face softened at once. "He will be asleep at this hour, but we shall just look in on him."

Inside, she led Winnie up two flights of stairs. "The trouble with these town houses is they have no room to sprawl as they do in the country, so the only way to go is up. We have four floors here, not counting the basements and attics, and you are on the top, I am afraid. But I have put you at the back, so... well, you will see. Here is the nursery."

They crept in, the curtains drawn against the afternoon sun making the room gloomy. There beneath the window, where a faint breeze could cool him, lay Master John Blackwood, a year and a half old, one thumb close to his mouth as he slept peacefully in his crib. The two women sighed over him, then left him to his nurse, sitting with her sewing in the corner.

Up another flight of stairs, Aunt Sofia threw open a door and ushered Winnie inside. As soon as she entered the room, Winnie gasped, for beyond the window there were no houses, no chimneys, no streets or rumbling wagons or noise, only greenery as far as the eye could see.

"Oh, the park! How lovely. So many trees! This is almost like being in the country."

"Yes, we chose this house because of its situation overlooking St James's Park. Our back garden, so to speak, for we have no garden of our own, nothing worth mentioning, anyway. But there is a gate into the park, and there we are. I walk there almost every day, and I am sure you will, too. You are such an indefatigable walker. But you must never walk alone, not here. Do not even step outside the door without a man to protect you."

"Is London so dangerous?" Winnie said, with some alarm.

"Oh, no, no, no! I should not wish you to think we live amongst savages here. It is true that there are pickpockets and worse in these streets, and in the parks, too. Anywhere with crowds, like the theatres and other places of entertainment. But during the day, if one is careful, it is safe enough. No, the greatest danger is to your reputation. An unmarried woman cannot walk about unescorted, and a man is better protection than another woman. I myself always take Percival with me whenever I go out without

Edmund's company, and you must do the same. You will not encounter any trouble when he is with you."

"I can imagine! He is the tallest man I have ever seen, and the darkest of skin."

"Have you never seen a Negro before?"

"No, never."

"Well, goodness me! One sees them everywhere here. Percival was brought to England as a boy to be a page to the Duchess of— Well, better not to name her, perhaps. But when he grew so tall, she tired of him and turned him out. Edmund's brother found him scraping a living as a prize fighter and offered him a more respectable job, then he came to us when we married, as a sort of wedding present. I must say, he is far more use to us than all the silver and plate we were given, although more expensive to maintain. Quite apart from his exorbitant wages, almost twice the usual, he eats a mountain of food every day. But worth every last farthing."

"The indispensable Percival," Winnie said, smiling.

"He is that. Anyone may have a footman of the ordinary sort, but few have one like Percival. Sadly for us, he is saving up his wages to open his own boxing academy, like Gentleman Jackson, so we shall lose him eventually, and then we shall be reduced to taking on an ordinary footman again. Ah, Martha has found her way up here, so I shall leave you to wash and change, and rest after the travails of the journey. Whenever you are ready for company again, I shall be in the drawing room, two floors down. We dine late, at seven, so there is no need to rush."

Impulsively, Winnie crossed the floor and wrapped her aunt in a tight hug. "Oh, I am so glad to be here, Aunt! I am going to enjoy myself prodigiously."

"That you may depend upon," her aunt said, with a wide smile.

16: The General Post Office

For Captain Michael Edgerton, breakfast always set the tone for the day. A snatched meal at an inn or, even worse, under a hedge somewhere, and the day was bound to be difficult. A proper meal with white linen on the table, silver spoons and his wife sitting opposite him, and the hours were bound to unfold smoothly. That was how it was supposed to be, anyway. But today, he felt, was not going to plan.

Miss Peach was there, for one thing, and that was by no means usual. Being a lady of a certain age, she tended to keep to her bed until a late hour, enjoying a tray in her room and the attentions of a maid to help her dress, for a retired governess was by no means accustomed to such ministrations. Lately, she had seldom been seen in the castle at all.

But today, there she was, and all of a flutter. "Two days before the murder, Captain — *two* days! It cannot be a coincidence, can it?"

"Peachy, dear, we have understood that part very clearly," Luce said, in her calmest tones. "You have said it several times now, after all. But you will need to explain a little more clearly what it was that happened two days before the murder."

"Why, the meeting at the White Horse, my dear. Did I not say so? All the men of the village — the working men, that is, not Mr Dewar, naturally, or any of the *gentlemen* of Birchall. No man of principle would involve himself in such an enterprise, would he? I mean, it stands to reason."

"What sort of enterprise, Peachy?"

"I have told you... have I not? Well, I am not terribly clear what precisely they planned to do, but Mr Nicholson's name was mentioned... I am sure Mrs Haslet said Mr Nicholson, although sometimes she speaks very fast and the accent, you know... But I am quite sure Mr Nicholson came into it somehow, and they were very angry about it... whatever it was. But then Mr Oakes... the curate, if you remember... came in with a message for Mrs Haslet, and so I heard no more about it. Or was it for Miss Mary Haslet... I cannot quite recall. A message for someone, anyway, and so the subject was dropped and I did not feel I could ask directly about it. But I wanted you to know at once, Captain. This is why I go to Birchall and sit with my sewing in Mrs Dewar's parlour, to hear the gossip, you see. I hope it is helpful?"

"Very helpful, Miss Peach," Michael said at once, as he knew he was expected to do. But after Miss Peach had drunk her tea and departed for the village, he said to his wife, "Should I stop her from all this creeping about listening to gossip, do you think?"

"Why spoil her enjoyment?" Luce said, with her lovely smile. "She was bored here, and it brings a little excitement into her otherwise very dull life.

Chatting with the ladies of Birchall village is a harmless enough occupation, and she is making garments for the poor at the same time."

"Very well, my dear. It shall be so."

But it set him all on edge for the day, nevertheless, and he was obliged to abandon his unproductive work in the castle and go for a long ride on the moors to clear his head.

***

Winnie's desire to enjoy herself was fulfilled in every respect. For several days, Aunt Sofia swept her off to the draperies and modistes and milliners and haberdashers that London offered in abundance, and her room began to fill up with hat boxes and interestingly shaped packages, and the delicious difficulty in choosing which new gown or spencer or bonnet to wear for which occasion. There were long walks in the park with her aunt, catching up on three years of news, with the indispensable Percival following them. There were cheerful breakfasts and lively dinners, sometimes with friends of Uncle Edmund and Aunt Sofia, invited to meet the visitors, and sometimes just themselves. Even the hours spent in the library acting as secretary to Uncle Alfred were delightful, because Walter was there. And although she missed her family, and wrote a long letter home every day, it was pleasant not to have Mama's admonishments ringing in her ears, and to be treated as a valued and most welcome guest.

One of the advantages of her new situation was having Martha's undivided attention when she was dressing for dinner. Instead of rushing in at the last minute, so that she had to scramble into a gown to avoid being late, she had the maid for a whole hour, if she wanted, with time to try a new style to her hair, or different ornaments. And Martha liked it too, for she became very chatty, asking about things she had seen on the journey, or explanations for remarks by the other servants. And sometimes, she talked about the other members of the household.

"Poor Mr Atherton," she said one evening, with a heavy sigh. She never mentioned him now except as *'poor Mr Atherton'*. "To be all set to be an earl, an' then find you're nobbut a bastard. It's hard, that is. Yet he seems very cheerful. Mr Rashleigh, his man, says he's always cheerful, never gets down about it."

Winnie disagreed with Rashleigh, but she was not about to gossip about Walter so she let Martha rattle on, her fingers busily arranging Winnie's hair as she chattered.

"Has his father thrown him out, then, bein' as how the poor man's a bastard now?"

"The earl? No, he has not thrown Mr Atherton out, as you put it. He is still a part of the family, but he will have to earn his own living now that he is not to inherit. He is to see if my uncle's line of work in the Treasury might suit him. If it does... well, I suppose he will live in London, most of the time." A pang of grief at the prospect — never to see Walter again! Never to meet him at the tree house... a horrible thought. But she must not give way... "If it does not suit him, then he will go home and look about him for something else, but his father will never repudiate him. No man of his standing would do so. It is a matter of honour to take care of all their children, even the illegitimate ones. That is how a gentleman behaves."

"Not all of 'em," Martha muttered.

This was so startling that Winnie spun round on the stool, so that Martha's brush and comb were left stuck in Winnie's hair. "Not all of them? You know of a gentleman who abandoned an illegitimate child?"

"Forget I spoke, Miss Winnie, please. It's supposed to be a big secret, I shouldn't'a said nothin'"

"We are speaking about your sister Maisie, I take it," Winnie said musingly. "John is sixteen now, so…" It was not Walter, that was her first thought, as relief washed through her. Not any of the younger generation. But who else? Surely not the earl… the old earl? He would have been a very elderly man at the time. Then, with a squeak of alarm… "Not my father!"

"No, Miss Winnie, no! Not any o' your family."

The Franklyns had not been there, then, so it could only be the earl's family… or someone from further afield, or even a stranger.

"Why was it supposed to be a secret? Are not these things usually known, somehow?"

"Aye, but Maisie said nowt, just that he were important an' married, so no one knew until a few months ago, when Jack Wishaw gave her a whole bottle of his ma's gooseberry wine, an' she got snuffy an' told everyone it were— Oops. Better not say, Miss Winnie. There's enough trouble at the castle without stirrin' up old tales, an' besides, he's dead now."

"Martha, if it involves the castle, I had much sooner know."

"Oh, Miss Winnie, Maisie'll be so cross wi' me!"

Winnie turned back to face the mirror. "Then I shall not ask any more about it, Martha. I would not dream of insisting you break a confidence. Besides, if I am late for dinner tonight, everyone will be cross with *me* so we had better get on with it."

"Yes, Miss Winnie. Thank you."

But Winnie was satisfied. There were only two gentlemen who had lived at the castle at the appropriate time who were now dead — the old earl and the chaplain. She could not be certain which of them it was but she was very sure that, armed with this information, Captain Edgerton could find out. And if it should emerge that Mr Nicholson had had an illegitimate son with Maisie Whyte, that would be a matter of great interest to the captain. She would write to him first thing tomorrow.

***

'To Captain Michael Edgerton, Corland Castle, nr Helmsley, North Riding. Captain, I hope your investigations are proceeding well. A discussion with my maid, Martha Whyte, revealed some information that I believe will interest you. The Whyte family is long established at Birchall, and Martha's father, Joe, is the blacksmith. Martha's sister, Maisie, has an illegitimate son, John Whyte, now aged sixteen or so. He works as a groom at Westwick Heights, the home of Mr George Atherton, the earl's brother. Martha told me that the identity of John's father, long held secret, was recently revealed to the family, at least. She would not tell me who it was, except that he was someone important, who was married, lived at Corland Castle and is now dead. I can think of only two people who fit all of these criteria — the old earl, and Mr Nicholson. I am sure you will be able to find out which of them it is. With good wishes and my regards to Mrs Edgerton, Miss Peach, Mr Alexander and to you. Respectfully yours, Winifred Strong.'

***

One day, when Winnie had written yet another long letter home and took it down to the hall to be taken to the post, she found Uncle Edmund on the point of departure, all the day's outgoing letters in his hand, as Percival held the door for him.

"Are you going to the Post Office now? Can you take this one, too?"

"Of course. It is a bit late in the day, I know, but I have an important letter to send, and if I can get it to Lombard Street in time, it will go off tonight. I am only waiting for the carriage to be brought round from the yard."

"Oh... the Lombard Street Post Office. I should so like to see it, but—"

"Then run and get your bonnet," he said, with a smile. "Percival will tell your aunt where you have gone."

Winnie ran up the stairs at an unladylike rate that would have given her mother an apoplexy, and was downstairs again, ribbons still dangling, just as the carriage arrived at the door. The early part of their journey was along streets she had seen before, but then they came upon the magnificent edifice of St Paul's Cathedral, and Winnie gazed in awe as they rattled past. Then they reached a narrower, much more crowded street, where Edmund halted the carriage.

"We will walk the rest of the way. John Coachman will wait for us round the corner in Cornhill. The Post Office is just along here."

The pavement was crammed with hackney carriages, wagons, a few private carriages and a great multitude of people, all rushing hither and thither, and Winnie and her uncle only made progress because the flow of people was largely in one direction. They came at last to the imposing frontage of the General Post Office and made their way inside, where they halted, dismayed. The main hall was a sea of people, all jostling to get near the counters at the far end as the final hour for that day's collections approached.

"Hmm. I do not like to take you into such a mêlée," Uncle Edmund said. "If you step aside, just over there where it is a little clearer, you may wait safely for me. I shall be as quick as I can."

Winnie stationed herself against the wall in a corner that was outside the usual flow of customers, and gazed in admiration at the noble proportions of the hall. When that palled, she amused herself by watching Uncle Edmund's hat disappear into the crowd and inch its way towards the counter where letters and parcels were being assessed and stamped and sent on their way. Where might they be going to? All parts of London, or perhaps to Penzance or Edinburgh or Dublin. Or beyond Britain altogether... Paris or Brussels or Constantinople or Moscow or Charleston or... what was the name of that place on the far side of the earth? New South Wales, that was it, but she could not remember the names of the settlements there. Where was Uncle Edmund's hat? There it was, almost at the counter.

She was so absorbed in her thoughts that she did not notice the group of ragged urchins chasing each other around the pillars nearby, until one of them barrelled into her.

"Beg pardon, mum," he said, grinning at her, and at that precise moment, she felt a sharp tug on her wrist. Her reticule! One of the boys had hold of it and was trying to pull it off her arm.

"Stop that!" she cried, grabbing the reticule with her other hand and pulling it hard. But the urchin had a firm grip, and she failed to dislodge him. "Go away!" This time she gave him a firm shove in the chest.

She was only partly successful. The boy toppled backwards, but his grip on the reticule was so great that Winnie herself was pulled forwards, falling to her knees. By this time she was so incensed that she gave the boy's wrist a violent blow with the side of her hand and with a shriek of pain he released her reticule. Scrambling to her feet, boiling with fury, she prepared to do further battle, but unexpected reinforcements arrived in the shape of a finely dressed young man wielding a cane with vigour. Within moments, the urchins had fled, the startled faces watching the altercation turned away, and Winnie was left staring at her rescuer.

He had a pleasant countenance, but he was not handsome, or at least, not nearly so handsome as Walter, and was not above average height. If it had not been for his fashionable attire, she would not have noticed him in any gathering. As it was, his high shirt points, wide lapels, brightly coloured waistcoat and multitude of fobs would turn heads anywhere.

At that moment, as they caught their breath after the scuffle, there was a look in his eyes as he gazed at Winnie that almost made her blush. How long was it since a man had displayed such obvious admiration? But then, she wore one of her new gowns and a particularly flattering bonnet, and she was aware that she looked unusually well. She should dress this way more often if it brought such pleasing effects.

"Madam, are you harmed?" he cried.

"No, not in the least. I must thank you for your timely intervention, sir. I should have been hard pressed without your aid."

"As you still carry your reticule, I must suppose that the thieves were unsuccessful."

"Indeed, although even if they had managed to steal it, they would have acquired nothing more than a handkerchief and the few coins I keep to reward the crossing sweepers."

"Yet even that is worth stealing, to such as they."

"Poor things," she said. "They are only children, after all, yet they were so thin and undernourished. If they had *asked* me for charity, I should certainly have given them something, but I do not like to be robbed."

"No, indeed! An alarming experience. But you are not here alone, I trust, madam?"

"I am awaiting my uncle, and I see him approaching now."

Uncle Edmund hailed her as soon as he was near enough. "Winnie! What has happened? I saw a disturbance... are you injured?"

"Not at all. I was set upon by street urchins, but with the aid of this kind gentleman, they were driven off."

He said all that was proper to the stranger, the two men bowed to each other and he then began to steer Winnie towards the street.

"Are you going far?" the stranger said in anxious tones. "I should be very happy to accompany you to your destination."

"You are most kind," Uncle Edmund said, "but my carriage is only in Cornhill."

The gentleman looked relieved. "Then I shall accompany you to your carriage, for the streets are excessively busy just now. I have never known such a crush."

"We would not for the world put you to so much trouble, sir, when you have done so much for my niece already. It is but a short distance."

He looked pleasingly disappointed, but to Winnie's delight, he said, "Perhaps I may be permitted to call upon the lady tomorrow, to assure myself that she has taken no harm?"

Uncle Edmund assented, they exchanged cards with a bow, and then Winnie was swept into the street and, at a smart pace, towards their waiting carriage. Her uncle said nothing of the stranger on the drive home, merely questioning Winnie closely on precisely what had happened.

With a sigh, he said, "Sofia will ring the most almighty peal over me for putting you in such a position, and she would be quite right to do so. It was unconscionable of me to leave you alone there like that, but I did not think you would be safe in the crowd, with so much pushing and shoving going on. I had no idea the Post Office became so riotous near to the closing hour. It is usually Percival who goes, and no one pushes him about! But who could have imagined that taking letters to the Post Office could be such an exciting business, eh? Now you have something more than scenery to put in that journal of yours."

17: An Admirer

The event was the talk of the household that evening. Winnie was obliged to describe every last detail of the encounter with the urchins over and over again. Everyone was shocked, everyone had an idea of how it could have been avoided if only they had been present and everyone agreed that it was entirely Uncle Edmund's fault.

He accepted this with good grace, but after a while, he said mischievously, "Winnie has an admirer." As Winnie blushed and disclaimed, he went on, "The person she modestly described as *'a stranger who came to my assistance'* is in fact a very personable young man who has asked if he may call upon her tomorrow, to assure himself that she has taken no harm."

This caused even more of a sensation, together with calls for a full description of the gentleman, and the rest of the evening passed in lively speculation on the matter. Winnie said little, apart from insisting that no one should make anything more of it than the kindness of a stranger, for she was persuaded that he would very likely not come at all. Even so, sleep was a long time in coming, and when she rose the next morning, she took care to wear one of her new gowns, and not the one she had worn the day before.

She was busy in the library with Uncle Alfred, Uncle Edmund and Walter, when a rat-a-tat-tat on the front door caused them all to jump.

"Your admirer, no doubt," Walter whispered, eyes twinkling.

"It could be anyone," she said, but her heart beat a little faster anyway. Her mysterious admirer — surely it must be him!

The door creaked open, there was a murmur of male voices in the hall, and then steps proceeding up the stairs to the drawing room. A few minutes later, Percival entered the room.

"A gentleman has called to see Miss Strong," he said, with a hint of a smile. "He is in the drawing room with the mistress."

Walter burst out laughing. "Well, well, well," he said. "Shall we go and view your Sir Galahad, Mouse?"

They all trooped up the stairs to the drawing room, and there he was, in a different coat and waistcoat, but every bit as fashionable. He leapt to his feet as she arrived, and bounded across the room, a posy of flowers in his hands.

"I do not need to ask how you are after the distressing events of yesterday," he said, pressing the flowers into her hands. "I can see that you are in the very bloom of health."

Winnie blushed, despite herself. Such a fulsome compliment, combined with the glow of pleasure on his face, quite undid her.

Aunt Sofia jumped in to rescue her from her confusion. "Winnie, this is Mr Rupert Lomax. Mr Lomax, my niece, Miss Winifred Strong, her uncle, Mr Alfred Strong, and this is Mr Walter Atherton."

Mr Lomax made Winnie a low bow, as she curtsied. She did not quite know what to do with the flowers — no one had ever brought her flowers before! Still clutching them, she sat down, he sat beside her, his expression animated, and began to ply her with questions. Had she quite recovered from her ordeal? Had she managed to snatch a moment of sleep? Was she not too disturbed by unpleasant memories? Interspersed with such enquiries were expressions of his own fears on her behalf and his wishes for a speedy return to what he was sure was her normal equanimity.

"I believe you make too much of what was a relatively minor occurrence, Mr Lomax," she said. "Thanks to your timely intervention, there was no harm done. Let us talk of other matters. Do you live in town?"

"My home is in Oxfordshire, near Abingdon. I would not normally be in town at this time of year, except that I had some business to attend to. Normally I account such visits a chore and cannot wait to return home, but... not on this occasion."

Such open compliments were delightful to Winnie. She basked in his attention, and they were soon on the easiest terms. She found herself telling him much about herself and her family, and discovered that he lived alone with his mother since his father's death three years earlier, and that he had two married sisters. At some point, Aunt Sofia gently removed the posy from Winnie's hands, and someone — perhaps Walter — pressed a glass of wine on Mr Lomax — but the conversation flowed on, uninterrupted. It was only when the clock on the mantel struck the hour that Mr Lomax leapt to his feet.

"My goodness, look at the time! What must you think of me, Mrs Blackwood, to be so lost to all good manners? More than half an hour!"

"It is not of the least consequence, sir. We do not stand on ceremony, not with Winnie's chivalrous knight errant."

"You are too kind, ma'am. But I shall not stay a moment longer, although perhaps... would it be presumptuous of me to invite you and Miss

Strong to take a drive with me tomorrow in the landau? Perhaps to Hyde Park? There would be room for one of the gentlemen also. If you have no other engagement."

With a quick glance at Winnie, Aunt Sofia agreed to it at once, and rang the bell for Percival to show Mr Lomax out.

"Well, Winnie," she said, as soon as the door had closed behind him. "A fine young man, your rescuer."

Walter burst out laughing. "Oh, very fine, Mrs Blackwood. He will poke his own eyes out with those shirt points, if he is not careful. And did you notice how he walked... like this." And he minced across the room in an exaggerated swaying motion.

"I did not notice anything odd about his manner of walking," Winnie said crossly, "and his style of dressing is very much in the height of fashion, I believe."

"He is a coxcomb," Walter said.

"I have no idea what that means," she cried, "but *I* thought him a most agreeable man."

"And so did I," Aunt Sofia said. "He clearly admires Winnie, and I am disposed to like him solely on that account, even without his very gallant intervention yesterday."

"Pft," Walter said. "He is a strutting coxcomb, and we know nothing about him, except what he has told us himself. Blackwood, do you know him or the family?"

"No, not at all," Uncle Edmund said, "but he is close to my age, I should judge, so we may have acquaintances in common. I am not sure that I would describe him as a coxcomb, precisely, for his clothing is not out of the way for a young man with pretensions to fashion, but you are right in one thing, Atherton — if he is going to pay court to Winnie and take her out for drives, we need to know more about him."

"I do not care about his clothes, except that I thought he looked very well in them," Aunt Sofia said, "but I agree we should be cautious. However, I confess that a drive in Hyde Park in a landau will be very pleasant indeed in this warm weather. Edmund, will you join us?"

"I will. I should like to know more of this Mr Lomax."

And on that point Winnie could agree with him wholeheartedly.

***

Michael read the letter with a smile on his face. "What a remarkable woman Miss Strong is."

"Miss Strong?" Luce said, looking up from sorting the rest of the day's letters. "Is she writing to you now? Oh! Sandy, this one is franked by your cousin. What news?"

He ripped the letter open eagerly. "The best — another son. Mother and baby both thriving."

"That is indeed the very best news. Such a blessing! How happy they must be! Are you never tempted to find yourself a pretty young lady and settle down, Sandy?" Luce said.

"Not unless I can find another you, Mrs Edgerton, who will follow me about uncomplainingly as I risk life and limb on Michael's reckless adventures. Although I have tae say that the greatest risk on our present venture is dying of boredom. We're not doing sae well, are we?"

Luce sighed. "I was so hopeful of the mysterious Lord Farramont, who appeared and then vanished in a single night, but it turns out not to be the right night after all."

"So he says," Sandy said darkly.

"But he is such a methodical man," Luce said. "His diary was very precise — it was the night *before* the murder, and he had left the castle before ever an axe was swung."

"Ah, but here we have new information," Michael cried excitedly, waving the letter about. "An illegitimate son, no less, and I would wager my favourite sword it is Nicholson's."

"Your *favourite* sword?" Luce said in surprise. "The one that has had all the adventures?"

"Hmm... well, perhaps my *second* favourite sword... no, I am very fond of all my swords. A pony on Nicholson, then."

Sandy laughed. "A mere twenty-five pounds? That is no wager at all. Make it a hundred and I will take you up on it."

"Done. But I must see the earl without delay."

There was no seeing the earl without delay, however, for he was out riding and then had appointments with an array of men dressed in solemn black, wearing lugubrious expressions. Michael was obliged to curb his impatience in the library awaiting the earl's pleasure for some time, which he did by pacing back and forth and then, when the temptation became irresistible, amusing himself with a rapier from the armoury display in one corner. He was deep into a fight to the death with an invisible opponent, when a voice came from the open study door.

"Planning a duel, Captain?" the earl said, his tone politely bland at this abuse of his library.

"Not planning, precisely, my lord, merely practising. One should be prepared for any eventuality, do you not agree?"

"I cannot see that preparing for a duel would be much use to me, but I dare say your way of life is somewhat different to mine. Do come into the study and tell me what the problem is, and if you can keep it brief I shall be very much obliged to you."

Michael heard the weariness in his voice, and kept it very brief indeed. "I have discovered that someone, either your father or Mr Nicholson, fathered an illegitimate child on Maisie Whyte, the smith's daughter, who lives at Birchall."

"The child's age?"

"Sixteen or so."

"Not my father, then. It must be Nicholson." The earl gave a bark of laughter. "Well! The old rogue! I would not have guessed it, I have to say."

"You did not know?"

"I knew nothing of it, and would not have suspected it of Nicholson. He always seemed such a devoted husband. But then, he was hand in glove with my father, and, much as it pains me to say it, my father was very lax about such matters himself. He had a succession of mistresses in his younger days, and thought me a positive slow-top for choosing to be faithful to my wife. Let us sit down, and discuss this more fully. I have neglected you rather, I regret to say, being caught up in my own affairs. We should have had this conversation earlier. Will you take a glass of something, Captain?"

Michael agreed to it, and sipped politely when the glass was pressed into his hand, but then set it down on a side table. "Did Nicholson have a mistress?"

"I never heard word of it, if he did. But then, if this boy is truly Nicholson's, I never heard word of that, either, and that was only at Birchall, right under our noses. You say the boy is sixteen? Then it was after..." He rubbed his nose, looking somewhat embarrassed.

"It was after Miss Teresa was born," Michael said in his blandest tones.

"Yes!" the earl said. "Exactly so! Everything changed... and Alice was quite unwell... naturally they decided..."

"To sleep in separate rooms."

"Precisely! Not that that excuses it, of course. Christian marriage vows take no account of difficulties of that nature... but it was a matter of Alice's health, you see. It was a great concern to all of us, and not least to my dear wife, who had no trouble in that way herself, but she sincerely felt for Alice. Motherhood brings such rewards, does it not? We were all so relieved after Tess was born, although... such a tiny creature! It was a miracle she survived. And after that... Nicholson would have made every effort to preserve his wife's health, as any husband would. I beg your pardon, Edgerton. I am rambling. This is a shock, as you may imagine. One thinks one knows a man well, and then to discover something of this nature. But it may have been a momentary weakness, bitterly regretted afterwards and perhaps never repe ated."

"Perhaps, my lord."

"You do not seem convinced."

"I see the worst of human nature, in the course of my work."

The earl chuckled. "I suppose you do. Murders and so on... but I cannot see that this news of the bastard advances your efforts at all."

"One never knows where a thread of new knowledge may lead, my lord. Perhaps the boy resented a father who misused his mother and then failed to acknowledge his own son. Perhaps there are other bastards to be found, other secrets to uncover. My lord, let me be frank. I and my associates have been here for four weeks now, and although we have been able to remove some persons from suspicion, there remain a great number w ho *might* have killed the chaplain. I have exhausted all enquiries within the castle, but there is still much that could be investigated. Mr Nicholson's financial position, for instance, his acquaintances beyond Corland, his family, the property he was left by the late earl, his dealings with local people… there are so many possibilities. If I am given a free hand, I believe there is much more to discover about Mr Nicholson, as this discovery of the boy suggests."

He paused, but the earl said nothing, merely nodding his head gravely, so he ploughed on.

"But so far, following your instructions, I have confined my enquiries only to Corland. I should like your permission to extend my enquiries beyond the castle, and also to interview the Lady Alice again, in light of this new information. The time has come, I believe, to decide whether you wish to pursue the matter further, following all leads wherever they may take us, or whether you wish this murder to be forever a mystery."

The earl rose, and walked to the window, gazing thoughtfully out. Michael rose also, waiting. From outside, he heard sounds of sweeping from outside the stables, and a groom whistling cheerfully. Someone hard at work, and enjoying it. There were times when Michael envied such men. How simple life would be if all one had to do was sweep out a stable, and care for a string of carriage horses and hacks. Horses were so much easier to deal with than people.

The earl slowly turned to face him. "I cannot see that grubbing about in Nicholson's bills and bank accounts will help. Surely Nicholson himself is irrelevant in this matter. It is obvious to me that a stranger killed Nicholson."

"Why?"

"What do you mean, why?"

"I mean, my lord, why would anyone do such a thing? This is the question that has haunted me from the very start. Nicholson appears on the surface to be an inoffensive man, dutiful, devoted to his wife, liked by everyone, or at least not greatly *dis*liked. And yet… there was more to him. He had no money of his own, but leaves a fortune to his daughter, and with odd conditions, which I have not yet got to the bottom of. The devoted husband leaves an illegitimate son. He was abnormally lucky at cards, which raises the possibility of cheating. The late earl left him a house — why? What sort of house, and what is being done with it? What was the great attraction of the political society at Pickering? It is my belief that Nicholson was a man with dark secrets, but I cannot find them out while I sit here, not allowed to look beyond Corland Castle itself. There is an answer to this murder, Lord Rennington, but it will not be found *here.* If I am to uncover the truth, I must start with Nicholson himself, lifting every stone to see what shadowy shapes lie beneath, for only that way can I answer the question of who wanted to kill him, and why, and only *then* can I be sure that there will not be another murder."

"This is more than a job to you, I think," the earl said gently.

"I hate mysteries, my lord — hate them with a passion. I always want to worry away at them until everything is clear to me, and especially so when a man has died."

The earl sighed. "It is not my responsibility to gratify your need for certainty, Edgerton, but if you can bring this matter to a resolution, it will be better for all of us. By all means endeavour to uncover Nicholson's secrets. You have my permission to talk to anyone, to go anywhere, to follow whatever trails you may find. I will write you letters of authority to the banks and attorneys that Nicholson might have dealt with. I was not close to Nicholson, but he was my brother-in-law, and for my poor dear sister's sake, I want his murderer found, however long it takes."

"It may be," Michael said cautiously, "that we will never find definitive proof — enough to hang a man, anyway. It may come down to mere supposition, in the end."

"Then let me put it another way — stay until you have satisfied yourself of the murderer's identity, even if it can never be proved. Or until you feel there is no longer any hope of resolving the question. The judgement is to be yours, and yours alone."

Michael bowed. "Thank you, my lord. I will endeavour to be worthy of your trust in me."

18: A Free Hand

Michael was excited. Finally, they were able to make progress on solving this difficult murder! He summoned all of his investigators to a meeting in the old nursery.

"At last we are free of the earl's restraints," Michael said, unable to suppress his grin. "The wonderful Miss Strong has helpfully given us the key to unlocking his lordship's hard heart."

He waved the letter triumphantly. Luce snatched it from his hand and smoothed the creases. "John Whyte... the smith's daughter... promising. Miss Strong writes a good hand. Oh, I like this! She says, '*With good wishes and my regards to Mrs Edgerton, Miss Peach, Mr Alexander and to you. Respectfully yours, Winifred Strong.*'" She looked up and laughed. "No good wishes for James, I notice."

James Neate smiled, and broke into dialect. "Aye, but I'm nobbut yer footman and groom, mum. Why'd a fine lady like that ever notice the likes o' me?"

"And that, my friend, is precisely why you are so useful to me," Michael said. "And so is Miss Strong useful to me, in a different way. Such precision in her mind! She narrows the likely father of this boy to just two possibilities, the late Lord Rennington and Mr Nicholson. The present earl agrees with me that it must have been Mr Nicholson. And, bless him, he has given me permission to widen the investigation beyond the castle itself."

"Very sensible," Pettigrew said. "After a full month here with little progress, we must begin to make enquiries elsewhere."

"We, Pettigrew?" Michael said, smiling. "Have you no urgent business at present calling such a distinguished barrister as yourself back to town?"

"Nothing as exciting as an axe murder," Pettigrew said, smiling. "I have never been minded to follow the Assizes about hither and thither, and the courts in town are full of petty thieves and cheating grocers, which hold little appeal. Besides, if you have authority to spread your net wider, that means attorneys and the like, and your only other lawyer is James, who is now firmly established as a footman. I am at your service for any legal or financial enquiries you wish to make."

"Excellent," Michael said, grinning in satisfaction. "I shall supply you with a list of banks and attorneys — Helmsley to start with, but we may need to look at Pickering and York as well, where Nicholson was known to go regularly. But this John Whyte... the illegitimate son... hmm, how to approach that? He works for Mr George Atherton, so we cannot barge in unceremoniously."

"His mother is the daughter of the Birchall smith," Luce said. "Perhaps a visit to the smithy?"

"And to the White Horse, which is directly across the road from the smithy," James said. "I have taken the odd tankard of ale there, but it would be livelier on a Saturday night. I might hear something about the argument Miss Peach reported."

"What argument, Mr Neate?" Miss Peach said, looking up from the child's nightgown she was stitching.

"Something you heard at the rectory, Peachy," Luce said. "About Mr Nicholson. You said everyone was very angry."

"Oh no, dear, no. There are never any arguments at the rectory. Mrs Dewar would never allow anything so unseemly."

The others exchanged glances. "You take the White Horse, James," Michael said, "and I shall talk to the smith. Luce, might you care to venture on a shopping expedition to Pickering?"

"Where Mr Nicholson owns a house? That sounds like fun. Peachy, will you come with me?"

Miss Peach shook her head, not looking up from her needlework. "Oh no, dear. I have made such good progress with Mrs Dewar and the Miss Dewars, and it could all be undone if I break with my routine."

"Not even for two or three days?" Luce said. "You are supposed to be my companion, after all."

"It would be very helpful," Michael said. "I believe, Miss Peach, that you have the same talent as James for passing unnoticed in company, which gives you an incomparable advantage over the rest of us. Luce could never pass unnoticed in any company, and anyone who dresses as Pettigrew and I do can never be invisible."

Miss Peach set down her sewing. "Oh... oh, yes, that is very true. So very fashionable as you gentlemen are, and Lucinda so elegant and lovely. No one takes any notice of *me.* Why should they? I am nobody, nobody at all. I wonder... Pickering... but I should like to be allowed to wander around on my own, Captain Edgerton. I can go into places… low shops, taverns and the like… which Lucinda would not wish to enter."

"Not if there is the slightest risk, Miss Peach," Michael said firmly. "It is one thing to join Mrs Dewar's sewing circle at Birchall, and quite another to go snooping round places where unsavoury characters may gather. That I could not permit."

"No, no, nothing of that nature. I was thinking more of the cheap haberdasheries and the like, or the common rooms of inns — not the tap rooms, I do assure you! But there is so much to be gleaned merely by sitting over a bowl of soup and listening, or chatting over a length of ribbon."

"Very well, but do be careful, Miss Peach."

"Oh, yes, Captain. I am a very careful person, always."

"Excellent," Michael said, folding away Miss Strong's letter again.

"And what about me, Captain?" Sandy said. "Ye'll have some plan for me, I'm sure."

"Ah, now you and I will start interviewing beyond the castle, so be sure to stock up on paper, quills and ink, and we shall start with Mr Eustace Atherton."

"Why him?" Sandy said, face lighting up with interest. "Do ye have some guid reason tae suspect the man?"

"None at all, apart from the small matter that the axe was his, and we have only his word that it was part of the display on the stairs," Michael said promptly. "Apart from that, he lives twelve miles away, and seemingly was tucked up in bed with a female at the time of the murder. However, it would be good to scratch him off the list of possible murderers once and for all. Everyone we can definitively place elsewhere can be removed from all suspicion, which reduces the pool of potential axe killers. And when we have done that, perhaps he will show us his collection of assorted weaponry. I have only had the privilege once, but I should dearly like another look."

"Ah, swords," Sandy said knowingly. "Ye's mortal fond of swords."

"Not mere swords... sabres, javelins, scimitars, falchions, cutlasses, halberds, claymores, broadswords—"

"Right, right... lots of swords."

"And firearms, too. He has any number of pistols, muskets and rifles, and a collection of cannons in his garden, although not all in working order. I could spend a month at his house and not exhaust my interest."

"Not all? Does that mean some *are* in working order?" Sandy said eagerly. "When can we go there?"

Michael laughed. "Soon, but I must write and give him notice of our visit first. We cannot descend on him unannounced."

"No?" Pettigrew said. "Is that not the best way to discover the truth, to arrive unexpectedly, so that the object of the visit has no chance to prepare?"

Michael frowned. "That is a good point, but then I have no reason to suspect him. Besides, he is the son of an earl and entitled to the courtesy of that rank, and no less because he is now illegitimate. We must be respectful to these people, otherwise the earl may close us down altogether."

***

Michael and Sandy rode out across the moors to Welwood-on-the-hill on a glorious summer's day that lifted their spirits immeasurably. At least, it lifted Michael's spirits, for the Scotsman never seemed downhearted.

Michael reined in his horse beside a narrow tower, a monument perhaps to some long forgotten battle.

"Look at this," Michael said, taking in the vista with an expansive sweep of his arm. "Is this not the most wondrous of views? There is something magical about moorland, do you not think? So much open space, just an occasional tree to disturb the skyline, birds flitting here and there, and the music of little streams."

"Aye, it's bonny enough," Sandy said, "but I prefer the works of men. Productive fields of corn or cattle, or the liveliness of a town suit me better. There's nothing but sheep here."

"Very profitable, sheep," Michael said, smiling. "But we had best get on. We would not want to keep Mr Eustace Atherton waiting. You remember the plan?" He urged his horse into motion again.

"Aye, I do. Ye've drilled it into me enough times, and I cannae see the point. Mr Eustace the Libertine was cosily in bed with his lady-bird at the time of the murder, wasn't he? And even if he'd been minded to murder the chaplain, he'd have had to find his way across the moor at night through this rabbit-warren of criss-crossing tracks, and back again. I dinnae see how he'd have done it."

"Neither do I, to be truthful," Michael said. "I cannot see any of the family slaughtering the chaplain in cold blood, but I have to be sure of that before I can move on to consider those from outside the family. And Eustace is *clever*. The earl himself and the eldest son are straightforward types, not well endowed with mental acuity, but the other two sons are more interesting. I think Eustace might be capable of this kind of convoluted murder, if he set his mind to it."

"Is it convoluted?" Sandy said. "Seems simple enough tae me."

"It is convoluted enough to appear simple," Michael said tersely. "Nothing about this case is simple. The sweet, saintly chaplain turns out to be anything but a saint, and who knows how many other secrets there are to uncover? No, there is more to this than meets the eye. Ah, that must be Welwood on that rise. He has a fine view, does Mr Eustace."

Welwood was an undistinguished house, of no architectural or historic importance, and surrounded by gardens that could most charitably be described as pleasant. There was a high wall around it, so Michael and Sandy were obliged to return to the road to reach the gates. Across the road, an elderly horse gazed mournfully over the hedge at them.

Mr Eustace himself emerged from the house to greet them, as grooms emerged to take care of the horses. "Welcome back, Captain. Welcome, Mr Alexander. I am quite ready for the inquisition. I have cleared the whole day for you. I trust that will be sufficient?"

"I sincerely hope so, sir," Michael said. "As for an inquisition, I prefer to call it a little chat. You have no objection if we talk to your servants, also?"

"Not the least in the world. I have told them of your purpose in coming here, and to answer your questions fully." He lowered his voice as he ushered them into the house. "I have taken the liberty of asking the young lady to be here — the one who was here on the night in question. It will save you the trouble of seeking her out, for I am certain you will wish to confirm my record of events."

"That was very thoughtful, sir. Thank you."

"You may use my study, Captain. I have cleared my desk for you. Shall I bring Daisy in first?"

"We will start with you, sir, if you would be so good."

"Oh. Very well. I shall just let Daisy know. She is a trifle nervous, you understand, having never been questioned in this way before."

The study was much like the rest of the interior of the house, furnished for comfort rather than elegance. It was neat and tidy, however, and the housemaid did her job thoroughly, for everywhere was clean, floors swept, wood polished to a high shine and windows spotless. Michael eased himself into a chair with slightly sagging upholstery behind a desk empty of all but a standish. Sandy pulled over another chair and laid out his writing equipment.

Mr Eustace returned quickly and settled without complaint into the visitor's chair at his own desk. "So you want to know about that evening, I suppose," he said. "I had dinner—"

"Tell me first about this house," Michael said. "How long have you owned it?"

"Oh. Let me see... three years now. A little over."

"You inherited it, I understand. From a relation?"

"Not a relation, no, just a friend. A bookbinder by trade, who moved here with his sister when he retired from the business. When the sister died, he befriended me and I was always happy to keep him company — read to him, play cards, discuss the state of the world, you know how it is. And when he died, he left the house and his modest fortune to me, having no relations close to him."

"How very fortunate for you, sir. I congratulate you," Michael said in his blandest tones.

Eustace smirked. "Thank you. It is more fortunate than I knew at the time, for it leaves me unaffected by this confounded business of Nicholson not being ordained."

"Except for the small matter of illegitimacy."

Eustace laughed. “Except for that. But I still have my house and a good income. Fourteen hundred a year, since I feel sure you will want to know. My illegitimacy need not prevent me marrying.”

“You have a young lady in mind, do you, sir?”

“Certainly. She will be young and fresh and very beautiful — blonde, I fancy, with a well-formed figure and graceful deportment. She will play two instruments, speak three languages and ride all day without tiring. If ever you should meet her, pray send her my way.”

Michael could only laugh and shake his head. “I have never met such a paragon, sadly. To return to the house... do you often visit your family at Corland Castle?”

“Oh, sometimes,” he said airily. “But you know how it is — they have their own lives to live, and I have mine.”

“And when you visit, you ride across the moors?”

“Sometimes, when the weather is fit, since it is the shortest way. In bad weather, I take the road.”

“Very well. Sandy, have you got all that?”

“Aye, Captain.”

“Let us turn to the night in question, beginning with the day before. What did you do that day, sir?”

“Lord, I barely remember now. I had not long returned from town... two days before the murder, I think... I had had some good fortune at the tables, so I was in cheerful mood and ready to celebrate. I sent for Daisy, and gave orders that the servants might have a bowl of punch that evening. Daisy arrived, we had dinner, we went to bed. And there we stayed until quite late the next morning.”

“Could you be more specific about the times at which you retired to bed and left it the next morning?”

"Let me see... we dined early, so that the servants could have their evening free. We must have retired at eight, and I did not wake until ten the next morning. Daisy was still asleep, but she woke shortly after."

"Thank you. May we see the young lady now?"

Daisy Marler was exactly as Michael had expected, a cherry-cheeked young rustic with no pretensions to ladyhood and clearly nervous. Eustace led her in and settled her in the chair, with the cheerful words, "Nothing to be in a pother about, Daisy. All you have to do is to confirm that I was here all night. I shall be right here if you get flustered."

"Actually, I should prefer to talk to Miss Marler alone, if you would not mind, sir," Michael said.

He frowned. "You will not harass her? She is a good girl, and I should not like her to become distressed."

"No harassment, I assure you. She is not in any trouble, and need only tell truthfully what she remembers."

"I shall be just outside, Daisy, if you need me." Still frowning, he withdrew, Daisy's eyes following him anxiously to the door.

"Now then, Miss Marler—"

"Everyone calls me Daisy, sir, if you don't mind."

"Very well, then, Daisy. Now, tell me first, you and Mr Eustace are old friends, are you not?"

"Oh, yes, sir! Known him years, I have, and he was always kind to me, even when old Mr Sinclair were here. I used to oblige Mr Eustace even then, when he asked... when he were staying here, like." She blushed as she spoke of *'obliging'* Eustace.

"And he was generous, I expect, when you obliged him."

"Oh yes, very generous, and we was always glad of the extra money. It got my little brother a good apprenticeship with a cobbler. There's not been so much lately… well, he's away a lot, isn't he, and I dare say he has other girls he likes, too, so I never minded, but I'm always happy when he asks for me."

"As he did on that night in June — do you remember the date?" A sudden look of panic crossed her face, and she shook her head. "It is of no consequence, Daisy. So Mr Eustace asked for your company. Did he send the carriage for you?"

"The dog cart. He always does, unless it be raining, and then it's the carriage. And home again afterwards," she added proudly. "He's ever so kind."

"Well, then, you arrived, you had dinner… do you remember what you ate?"

Another moment of panic, then her face cleared. "Mutton. It's always mutton."

Michael laughed. "An excellent choice. One can never go wrong with mutton. And then you went to bed at about eight o'clock and stayed there until ten the next morning?"

"I don't remember the times," she said warily.

"But you were with Mr Eustace the whole night."

"Yes. The whole night. We was awake for quite a long time, and then we was exhausted so we slept until late the next morning. We never stirred, neither of us."

"Thank you, Daisy. You have told us all we needed to know."

Relief flooded her face, and she dashed out of the room.

"She's lying," Sandy said at once. "That whole business of being exhausted and never stirring, that was rehearsed."

"Of course it was, and we expected that, remember? An uneducated girl like Daisy could easily get flustered and not know what to say, so anyone would put some words into her head. But do you know how I know she is telling the truth? She did not know the date or the exact times. If she had *not* been here, he would have told her all that and she would have come right out with it. No, she was here, and I am sure the servants will verify the story. The plan, Sandy... kitchens and stables next. Let us get all that out of the way, and then we can have a look at those cannons, eh?"

Sandy's face broke into a smile. "That's all ye's here for, isn't it?"

Michael merely grinned.

19: Walter Intervenes

The incident at the General Office began a pleasant interlude in Winnie's life. In one way or another, Mr Lomax managed to see her every day. Sometimes it was merely a morning call, but more often there would be a drive or a walk, with Aunt Sofia chaperoning them. When they went to the theatre, he joined them, and when they had dinner guests, he was invited too. When a party was got up to go to Richmond to visit Uncle Edmund's mother, the ladies drove in Mr Lomax's landau. When neighbours held an evening party, with impromptu dancing, he danced twice with Winnie and then hovered nearby for the rest of the evening, as if he wished he could stand up for every dance with her. And after ten days, the seriousness of his intentions became clear when Mrs Lomax arrived from Oxfordshire to inspect the young lady who was keeping her son in town. Two days later, they dined at Mr Lomax's town house on Charles Street, just off Berkeley Square.

It was gratifying, of course, but to Winnie it was also heartbreaking, for while one man courted her with flattering intensity, the other treated her with the same casual affection as always. Why, why, why could it not be Walter who drove her about, who brought her flowers, who looked at her with fire in his eyes? He was hurtfully disdainful of Mr Lomax, as if he thought that no sensible man could possibly want to pay her any attention. And he showed not one iota of jealousy.

Gradually it became clear that he would never change. If the long journey south and spending hours every day together did not bring him to see her in a different light, if even a rival for her hand could not inspire him to see her as a woman, then nothing would. And although these bitter reflections caused her to weep a little, she could not wait for ever for Walter. She knew what she must do. She was unsurprised, therefore, when Aunt Sofia came to see Winnie in her room one night.

"I think you will need to be ready, Winnie," she said without preamble.

"Ready?" she said, although she knew what her aunt was about to say.

"For his offer. Alfred tells me that Mr Lomax came to see him privately today, and was very open about his intentions. He has four thousand a year, and no debts or encumbrances. I believe he will speak before you leave town, so you will need to have your answer prepared."

"I know what I will say, if it comes to that point, Aunt. I shall accept him, of course, subject to Papa's approval, naturally. And I should like to see his house first, before I commit myself irrevocably."

"You doubt his description of it?"

"No, not at all, and I know that Uncle Edmund has verified everything from his friends at White's and the Treasury. No, I should like to see his house and estate to understand what sort of man he is. Are his lands in good order? Are his tenants well cared for? Are his servants contented?"

"And will his mother move out when he marries?" Aunt Sofia said with a laugh.

"She has already told me that she will. She seems to accept his choice. I assume that he has made the same enquiries of my family that Uncle Edmund has made of his, and is satisfied."

"Then you are decided," Aunt Sofia said, a hint of surprise in her tone. "I confess, this is not the outcome I expected when I first suggested you come to visit us. I thought..." She chewed her lip anxiously. "No, let us have no secrets between us. When I heard about Walter's situation, and that his engagement to Miss Franklyn was at an end, I saw the opportunity. I had Edmund write to Alfred to persuade him to bring Walter here on some pretext or other, and to invite you too. My hope was that a few weeks together would bring him to value you as he ought, and to begin to return your affection."

Winnie blushed at this frank speaking. "You know of... my affection for Walter? Did Mama tell you?"

"No, indeed, I observed it myself. Alfred has noticed it, too. You conceal it very well from the world at large, but those who know you best can see it. What I cannot understand is why Walter is unaware of it, and why he so stupidly does not snatch up the treasure that could be his. Bea Franklyn, indeed! Whatever was he thinking, when he could have had you? And then, when a respectable man courts you, what must he do but make fun of the poor fellow!"

"He treats me as a sister — exactly as a sister, for he used to tease Josie and Izzy about their suitors in just the same manner. It is only his way, and he means no harm by it, but he will never see me in a romantic light. Look at what happened at the Andersons the other night — he did not dance with me once, even though he stood up with all the other young ladies. I too thought that this journey might spark some response in his breast, but I have now given up all hope of it. I cannot wait for ever, so, if

Mr Lomax should honour me with a proposal of marriage, I shall certainly accept him."

"Very well, dear," Aunt Sofia said, but Winnie thought her tone was sad.

***

Michael left his horse at the inn in the centre of Birchall village, strapped on his sword, and strolled across the road to the smithy. There were three men hard at work, an older man easily identified by his size and strength as the smith, and two younger men, tending the forge and passing tools as needed. Michael waited patiently as the three finished the piece they were working on, admiring the silent but efficient way they moved around each other, like a strange dance punctuated by clanging metal, wheezing bellows and the hiss of hot iron in water.

"You wanting me?" the smith said eventually, tossing aside his gloves and wiping his sweating forehead with a meaty forearm.

"If you can spare the time for a chat, Mr Whyte. And perhaps a drink across the road?"

"I don't drink with no strangers," the smith said.

"Captain Michael Edgerton, formerly of the East India Company Army, and more recently, Tattersall's. Currently employed by the Earl of Rennington to investigate the murder of Mr Arthur Nicholson."

"Him!" one of the younger men said, and spat on the floor.

"Hush, Jack. The man's dead," the smith said. "Joe Whyte. These are my sons, Jack and Will. Tattersall's, eh. That's worth a pint. Jack, get the other hinge ready while I'm gone."

It cost Michael three pints in the end, and he had all but exhausted his stock of tales from his time at Tattersall's by the time the smith had slaked his thirst, but eventually he led the way back to the smithy, picked up his hammer and said, "So say what you want to say, Captain, while I work."

"I should like to talk about your grandson, John Whyte."

"Got three o' those."

"The illegitimate one."

"Got two o' those."

"The one who is a groom at Westwick Heights. Supposedly by Mr Nicholson, chaplain at Corland Castle."

"*Former* chaplain," Jack said, spitting again.

"You dislike him," Michael said.

"Aye. Hate the man's guts, and that's the truth."

"Did you hate him enough to kill him?" Michael said conversationally.

The effect was immediate. Jack picked up a heavy iron bar and closed the distance to Michael in three swift strides. He was not as muscular a man as his father, but he was taller and considerably more powerful than Michael, and he carried the metal bar as if it weighed nothing, tapping it menacingly against his other palm.

"Come closer, *Captain*, and say that to my face."

Michael smiled and in one smooth motion, drew his sword. "You come closer, Mr Whyte, and ask again."

"You want a fight, do you?"

"Do you? I should warn you that I keep my sword sharp. You might lose a hand or two."

Jack made a low growl deep in his throat, but he dared not move within range of the sword. For several heartbeats they stood motionless, Jack glaring and Michael in the casual pose that he had found most disconcerted those untrained to sword fights.

The smith tossed his hammer onto the anvil with an exclamation of disgust. "Give over, you two. You're like a pair of strutting cockerels fighting over the dung heap. No one hated the chaplain enough to kill him, Captain."

Jack grunted, and, hurling the metal bar onto a table with an echoing clang, picked up the bellows and began work on the fire. Michael felt it was safe to sheathe his sword.

"Then what was the discussion about in the White Horse? It was a couple of days before the murder, and people were angry, so I hear."

"There's plenty of angry talk in the Horse when folk get well into the ale," the smith said with a huff of amusement.

"Nicholson's name was mentioned."

"Ah. That. We'd just heard he'd fathered Maisie's bairn, so we was right angry, true enough. Round here, a bastard's no great grief. It happens, the parson rants a bit, life goes on. Every child's a gift from God, in or out of wedlock. But a man's expected to take care of his own. Wed the girl, if he can, and if not, then money or a bit o' meat now and then. My Annie, the cobbler put one in her belly, but that boy's been well shod from the day he could walk, and he'll apprentice to his father when he's old enough. But Nicholson! Not a word, not a coin, not a gift in sixteen years, and him the chaplain, too. Maisie's had nowt from him but a roll in the hay, and that's not right, is it? Aye, we were angry, and we thought we'd go over there and have a word with him... make a fuss, like, and get him to acknowledge his own flesh and blood, if nothing else. But Maisie talked us out of it, and now he's dead, poor man, but it wasn't nothing to do with any of us, I'll swear to that on the Bible. We've no book learning here, apart from the Holy Book, but we know right from wrong, and killing's wrong, and that's all there is to it."

"And the boy himself? Was he angry, too?"

"Nay, not a bit on it. He's got a good place with Mr George Atherton, and he won't do nothing to risk that."

"You will not mind if I go over to Westwick Heights to have a word with him?"

"I don't mind, but he ain't there just now. He's away with Mr Bertram to Lincolnshire — some duke's place. Left yesterday. Gone for a month, he i s."

A month! Michael cursed inwardly all the way back to the castle, but there was nothing further to be done about John Whyte until he returned from Lincolnshire.

***

Walter could not understand why Winnie accepted Lomax's attentions so complacently. Mere politeness, he supposed, although how she could stomach him was more than he could fathom. The fellow's ridiculous clothes, his odd, swaying way of walking, and his effusive compliments were nauseating. Winnie was an absolute saint to put up with him without laughing or kicking him in the shins. Walter was tempted to kick him in the shins himself, for importuning Winnie so offensively. Every day, there he would be, hanging around the drawing room or whisking her out in his landau, and then in the evening as often as not he was there for dinner, too. It was sickening. Fortunately, the day was fast approaching when they would all go back to Yorkshire and leave the obnoxious Mr

Lomax of Wallingham Manor behind. Walter was ready to go home, now that Izzy had been and gone from the castle.

The only good part of the journey south had been meeting Alfred Strong's colleagues in the Treasury. Walter had quickly realised that the supposed crisis was merely a ruse, although to what end he knew not. Still, it gave him an opportunity to understand how things worked and to see a glimmer of how he might fit into the workings of the place. Money, and numbers generally, were no mystery to him, so he grasped the essentials very quickly. Besides, a great deal of the work seemed to be meetings of one sort or another, and he was well qualified for that. It was a pity that none of the truly important personages were in town, but August was almost upon them and everyone had dispersed from the heat and incessant smells of town, preferring the sea air and gaiety of Brighton, or the cool greenery and gentler pursuits of the countryside.

There were no Treasury distractions in the evenings, however, and Walter was obliged to watch the Lomax blockhead buzz around Winnie like a persistent wasp. She seemed unable to deter him. The lowest point of the whole time in London was an evening party at some neighbours of the Blackwoods, who got up some informal dancing in one of the drawing rooms. Walter would have liked to join in the card games set up in the library downstairs, but he felt an obligation to keep an eye on Winnie, and make sure Lomax did not offer her any offence.

The fellow danced with her twice and then clung to her side for the rest of the evening, preventing her from being with anyone else. Only once did another man manage to muscle past Lomax and take Winnie off to dance, and as soon as she sat down again, Lomax was there. Winnie could not shake him off without being rude, which she was too well-bred to do. Nor could Walter intervene, since Winnie's aunt and two uncles were there with her, although he ground his teeth in frustration at their lack of care for her. Surely they could find some way to protect her from pretentious coxcombs like Lomax? Yet they did nothing.

It was in this black mood that Walter went out one morning. His mentors had graciously allowed him some little time to visit his tailor and boot maker, and, these tasks completed and with an hour in hand, he thought to look in at White's to see if any of his friends were in town. He almost groaned aloud when the first person he saw of his acquaintance was Lomax. Nor was there any opportunity to turn and leave at once, for Lomax saw him and hailed him cheerfully.

"Atherton! Just the man I had most hoped to see. Will you not come and take a glass of wine with me... if you are not engaged on any more urgent business?"

Several excuses rose to Walter's mind, but it occurred to him that here was an opportunity to turn Lomax aside and free Winnie from his cloying attentions, so he agreed to it. As soon as they were settled, and the wine poured, Lomax turned to him eagerly.

"I hope, sir, that you, as Miss Strong's good friend, will be able to give me some hint... some slight indication... of her mind. Have I any chance, do you think? Can you give me any cause for hope? I fully intend to put it to the touch regardless, but it would be less nerve-wracking if I could be sure... Or perhaps I should wait? It is very soon, I know... too soon, perhaps. Her relations might think so. She has been tolerably encouraging, but... oh, but I do not know! What do you think?"

For a moment, Walter was almost too astonished to speak. The man wanted to *marry* Winnie! At least he could disabuse him of any notion that Winnie was encouraging him. "I am not in Miss Strong's confidence in the matter, sir, but I confess that I see no sign of great attachment in her. She is her usual even-tempered self with you as she is with everyone."

His face fell. "You do not think...? But she has allowed me to take her out driving several times. That must be regarded as encouragement, do you not think?"

"Her aunt and uncle have no open carriage, so your landau is a great attraction in this warmer weather."

"Oh. Yes, of course. That must be it. And Miss Strong is too kind-hearted to hint me away, perhaps."

"There is also the fact that she will be leaving town very shortly," Walter said. "She will not feel the need to hint you away when she is so soon to be gone from your company."

He sighed. "Such a gentle lady... she would suit me perfectly. Mater thinks so too, and that must be my guide in all things. So you do not think...? Still, one must be positive. I am determined to speak and if she rejects me, perhaps I shall follow her to Yorkshire and try again. Her father, I am sure, will not refuse to countenance the match. After all, a lady who is still unwed at twenty-four cannot reject a perfectly good offer without careful thought. Yes, that is what I shall do. It is better so, in fact, for although I have the sanction of her uncle, it would be better to talk to her father. If he approves, then Miss Strong cannot refuse, surely."

"Her uncle has given you permission to pay your addresses?"

"Indeed he has. I saw him privately yesterday, and he was most encouraging. He could not vouch for Miss Strong's answer, he told me, for ladies can be unaccountably capricious — his word, not mine — but for himself, he was satisfied that I am well qualified to make Miss Strong an excellent husband. Again, these are his words, not mine. On my part, he told me everything that remained unknown about Miss Strong, in particular, her moral character. That was my principal concern, naturally. Her modest dowry is not of the least importance to me, for I am in the fortunate position of not needing to augment my wealth. Her manners and pleasing style of dress I can see for myself. Her mind is tolerably well-formed, and although her education has been deficient in some areas, she shows a pleasing willingness to take instruction."

That made Walter smile. How often had he heard Lomax pontificate on some subject or other of which he professed great knowledge, and Winnie, not wanting to argue with him, had said peaceably, "I am sure you are right, sir." If he ascribed that to a willingness to take instruction, then so be it.

"On one point in particular, Strong was able to set my mind at rest," Lomax went on. "I was concerned, you see, that a young lady of four and twenty years, as yet unmarried, might have some... some *taint* in her background such as to render her ineligible as the wife of a respectable man. One must consider very carefully, after all, to whom one entrusts one's children. A mother must have an entirely unblemished reputation, with not a single stain upon it. So it has always been in the Lomax family, and I hold to the same standard in my choice of wife. I was delighted, therefore, when Strong assured me that his niece is entirely pure, as innocent as the day she was born."

Walter was speechless. The shock must have registered in his expression, for Lomax said nervously, "Atherton? You know something to the contrary?"

It was hard to believe. Surely Alfred Strong must know the truth, and to lie about such a matter was disgraceful. It was one thing to say nothing at all and hope Winnie could be safely wed before her husband discovered her history, but when asked directly and then lie openly about it was utterly dishonourable. And it could only mean that Strong was determined that Winnie should marry Lomax. Whatever her feelings on the matter, she would be hounded and harried until she gave in, and she, sweet girl that she was, would not be able to withstand the pressure.

But Walter could save her, and he did not hesitate. "I am afraid Mr Strong has misled you, sir. I tell you this in the strictest confidence and only because of the exceptional circumstances, for it is not common knowledge, but it came directly from the gentleman concerned to his father and thence to mine. His name was Seymour, and he met Winnie at York, in her second season there. She has an aunt living in the town, a rather ramshackle lady, to speak truth, who perhaps did not guide Winnie correctly, and certainly did not chaperon her properly. Seymour became enamoured of Winnie and was proceeding towards making her an offer, until... well, let us say merely that Winnie behaved in a way that no well brought up young lady should behave. Seymour withdrew at once, naturally, and Winnie left York and never returned. That, sir, is why she has never married. It brings me no pleasure to say this, and I should not have raised the matter for the world, except for Strong's deception. That is no way to deal with an honest man."

"And I thank you, sir, from the bottom of my heart!" Lomax cried. "It is, then, as I suspected all along, but she seems so meek, so dutiful... yet I always suspected something amiss. You have spared me from a grave error, sir, and I am deeply grateful."

"You will not, I trust, mention this to anyone?"

"Indeed not. Such tattling is of all things repugnant to me."

They parted in mutual satisfaction, Lomax removed from the danger of an injudicious match, and Winnie removed from the irritation of Lomax's company. Walter walked back to Park Street very pleased with himself.

20: Return To Yorkshire

Every Saturday afternoon at Corland Castle, Michael summoned all his fellow investigators to discuss progress. For the first month or so, there had been little to report, but now that the earl had allowed him to widen his search for information, he began to feel more optimistic.

"Sandy, summarise our interviews if you will," he said, as Luce handed round glasses of Canary.

"Aye, Captain. We've talked to everyone, above stairs and below, at Birchall House, Westwick Heights, Highwood Place and Welwood-on-the-Hill, without finding any suspicious behaviour or obvious lies or any cause which might drive someone to murder the chaplain."

"Are you satisfied that Mr Eustace had nothing to do with it?" Pettigrew said. "You said the girl was rehearsed."

"So she was," Michael said, "but that means nothing. She would say whatever Eustace told her. It was the servants who were the key to it. Our plan was to interview them individually, but then get them all together and talking informally, and see if we could spot any discrepancies or signs of nervousness. *One* servant might be loyal enough to lie for his master, but there are eight of them there, two of them young enough to get flustered if asked to lie, several who were very indignant at even the suggestion that they might cover up a murder, and one old fellow who used to work for Sir Hubert, who vouches for his impeccable character. They all swear on the Bible that Eustace was there until mid-morning and that no horses left the stables in the night, so unless he grew wings and flew to Corland, I think we must scratch him from the list, especially since we cannot find a reason why he would have wanted Nicholson dead."

"The list is getting rather short," Luce said with a wry smile. "The Lady Alice is still on it, I notice."

"If I ever get to talk to her again, I may be able to cross her off," Michael said. "Tess Nicholson, too, but she is still away. And our only other suspect, the illegitimate son of the chaplain, is also not here. He is a groom at Westwick Heights, but he has gone off with Mr Bertram to Lincolnshire, which is annoying, to put it mildly."

"Ye didnae put it mildly when ye found out," Sandy said, grinning. "Ye never heard such language. I was shocked, I tell ye."

"I confess I expressed my opinion robustly," Michael said. "We only missed him by a day. But perhaps it is as well he is not here. I am not sure that a boy of sixteen is our likeliest suspect. We have plenty of other trails to follow for the moment, so Mr John Whyte can wait a little longer. So next week, we start on the lower gentry at Birchall village."

Sandy grunted. “Where we’ll undoubtedly find they’re all upstanding Christians who wouldn’t hurt a flea, never mind attack a chaplain with an axe, but I suppose it has to be done.”

“Indeed it does,” Michael said. “If they can look me in the eye and tell me without hesitation that they would not hurt a flea, I might just possibly believe them. Until then, we should remain suspicious of everyone. My own feeling is that the murderer is from quite outside this area. Perhaps around Pickering, where the sainted Mr Nicholson was so frequent a visitor. Luce, tell us the results of your jaunt to Pickering, apart from no fewer than three new hats, I notice.”

“The milliner was excessively fond of gossip,” Luce said. “Unfortunately, she was more interested in what I could tell her about the Atherton family than in revealing anything, so perhaps it was a waste of ten guineas. However, I saw the house that Mr Nicholson owned, and I have to say, it is as nondescript a house as ever I saw. Run down, with peeling paintwork, although the gardens are tidy. Why would the late earl ever buy a place like that, and why would he leave it to his chaplain, of all people?”

“A dower house, perhaps?” Michael said.

“Not grand enough for a dower house,” Luce said, with a decisive shake of the head. “A grace and favour house for a relation would have a certain style, I should have thought.”

“It is let to a charitable case, supposedly,” Michael said. “Did you find out anything about that, Luce?”

“Nothing at all, for my own part, although I walked past the house two or three times every day. However, Peachy is more enterprising. She spotted a lady at work in the garden and they fell into conversation over the ten week stocks. She is a Mrs Mayberry, a widow, who has lived there for fifteen years, and has never seen her landlord — that is Mr Nicholson now, I presume. Peachy reported that she seemed a very respectable sort of woman."

"Where is Miss Peach, by the way?"

Luce rolled her eyes in a most unladylike way. "I am becoming concerned about her, Michael. I only brought her here as my companion to puff myself up for the earl and countess so they would treat us like guests, which worked gratifyingly well. I thought it would be a pleasant little holiday for her, and she would enjoy sitting about doing nothing, being waited on hand and foot. Instead, she has hurled herself into the enquiries with abandon. She is still in Pickering, and do not ask me what she is doing there, for I cannot tell you. She has found lodgings above a chandlery and frankly, she may stay there as long as she pleases. I am quite out of charity with her."

"You just like having someone on hand to fetch and carry for you," he said, smiling affectionately at her, pleased to see the scowl soften at once.

"Oh yes! *Such* a convenience, and it was very pleasant always having someone to talk to me. Poor Peachy! But she is enjoying herself, and will have a stock of stories to astonish her Harrogate friends with when this business is over. A month or two more of this, and she will have tales enough to last her for the rest of her life. Will it ever be over, Michael? I thought we would be in and out in a week."

"So did I," he said regretfully. "I thought it would turn out to be a drunken valet or some such, and we should find his blood-stained nightshirt stuffed under his bed. But I must confess, it is far more interesting than that. Since the only bloodstained garment to be found belongs to the Lady Alice, and I cannot really see her carrying off such a crime, then it was a carefully planned affair. And how that was done, and more to the point, *why* it was done, are fascinating questions." He sighed. "Pettigrew, you are looking decidedly smug. Please tell me you have discovered some irregularities in Nicholson's financial affairs."

Pettigrew Willerton-Forbes beamed at him. "It is remarkable the effect that a letter of authority from an earl can achieve. I started in Helmsley and very quickly found an attorney with whom Nicholson had a financial arrangement. The attorney acts as a small local bank. Nicholson would deposit money with him and then withdraw small sums when he needed to settle bills. He always paid his bills on time, by the way. The tradesmen spoke well of him."

"So no unpaid tailor seething with wrathful indignation?" Michael said.

"Sadly, no. He might quibble over an item here and there, but he always settled in full in the end. The attorney directed me to the bank in York where Mr Nicholson held an account. They also had charge of the amount of Lady Alice's jointure, fifteen thousand pounds, the exact dowry that her father had bestowed on her when she married. Mr Nicholson never touched a penny of it, although naturally he took the interest. His own account contained a sum slightly above ten thousand pounds."

"That is not very much," James Neate said at once.

"It is a not insignificant sum," Pettigrew said mildly.

"But consider, sir," Neate said. "He has been chaplain here for thirty years, with no doubt a substantial stipend, as well as the interest from his wife's money. He is known to be unusually lucky at the card table, too, so his income must be well over a thousand a year. Yet what are his outgoings? He is housed and fed, probably provided with horses, too, his only expenses his clothes and perhaps his own valet, and his wife's pin money. No more than a few hundred a year. Yet he leaves only ten thousand?"

"And his will left his *fortune* to his daughter," Michael said eagerly. "That word is highly significant. Ten thousand is a rather trifling amount to be described thus."

"Not to a chaplain's daughter," Luce said. "It is a good dowry for a girl of modest rank and expectations, and she will no doubt inherit her mother's fifteen thousand, in time."

"But there is something you do not yet know," Pettigrew said smugly. "There was a second account, for some kind of charitable institution which Nicholson set up about ten years ago. Every quarter, sums of money were deposited into the account — anything from ten pounds up to thirty, from local worthies, amounting to more than a thousand a year, and Mr Nicholson withdrew the full amount each quarter."

"That is a great deal of charity," Luce said. "The house in Pickering could not cost anything like so much."

"Then where did it go?" Neate said. "Did he spend the surplus? Or squirrel it away somewhere?"

There was a long silence as they all looked at each other.

"He must have been lining his own pockets," Michael said slowly. "Mr Eustace suggested something of the sort — Nicholson was managing the late earl's financial affairs, and there was not so much money as there should have been when he died. The late earl died ten years ago, and perhaps he has less opportunity with the present earl, so he accumulates money this way. But where does it go to?"

"There *may* be other banks," Pettigrew said. "I could not find any in York but in Scarborough, perhaps? Or further afield? I shall continue to investigate. There was no money found here, I take it?"

"No more than a thousand pounds in the safe," Michael said. "Not these excessive amounts. But this is excellent work, Pettigrew. The sainted chaplain was as straightforward as a corkscrew, if you ask me, and this sounds exactly the sort of devious trick he would get up to."

"Is it enough to get him killed?" Pettigrew said.

Michael chewed his lips thoughtfully. "Perhaps. At the very least, it gives us a thread to follow, and it may well account for this mythical fortune. If only we knew where it was tucked away."

***

It was two days before Winnie realised. On the day after the dinner at Charles Street, she wrote her note of thanks to Mrs Lomax and went shopping with Aunt Sofia for some last minute items before their return to Yorkshire. She had wondered if she should stay at home in case Mr Lomax rushed round to propose, but Aunt Sofia insisted they go about their normal business.

"He will come whenever he comes," she said. "We do not leave for two more days yet. Besides, he may not want to speak until he has seen your papa, which would be very correct of him."

It was not until late in the afternoon that she realised he was not coming at all that day. When he did not come the next day either, nor send word, Winnie's spirits sank alarmingly. Since the day they had met at the General Post Office, not a day had passed without a call or a drive or a dinner with Mr Lomax. Now, all of a sudden, he had abandoned her.

Edmund walked round to Charles Street to investigate, returning with the gloomiest news — the house was shuttered and closed up, the knocker off the door. The Lomaxes had gone.

Winnie was determined that she would not cry. She was no worse off, after all, and it was not as if her heart was broken. She had never been in love with Mr Lomax, and marrying him would have been a pragmatic matter — an eligible match, but not a romantic affair, not on her side. Yet she had thought that his affections, at least, were engaged. He had given every sign of being a man head over ears in love, and now he had gone away without a word.

"I expect he has gone to Yorkshire to talk to your papa," Aunt Sofia said optimistically, but Winnie was too realistic to give the idea any credence.

As they packed and bade farewell to Aunt Sofia and Uncle Edmund, and began the long journey back to Yorkshire, Winnie's mind spun with dark thoughts. What could she have done to drive Mr Lomax away? It must have been something very dreadful to deter a man pursuing so determined a courtship. She went over and over every moment of their last few meetings, but could think of nothing. It nearly drove her insane.

As if in tune with her mood, the journey north was nothing like as smooth as their southbound travel. A horse went lame, the carriage windows stuck closed, so that they sweltered, they took a wrong turning, losing two hours, and at their final overnight stop, the inn had not received Uncle Alfred's letter. Being almost filled by a large, rowdy party, there was a scramble to find enough rooms for them, and the only parlour free was a poky little place with a smoke-grimed ceiling and battered furniture. The innkeeper was profusely apologetic, for Uncle Alfred was a regular and much valued customer, but nothing could be done.

"We shall manage very well," Uncle Alfred said. "The dinner will be as good as usual, so we will not be dissatisfied, I assure you, my good man, especially if you bring us a bottle of your best claret and another of brandy. And tea for the lady."

"At once, sir," he said, bowing himself out.

"Well, it is only for one night," Uncle Alfred said. "I must go and see about securing horses for tomorrow. Stay here, Winnie, and do not wander about, not with this rabble here. Walter, take care of Winnie. I shall be as quick as I can."

Winnie had providentially brought a shawl down from her room, for even in summer there was rarely a day when such precautions could be abandoned. Now she was glad of it for the room felt damp.

"You look chilled," Walter said. "Shall I get someone to light the fire?"

"No, it is just the change from the stuffy coach to this place."

"A cup of tea will warm you up."

"A glass of wine would warm me better."

A couple of servants came in just then with tea, wine and brandy, and a plate of bread, ham and cheese. "To put you on till dinner," one of them said. "Kitchen's busy just now, so it'll be a while."

Walter poured wine for them both, and set about the bread and ham, but Winnie sat dispiritedly by the window, huddled in her shawl. It was just starting to rain, a few drops streaking the dusty panes.

"Will you not eat?" Walter said. "The ham is very good."

"I am not hungry."

"You have eaten nothing since breakfast."

"I am still not hungry."

"You are very out of sorts, Mouse. Your little journal has hardly put in an appearance today, nor the guide books."

"We have already seen everything of note on the way south," she said tiredly.

"Then why so glum? One more day of this, and we shall be home."

She spun round, then impulsively picked up her glass and sat down opposite him at the scratched oak table. "I keep wondering why Mr Lomax would just vanish like that, without a word. It seems so unlike him. Do you think something has happened — something dreadful? An accident?"

"You would certainly have heard about that. It would have been in the newspapers."

"So it would. Then it must have been something I did — something that gave him a disgust of me and drove him away."

"Really, Mouse, he is not worth all this worry. Put him out of your mind."

She huffed impatiently. "I cannot do so. It is the not knowing that keeps me awake at night, Walter. Every day he came to see me, every single day, and then one day — he is just *gone.* Why? Why would a man do that? It *must* have been something I did!"

"It was nothing you did. *I* was the one who got rid of him for you."

All the air whooshed out of Winnie's lungs, as if the very floor beneath her feet had melted away and she was hurtling into the void. "What... what do you mean?" she whispered.

"The fellow was nothing but an annoyance, so I sent him packing."

"But how? What did you do?" So hard to believe that Walter — her *friend* — could say such things and seem so pleased with himself, as if he had done her a favour. And what on earth could he have done to make Mr Lomax turn away from the brink of a proposal and leave without a word? "Walter, *what did you do?"*

He sighed. "I met him in White's, the morning after we had dinner with him. He wanted to talk about you, naturally, and it became clear that he was planning a proposal."

"I know. Uncle Alfred told me."

"Yes, your uncle... who seems to have told him a pack of lies."

"What! No, that I cannot believe!"

"Well, he did. Lomax was concerned, you see, that there should be no blemish against your name, so he asked your uncle, who told him you were as innocent as a newborn babe. Well, it would be dishonourable to let that stand, so I told him about Seymour."

Whatever Winnie had been expecting, that threw her into total confusion. "Mr Seymour? What does he have to do with any of this?"

"You have to admit, Winnie, that was not your finest hour."

Her head was spinning. Mr Seymour? A blemish against her name? Her uncle lying? "Walter, I understand none of this. Whatever you said to Mr Lomax drove him away, so please will you tell me exactly what passed between you."

"I have told you already — I told him about what happened with Seymour, and that got rid of him for you."

Fury rose up inside her. The nerve of the man, to speak to Mr Lomax about her at all! And now to hedge and prevaricate, and to boast — *boast!* — that he had got rid of Mr Lomax for her! The man who had wanted to marry her, driven away by something Walter had said, and how insufferably pleased he looked with himself.

Slamming her wine glass down on the table so that a little splash of red marred the table, she marched round to Walter's chair and poked him angrily in the chest.

"How dare you!" Poke. "By what right do you interfere? Who are you to decide who proposes to me and who does not?" Poke, poke, poke.

"Steady on, Winnie! I am only looking out for your best interests, you know."

"What did you tell him?"

"Calm down, for heaven's sake! I only told him about the Seymour business."

"*Precisely*, Walter."

"Precisely. Very well. I told him that you met Seymour in York during your second season there, he was on the brink of a proposal and then you behaved badly and he took off."

"*Behaved badly?* What is that supposed to mean?"

"Something no innocent girl should do, Winnie. You... allowed him to take liberties. I am sorry to drag it all up again, but Lomax raised the subject and he needed to know the truth."

"But it is not true! I have never done anything of the kind."

"Winnie, there is no need to pretend, not with me. *I* do not think any the worse of you for—"

"*It is not true!*" Hot tears stung her cheeks. How could he betray her so?

"Hush, Winnie, for goodness sake! Look, Seymour told his father, and he told mine, so I know—"

"Mr Seymour offered for me and I rejected him."

"What! No, that cannot be right."

"It is the truth, Walter. Aunt Minna will tell you, for she was outside the parlour for the two minutes it took, and that was the only time I was ever alone with him in the whole of our acquaintance, so whatever he told his father was a foul lie. Why would anyone do a thing like that, when he professed to *love* me." She could barely catch her breath for crying. "Oh, what have you *done*, Walter? What have you done?"

"I am very sorry if I have been misled, but I only acted in your best interests, Winnie. At least now you will not have to put up with that travesty of a man."

"I *liked* Mr Lomax! He was going to propose, and now you have ruined it, and I will never get another offer."

"But... you would not have wanted to marry him... would you?"

"Of *course* I would!"

"But why? He is a coxcomb, Mouse."

"Stop calling me Mouse! I hate it!"

"Do you? But you cannot truly want to marry a man like that. For God's sake tell me you are not serious."

"He is a respectable and educated man of independent means, who has never shown me anything but kindness. Any sensible woman would take him in an instant, but especially so when she is twenty-four years old, with no other prospect in view but a lifetime of racing from one sister or brother to the next. Dependable Aunt Winnie, always ready to help out with other people's children. *Of course* I wanted to marry him, and have my own house and my own children, and be the centre of a family instead of always being on the margins. And now you have spoilt it and I shall never get another offer. I will die an old maid and it is all your fault, Walter Atherton."

He looked stunned. Clearly it had never crossed his stupid mind that his view of Mr Lomax was not the only possible one, or that anyone would want to marry him. How could he betray her so? Walter, her dearest friend, who would never be more than a friend, never be the husband she longed for, yet seemed determined to prevent anyone else from assuming that rôle.

"If it is a husband you want," he said slowly, "then I will marry you."

"Oh!" She almost screamed in frustration. "After what you have done to me? I would not marry you if you were the last man on earth!"

And she ran sobbing from the room and up the stairs to her chamber, where she threw herself onto the bed, spilling the endless tears into the pillow.

21: Home

Walter sat, heart pounding. Dear God, what had he done? He had ruined Winnie's life, all unwittingly and with the best of intentions, but he had done it, nevertheless. His dearest friend, who had every right to look to him for protection, and he had destroyed all her prospects of happiness. If he could only go back and undo his mistake! If he could make it right again... but it was too late.

She had cried. He could not remember the last time Winnie had cried. Not since childhood, perhaps, when she scraped a knee, or that time she fell out of the tree house. No, he rather thought she had only laughed about that, and showed him the bruises on her arms the next day. But about this, she had cried, and it was his fault. He had made Winnie cry, and that was the most unbearable part of all of it.

How foolish he had been not to realise that she liked Lomax. He had allowed his own prejudice to blind him to the truth — that for Winnie, he was an extremely eligible suitor, to be encouraged at every turn. He had thought her merely polite in allowing Lomax to pay court to her, but he realised now that she had seen him in a very different light. Was she in love with him? Would she have cried so much if she were not?

After a while, he remembered that he was supposed to be taking care of Winnie, and he had let her run off... somewhere. In her room, most likely, but he needed to be certain. He half ran up the stairs to Winnie's room, then paused to listen at the door before knocking. Even through the solid wooden door, he could hear the muffled sounds of weeping.

Oh, Winnie! What an absolute heel he was, to make her cry so long and so passionately! He leaned his forehead against the door, and closed his eyes. In that moment, he hated himself for what he had done to her, hated everything about himself. He had never accorded her the respect that was due to her... had never seen her as anything other than good old Winnie, his best friend. Now, to his astonishment, all he wanted was to take her in his arms and comfort her. Dear Winnie! Sweet Winnie, who had never harmed a soul, who had trusted him, and he had betrayed her trust. He was despicable.

Eventually, he crept downstairs again and into the parlour.

"Ah, Walter, there you are!" said Alfred Strong. "Have you—? But whatever has happened, boy? You look as if you have the weight of the world on your shoulders."

"I have done a dreadful thing, sir," Walter said, too grief-stricken to dissemble.

"To Winnie?" Strong said sharply.

"Yes... oh, no, no! Not anything of that nature!" he cried, seeing the thunderous expression on Strong's face. "You know I would never harm Winnie, not for the world. But I have done her the gravest disservice, regarding Lomax."

"Ah." Strong pushed a glass towards him. "Is this your wine? Sit down, calm yourself and tell me the whole."

And Walter did, although his mind was in such confusion that the story came out jumbled and barely comprehensible. But by asking a question here and there, Strong got the gist of it. For a while, he sat in silence, his face... not angry or disgusted, but merely thoughtful.

He sighed. "Well, I guessed something of the sort must have occurred, something that made Lomax veer away at the last moment. He actually asked my permission, you know, and said, very properly, that he would submit himself to Sir Hubert as soon as he could, but he wanted to settle matters before Winnie went north again. And then he vanished, so there had to be some reason for it, some incident that made him think better of i t."

"It was entirely my fault," Walter said despondently. "I have ruined Winnie's life through my stupidity."

"Hmm. As to that, I am not sure that a man who shies away from matrimony merely on the hearsay of one person is worth having. Do you not think that, if he were truly, deeply in love with Winnie, he would have disbelieved the story instantly? At the very least, he could have come to me and said — I have heard a different story, so what is the truth? We could have sat down, you, me and Lomax, like sensible men, and discussed the business rationally, and if he still felt he could not marry Winnie, then good riddance, I say. I have never been entirely easy about him, to be honest. Oh, it would have been a wonderful match for Winnie, and if it were her choice, I should say nothing, for I saw nothing objectionable in the man, nothing to cause me concern."

"He is a coxcomb," Walter said, with a glimmer of his old spirit.

Strong gave a bark of laughter. "Yes! Never trust a man who cares quite so much about his appearance, that is my motto. But that alone is not enough. Now we can see that his supposed love for Winnie is not strong enough to sustain the least knock. You told him of the rumours, he believed you without hesitation and threw away his own happiness as well as Winnie's. That is foolish. Besides, even if it were true, marriage would restore her reputation. He had it in his power to wipe away any stain, if such a stain existed. Walter, how could you believe such a thing of Winnie? You, who have known her all her life, must know how strong her moral sense is."

"The tale came to me from my father who had it from Seymour's father who had it from Seymour himself. I should not have given it credence had it not originated with Seymour."

"Yes, and even if it had been true, what sort of man would circulate such a story about a lady? That is despicable behaviour."

"It is, but so is mine, in repeating it to Lomax."

Strong sipped his wine thoughtfully. "I am not sure that I agree with you. If I had been in your position, and a man had made it clear that the purity of his bride was an absolute requirement, I might very well have given him a hint, too, although hedged about with caveats — only rumour, not sure of the exact circumstances and so on and so forth. But I should certainly have told him. There should be honesty between gentlemen, I feel, and you did not know the story was untrue."

"Oh." Walter's spirits lifted marginally. "Then... you do not blame me?"

"Not entirely, no. Your reasoning was faulty, in assuming that Winnie saw him as you did and would be glad to be rid of him, but your heart was in the right place, and perhaps she is better off without him. So in the end it may turn out that there is no harm done."

"But there is," Walter said sadly. "My friendship with Winnie is quite broken, and I do not think it can ever be repaired. Lomax may have lost something exceptionally precious, but so have I."

"Now there I cannot help you," Strong said. "You must trust to time to heal the breach. Winnie is sensible, and will come round eventually."

"No. You are very kind to say that you would have done the same, but you would not have barged in with my unspeakable arrogance, assuming that I knew the truth and that I had any right to interfere with Winnie's future. It was quite unforgivable, and I do not expect to be forgiven. Winnie is the very best of creatures, and I am only now realising what a treasure she is, just when she is lost to me for ever."

***

Walter spent the final day of the journey squeezed into the second carriage with the two valets, Winnie's maid and an assortment of oddly-shaped packages that could not be put elsewhere. It was not comfortable for any of them, the servants rendered silent by his presence and Walter himself too miserable to do more than stare out of the window as the rain trickled relentlessly down.

He had decided to relieve Winnie of his obnoxious presence even further, by spending a few days at the castle with his father, but as the footmen manhandled his boxes across the bridge and into the entrance hall, and he watched the two carriages drive away without him, he felt oddly bereft. It was as if Winnie were disappearing from his life for ever, and no amount of rational thought could disabuse him of the notion.

"We are delighted to have you home, sir," Simpson said, as Walter entered the hall. "The castle is not the same without you."

"Thank you, Simpson, but I shall only be staying a few days to catch up with family news before I return to Birchall House. You survived the visit from Lady Farramont, then?"

"Oh, yes, sir," the butler said, smiling fondly. "We are used to her ladyship's ways. She did not stay long, unfortunately, so Lord Farramont, who was following behind, missed her altogether."

"Oh dear. And how is my father?"

Simpson hesitated. "His lordship bears up wonderfully well, sir, but he would do better if Lady Rennington were here."

"My mother is not home yet?" Walter said sharply.

"No, sir. I believe she has left Harfield Priory and gone to Lochmaben, sir."

"Where is my father?"

"In his study, sir. He spends a great deal of time in his study."

Walter tossed his hat and gloves to the nearest footman, and went at once to the study. The earl was sitting in his favourite chair, positioned beside the window at this time of year, gazing into space. He looked about ten years older than when Walter had last seen him, barely a month ago.

"Father?"

"Eh? Oh, it is you, Birtwell— Walter, I mean." Then his smile was replaced by a puzzled frown. "Were we expecting you?"

"No, but I am just back from town and thought I would spend a few days with you before I return to Birchall. How are you, Father?"

"Oh, well enough, I suppose. You know that Izzy has gone, I take it? It is safe to come back." For the first time, there was a glimmer of amusement in his eyes.

"Was it dreadful?"

"It was... trying. And exhausting. But you know Izzy, she can never settle for long, so off she went, with Farramont in hot pursuit."

"I cannot imagine what Farramont, or any man, sees in her," Walter said. "Most men want a conformable wife, or at least one who is restful to be with."

The earl chuckled. "And yet she had half the men in town in love with her when she first came out, and four serious suitors. Farramont was not the only one, by any means. He is still besotted with her, unfathomable as it may seem to the rest of us. But what of you? How did you get on in town? Sofia Strong lives in Westminster now, does she not — a trifle out of the way
"

"She is Sofia Blackwood now, and has a pleasant house backing on to St James's Park, a very convenient location for those engaged in government business. They have offered me a home there, if I decide to pursue a career in the Treasury with Alfred Strong and Edmund Blackwood."

"A career! You should not have to earn your bread like a nobody, but if you must do it, you must. Still, I do not like a son of mine living so close to the river. It is not healthy. You could easily have rooms in Grafton Street, if you want. That would be more appropriate for your station in life."

"My station in life? A bastard son?"

"The son of an *earl*, Walter. I shall not treat you any differently, just because of this stupid business. You are my eldest son, and I will have you held in respect. You may keep your allowance for ever, if you want, and Langley Villa is still yours whenever you marry. You do not need to grub about in the Treasury."

"It would hardly be right to hang on your sleeve for the rest of my life, Father, and Uncle George after you."

"Then marry a woman of fortune. With your looks and address, you would have not the least difficulty. Twenty thousand would set you up perfectly well to live as a gentleman."

"Father, I have been idle too much. I want to work for a living, and I believe I shall like grubbing about in the Treasury. Now tell me about everyone else. How is Mother?"

A shadow crossed the earl's face. "I wish she would come back, Walter," he said, his voice as querulous as a man of eighty. "I miss her abominably. I feel like a rudderless ship without her. But she has this bee in her bonnet and nothing I say makes any difference to her."

"About you marrying a younger woman? There is a certain logic to it, I suppose. One of the duties of the earldom is to sire a legitimate son to inherit."

"Which my father did by producing George as well as me. He would make a fine earl, and Bertram after him... or Lucas or little Philip. That is how it is supposed to work, Walter. There is always another male heir somewhere in the many branches of the family diverging from the first earl."

"What does Uncle George say about it?"

"He would be delighted were I to marry again and cut him out, frankly, but he tells me I must not regard his wishes at all. He will do his duty, if it should come to that, and besides, I am not yet in my dotage. He has plenty of time to grow accustomed to the idea."

"Then it is up to you to do whatever you feel is best."

"If it were entirely my choice, I should not hesitate to remarry your mother as soon as may be, but she tells me..." He passed a hand tiredly across his eyes. "She says it is the only way she can now help the family, by standing aside. She has sent me a list of suitable candidates, you know. Now where is it? Ah, there now. What do you think of that?"

Walter took the paper, recognising his mother's elegant hand. There were six names on it, each with age and lineage and a few words describing the disposition of each. "Well, at least they are not schoolroom chits."

"No. She said she thought that would not suit me. Two of them are widows, you see. With children already."

"Typical of Mother," Walter said. "So very organised."

"She is a managing kind of female — always has been," his father said sadly. "I was all set to marry someone else, you know. Not officially, but my father and the lady's had had some discussion about it. Then along came Caroline with her sweet smile and her trim figure, and there we are. I never regretted it, not for a moment. We have been as happy as any two people could be all these years. I cannot imagine what I shall do without her, and that is a fact."

Walter merely smiled, having heard the story many times. "Can you not persuade her?"

"She is adamant, and you know what she is like once she has made up her mind. I suppose I shall have to do what she wants. I generally do, and she is invariably right. Do you know any of these women? They are more your age than mine."

"Not really. These are all Yorkshire women, Father. Good, solid families but not the top drawer."

"Your mother is trying to spare me the indignity of submitting myself to the London season. Your Aunt Jane knows them, for she is from a good, solid Yorkshire family herself. She is to invite them to stay with her, one at a time, so that I can meet them informally."

"Father, must you do this? It seems so heartless, to set Mother aside in this way."

"It is her own choice, Walter. She wants it, George, Jane and Bertram want it, even your Aunt Alice thinks it a good idea, so what can I do?"

He shrugged helplessly, and Walter understood all too well the futility of arguing with a woman who had made up her mind about something. It had led him into his ill-fated betrothal, after all. Sometimes it was simply easier not to fight against the inevitable.

With Winnie still dominating his mind, Walter said, "Father, do you remember that tale we heard of Winnie Strong — that there had been some improper behaviour? Well, it was all a hum, which we should have known, of course. Winnie is too good ever to allow a man to take advantage of her."

The earl frowned. "Truly? No truth in any of it? You know what they say — no smoke without fire. And it came from the fellow concerned — what was his name?"

"Seymour, and it was a lie from top to bottom. He actually proposed to Winnie and she rejected him, and he told his father that he had decided not to marry her because of her impropriety, the scoundrel. To say such things of a sweet, innocent girl like Winnie!"

"That is very bad, if it is indeed so," the earl said thoughtfully. "Do you know, we thought of a match for you there, at one time."

"Winnie... and me?" Walter said, startled.

"Exactly. Strong suggested it, but you were only twenty-three at the time, and I thought you too young to settle to domesticity. Then we heard this rumour about Winnie, from Seymour's father himself, so how were we to know it was untrue? Then there was that business of yours with that girl..."

Walter sighed. “Father, it is not unusual for a man to take a mistress, and I took good care of Maria. Better that than brothels and chambermaids. Grandfather would have approved.”

“His was a different generation, Walter. Neither your mother nor I approved of it, and Lady Strong was adamant that no daughter of hers would marry a man of loose morals, so what with that and this rumour, any idea of a match between you and Winnie ran aground.”

Walter was left to digest the startling information that, if matters had gone otherwise, he might now be married to Winnie. It was the strangest thought.

22: Love And Honour

Winnie was filled with sorrow as she saw Walter's luggage being unloaded at Corland Castle. Her last sight of him as the carriage rolled away down the drive showed her a man standing as if lost, an island of stillness in the ocean of bustling footmen. Then the drive curved away and he was lost from her sight. She wondered wildly whether she would ever see him again, before reminding herself sternly that he had agreed to return to Birchall House in a few days.

Uncle Alfred's voice startled her out of her reverie. "Winnie, what do you wish to tell your parents about all this? Your Aunt Sofia has been keeping your mama informed of every last nuance of Mr Lomax's behaviour, and I have myself written to your father to tell him that an offer was imminent, but we can simply tell them that he was obliged to go out of town, if you prefer."

"What is your opinion, Uncle?"

"I do not feel it wise to deceive them regarding Mr Lomax's absence. If they imagine that he will turn up on the doorstep at any moment—"

"They will plague me to death! Yes, they had better know the truth, then."

"And what about Walter?" he said gently. "Perhaps you may feel that there is no need to reveal Walter's rôle in Lomax's departure? He meant no harm by it, after all, and—"

"Oh, do not defend him!" she cried. "What he did was unconscionable! To pass on rumour and hearsay, and of such a nature! It is bad enough that Mr Seymour, a man who wished to marry me, for heaven's sake, should speak so of me, but for Walter to repeat such tales, and not once to ask me the truth of the matter... for him to *believe* it of me, when he has known me for so many years, and must know my character better than anyone outside my own family... Oh, it is beyond anything! You must not — *cannot* defend such behaviour!"

The tears were falling again, so he patted her hand and murmured, "There, there, dear. Never mind, now," in the vaguely embarrassed way of men faced with a weeping female. And since she had no wish to return home with the tear-stained appearance of a broken-hearted woman, she dried her eyes and watched the familiar fields and farms and cottages pass by, telling herself sternly that she was nearly home and the distress of Walter's betrayal was behind her. She had now only the ordeal of telling her family of it, and dread settled in the pit of her stomach like a cannonball.

The sound of the carriages on the drive brought the whole family and half the servants out to greet them, but there were no smiles. Mama held a handkerchief to her eyes, and Lily, never able to restrain herself, rushed forward and flung her arms around Winnie, weeping copiously.

"Oh, Winnie! You poor, poor thing!"

It was clear that she was forestalled. Aunt Sofia, it must be supposed, had been busy with her pen and the rapidity of the Royal Mail had brought notice of Mr Lomax's defection before her own arrival.

Uncle Alfred at once said, "Now, now, Lily, let your sister into the house before you drown her in your tears. Come, now, inside if you please."

Mama stepped forward to hug Winnie fiercely and kiss her on the cheek, leading her up the steps and into the house, with Lily, still lachrymose, hanging on her other arm. Meanwhile, Harris and Lionel, not in the least interested in their older sister's matrimonial prospects, competed to execute handstands on the wide top step and generally hamper the footmen unloading the luggage.

"Winnie, why do you not go upstairs and put on one of your pretty new gowns to show everyone, eh?" Uncle Alfred said. "When you have changed, you can join us in your father's book room. Kitty, Hubert, Lily... shall we await her return in the book room? I could do with a glass of something. My throat is quite parched, for I never saw so much dust thrown up by the horses."

Grateful for her uncle's good sense, Winnie went, and before long her boxes arrived, followed by a rather breathless Martha, and there was the very mundane business of choosing a gown to wear, and then extracting it from the luggage, and getting washed and changed, and tidying her hair. By the time all was done, almost an hour had passed, and that was, she presumed, precisely as Uncle Alfred had intended.

When she finally descended to the book room, only Papa and Uncle Alfred were there, quietly sipping wine. Her father at once set down his glass and crossed the room to wrap her in a tight embrace before the door had well closed behind her.

"My dear girl!" he said, his voice thick with emotion. "What a dreadful business! How distressed you must be! The scoundrel, to treat you so! What a knock you have taken, to have your hopes raised like that and then dashed to pieces. But you will recover. You must not let him destroy your happiness for ever. The heart is resilient, and you will learn to smile again and to enjoy life. We will help you to recover, and your mother already has plans in mind."

"Plans? Oh dear," Winnie said, unsure quite what to say, for it was not at all clear to her whether her father's ire was for Mr Lomax or for Walter.

Uncle Alfred chuckled, and even Papa smiled wanly at this feeble sally, and released her.

"Ah, that is like you, to make a jest of it, but your spirits must be low indeed. Were you very much in love with Lomax?"

"No, Papa. I liked him well enough, but I was not at all in love with him."

"Oh." He looked taken aback. "Then why encourage his advances?"

"Because he was eligible and I should like to be married. I am twenty-four, after all, and it is not as if offers grow in every hedgerow, waiting to be plucked."

"But to marry without love, Winnie! It is not at all what I should wish for you."

"I think there *was* love, but it was all on his side. He certainly showed every sign of a strong attachment. If he were indifferent to me, then I should not contemplate matrimony with him, but he was extremely attentive... until he left town abruptly."

"Hmm. Your Aunt Sofia thinks he has gone to put his estate in order for you, and will turn up here before too long, but I think we should not depend upon it, and from what your uncle tells me of Atherton's involvement..." His expression was pained. "When I think how that boy has run tame in this house, treated almost as my own son, and always trusted implicitly, because of his father, and then to turn round and abuse you so wickedly! To scotch all your hopes, and so maliciously!"

Despite her own anger with Walter, despite all she had said to her uncle, Winnie could not help defending Walter from such an accusation. "I do not think it was malicious, Papa. Thoughtless, perhaps, and... and disloyal, but he truly thought he was acting in my best interests. He dislikes Mr Lomax himself, so he could not imagine that I might want to marry him."

"That does not excuse it! To say such things of you— But that is all water under the bridge. What is done is done, and if your heart is not broken... well, perhaps it is not so bad as I feared. But still, I have told your mama and Lily that they are on no account to ply you with questions, or even mention the subject in your presence. If *you* should wish to speak of it, that is another matter, but I will not have you plagued by Lily's excessive sensibility. They need not know of Atherton's part in all this. Your mama already has a poor opinion of him on account of— well, no matter. He is still an earl's son, and I should not care to set myself at odds with Rennington. But your Aunt Sofia has suggested that you might like to go to your Aunt Esme in Scarborough for a month or so, and your mother thinks it an excellent idea. These bathing resorts are very lively in the summer, and with these new gowns you have... and your hair has been cut, too... I must say, Winnie, you look very well, very well indeed."

"Thank you, Papa. Aunt Sofia bought me some new gowns and bonnets and suchlike fripperies."

"Well, she has done you proud, I must say. You have a little London polish, no? But you see, Winnie, after you turned down Seymour — a most eligible match, and all that a young lady would admire, or so Minna said — we supposed you were not much minded for matrimony. You stood aside for Hebe and Mabel, and made a comfortable life for yourself here ... well, we thought you were content to stay unwed. But this Lomax fellow has changed the landscape. It seems that you would care to marry after all, and since Sofia has rigged you out in prime style, it would be a pity not to take advantage of the situation. What do you say? A month or so at Scarborough, assemblies, evening parties, riding expeditions... you might meet someone of greater worth than this Lomax fellow, and more steadiness of character, too."

"Thank you, Papa, but I am quite content to stay at home. I am not fond of dancing, you know, or of meeting new people. Mr Lomax was... fortuitous, but I cannot expect to meet another such so soon. It is six years since Mr Seymour offered for me, so perhaps in another six years, I may be lucky again."

"But you will be thirty!" her father said, aghast.

Winnie laughed. "And Aunt Sofia was thirty-nine when she met Uncle Edmund. I have plenty of time yet. I can wait."

Her father smiled. "You are a good girl, Winnie, have I not always said so? I am very glad your heart is not broken, but I wish beyond all things that you could find a man you could love who would make you as happy as I am with your mama."

"I wish that too, Papa, but we cannot all be so fortunate as you and Mama. A good, honourable and respectable man would serve me perfectly well."

"And rich," put in Uncle Alfred.

Winnie nodded. "And rich," she said, laughing. "Definitely rich. Now that I have discovered the pleasure to be had in a fashionable bonnet, I should very much like to continue in the same manner. Are you going to pour me some wine, or must I go thirsty?"

***

Walter lost no time in going to see Aunt Alice. She still kept to her room, but she welcomed him with a smile, one hand held out towards him.

"Walter! How lovely! How was London?"

He took her hand and kissed it lightly. "Oh... very quiet. No one is there at this time of year."

"But you did not go there for the society. Do you think you might like the work that Alfred is offering?"

"Indeed I do."

"Then you will go away to live in town," she said sadly.

"For part of the year, certainly. But what about you — how are you, Aunt? Are you well?"

"As well as I can be. I shall never be entirely well again, not without my Arthur." Her voice wobbled, but she took a deep breath and went on more strongly, "This captain fellow is no further forwards in finding out who killed him. He is very lax, it seems to me. Weeks and weeks he has been here, he has talked to everyone, sometimes several times, and he has discovered where the axe came from, yet still he has not the least idea. Will you talk to him, Walter? I cannot bear to see him again, but you could do it for me. Push him into a little more exertion, for my sake."

"I will certainly do so. But why do you hide yourself away like this, Aunt? Why not sit in the drawing room, or out in the garden? Do you not even come down to dinner?"

She shuddered. "And eat at the same table as the man who has failed to find my husband's murderer? I could not. Every room in this castle reminds me of Arthur, and brings only the most grievous thoughts to my mind. This is the only room he never entered, so here I stay. Like Mama, I am shut into my tower room, and perhaps, like her, I shall leave it only to be buried."

Walter could not answer such dark thoughts, so he talked instead of London, at least those parts of the visit that he felt able to tell. But Aunt Alice knew him very well.

"There is a great sadness in your voice, Walter. Did something bad happen in town?"

He hesitated only a moment. Aunt Alice had always been a great dispenser of wisdom. "I did something abominable, Aunt," he said in a low voice, and set about telling her the whole story, holding nothing back. His aunt listened in silence, and even when the torrent of words finally trickled to nothing, she sat thoughtfully.

Eventually, she said, "What are you going to do about it?"

"What can I do?" he said helplessly. "How can I mend something which is irrevocably broken? God knows, I wish I had never interfered, but it is done and cannot be undone. Winnie will never forgive me, and she should not."

"Oh, Walter! I think you are in love with her."

"Is that what this is — this pain that never leaves me?"

"Love is pain, yes," she said softly. "It can also be the greatest joy imaginable. But Walter, answer me this — do you love her enough to give her up to another man?"

"To Lomax? He is an idiot. She deserves better than a muttonhead like that."

"But if Mr Lomax is the man she wants...? Even if you think she is crazy to want him...?"

Walter let out a long, slow breath. "Yes... I want her to be happy, Aunt Alice. I want her to have whatever she desires — a husband, her own establishment, children. She *deserves* that and if Lomax can give her those things... yes. But he is gone, and—"

"And he may never return, that is true. Perhaps his trust in her goodness was too fragile to be rebuilt. But even without considering Winnie's future, the fact is that you told him something that was untrue. You believed the rumours that Mr Seymour put out, but since it now appears there was not a word of truth in them, you are bound in honour, I believe, to inform Mr Lomax of that."

"He may not believe me... but you are right, Aunt, as usual. He should be told the truth. What he chooses to do then is entirely a matter for him to decide."

"And you may judge him by his actions, Walter. A man's honour is seen in his behaviour towards a lady. However badly he behaves in other areas of his life, if he deals righteously by the female sex, I shall account him an honourable man."

23: A Clever Man

Walter did not forget his promise to Aunt Alice to talk to Captain Edgerton about the progress of his investigations, but the fellow was abominably close-lipped. He would say only that he had not yet discovered a reason for Nicholson's murder, but the earl had given him permission to stay until the matter was resolved to his satisfaction.

"To your satisfaction?" Walter said sharply. "So you are to be judge and jury, are you?"

"No, sir, but it may be that we shall never know the truth, so I shall have to settle on whatever seems to me to be a reasonable explanation."

"Surely it is obvious? Some lunatic broke in overnight with an axe and then attacked Nicholson as he slept."

They were seated in the old nursery, Edgerton's colleagues having diplomatically vanished. Edgerton had poured wine for them both, but had not yet touched his.

"We can all agree that he attacked Nicholson as he slept," Edgerton said easily, "but the axe came from inside the castle. It was part of the display of armour and weaponry on the stairs."

"Was it?"

"So Mr Eustace said."

"Well, he would know, but that makes no difference," Walter said testily. "So the culprit broke in, snatched up the axe as he ran up the stairs and then attacked Nicholson as he slept."

"How did he know the axe was there?"

"He saw it, of course. He must have gone up the main stairs, then he would have seen it right in front of him."

"It was the middle of the night. How did he see?"

"He carried a light. He must have done."

"Very well. So he breaks in… how does he break in, by the way?" Edgerton's tone was bland, but Walter thought he was enjoying himself.

"By a door into the basement. Not the drainpipe, and not the scullery window, because of the dogs that sleep nearby, you have proved that, so it would have to be the garden door — that is as far as it is possible to get from the dogs, and there are service stairs right beside it."

"It is supposed to be kept locked, but let us suppose that it has helpfully been left unlocked, or perhaps with an idea that he might need it, he arms himself with one of the spare keys. He breaks in, stops to light a lantern or candle — we cannot be sure which — managing not to wake the kitchen boy or the dogs, and then up the service stairs to the upper floor… but no, he goes only so far as the ground floor, then for some reason enters the great hall in order to take the main stairs, where he finds a handily placed axe. He then goes to Nicholson's room, sets his candle, or possibly his lamp, on a table without leaving any trace of dripping wax or smoke and without waking his quarry. *Then* he attacks Nicholson as he slept. Then he leaves again, taking his candle or lantern with him, and vanishes without trace."

He smiled benignly, and Walter could not help but laugh. "You are very clever, Captain."

"Indeed I am not," he said with some vehemence. "If I were clever I would already know who had done this evil deed, even if the motive for it yet evaded me, but I have not the least idea. I believe you can understand why I am not convinced that the murderer is a passing lunatic. If he indeed came from outside, then he must know how to get in, how to move around undetected and where Nicholson slept. The axe I grant you may have been fortuitous, but there are hundreds of other weapons on the walls. And if it were someone from within the castle, it could have been absolutely anyone, even you, sir."

Walter opened his mouth to protest, then laughed again, shaking his head. "Your argument is well made, but is there no one you can point a finger at and say *'There! That fellow is the most likely to have done the deed*?"

"Certainly there is," Edgerton said, the smile dropping away. "There is most definitely one person at the top of my list, the one who was discovered beside the body covered in blood and with an axe in her hand. The Lady Alice is the very last person I want to accuse, but until I can say for certain that she did not kill her husband, I can make no progress on this case."

"But surely... how could she possibly?" Walter said. "She is *blind!*"

"Yet she can move freely about the castle, even at night without needing a candle. The axe is light enough to be wielded even by a woman, and she knew precisely where her husband would be."

"Why on earth would she kill him?" Walter burst out. "She depended on him to read and write for her, to prepare food at table, to ride with her… everything. They were together for many hours a day. She *adored* him."

"I know all that," Edgerton said tersely. "She is also a very composed person, well in control of herself. I cannot see her losing her temper, but then this is not a case of a sudden quarrel flaring up. Nicholson was fast asleep in his bed, killed not in a rage but coldly, calculatedly. Yes, the Lady Alice would be capable of that."

"Are you assessing all of us by the same measure?" Walter said, horrified. "Do you think *I* am capable of such a murder?"

"No," Edgerton said promptly. "You might get into a quarrel, you might even hit a man in a fit of passion, but then you would haul him back to his feet, apologise and pass him a glass of brandy, laughing at your own foolishness. I cannot see any circumstance when you would plot a murder of this kind."

"Well, thank you for that, at least! I shall not ask your opinion of the rest of my family. I am not sure I want to know."

"A wise decision, sir. Pray convey my apologies to the Lady Alice, and assure her that I am doing the very best I can to find her husband's killer. You may also mention to her that I would proceed more swiftly if she herself would agree to talk to me again."

Before Walter could answer, there was a knock on the door and Aunt Alice's maid entered, a small box under her arm.

"Yes, Malling, what is it?" Walter said, forgetting the room was not his.

She seemed surprised to see him there. "Oh! Beg pardon, my lord… sir, I didn't know… I'll only be a moment. Captain, I believe you have the key to Mr Nicholson's safe? I have some jewellery to deposit there, just back from being cleaned."

"Nicholson had his own safe?" Walter said, frowning.

"Oh yes, sir," Malling said. "He had it fitted in his room for convenience to keep her ladyship's jewels safe. Being the only daughter, she had all her mother's jewellery. Mr Nicholson always chose what her ladyship wore. He had excellent taste. It is odd, though..." A frown flitted across her face. "Mr Nicholson arranged for this to be cleaned, and I never knew him do such a thing before. I usually took care of the cleaning, with a man in Helmsley, but this fellow has come from York to—"

"From York!" the captain exclaimed. "That seems a long way to go to have a piece cleaned. And has it been cleaned, Miss Malling?"

"Oh, yes, sir, very well cleaned. It looks just like new... see?"

She opened the box, and nestled within was a diamond necklace Walter remembered seeing his aunt wear. It did indeed look like a new piece, every stone shimmering, and the gold gleaming brightly.

"He asked for Mr Nicholson at first," Malling said. "Seemed very upset to hear he was dead. Then asked for my mistress, but of course that was denied, so it fell to me to deal with him."

Captain Edgerton lifted up the necklace carefully, turning it this way and that, examining the hallmarks and the clasp, and gazing intently at the largest stone, attached as a pendant. Quickly he lifted the stone to his lips and breathed on it, then held it close to his eye. With a cry of "Aha!", he carried it to a side table and examined it more carefully with a magnifying glass.

"As I suspected," he said. "This necklace is a fake."

Malling cried out in shock. "No, sir, no! Surely not! Then this man has stolen my lady's diamonds."

"I suppose he is not still here, is he?" Edgerton said hopefully.

"He might be. I sent him downstairs to have a bite to eat."

“Ha!” was all Edgerton said, setting off at a run, the necklace still in his hand. Walter tore after him, following as he dived down the spiral service stairs, down and down, their boots thundering, the captain’s sword sheath clattering against the stone walls now and then. Walter burst into the kitchen, seeing Edgerton already at the far side, anxiously asking something of the cook, who pointed down the passageway. They ran on, bursting into the servants’ hall with its long table, almost empty at this hour.

But there at one end sat a small man of sixty or so, with wispy grey hair and a coat shiny from long use, spooning stew rapidly from a steaming bowl. He looked up in surprise, saw Edgerton bearing down on him, necklace in hand, and dropped the spoon, jumping to his feet.

“I only did what he told me!” he cried, eyes wide with fear as he took in the businesslike sword at Edgerton’s side. “Truly, sir!”

“Nicholson told you to do it?” Edgerton said in such stern tones that the man visibly shook.

“Yes, sir! As God is my witness, and may He smite me down on the spot if I lie.”

“I may smite you down myself, lying or not,” Edgerton said tersely. “What are you about, man, to be taking a fine necklace such as this must have been and creating a paste version of it? Even if a man tells you to do it, that is a perversion of your craft.”

“I don’t do it myself,” the jeweller said, in less agitated tones. “I know a man who does, though, and if a gentleman comes to me — a *respectable* gentleman, and a parson, no less — and says that his wife’s a bit short of the readies and can I make a fair copy of a piece, well… I’m not going to say no, am I? Not when he’s willing to pay a ton for it.”

“A hundred? Is that all the profit you make?”

"It is, sir, I swear, and I give most of that to the man who does the crafting. It's skilled work, that, and takes him a while to do properly."

"So you make nothing for the stones or the gold?"

"No, sir! The gold's used in the copy, for the proper marks, and we gave the parson the full reckoning for the stones."

"The full reckoning? Not a penny more for yourselves?"

"No, sir. He was an astute one, and knew their worth. It was all agreed before he handed over the necklace. I'm an honest dealer, sir, and I've never played any tricks on Mr Nicholson. Here... here is the money from the stones from this piece."

He laid a roll of money on the table. Edgerton unrolled it, examined the values and then passed it to Walter. Six hundred pounds. He tossed it back on the table in disgust, but Edgerton scooped it up, and tucked it away in a pocket.

"I shall put that in Nicholson's safe," Edgerton said. Then, to the jeweller, "Sit and eat your food, and you can tell me how it worked. When did Nicholson approach you?"

"The first time was seven... no, eight years ago, sir. That was diamonds, too. Then about once a year, it would be, he would arrive in my little shop with another piece. The arrangement was just as I told you — a hundred pounds for me and Glover, and we would buy the stones to reuse or to sell on, but discreetly. We were very careful. Unusual sales get talked about, as you might imagine, sir."

"So what were you planning to do with this money, given that Nicholson is dead?"

"Well, we never knew that, sir. I heard there was a murder, but never realised it was him. Once a piece was finished, it went into my strongbox and waited for Mr Nicholson to come and collect it. That could take a while, and I wasn't allowed to write to tell him it was ready. It was only yesterday I noticed it was still there, had been there for a couple of months, so maybe he'd forgotten about it, so I thought I'd bring it out to him. Gave me such a turn to hear he was dead, I can tell you! I wasn't allowed to see her ladyship that was married to Nicholson, and that haughty maid of hers just took the box from me as if it was perfectly normal, but never mentioned the money for the stones. I had no idea what to do, to be honest, so I'm right glad to hand it over to you, sir, for you'll know just what to do about it, except please don't set the magistrate on me, nor on Glover neither, for I've a wife and seven little ones to feed, and he's got five and another on the way, and we haven't done anything criminal, sir, only what we were asked to do."

"No, it is not your fault," Edgerton said thoughtfully. "But I shall check on you, mind! And Mr Glover, too, so write his direction and a list of all the pieces the two of you have worked on, with the dates and the money that changed hands. Atherton, have you a notebook on you? I left mine upstairs."

The jeweller wrote, and Edgerton pocketed the paper with a smile of such malicious glee that the jeweller abandoned his stew, and scurried away, relieved to be free from Edgerton's baleful glare and barked questions.

"Well!" Walter said. "This is a startling development. What was Nicholson about, to be getting copies made of Aunt Alice's jewels? Do you suppose she knows about it? Is this the reason for Tess's unexpectedly large inheritance?"

"These are all excellent questions," Edgerton said, absent-mindedly tapping his fingers on the table. "There is so much about Mr Nicholson we still do not know. But there is one very good outcome from all of this. I now have the best reason in the world to talk to the Lady Alice again. This needs to be explained, and she will not deny me this time."

He grinned in delighted anticipation.

24: Regrets

AUGUST

The familiar routine of the house rose up to enfold Winnie in its welcoming arms. While she was busy in the kitchen or the hen house or the still room, she could not brood over what might have been. Callers came to welcome her back to Yorkshire, and that, too, was a distraction, and although they wanted to talk about Mr Lomax, they skirted delicately around the subject. Or most of them did. Not all were so considerate.

"Do tell us all about Mr Lomax. Was he very handsome? And rich! His own estate, Winnie — how wonderful for you. When do you expect him here?"

Mama fluttered in alarm, but Winnie answered calmly. "He was certainly handsome, and he dressed well, like a man of fashion, but I have no expectation of seeing him again," she said with perfect truthfulness. "I doubt I shall go back to London, I am most unlikely ever to go to Oxfordshire and he is not likely to travel to Yorkshire."

"Not travel to Yorkshire? But how can that be? I thought he was on the brink of a proposal."

Her mother smoothly intervened and the subject was dropped, but after the visitors had departed, Mama said quietly to Winnie, "I was very proud of you today, my dear. Such questions would try the patience of a saint, heaven knows, but you answered very properly and without the least display of unbecoming sensibility, which is just as it should be. Lily, I hope you observed your sister's behaviour, and will take it as your model from now on."

"Winnie shows no sensibility because she feels none," Lily said, lifting her chin a little.

"Nonsense, child! Winnie feels her loss as deeply as anyone could do, and if you cannot see that, you do not understand your sister at all. Whatever she feels, however, she conceals from the world, as a lady should. Really, Lily, when you talk in such a wild manner, I cannot but think you are not yet ready to be out in society at all. Do try for a more refined and thoughtful attitude. You will find a suitable passage from the Holy Book, and memorise six verses to recite to your father before dinner. Something about duty or demure behaviour or about Mary, the dear mother of Our Lord, who is the shining example to all womankind. Run, now, and fetch the Bible. You may work on it while I tackle the last flower on my cushion cover. Winnie, you may return to the still room."

Obediently the sisters separated about their appointed tasks, Lily with a sullen expression, Winnie keeping her resentment well hidden. Yet she *did* resent it. Long years now stretched before her of subservience to her mama's orders. Have you made the damson jam, Winnie? Select a goose for the table, Winnie. Run down to the kitchen and see about the pies, Winnie. Not that gown, Winnie. Go and change into something less ancient. Oh, to be mistress of her own establishment, to make her own decisions for a change! She would have had Mr Lomax's wishes to take into account, but a doting husband would perhaps be less oppressive than her watchful mother.

She made no complaint. She had never complained, for a dutiful daughter did as she was bid, but she would have relished her freedom, if Mr Lomax had made his offer. It was not the man himself who haunted her. Occasionally fleeting memories passed through her mind of his pleasant smile, or the warmth of his gaze, but they held no charm for her. It was the life he might have given her that she grieved for — the house in Oxfordshire, with fourteen bedrooms and two thousand acres, as he had told her more than once. The servants who would have danced to her command. The children who would never now be born. Sometimes she imagined them running about, chasing each other across the south lawn, or hiding in the shrubbery. Perhaps one would fall over, and come crying to her for comfort, and she would lift him onto her lap and sing lullabies to soothe him.

That dream was quite gone now. And yet, that was not the sharpest grief. Buried deep within her, never to be spoken of, even to Mama, was the pain that kept her awake at night. As soon as Winnie lay down in her bed and blew out the candle, her darkest thoughts emerged from the deep shadows where they had hidden, and danced around her wakeful mind gleefully.

Walter. It was always Walter who filled her mind and caused her public composure to crumble so alarmingly. Walter who had so casually destroyed her chance of marriage. Walter who had been so oblivious of her feelings. Walter who had believed such terrible things of her. Yes, all of that was bad, but it was not the worst... it was far from the worst.

The real grief, the pain like a knife in her heart, was that Walter had offered for her. Walter, whom she had loved passionately and devotedly for ten long years, had proposed to her. Ungraciously, casually but without hesitation — *'If it is a husband you want, then I will marry you.'*

And she had turned him down.

If she had hesitated just for a second... if she had not been so *angry* with him... if only, if only... perhaps she might now be betrothed to him. And perhaps, finding himself betrothed, he would have accepted it, just as he had accepted the inevitability of his betrothal to Bea Franklyn. Honour would have held him to his word.

How different her world would have been! She would have stepped through the days in joyous anticipation of the halcyon time to come. He had no great house or estate, but what did that matter? They would live on love and smiles and long walks hand in hand.

Instead she had nothing, not the man she loved nor the man with the great house, nothing but a lifetime of dancing to her mother's tune, and periodically being summoned by one or other of her sisters to help with their growing families. Winnie was not one to fall into despair, but in the wakeful hours of the night she came close to it.

Each morning, however, she rose at her usual hour and read a little from the Bible, which comforted her. Then she donned a plain gown and cloak, and her comfortable half-boots, and set off into the garden. She walked briskly, because that felt as if she were accomplishing something, instead of merely dawdling away an hour before breakfast. She marched, therefore, through her mother's neat flower garden, skirted the lily pool, and took the path between the walled garden and the orchard. Then she was into the woods, and she could wander at will, unseen, unnoticed, like the little mouse that Walter called her. With her old brown cloak, and brown hair uncovered by any bonnet, which was how he had so often seen her, she supposed she looked a little like a mouse.

On the first days after her return, she had avoided the tree house, terrified that Walter would be there. She had appreciated his forbearance in travelling in the other carriage and then staying with his father for a while, for she was not at all sure she was ready to face him yet. But there came a day, however, when she was so lost in her thoughts that her feet carried her to the tree house all by themselves, and she jumped in shock when she rounded the corner and saw Walter sitting on the swing.

She stopped, irresolute. He sprang to his feet, twisting his hat in his hands, with such a look on his face! Such abject despair. Her heart turned over at the sight, but she could not talk to him, not here, not in the very place where they had confided in each other over the years. It was too intimate. In a drawing room with other people — yes, she could maintain her composure in his company then, but not here, certainly not here.

She turned away.

"Ah, Winnie, no! I shall leave... I would not for the world... this is *your* place, and I will not intrude."

Slowly, she turned back. Now his face was alight with... something. Something she could not name. He reached out a hand imploringly, then let it fall again.

"Winnie," he said in a low voice, "I do not expect your forgiveness. I cannot forgive myself! But I hope one day, if I try very hard, to restore your good opinion of me far enough that we might be friends again, as we once were. I... I cannot bear to lose your friendship. It means all the world to me. But for now, I shall leave you. Good day, Winnie."

He bowed to her formally, then turned on his heel and strode away, hidden by the trees in moments.

Winnie stood frozen. That formal bow… not cold, not impersonal but showing her how much he respected her… it twisted her inside as nothing else had done. How could she *not* forgive him when he was in such despair? *'Your friendship means all the world to me'*, he had said.

"As yours means to me," she whispered to the trees, and they soughed softly in a consoling chorus.

Friendship… yes, she would accept that, if it were all he offered. But on one point she was grimly certain — if ever Walter should ask her to marry him again, however casually it might be, she would accept instantly. She would not waste a second such opportunity.

If it should ever come.

***

Walter returned to Birchall House the following morning, but Winnie knew nothing of it until Lily bounced into the housekeeper's room, where Winnie was discussing the dinner menu with Mrs Penfold.

"Have you heard? Walter is back."

Winnie dropped the pencil she was holding, and it rolled noisily across the wooden table and clattered to the floor. "Is he?"

"Not to worry, Miss Winnie," Mrs Penfold said, as she bent to retrieve the pencil. "His room is ready for him, just as he likes it."

"Well, he may not be staying," Lily said. "He has no boxes, and he has been stuck in the book room with Papa for an hour, at least."

That was strange! Winnie could not decide whether it was good news or bad. Good that he came at all, but bad that he only saw Papa and brought no boxes. That quick glimpse of him at the tree house was like a single spoonful of damson pie, not nearly enough. Having spent several days being terrified of seeing him again, now she longed for a sight of him, however fleeting. She had not realised until that moment just how much she had depended on his return to Birchall. But he might not. He might decide that working with Uncle Alfred was not what he wanted to do with his life, and then she would be reduced to only seeing him now and then, at an evening party, perhaps, or at church.

Pushing such dispiriting thoughts to the back of her mind, she finished her business with Mrs Penfold and went back upstairs, meeting Maynard on the way down.

"Ah, there you are, Miss Winnie. Your father wishes to speak to you in his book room."

"At once?"

"As soon as convenient."

Winnie's insides churned alarmingly. Walter here but not staying, only seeing Papa! And now she was sent for! What else could it be? He had offered for her, and properly this time... what else could it mean? Oh, please, please, please, let it be so!

All the way up the stairs, her stomach roiled about and her legs were as shaky as jelly. Maynard preceded her, knocked on the door and then announced her.

"Ah, Winnie! Come in, my dear."

He was alone. But that did not necessarily mean anything. Perhaps Walter was waiting in another room. Or had left and would return later, and this interview was merely to warn her what was to come. She did not quite trust her voice, so she said nothing.

"You will be aware, I expect, that I have had Walter here this morning. He came like the honourable man he is to make a full confession of his part in the retreat of your gentleman from London. I knew the whole story, of course... or almost all, from your uncle, but Walter held nothing back. He is in the utmost despair, and not the least part of it is that he knows he has lost your good opinion. He values your friendship very highly, and he is aware that he has now forfeited it. However, he wishes now to do what is right."

Winnie's heart lurched violently. This was it, the moment she had waited for...

"He would like to return here to continue his tuition under your uncle, but not if that would distress you, my dear. He has behaved very thoughtlessly in his dealings with Lomax, but this shows a pleasing consideration for your feelings. I wonder if he is finally growing up a little." He chuckled genially. "What do you say, Winnie? Will his presence here distress you? What shall I tell him?"

Winnie's disappointment was so acute that for a moment she could neither speak nor breathe. Were all men so blind as this? Walter had never seen what lay in her heart, but that her father should be just as oblivious was a little surprising. How could they not know the emotions which gripped her so fiercely? She turned away and walked to the window to give herself time to compose her disordered mind.

"Winnie?" her father said, suddenly uncertain. "This troubles you?"

With a supreme effort of will, she composed her features and turned to face him. "No, not at all. Let him return here, if he will."

"You do not object to his presence here?"

"By no means." And that was the truest word she had spoken. If she could not marry him, and perhaps could not even be his friend, at least she could see him, be under the same roof and breathe the same air as him. If that was all that was allowed her, then she would take it, and cherish it.

The interview being over, she went quietly to her room and wept in solitude for half an hour. That was all the time she allowed herself to grieve. Then she washed her face, tidied her hair a little, and went down to the still room to continue her morning chores.

***

The note from Sir Hubert was brief — *'You may return here whenever you choose.'* Walter breathed a sigh of relief. Winnie had, if not forgiven him, at least permitted him to resume his attempt to scratch out a career for himself. It was something, at least. He ordered his boxes packed and returned to Birchall House late in the afternoon, just in time to change for dinner, for the Strongs dined early.

Winnie was already in the drawing room when he entered, but there was no opportunity to speak to her, for Lady Strong descended upon him and engaged him in conversation as if nothing had ever happened to disrupt the smooth flow of good relations between his family and hers. As if he had not destroyed her daughter's hopes of a good marriage by his stupid, *stupid* arrogance. He could not decide whether her behaviour arose from ladylike good manners, or whether perhaps she was not even aware of all that he had done.

He was still undecided when the arrival of the Cathcart family was announced, followed almost immediately by the rector, Mr Dewar, and his family, and he was drawn into the business of being a good guest and making conversation, with no more than an occasional glimpse of Winnie moving about the room. She seemed pale tonight, and perhaps a little distracted, but no doubt that was due to his unwelcome presence. He wished he could speak to her, to thank her for her forbearance, but then it occurred to him that any attention from him might distress her, so perhaps he would be best advised to keep her at a distance. It was so hard, when he had been used to be on such easy terms with her! Now he hardly knew how to approach her.

For one reason or another, he had not seen any of the Cathcart or Dewar families since the discovery that he was no longer the heir, and discovered that he was now a person of the greatest interest to the young ladies. The older members of the two families were more interested in Winnie and her visit to London, but Miss Cathcart and the three Miss Dewars clustered about him, handkerchiefs at the ready to hear the whole of the affecting story.

Their breathy gasps and murmurings of *'How terrible for you!'* grew tedious in very short order. It was hard for him to see the horror in his situation that they clearly expected him to feel. It was a shock, of course, to find himself suddenly cut off from all that he had expected, but at the same time, it was curiously freeing. Until now, his whole life had been planned out for him — his school, his college at Oxford, his membership of White's, his introduction into society all mapped out from the moment of his birth. He would marry suitably, produce the requisite heir, and in time assume the mantle of Earl of Rennington and all the responsibilities that entailed. He would take his seat in the House of Lords and vote Tory, just as his father did and his grandfather before him. His suitable wife would raise the next heir to follow in his footsteps. And because he was a dutiful son, he would have done it precisely thus. Or perhaps it was inertia that had held him fast.

But now — he was free! He could make his own life, marry where he chose, live where he wanted. His father was generous enough to support him while he found his way, but in time he would be independent, not beholden to anyone... not constrained by tradition or his father's wishes. So as he explained it all to his intent audience, he could see bewilderment on their faces. *'So brave!'*, one of them murmured, patting his arm gently. He hardly knew what to make of it, but as they clustered around him, a dreadful fear grew in him that he now featured in their matrimonial ambitions. Viscount Birtwell, the heir to an earldom and vast wealth, was far out of their reach, to be treated only with the deepest respect, but the illegitimate Mr Atherton had been sufficiently reduced in rank to be attainable, in their eyes.

It was horrifying. Having only just been released from one ill-fitting betrothal, he was by no means inclined to rush into another. He had passed many seasons in London and not been drawn to any of the daughters of the aristocracy, so he was hardly likely to take up with a provincial miss. But instantly the image of Winnie flashed into his mind. She was one provincial miss it would not be a penance to wed. It had almost happened, five... no, six years ago! Astonishing thought. And he had impulsively offered her marriage just a few days ago, although—

'I would not marry you if you were the last man on earth!' she had screamed at him.

Her rejection was as painful as if she had stabbed him through the heart. Such pain! Why did it hurt so much? Perhaps Aunt Alice was right. Perhaps he was in love with her... dear, dear Winnie. Whom he could not even go near any more, for fear of distressing her. It was unbearable.

Fortunately, dinner was not as late as usual, and Walter was relieved to be summoned to sit beside Lady Strong, who directed the inoffensive Miss Parish to take the seat alongside him. She was some sort of cousin to the Cathcarts, and had come to live with them three months ago after her father died. Walter had never managed to get more than three words in succession out of her, and had no expectation of exceeding that number on the present occasion, but a silent dinner companion was better company than one who wanted to flirt inexpertly through two full courses.

Not that he minded flirtation, in the general run of events. A slow evening could be immeasurably enlivened by a little delicate badinage, preferably witty. Just at the moment, however, it was the last thing he wanted. He could not see Winnie at all, for the table was fully extended and she was at the far end of it, but he was content to know she was there. Better not to see her, in fact, for her pale face and those huge eyes were a constant reproach. But he would do better... he *would* be worthy of her, on that point he was determined.

So he applied himself diligently to being a good dinner guest, asking Lady Strong about her married daughters and receiving a great deal of unwanted detail about the progress of their present delicate conditions, although all couched in roundabout terms. Lady Strong was far too polite ever to mention such indecorous terms as *'baby', 'pregnancy' or 'confinement'* to a gentleman, so it was a testament to her conversational skills that she could talk at such length on the subject.

Nor did Walter neglect Miss Parish, finding her more than willing to talk about her recently deceased father, her long dead mother, and the older brother tragically killed at sea. But he was able to express the usual platitudes appropriate to a man who had served his country admirably by joining the Royal Navy, and although she was too downcast to enjoy the fish, by the time it had been removed with a loin of beef, she had cheered up enough to eat a tolerably hearty meal.

Afterwards, Walter listened to the ladies' musical performance, and applauded with enthusiasm, although only Miss Parish on the pianoforte and Lily on the harp showed any aptitude. After that, he willingly joined a group playing whist, until the ladies withdrew, and shortly after that he himself went upstairs.

"A good evening, sir?" Rashleigh said, helping him out of his coat.

"Very pleasant," Walter said, in surprised tones. It *had* been pleasant, in fact, despite not exchanging a single word with Winnie. But she had been close by, she had sung very prettily after dinner, and he had heard her laughing once or twice at the large table where most of the young ones were engaged in a round game. So that was a relief.

Tomorrow, he would begin work again with Mr Alfred Strong, and there would be breakfast with Winnie and another whole evening for him to show her that he was a reformed character. He was no longer the arrogant, selfish, inconsiderate lout she thought him. He was humble and considerate and willing to please, and sooner or later she would notice and approve.

And perhaps, one day, far in the future, he might have sufficiently redeemed himself that she might look on him with favour. Dared he aspire to her hand? That might be too ambitious, but he could hope, surely. There was always hope.

25: An Imperfect Man

Captain Michael Edgerton had a great deal of experience in interviewing those he suspected might be able to help him investigate a crime. Some were enthusiastic, spilling every detail of their lives, and the lives of their friends, relations and casual acquaintances. Some were taciturn or sullen or argumentative or resentful. Generally, they were co-operative, and the higher up the social scale, the more likely to put a good face on it. But never before had he come across a noblewoman who simply barricaded herself in her boudoir and refused to speak to him at all. Whenever he asked, he received a swift response by way of the maid — the Lady Alice sends her regrets but is unable to oblige Captain Edgerton with another interview. Once was quite enough.

After several days, Michael went to the earl. "Can you not persuade her, my lord? I cannot move forward without speaking to her again."

The earl heaved a sigh, a hunted look in his eyes. "The poor woman is grieving for her husband, Edgerton. Surely—"

"She has had almost two months to grieve in seclusion," Michael said. "I need to talk to her."

"But you cannot surely suspect her of—"

"I suspect everyone, and *especially* the one person discovered standing beside the body, axe in hand, covered in blood," Michael said sharply. "Whoever killed Nicholson would be coated in blood, but I have asked every single person in this castle if they saw any bloodstained garment, or any remains of one burned, or any item of clothing missing, and no one reports a single such case — except for one. I need to talk to her, my lord."

"You have already talked to her at some length."

"I have new information. There is the fact that the Lady Alice's perfect husband sired an illegitimate son, and was having her jewellery copied, which is something that a lady might justifiably resent."

"You cannot seriously suggest— Oh, this is ridiculous, Edgerton! Leave Alice alone. The answer lies outside this castle, we can be certain of that."

"Can we? I wish I had your confidence, my lord. Very well, you leave me no choice but to ask the magistrate to arrest Lady Alice and take her to York gaol."

"Arrest her! *Arrest the sister of an earl?* You exceed your authority, Edgerton. Besides, Strong will not act without my approval. My views do carry some weight in the county, you know. Neither you nor anyone else can gainsay a peer of the realm."

"I believe Strong will do what is right, my lord, but if you choose to wave the flag of your rank at me, then I shall summon the Marquess of Carrbridge to my cause, and then we shall see who can gainsay whom."

For a long moment, the two men glared at each other, the earl with all the hauteur of nobility, and Michael with what he liked to think of as steadfastness, but was probably pure obstinacy. How he hated to be denied! And yet how could he possibly do the job for which he was engaged without the support of everyone involved? If this went against him, he would be forced to withdraw from the investigation, if the earl did not throw him out on his ear first. He might even be the one to end up in gaol! Was Strong truly in the earl's pocket? He had wagered on it not being so, but now he was driven to doubt.

Abruptly, the earl broke into laughter. "You are a very determined man, Captain Edgerton. You must have terrified the restless natives in India. Do you truly know Carrbridge?"

"I have that honour, my lord. I have been of service to him and his family on more than one occasion. I believe he would come if I asked it of him."

"We shall not put him to the trouble. What time will be convenient for you to see Alice?"

"The lady may set her own time, today or tomorrow, so long as she comes."

Within the hour, Lord Rennington had brought his sister, pale but composed, to the old nursery, seated her on a chair and then pulled forward a chair for himself.

"No, Charles, you may leave me," Lady Alice said.

"I have no intention of leaving you alone with this man. He may have his interview with you, but I will not allow him to browbeat you."

"Go. Tell Malling to wait outside for me, for such time as the captain has run out of questions." Her well-modulated voice was low, not raised in the slightest, but he accepted his dismissal with a grunt and a curt nod.

When the door had closed behind him, Michael said, "We are quite alone, my lady. May I offer you any wine or—?"

"I want nothing. Are you going to browbeat me?"

"Only if I am obliged to, my lady."

Not a flicker of reaction crossed her face. "Why are you questioning me again, Captain?"

"Why are you so reluctant to talk to me?" he said in mild tones. "An innocent woman would surely wish to do everything possible to help catch her husband's killer."

That brought a reaction! Her bosom heaved as she said icily, "You are insolent, sir! How dare you accuse me!"

"I accuse no one, merely I wonder at your attitude, Lady Alice. Your husband was brutally murdered, and no one knows why. That means that the killer may strike again, and next time it might be you, or your brother, or your daughter. I very much want to prevent that. Will you not help me?"

"I know nothing that can help."

"You cannot be sure of that, and since our last conversation, new information has come to light. Were you aware, for instance, that your husband had fathered a child on a local girl?"

There was a long silence, as the colour on her cheeks flared up and then paled again. Her breathing was rapid at first, but then she brought herself under control.

"I find that... unlikely."

"What makes you say that?"

"My husband was faithful to me. He was a clergyman, a man of God who took the tenets of Christianity seriously. He would never commit adultery."

"You oblige me to point out, my lady, that Mr Nicholson was not a clergyman at all. His life here was a lie. Is it not possible that there were other lies?"

"No!" she said, with some force. "The ordination... perhaps there was a misunderstanding there, for I am sure he did not mean to cause such trouble for Charles, but in every other respect, Arthur was a man of the most upright principles. He was a good man, Captain Edgerton, and did not deserve to die in such a horrible way."

"No one deserves to die that way," Michael said quietly. "Lady Alice, were you aware that your husband had been systematically replacing your jewellery with paste copies, and keeping the value of them himself?"

She actually laughed at that. "Paste copies? What nonsense!"

"It is not nonsense. I have had two separate jewellers, one from Helmsley and one from Pickering, examine all the jewels in your husband's safe, and they have identified eight pieces or sets which have been replaced. I have not yet located the proceeds, however. The amounts of money raised were substantial, yet there is no money to that value deposited in the bank, nor does it remain in your husband's room, and believe me, we have searched very thoroughly, even removing the floorboards and looking up the chimney."

There was a long silence. Lady Alice sat, ramrod straight on her chair, her sightless eyes fixed on a point somewhere to the left of Michael's face. Only her breathing, slightly faster than usual, betrayed her agitation.

"I always knew he was not perfect," she said eventually, with a sigh. "He told me as much before we married — confessed all his sins, if you like. He spoke of women, a little creativity at the card table, pocketing coins left lying unattended... that sort of thing. I was not exactly perfect myself, so I understood. But when we married, he told me repeatedly that I had made him a better person, that he was a reformed character, and I believed him. Well, I would not be the first wife to be fooled by a plausible rogue, would I?
"

"It is very common, unfortunately," Michael said sympathetically.

"But this!" she cried. "The child… I confess, I suspected something. Having no sight, I am unusually alert to the other senses, and sometimes I thought… sometimes there was a hint of female perfume about him. I chose not to think about that. Well, men will be men, and sometimes they cannot help themselves. I told you of our arrangement after Tess was born, so it does not surprise me to learn that Arthur was unable to restrain himself. Celibacy is not a natural state. But my jewellery — that is a very different ma tter."

"It is theft, and a capital offence, if it had been discovered and you had chosen to pursue the matter."

"Which I never would, of course. He must have known that." She paused, then said slowly, "How much? How much money did he raise from selling my jewels?"

"In all, eight thousand pounds."

She fell silent again, and Michael said nothing, allowing her to come to terms with this discovery in her own way.

At length, she sighed again. "He has a house… in Pickering," she said in a low voice. "Perhaps the money is there?"

"It is leased to a Mrs Mayberry, a widow, who has been in residence for some fifteen years now. She says that Mr Nicholson has never been there. Her dealings are all with the attorney."

"Perhaps he has an account with another bank?"

"We have only found two, one in York where the bulk of his fortune is kept and a smaller account with an attorney in Helmsley, which he used for small expenses — paying his tailor and so forth."

"How large is this fortune?" she said, frowning. "His will said that Tess was to have the residue of his *fortune*, but it seemed an odd word to use. I had never suspected he had a fortune tucked away."

"After your jointure is accounted for, and the small bequests, it amounts to almost ten thousand pounds, accumulated slowly in small amounts over the years."

"That is... not a vast deal of money," she said thoughtfully. "A modest dowry for Tess, but not a fortune. I suppose he saved a little from his stipend as chaplain and his winnings at the card table. Over thirty years, it might add up to that amount."

"It might," Michael said. "But it does not include the eight thousand pounds."

Again she lapsed into silence.

When it seemed that she would not speak again, Michael said gently, "Do you see in what a quandary this places me, Lady Alice? If you had discovered that your husband was systematically stealing from you, might you not have wanted to kill him?"

"But I did not know about this!"

"So you say, but—"

"Do not *dare* to call me a liar, sir!" she cried, quivering with indignation. "*I did not kill my husband!* I knew nothing of the jewellery, nothing of the child, nothing of this axe that the murderer used. How do you think I could possibly get hold of an axe I did not even know existed?"

"Do you want my honest answer, my lady? I think you are an extremely resourceful woman, who can do far more than most people imagine. It would be very easy for you to sit quietly in a corner, listening. No one needs to tell you anything, you would just overhear it. You know every inch of this castle, but only you can creep around at night without needing a light. Only you could enter your husband's bedroom unobserved. Anyone could have wielded that axe, even a woman, but only you could murder your husband and then say, with perfect plausibility while covered in his blood, that you discovered him already dead. And only you have a reason to hate him, for stealing your precious jewellery." He hesitated, but he had gone too far now to withdraw. "And I have to say, my lady, you are by far too calm for a new w idow."

As he spoke, he saw her gradually crumple, her hauteur melting away. "Too calm?" she whispered. "Do I seem calm to you? Oh, if you could only see the agony in my mind! My husband was not perfect... was very far from perfect, but I never saw that side of him. To me he was everything that was good and kind and devoted, and I loved him... I *adored* him with every fibre of my being." She paused, with a little sob, tears coursing down her cheeks. "He was my sun and moon and stars... my entire world. My life was immeasurably brighter when he came into it, and now... now I am condemned to live in darkness for ever."

For a moment, her tears overwhelmed her, and she rummaged in her sleeve for a handkerchief, her whole body shaking as she wept piteously. Abruptly, her head lifted.

"What am I to do without him?" she cried. "I cannot live... cannot *exist* without my darling Arthur! Oh God, what is to become of me? I almost wish..." She heaved a breath, then said more moderately. "I should not say this, for it is wicked, but almost I wish you would send me to the Assizes for this crime, for then I would hang and I would be with my beloved Arthur all the sooner. But I do not believe you truly think I killed him."

Michael knelt at her feet, pushing his own larger handkerchief into her hands, and speaking with the utmost gentleness. "I do not believe it, no. But if not you, then who was it? Who hated him enough to kill him?"

"No one *hated* him. He had no enemies that I know of, but you have already demonstrated that there was much about him that I did not know."

"Then who disliked him? Who quarrelled with him? Who did *he* dislike?"

She mopped her eyes with his handkerchief, and took another long breath. "Quarrels... there have been quarrels. He and Tess fell out last year, but I hope you are not suggesting that his own daughter killed him."

"What was the quarrel about?"

"A man... not surprisingly, given her age. Girls of nineteen can be very foolish. Tom Shapman, a woodworker in Birchall village. Entirely unsuitable, and Arthur put a stop to it at once, which Tess was not at all happy about. Who else was there... let me see... Lord Farramont never got on with Arthur, but then Farramont is a dull, humourless man, so they had nothing in common. Kent... they did not exactly quarrel, for Kent never quarrels with anyone, but Arthur had some concerns over him, all the same. Charles and Caroline... no, they never quarrelled with Arthur, not even the mildest disagreement, but they were never close to him, either, which was odd when he was their brother-in-law, and much the same age. Arthur was closer to my father, in fact. They were such good friends, you cannot imagine. But when he died... Charles and Arthur were never close."

She lapsed into thoughtful silence, and after a while Michael thought it necessary to say, "Anyone else? Mr Walter or Mr Eustace? Any of the girls?"

"No... well, Izzy, but Izzy quarrels with everyone, and especially with her husband. Poor Farramont! A merry dance she leads him! Olivia took Tess's part in the business over the woodworker, but they are as close as sisters. Walter... Walter truly loved Arthur, I think. Eustace is a strange boy. He has had his differences with Arthur, but since he came into his little inheritance and moved out of the castle, they have not fallen out at all. As for the servants, I never heard of any quarrel. Arthur was always a considerate employer, not demanding or difficult. His valet had been with him for more than twenty years, so he must have been contented in his employment. Is this what you want, Captain? These trivial disagreements that occur in every family? None of these are cause for murder, I should imag ine."

"No, but it gives me a reason to ask questions... to poke and prod at people until they tell me something interesting."

"Ah. That is exactly what you have been doing to me, is it not? Poking and prodding."

He chuckled. "And just see how much you have given me to think about. Now I have lots of interesting little threads to tug on, and see what emerges."

"Is it enough?"

"It is a start. Each little thread unravels something else, and so it goes on until the big secrets come out. Sooner or later I will find out who killed your husband, Lady Alice."

Finally, Michael had material to work with, enough to keep him busy for months. But still at the back of his mind was a nagging doubt — could Lady Alice have murdered her husband? He did not want to believe it... he did *not* believe it, not in his heart, but it remained a possibility, and until he could be sure of her innocence, sure beyond all doubt, he could not quite leave the idea behind.

Yet no matter how he tried, he could see no way to prove it.

***

Michael's first task was to talk to Tom Shapman, the unassuming man who had mended the scullery window and changed the locks, and had failed to mention that he had wanted to marry Tess Nicholson. Tess herself was out of Michael's reach, but he remembered her anger about the will which had left her a fortune, but only if she married a gentleman. Now he saw the reason for that anger.

Shapman was often out and about, but at the third attempt Michael found him at home, at a small workshop just off the main road through Birchall. It was a small place, with a tiny kitchen and a store room at the back, and stairs to a room above, but adequate for a single man.

"Good day to you, Mr Shapman. A neat little place you have here. Do you sleep upstairs?"

"Aye."

"And cook here?"

"Nay. I eat at Ma and Pa's."

"Have you a few minutes to talk to me?"

"If you don't mind me working while we talk," Shapman said. "D'you need some more locks changed?"

"No. I wanted to talk about you and Miss Nicholson."

Shapman looked up from planing a length of wood with a wry smile. "Ha! Nothing came of that."

"So you simply gave up the idea, is that it? Or did the two of you resent Mr Nicholson for interfering?"

"Tess did," he said, bending his head to his work again. "I always knew it was a wild idea, but you know what she's like."

Michael pulled forward a wooden stool and sat down. "Tell me what she is like."

"Like all rich girls, she wants what she wants and she wants it now."

"And what would she do to get what she wants?"

He looked up again. "Are you trying to trick me with words? Not kill her own father, that's for sure."

"But maybe you would, to get yourself a rich wife, eh?"

Shapman straightened himself and stared at Michael. "Me? Ha! No. Look, Tess was the one who had the idea we could wed, not me. Her father said no, and that was it, as far as I'm concerned. Never blamed him, never wanted to do anything about it. Wished she'd let it go, frankly. I'm content here, making my doors. Don't want no rich wife, and certainly not one as slippery as Tess."

"Is she slippery enough to plan a murder?"

"No. She's always up to some scheme or other, but she'd not kill anyone and that's a fact."

"Do you know where she is?"

"Aye. She writes to me."

"And do you write back to her?"

"Sometimes."

"Well, next time you write, Mr Shapman, tell her that I want her to come back here and talk to me. And if she is not minded to do that, I shall take it as a sign of guilt and put out the word to have her arrested. Understand?"

He nodded, but his eyes were wide. Michael left in a slightly better mood than he had arrived.

26: A Family Visit

The day after Walter's return to Birchall House, Winnie's sister Hebe came for a visit, together with her meek husband William Plaister, and their baby, Prudence. Theirs was a love match, and it always delighted Winnie to see the little glances they exchanged, the intimate smiles over the top of the baby's head and the way they would accidentally touch hands now and then, as if they could not bear to be disconnected. How she envied them their closeness. If only she could aspire to such a marriage!

It was astonishing just how much disruption one small child, barely able to walk, could cause, considering that at one time there had been six children in the Birchall House nursery, yet creating one tenth of the noise and general disorder that now prevailed. Prudence, it seemed, was a wailing sort of baby, and so there was a constant flurry of nursemaids and anxious relations up and down the stairs at all hours of the day and night.

After an exhausting day spent repeating news already told by letter, admiring Prudence's most effective lungs, and being wept over by Hebe, Winnie was then woken several times during the night. Eventually, realising that more sleep was impossible, she donned a comfortable old gown and shawl, and set off for her morning walk.

She found Hebe before her, loitering expectantly by the garden door.

"I knew you would be up early," Hebe said, tucking one arm into Winnie's. "Now we can have a comfortable coze, sister, and you can tell me all the little details of London that were left out of your letters, for one can never write everything, can one? But I am pleased to see you still have some of your old gowns. That one must have been tolerably flattering when you were twelve. I could scarce believe my eyes when I saw you yesterday — I almost turned to Mama and said, *'Who is that fashionable stranger in our midst?'* Truly, I hardly recognised you, sister. When you wrote that Aunt Sofia had rigged you out in prime style, I thought perhaps it was your little joke, for she was always used to be a dowdy creature, worse even than you."

"She is not dowdy any longer, I assure you," Winnie said, as they left the house and set off into the gardens. "We did so much shopping, I cannot tell you the half of it! But her dressmaker was very glad of the business at this time of year, and made everything in no time at all."

"But I suppose you do not care much," Hebe said, laughing. "You never agonised over wearing last year's gown as I did, or Mabel."

"No, it does not trouble me. Gowns can always be reworked, and I feel more at ease in company in a familiar old gown."

"You were very quiet last night, but whether that was that very fetching gown or some other reason must be all conjecture," Hebe said, with an arch glance at Winnie. When no answer was forthcoming, she went on, "Now, Walter was surprisingly good company. He never used to make much effort to please, but he was very agreeably disposed, I thought. I had imagined he would be in the most enormous sulk, but no one would have guessed by his manner that anything untoward had occurred."

"He is a gentleman, and gentlemen do not fall into sulks," Winnie said, a touch of pride in her voice, for she had been greatly impressed by Walter's composure herself. He had avoided her, she noticed, and even though she would very much like to have talked to him on their former easy terms, she honoured him for his consideration for her feelings.

Hebe only laughed. "Really? Oh, you have a lot to learn, Winnie. But how are they going on at the castle? Izzy passed through like a whirlwind, by the sound of it. What a dance she leads that husband of hers! But what is the latest? Tell me everything."

For some time they talked of the Corland family and the great change in their circumstances, and Winnie told her of Bea Franklyn's new plan to persuade Bertram to marry her. They reached the tree house, and sat companionably side by side on the swings, Winnie moving with some vigour and Hebe, in deference to her delicate condition, merely rocking gently.

Eventually they reached the real purpose of the outing, as Winnie had known they would.

"Winnie, you are remarkably composed considering... well, recent events," Hebe said, with a nervous glance at her sister. "Mama has told us under no circumstances to mention the subject to you, and I shall say nothing more, only that I am very pleased that you are bearing up so nobly after the tragic defection of... of a Certain Person."

Her voice wobbled, and she fumbled for a handkerchief as a great tear rolled down one cheek.

"Oh, Hebe!" Winnie said, trying not to laugh. "It is hardly a tragedy. No one has died, after all, and I am no worse off than before."

"But the dashing of all your expectations! And to leave so abruptly, with not a word! Is it all irrevocably over, dearest, or do you still harbour any hope of a reconciliation?"

That was a question Winnie could not answer. Her realistic self told her that Mr Lomax had gone for good, and that it would be foolish to think otherwise, so she sensibly suppressed any thoughts that held the least optimism.

"I do not think about the matter at all," she said firmly.

This was not nearly romantic enough for Hebe, whose sensibilities demanded that Winnie weep copiously into her pillow every night. She would not have been surprised to find her sister entering a devastating, and perhaps even fatal, decline. She sighed in disappointment at her sister's pragmatic response.

"But why would he simply leave like that? That is what I cannot understand. To be on the point of making you an offer... to have declared his intentions to Uncle Alfred... and then... to vanish! Why would he do that?"

Winnie could not answer honestly without dragging Walter's name forward for Hebe to abuse, and she could not lie. She contented herself with saying uneasily, "Does a man need a reason? He thought of offering and then decided, upon reflection, that it was not what he wanted."

"Yes, but—"

"And think how quick it all was," she went on hastily. "Not even two weeks from the first meeting. One does not make so momentous a decision on so short an acquaintance. One *should* not, anyway. He thought better of it, that is all."

"You are more forbearing than I should be," Hebe said, still weeping slightly. "Dear, dear Winnie! Such an angel! But you never described him in your letters, dearest. Was he so very handsome?"

Winnie tried and failed to recall Mr Lomax's face to her mind. How odd that he should have faded from memory so soon. Some aspects of him were very memorable, but not his face.

"I cannot say," she said cautiously. "His features were... pleasant, I should say. His manners were excellent, and he was a very stylish dresser, quite in the height of fashion. He wore those shiny boots with tassels, and his shirt points were up to here." She waved her hands vaguely about her cheeks. "Walter used to make fun of him, but I thought he looked very well. But then Walter has always been such a careless dresser. He and fashion are entirely unacquainted."

She stumbled to a halt. Why was she talking about Walter? She must be careful not to say too much.

"But was he tall? Dark or fair? What colour were his eyes?"

"Not above average height. His hair was a medium brown, and as for his eyes... I cannot tell you."

Now if it were Walter, she could talk all day about his imposing height, his broad shoulders, his not-quite-blond hair that fell across his forehead so boyishly. He had eyes the colour of the sky on a warm summer's day, and long, long lashes darker than his hair. His hands, too... he had lovely hands with long fingers, strong, masculine hands. His nose was perhaps a shade smaller than perfection demanded, but his chin was a charming shape and his lips— She shivered suddenly. This was not a sensible line of thought.

"Let us not talk about Mr Lomax," she said quickly, seeing Hebe ready to settle in for a long discussion. "Tell me instead about Prudence. Does she always scream so, or is it merely that she dislikes so much fuss? She was passed from hand to hand like a parcel yesterday."

"Oh, she will settle soon, I am sure," Hebe said easily. "The disruption, you know… being jounced about in the carriage, and then all the new faces… yes, I am sure she will settle very swiftly."

"Perhaps a quieter day with Aunt Winnie would suit her? I can try out my repertoire of lullabies."

"Oh, no, no, no! You must not… so distressing for you, when you have been denied the chance for babies of your own." Hebe's tears were threatening again. "Nurse knows how to deal with her. There is no need for you to have anything to do with her."

"No, indeed, I shall very much enjoy playing the rôle of aunt again. She was so tiny last time I saw her. There will be so much more we can do together now that she is more active. I can bring her out here and introduce her to the swings. She can sit on my lap and see how she likes the motion. It is a family tradition for the young ladies of the family to come here. You must not deny poor Prudence her birthright."

Hebe smiled through her tears. "So brave, dearest!" she whispered.

***

With visitors to be entertained, Lady Strong had devised a full program of amusements. Every day had its outing or some gathering at Birchall House, and every evening the covers were increased for dinner to the greatest extent the dining room would permit.

Winnie had little part to play in these events. Whenever the carriage was summoned for some expedition or other, Mama would say, "Shall you accompany us, Winnie?", but when she declined, nothing further was said.

Mama merely murmured, "Very well, dear," and patted her sympathetically on the shoulder. And if everyone supposed she was pining for Mr Lomax and not ready for much company, that suited her very well. She spent her days with little Prudence, or catching up on still room tasks, and occasionally she was called in to take notes for Uncle Alfred. This was a particular pleasure, since Walter was there.

She felt they were gradually regaining their former easy companionship. Indeed, it was impossible to live under the same roof as Walter, to meet him at breakfast and again each evening, and occasionally bumping into him on the stairs or at the stables, without lapsing back into friendship, for he was the most easy-going of men. Each time they met, he was a little less aloof, and when, eventually, he felt sufficiently unconstrained to flick her on one cheek and call her Mouse in the old way, she was thrilled.

Breakfast was the best time of the day, but evenings were pleasurable too, for at least she was in the same room as Walter. She was able to admire him from afar, for he was easily the best looking and most imposing of all the men present. And sometimes there was the great joy of sitting beside him at dinner, or at the card table later.

On one such occasion, Winnie was partnering Hebe's husband, William, at whist, and Walter was gamely trying to instil the basics of the game into Lily, albeit without much success.

As Winnie shuffled inexpertly, Walter said to William, "You live at Pickering, I understand, Mr Plaister. Is there much to do there at this time of year? It always seemed rather a dull place to me, nothing like so lively as Scarborough."

William smiled. "It is true that Scarborough is livelier, but Mrs Plaister and I do not much care for that sort of liveliness. Mrs Plaister has her music society and her sewing circle and her work for the church, and I have my philosophical society and my political society. Not that I am strongly political myself, but I like to know what is happening in London and the colonies."

It was so much of a piece with the characters of both that Winnie could hardly suppress her own smile. William was a meek, bespectacled man whose quiet ways exactly suited Hebe's timid nature. They would never set the world on fire, but they would live retired, contented lives together, attending their little societies and raising a brood of equally timid children. Winnie could never imagine herself in such a situation.

"Is that the same political society that Mr Nicholson attended?" Walter said.

"Oh, yes. He was a very well-known personage in Pickering on account of the political society, and his businesses."

"His *businesses?*" Walter said, his tone suddenly sharp. "A man of God, chaplain to the Earl of Rennington, owned businesses in Pickering?"

"Indeed. A chandlery and an ironmongery, that I know of. There was talk of a haberdashery, too, but that was not certain. They did not operate under his name, but it was widely known that he owned them."

"Well!" Walter said, leaning back in his chair. "That is a surprising turn. I wonder if Captain Edgerton is aware of this."

"Is it important?" William said. "A man may own a business or two without censure, I believe."

"Certainly, but still... it is interesting. And he owns a property there, I believe. A house, rented out to a respectable widow."

And for some odd reason, William blushed furiously, even the tips of his ears reddening, and murmured something inaudible.

Walter merely raised an eyebrow, but Winnie was instantly curious. "What is so strange about that, William?"

"Oh... nothing, nothing at all, sister. Indeed it is rented out to a widow."

"But not a respectable one?"

Walter laughed. "You should not ask, Mouse."

"Why not?" Lily said, suddenly alert. "What is the great secret?"

"Because it is a subject not fit for discussion in the presence of young ladies," William said primly.

"Pft!" Lily said in disgust. "Gentlemen are always saying that, or else it is Mama says I am too young to know this or that."

"And she is quite right," Winnie said quickly. "There are many subjects which are not fit for the ears of an unmarried woman, and a well-brought-up young lady does not enquire further. Are we to play another rubber, or shall we abandon play for tonight? I am sure the tea tray will be appearing at any moment."

Lily was quick to declare a wish to move on from cards, and William too jumped up and hastened to his wife's side, leaving Winnie momentarily alone with Walter. She could not resist. Leaning towards him, she whispered, "Whatever is the widow up to, do you suppose?"

"You *really* should not ask," he whispered back, his face alight with mischief. "A well-brought-up young lady—"

"Very amusing. But my curiosity is roused, and I shall imagine all manner of activities if you do not enlighten me. Is it something illegal?"

"Possibly, but judging by Plaister's embarrassment, it is more likely to be immoral." He hesitated, then said in a lower tone, "I suppose the widow entertains gentlemen. Alone. At night."

"That would be very bad," Winnie said thoughtfully. "I suppose she must be lonely, being a widow."

Walter smiled at her, and, reaching across the table, took her hand. "You put a kindly light on such behaviour — would you then forgive her for her sins?"

"Of course. God forgives all, and we should do the same. Nothing is unforgivable, Walter."

"Nothing?" His voice was barely audible.

"Nothing at all," she said firmly.

***

This conversation raised Walter's spirits so much that he was humming quietly as Rashleigh helped him undress that night.

"A pleasant evening, sir?" Rashleigh said, with a benevolent smile.

"Very pleasant indeed."

She would forgive him, in time. Perhaps she had already forgiven him, although that might be too much to hope for. But in the future, after a few weeks or months... surely not years? And whenever that time came, he would be waiting, ready to offer her his heart.

It was strange to think that he had known Winnie all his life and never thought of her as more than his good friend. There had been long spells, months sometimes, when he had not seen her at all, and had not even thought about her, except an odd fleeting memory now and then of something funny she had said, or an example of her intrepid nature, or a joke they had shared. Then, when they did meet, it was as if they had never been apart.

Yet now... thoughts of her filled every free corner of his mind. When he woke each day, she was the first thought in his head, and he could barely wait for breakfast to see her again. Then there might be precious moments during the day when they would meet, and eventually a whole evening together. Tonight he had even managed to share a card table with her, although his penance for that had been Lily as a partner. Not that Lily was unintelligent, but she was by far too interested in the conversations on other tables to attend to the game. Not like Winnie, who could hold a conversation while playing an excellent game, and yet always aware of others. She it was who had noticed that Mr Alfred's wine glass was empty and had waved to the footman to attend to it.

Winnie... dearest Winnie, who perhaps would be *his* Winnie one day, if he were very fortunate. Winnie with the glossy brown hair that never quite behaved as it should, for there was always a lock or two adrift from the pins. Winnie with the shining eyes, and the smooth cheeks... how he would love to touch those smooth cheeks, to feel their softness... to press his lips against them. How would she react if he did so? Would she laugh and tell him not to be silly? Or slap his face? If she were shocked... no, he could not bear to see that expression of hurt dismay on her face, not again. Nor her anger.

'I would not marry you if you were the last man on earth!'

But she did not mean it... did she? No, he would not allow himself to think it, for if his case were hopeless, how could he bear it? He had to believe he could win her one day, or he would go mad.

Such thoughts were not sensible. Today had been good, for he had enjoyed a delightful evening with her, and tomorrow might be even better. Each day brought him a little closer to the restoration of his former friendship with her, and perhaps to something more, but he must not allow his thoughts of Winnie to distract him from his other responsibilities. His work with Mr Alfred, for instance, which was proving unexpectedly enjoyable. If it were not for leaving Winnie behind, he could happily leave for London tomorrow to begin his new career. And then there was his own family... which reminded him of something.

He lit an extra candle, and sat down at the small writing desk in his room. Pulling out a sheet of paper, he began to write.

'To Captain Edgerton, Corland Castle, Corland. Captain, I have today discovered that Mr Nicholson owned two businesses in Pickering, a chandlery and an ironmongery. Possibly a haberdashery, also. In addition, the property which Nicholson owned, which is leased to a widow, may be in use as a house of ill repute. This may be of interest to you, if you are not already aware of it. Yours, Walter Atherton.'

***

One afternoon, Lady Strong had invited a number of the local ladies to enjoy what she described as a garden party. There was to be a picnic, an archery competition for the energetic and gentle strolls to admire the flowers, the new water garden and the statue of Pan recently commissioned from a York sculptor. By the middle of the afternoon, the heat having driven almost everyone to the shade of the terrace, a large pine tree or the pavilion erected for the occasion, tea was brought out, along with wine for those of a more robust constitution.

Winnie was engaged in walking backwards about the lawn holding Prudence's hands so that she might perfect her walking technique, but as often as not she would tumble over, and eventually, when Prudence decided that crawling was the better option after all, Winnie simply lay down and allowed the child to clamber all over her.

She noticed James emerge from the house with the small salver used to convey calling cards, which was not unusual, but when her mother read it and gave a little squeak, Winnie grew interested. Someone important, then. Lord Rennington, perhaps? Not Lady Rennington, for she was still away, and Lady Alice never made calls.

Her mother composed herself very quickly. She rose and came with unhurried steps, the card in her hand, across the lawn.

"Winnie, dear, come with me. Nurse! Take the baby, will you?"

At once Winnie rose, brushing herself down as best she could, and followed her mother into the drawing room. Before she could speak, her mother turned to her, her eyes afire, and whispered in dramatic tones, "Oh, Winnie! He has come!"

"Who has come, Mama?"

She thrust the card into Winnie's hand.

'Mr Rupert Lomax, Wallingham Manor, Oxfordshire and Charles Street, London'

"Mr Lomax," Winnie said, stupefied. "Well!"

27: A Magnificent Creature

Winnie was almost too agitated to speak. Mr Lomax here! Had he made enquiries, and realised that the story Walter had told him was untrue? Or had he perhaps decided that it did not matter after all? What did it mean? Was he going to propose after all?

Mama was excited, but also practical. "At least you have on one of your new gowns, so you look very well, as far as that goes, and there is no need for you to change. But your hair! Still, I may be able to fix it. Hold still a moment."

With deft fingers, she pulled and tucked and pushed, and shifted pins around until she was satisfied.

"There! You will do. He is in the book room with your father. Let us go and greet him, shall we?"

Winnie's nerves almost got the better of her as she followed her mother with shaking legs across the hall and into the book room. What would he be like? Would he smile or be stern? What would he say? Would it be awkward? How would—?

He looked exactly the same. As soon as she entered the room, he jumped to his feet, a beaming smile on his face, and crossed the room to grasp her hands.

"Miss Strong! How delightful to see you again, and looking just as charming as ever. I need not ask if you are well, for I can see that your native Yorkshire air agrees with you. How pleased I am to be here, in this most interesting of counties. You spoke of it so much and extolled its great beauties, so here I am to see it for myself."

He raised both her hands, and kissed them, one after the other, keeping hold of them afterwards. There was no denying his genuine pleasure, or the admiration in his eyes. He was just as ardent as he had been in London.

Behind her, her mother coughed gently.

"Oh... Mama, may I present to you Mr Lomax. This is my mother, sir."

Finally, he released Winnie's hands, and made his elegant bow to Mama. They all sat, and began the usual conversation for callers newly arrived after a journey — the roads, the difficulties of travel, the dust and heat and flies, the indifference of the inns, the pleasures of the scenery. He enquired after the health of Aunt Sofia and Uncle Edmund. Winnie enquired after his mother. Uncle Alfred and Walter arrived, summoned from their study to greet an old acquaintance, and began another round of the same remarks. The roads, the dust and heat and flies... Winnie supposed she answered rationally, but her thoughts churned in her mind so greatly that she could not be sure of it.

And now she had Walter to worry about, for his face was grave, and she recalled how he had mocked Mr Lomax and called him a coxcomb. He disliked the man, for some reason she could not quite understand, and although he would offer him no insult, his quietness disturbed her. She had thought they were growing closer again, but now his silence and stern expression was a return to the worst days after they had arrived from London, when she had feared they would never be on a friendly footing again.

Mama asked Mr Lomax if he would like to meet the other members of the family and the garden party guests. He professed himself willing, offered his arm to Winnie, and they progressed through the hall and the drawing room and thence to the terrace. To say that their arrival caused a sensation was something of an understatement. Mama took him triumphantly from group to group.

"This is Mr Lomax, who rescued Winnie from thieves in London. Mr Lomax, who became acquainted with Winnie in London. Winnie's friend, Mr Lomax of Wallingham Manor in Oxfordshire."

He bowed repeatedly, murmuring each name that was tossed at him, although he could not possibly remember even half of them. The matrons inclined their heads regally to him, the younger women rose to curtsy, Harris and Lionel shook his hand and everyone ogled him shamelessly. He seemed not to mind.

Winnie hardly knew where to look or how to behave as she followed him around. Although he was the centre of attention, for surely the North Riding had rarely seen such a stylishly dressed man, she was herself the focus of many a knowing glance as well, and she was most unused to such direct observation. She could see the speculation in their eyes as they looked at him, and then at her, and then again at him.

For fully half an hour, Mr Lomax made himself agreeable to the ladies, and when it looked as if he might leave, Mama said brightly, "Perhaps you would care to see some of the garden, Mr Lomax? The water garden is a refreshing sight in such heat. Winnie, why do not you show Mr Lomax about? I am sure he must be pleased by the rose wall."

Mr Lomax smiled and said that it sounded charming, offering his arm to Winnie with a little bow. Whatever came of this visit, it was pleasing to be the recipient of so much attentiveness from a man. Apart from Mr Seymour, no one had ever courted her before, and he had been so discreet that his offer took her entirely by surprise. So they walked about the gardens, while various others of the ladies walked about too, talking about the blooms and the charms of the water garden, but all the while watching Winnie with Mr Lomax.

After a while, when they had left the others a little distance behind, he said quietly, "You must have wondered greatly at our leaving London so abruptly last month, and without so much as a word of explanation, too."

Winnie hardly knew how to answer him, for she knew perfectly why he had left, but the lack of any note or letter of explanation was worthy of comment. "We were concerned for you and Mrs Lomax," she said. "We feared an accident, or a severe illness."

"Indeed there was an illness, but not in my mother or myself, I am happy to report. A cousin of ours, to whom my mother is greatly attached, almost a sister, suffered an apoplexy, and Mother was in such agitation that she must needs depart at once, instantly, with not a moment to lose. Naturally, I could not object, and we left in such great haste that there was not even time for me to write to let you know what had occurred. I told myself that I should write the instant I reached Oxfordshire, but then I remembered that you would already be on your way back to Yorkshire and would not receive the letter for some days. And there was the awkwardness of writing to you when I have no right to do so. You may imagine the quandary in which I found myself. And then, of course, I found the very idea of a letter became unnecessary, for I had the happy idea of coming myself to surprise you."

It was all a lie, a complete fabrication, and not even a very good one, and at first she was shocked. Then she was angry. Why did he think it necessary to deceive her? He could have created some vague excuse... urgent business at home, that was the usual way.

When she could command her voice, she said, "Your coming was certainly a surprise, sir."

"I hope a pleasant one?" he said, and for the first time there was a note of uncertainty in his voice.

"Indeed it is," she said, for whatever his excuses for abandoning her, or his reason for changing his mind, she was very glad to see him. No woman could be displeased by a man who travels two hundred and fifty miles to see her. "I hope she is much recovered?"

"I beg your pardon?"

"The cousin who suffered the apoplexy."

"Oh... oh, yes, well on the way to a full recovery, happily. It is often the way, is it not, that these events are not so bad as one fears when one first hears the news. This is a very pretty garden, Miss Strong. It is all Lady Strong's work, I understand?"

"She is never happier than when she is on her knees with her hands in the soil."

He stopped. "Shall we turn back now? It is too hot to spend too long in the sun, I feel, even with a parasol to shade you. I am so happy to be in your company again that I scarcely notice the time passing, but I do not wish to exhaust you."

She denied any exhaustion, but he was adamant, so they returned to the terrace. His carriage was ordered, he made punctilious farewells to the ladies, and even remembered many of the names. Winnie and her mother escorted him to the front door, trailed by Lily and Hebe, and even Papa emerged from the book room to see him off. An invitation to dinner that evening was issued and accepted, his carriage arrived, he kissed Winnie's hands again, and then he was gone.

"Winnie, a word in my book room, if you please," Papa said. "No, not you, Kitty, I want to talk to Winnie alone."

"Very well, Sir Hubert," Mama said with dignity. "Come along, Lily. Come along, Hebe. We have guests to attend to."

When Winnie followed her father into the book room, he poured two glasses of Madeira and sat her down opposite him on a chair beside the window, from which vantage point the dust cloud from Mr Lomax's carriage was still visible on the drive.

"Well, Winnie, so that is the famous Mr Lomax. I am disposed to like him, despite the excessive number of fobs he wears, since his attachment to you shows commendable good sense."

Winnie laughed, but said nothing, merely sipping her Madeira.

"He has not said anything formal to me, but I think we may assume that he has not come all this way merely to enquire after your health. It would certainly be a good match for you, if you choose to accept him. Four thousand a year, I understand from your uncle. However, you do not have to rush into a decision. You will want to be reassured of the strength of his attachment, I imagine, and for myself, I should like to know that there is more to him than the fashionable appearance."

"I believe you will like him when you get to know him better, Papa."

He smiled at her, setting down his own glass and steepling his hands. "I believe so, too. The reports I have had from your Uncle Alfred, and also from the Blackwoods, reassure me that his mind is well informed, and by no means as frivolous as his appearance. As you consider your future, there is something I think you should know. You are aware that Walter was the cause of Mr Lomax leaving London in such haste. When Walter realised that the rumours he had passed on were completely untrue, he wrote to Lomax to tell him so. It is for this reason, I believe, that Lomax has changed his mind and sought you out again."

"Walter wrote to him?" That was a surprise!

"He did. It was a very proper and honourable action, and I think the better of him for it. When he first returned here, his first action was to come to me and make a full confession of all that he had done. Most of it I knew, of course, but he withheld nothing, and expressed himself very well. He is very remorseful, Winnie, for he never meant you the least harm, and would be delighted to see you well settled. He has been very thoughtless, perhaps, but he has seen his mistake, and is determined to do better. He is working hard to learn under Alfred's tutelage, and I truly believe he will make something of himself yet. It may indeed prove that losing his inheritance is the best thing that could have happened to him, for it has made him address his own weaknesses and become a better man. Possibly his first reward for that improvement is to see you happily married to Lomax. If so, he will have earned our gratitude. Winnie, you are very quiet. You are pleased that Lomax has come, I take it?"

"I am, but... Papa, he lied to me! He told me some fanciful story about a cousin being taken ill, and that was why he left town so hastily, but it is not true! He left because of what Walter told him."

"Well, perhaps there was illness as well, and he chose to use that as an excuse."

"No, for he said it was an apoplexy and his mother was too agitated to stay and wanted to leave instantly, and there was no time even to write a note to tell us, and that cannot be true. There is always time for a brief note! Even if he did not wish to write anything, he could have said to the butler as they were leaving, *'Run round to Park Street and tell Mr and Mrs Blackwood that I have had to go out of town.'* He could have done that while he was putting on his gloves, for you are not going to tell me that he ran out of the house without his gloves on! He would never do so."

Her father laughed, but said, "Winnie, do but consider. He cannot possibly tell you the real reason, and he probably imagines you know nothing of that. So he tells a little lie to cover it."

"A lie is still a lie, Papa, large or small. One should always tell the truth, is that not what Mama says? One does not need to tell the entire truth, that is all. When a lady asks if one likes her hideous new gown, one says that it is a beautiful fabric or a striking colour or the sleeves are very pretty. One need not actually say that it is hideous. So Mr Lomax could have said, quite truthfully, that he had doubts as to the wisdom of the step he was about to take, and needed a period of reflection. He could have said that everything was moving too swiftly. He could even have said that he panicked. I would have respected him a great deal more if he had only been honest with me. Or said nothing about it at all. He did not need to explain himself to me, after all."

"No, but he needed to explain himself to your uncle, to whom he applied for permission to pay his addresses. When permission is granted, it is customary for those addresses to be paid. He had declared himself, even if only to your uncle, and therefore created the expectation. He must have known that you were awaiting his proposal of marriage, and that he was therefore giving you a severe disappointment. I should not have mentioned the matter myself, but since you have raised the subject, I do not think he has acted as a gentleman should. If he now intends to pay those addresses, then he will redeem himself somewhat in my eyes, but I can tell you now, that if he comes to me for my permission to speak to you, I shall ask him outright for an assurance that he will not run away this time."

"Oh, Papa! I am sure he has not come all this way just to turn tail and slink away again. He will make the offer, but in his own time, and without the pressure of time that weighed on us in London, when he knew we were about to leave. He felt rushed, I think, and when Walter said... those things to him, he panicked. He did not know what to do, so he did nothing. It is a momentous decision for a man to take."

"And for a woman also," her father said gently.

"I am *almost* certain that I will accept him," she said.

"Almost?"

"I am still not entirely confident of his character, but I am not minded to be harsh. I want to be married, Papa, and I shall never get another offer so good. He will have to do something quite unforgivable for me to refuse him now."

He nodded. "You are a sensible girl, Winnie. I can depend upon you to make a wise decision. And now, judging by the chatter in the hall, the guests are departing. Why do you not go and bid them farewell, eh? And if you have any concerns about this man, or wish to talk about anything at all, my door is always open to you." He picked up his glass again, and reached for his book.

"Thank you, Papa."

She curtsied and opened the door, where the noise of many conversations in competition with each other assaulted her ears. She was absorbed effortlessly into the throng, and for perhaps twenty minutes a succession of carriages drew up on the drive and were filled with cheerful ladies. Only when the final carriage had been waved away did Hebe and Lily grab an arm each, and drag Winnie, laughing, into the drawing room, where Mama firmly closed the door on the interested Maynard.

"Oh, Winnie!" they breathed, almost in unison.

"What a fine man!" Hebe said, sentimental tears filling her eyes.

"How lucky you are," Lily said, with a great sigh. "I wish I may find such a husband."

"She is indeed fortunate," Mama said, smiling benevolently. "Four thousand a year, and a fine estate, by all accounts. It is mentioned in all the guidebooks."

"He is so handsome," Lily said.

"So splendidly attired," Hebe said. "I never saw boots shine so much. But where were the tassels, Winnie? You said he wore boots with tassels."

"Hessians?" Lily said. "But that would be town wear. For the country he wears top boots and breeches like everyone else. It is in all the journals."

"Not at all like everyone else," Hebe said. "I never saw anyone so smart, even in York. His waistcoat — did you observe it? And the lapels of his coat! He must have the finest tailor in London."

"His manners were everything they should be, too," Mama said. "I rate good breeding far above coats and tassels on boots."

"He is magnificent," Lily said, in tones that brooked no argument. "You lucky, lucky creature, Winnie."

28: Distant Rumbles

Winnie's head was in a whirl. Her life had always been so placid, with nothing to ruffle the smooth surface of her days, and now everything was in turmoil. She had careered from one excess of emotion to another, with no respite. First the flare of hope in finding that Walter was freed from his betrothal to Bea Franklyn. Then the slow, dreary recognition that he still did not see Winnie as more than a friend. Then Mr Lomax and the prospect of a different husband, very much second best, but still a desirable object. That, too, had faded to nothing, before exploding in rage at Walter's interference, which had ended in his totally unexpected offer. Which she had rejected! But it had given her hope... and now Mr Lomax again, and a dilemma.

Walter had offered for her once, albeit spurred by guilt. Could he conceivably offer for her again? Was there any corner of his heart where Winnie lurked, curled into a tiny mouse-like ball, perhaps, but lying there inside him, prodding him to offer for her again, properly this time? She had thought she had plenty of time to find out, but now there was no time left.

If — *when* — Mr Lomax made his offer, she had to reply, once and for all. Yes or no. Mrs Lomax or... possibly Miss Strong forever more. If Walter were ever to offer for her, it had to be now, but she could not see how it could be done. For three days, Mr Lomax came to call, and there were outings and walks in the garden and long evenings when he monopolised her attention, and there was not a single moment alone with Walter. Even her morning walks were accompanied by Hebe, so even if Walter had gone to the tree house too, there would have been no opportunity for private conversation.

But one morning, waking unusually early, she managed to evade Hebe and escaped alone for her walk. That at least was something! She needed time for quiet reflection to decide whether she could live with a man who lied to her. What would happen if he carried such dishonesty into their marriage? If she came to suspect him of gambling debts or unfaithfulness or some other misdemeanour, and asked him if it were true — would he look her straight in the eye and lie? Yes, she rather thought he would. He would consider that he was protecting her from unpleasantness, perhaps. It would not occur to him that she did not need protecting.

So her thoughts ran as she reached the tree house, and settled herself on her usual swing. She had not been there more than a few moments when she heard rapid footsteps approaching. Hebe, perhaps, chasing after her.

But it was Walter. "There you are, Mouse. You are a fast walker. I was sure I would catch up with you long before this."

"You have been following me?"

"I saw you leave, and I wanted an opportunity to talk to you without— alone. You are never alone these days." Then, hesitantly, "May I?"

"Of course. I am glad to see you alone, too. I understand I have you to thank for Mr Lomax's unexpected appearance on the doorstep. You wrote to him, I believe."

He sat down on the other swing, not looking at her. "I did. Once I understood the truth about all those foul rumours about you, I felt obliged to undeceive Lomax. Your father said not to tell you, in case it raised your hopes, but I am glad Lomax has seen sense at last." He raised his head and looked directly at her. "I am pleased for you, Winnie. He will make you an admirable husband."

"Will he? You had a very low opinion of him at one time."

Walter gave a slight chuckle, looking embarrassed, his head sinking again. "It was arrogant of me to presume to judge a man of whom I knew nothing except that he wears a great many fobs. A man's worth is not measured by the number of his fobs."

"Nor by the width of his lapels or the shine on his boots."

He laughed properly at that. "Especially not that. All his boots prove is that he employs a competent valet. Winnie, I may not greatly admire his style of dress, but I hope I am not so unjust as to condemn him for such a trivial matter. He holds you in the highest esteem, and that alone engenders my respect for his good judgement. You will be very happy as Mrs Lomax."

Winnie could not let the moment pass. He was saying everything that a good friend would be expected to say, but did his words hide anything deeper? Or was he exactly as he appeared — nothing but a friend? She took a deep breath. "It is by no means certain that I shall accept him."

Walter's head shot up. "What? I thought you *wanted* to marry him."

"I want to marry *someone*, Walter. I want a husband and my own establishment and my own children, and not merely play the aunt for my nephews and nieces, so I shall probably accept Mr Lomax if he offers. He is not perfect — he is very far from perfect. He has not been honest with me, and I cannot like that he believed those foul rumours about me. He feels... alien, somehow, not comfortable like a friend. He makes me feel odd, as if

I am not quite me when I am with him. But he is the best that is on offer. I cannot expect to find a man more to my taste, not at my age, and without anything to boast of in the way of looks or dowry or accomplishments, so I shall take him, I suppose."

She dared not come closer to the truth. If Walter did not respond to such an obvious opening, then she would give up all hope of him once and for all.

He was silent for a long time, then he said slowly, "You *are* different when you are with him, Mouse, but I think it is as much those fancy new clothes of yours as anything. You look so fashionable in your London gowns, and with your hair done just so. You are a perfect match for him, you know. You look well together."

"It is not about clothes!" she said impatiently. "Why does everyone judge by clothes? I am still *me* inside, whatever I wear."

"I hate to disagree with you, Mouse, but I think you *are* different. Look at you now, for instance — a dilapidated old gown, a cloak that is so old I cannot even tell what colour it is and your hair just bundled up on your head anyhow, with bits of it falling down. And here you are, completely the familiar old Winnie to me. Whereas when you put on your new gowns and walk around on Lomax's arm... well, you seem very different. Very ladylike. Very refined. Just like your mama."

She pulled a face. "But I do not want to be like Mama. Ladylike... perhaps. I should not like to be *un*ladylike. But in my own family, may I not be at ease and behave in a more relaxed way? Yesterday, for instance, when everyone was playing cricket on the lawn. Even Papa and Uncle Alfred and Hebe. Even William Plaister! I wanted to play, too, as I always had before, but Mr Lomax wanted me to sit with him and I did, but it made me feel... so strange. To be sitting on the terrace with him and Mama and Lily like a useless ornament instead of running about enjoying myself… I have always been a doer, Walter, not a watcher, and he is turning me into a watcher like h im."

"And is that not how it should be?" Walter said gently, his expression earnest. "A wife should follow her husband's lead in all things."

"As Bea Franklyn would have followed your lead, I suppose? No, Walter, a woman, be she wife or spinster, should always follow her own principles before all else."

"But a wife must be guided by her husband, do you not agree? You may argue as much as you like with *me*, but when you are married to Lomax you must abide by his wishes. It is a part of growing up, I think. I have had to grow up by losing my inheritance and carving a new path in the world, and you will have to grow up when you become Mrs Lomax. You are nervous about it, which is perfectly natural, for you are already feeling the changes that will be necessary, but it will all be worth it, Winnie. Lomax will make you very happy, and no one deserves that more than you."

That was the point at which Winnie gave it up in despair. If Walter had nothing to say to her except to push her towards Mr Lomax, then it was clear he had no attachment beyond simple friendship. They walked back to the house together in uneasy silence.

***

It was more than a week before Mr Lomax came to the point, and then it almost came as a surprise. The whole family had gone on a long drive up onto the moors for a picnic, arriving home grubby, hot and dishevelled late in the afternoon. Mr Lomax, his shirt points wilting in the heat, had retreated to the inn at Birchall to restore himself to his usual sartorial glory, returning only shortly before dinner. For once, he did not sit beside Winnie, choosing instead to sit between Mama and Lily, which was something of a puzzle. Winnie refused to allow her imagination to speculate on the reasons for that, but Lily had no such inhibitions.

"Is he going to run away again?" she whispered to Winnie, as the ladies withdrew after dinner, but Mama shushed her at once, for which Winnie was grateful. It was bad enough waiting for a proposal that might never come without Lily trying to read the poor man's intentions from every trivial deviation from routine.

So she sat and pretended to read a newspaper, while all the time wondering how many more days must pass before he made his declaration. The summer was drifting away and he showed no sign of progress. There had been no words of love, no tender looks, no meaningful pats of her gloved hands. Just the obvious admiration in his eyes and his eagerness to be with her. Most of the time.

It was rather like waiting for the thunderstorm at the end of a long hot day. Even now she could hear distant rumbles, but perhaps it too would come to nothing, fading away into the night. Hebe and Lily were playing together, Lily's delicate harp all but drowned out by Hebe's enthusiastic efforts on the pianoforte, but no one asked Winnie to join in. They understood, and respectfully left her to her own thoughts. Another day gone and she was still not betrothed.

Mama was called away by Maynard, and then, a few minutes later, Maynard returned. "You're wanted in the book room, madam," he said to Winnie.

Madam. Even the butler knew something was afoot. Her stomach suddenly tied in knots, Winnie left the room to sudden silence. Her sisters knew the significance of this moment.

Mama and Papa were both in the book room, sitting side by side and smiling at her. Mr Lomax stood beside the fireplace, one arm resting on the mantel, as if he were too anxious to sit, but he was smiling, too. The time had come, then. This was the moment when her life would change irrevocably.

She was aware of a sudden terror of him, this stranger to whom she was about to bind herself. What did she know of him, in truth? Very little beyond what he had told her himself. This was a mistake! She should run away as fast as she could... she should tell Walter outright that she loved him. And then what? He would feel obliged to offer for her, obliged to marry her and he would resent her for the rest of his life.

The thought steadied her. Walter had had his chance, and had chosen not to take it. So be it. She would marry Mr Lomax instead. Lifting her chin, she curtsied. "You wished to see me, Papa? Mama?"

"It is Mr Lomax who wishes to see you, Winnie," her father said, still smiling. "He has something very particular to say to you. I would have you understand, Winnie, that this has the approval of both of us, but the decision is yours to make. We will accept whatever you choose to do."

Mama gave him a quizzical look, but Winnie said, "I understand."

"Very well," her father said. "We shall await news in the drawing room."

Then she was alone with Mr Lomax. Her future husband.

He came towards her, and took her hands, kissing one after the other. "My dear Miss Strong... Winifred," he began.

She was startled to be called *'Winifred'*, a name probably not used since her Baptism, but made no comment, not liking to interrupt his speech.

He pulled her to a sofa and sat down beside her, still holding her hands. "You will have been aware of my intentions for some time, delayed only by..."

Would he lie to her again?

"...by the illness of my aunt..."

Yes, he would, and surely it was supposed to be a cousin?

"...but finally I am able to say to you the words you have no doubt been long expecting. Winifred, my very dear Winifred, I knew from the instant I saw you in the General Post Office, so in need of a gentleman's support, that I wished to protect you and keep you safe for ever. Will you allow me to do so? Will you be my wife?"

Quite apart from the name, there was something in his manner that set her back up. Whatever made him imagine she needed protection? She had fought off the urchins by herself, after all, and although she had been very glad of his cane to finally drive them away, she felt she had managed well enough on her own. And then the presumption that she was complacently waiting for him to speak! It was true, of course, but it was not polite to say so. And not a word of love!

Had her circumstances been different, perhaps even now she would have given him a different answer... had she been younger, or had another suitor, or not cared about marriage quite so much. But she was twenty-four, Walter was lost to her and she could not give up, perhaps for ever, the chance of having a little Prudence of her own, or several little Prudences. One could never have too many children to cherish. Mr Lomax was not perfect, but what man was? And if she was not in love with him, at least there was nothing about him to give her a disgust of him. He was fastidious about his person, so she knew he would always be clean and sober.

It was as good an offer as she would ever get. So she bowed her head demurely, and thanked him, and told him that she would be honoured to be his wife.

"Excellent!" he said cheerfully. "Let us go and tell your family, shall we?"

A little bemused by the lack of lover-like impulses, for surely this was the moment for him to speak of love, she allowed herself to be steered into the hall and then into the drawing room. Most of the men had joined the ladies by this time, and every face turned expectantly to the door as they entered. The music stopped abruptly, and several conversations died away to nothing as they waited.

"Miss Strong has consented to be my wife," Mr Lomax said loudly into the lull.

At once there was a hubbub, with congratulations hurled about, and Papa calling to Maynard to bring something up from the cellar for a toast. Mama and Lily and Hebe hugged Winnie and smiled and wept and laughed and wept again, and Winnie could not prevent herself from smiling and laughing too. She could not quite weep, however. A betrothal was hardly a weeping matter. The men patted her genially on the shoulder or kissed her cheek and pumped Mr Lomax's hand, wishing them both joy.

Glasses were filled, toasts were drunk and Papa made a sad little speech which was more about how he would miss Winnie than anything else, and that did bring her perilously close to tears. Then Mr Lomax made a speech in return, telling them how well he intended to look after Winnie. Then Hebe sat down with a whoosh, complaining of the heat which was making her feel dizzy, and before Winnie knew it the whole party was stepping out onto the terrace to walk in the cooler air of the garden. The sun was close to setting, but there was still enough light to see the paths clearly. Far away in the distance, thunder still rumbled gently, like the soft noise of a sleeping do g.

The gardens were large and criss-crossed by a multitude of paths, and within a very few minutes the multitude had dispersed and Winnie was alone with Mr Lomax. That was undoubtedly the purpose of this sudden walk, to allow the newly-betrothed couple a private interlude. Mr Lomax seemed unaware of this intention, however, for he talked without pause about nothing in particular. The flowers, mainly, for the evening air was heady with their scent. It was quite intoxicating, and a romantic man would surely have seized the moment. Disappointingly, Mr Lomax appeared not to be a romantic man. Not only did he not take the opportunity to play the lover, he did not even talk about subjects that might be supposed to interest Winnie, like their future life together, or when they might be married. Nothing but chatter about flowers, on which subject he appeared to know not hing.

Eventually, he ran out of things to say about the flowers. "It is getting dark," he said. "I do not want you to be quite exhausted, my dear Winifred. Shall we turn back now?"

"I am not at all exhausted. Why do you call me Winifred? No one calls me that, except old Mrs Lennon, who hardly knows what day of the week it is. I much prefer Winnie."

"Winifred is a very pretty name," he said, sounding puzzled. "It is your Christian name, after all. Winnie sounds like a horse. Mother and I have agreed that we will call you Winifred."

He had agreed it with his mother, had he? She did not like the sound of that. However, she did not quite like to quarrel with him on the very day of their betrothal, so she merely made a mental note to raise the subject on another occasion. After twenty-four years as Winnie, she was not sure she could stand twenty-four years as Winifred. She felt a little like Walter, losing his name after ten years as Lord Birtwell.

She turned and prepared to return to the house, but he stood irresolute, gazing at her, his fists clenching and unclenching.

"What is it, sir? Are you quite well?"

Before she could grasp what he was about, he had grabbed her by the shoulders, and pressed his lips hard against hers. Taken by surprise, she instinctively leaned away from him, only to find a tree behind her, impeding her. The more she tried to move away from him, the harder he pushed her against the tree, so that she was pinioned there, the gnarled bark pressing painfully into her back, his lips forced against hers.

Abruptly, she was free. He laughed, then offered her his arm. "Shall we return to the house, my dear?"

Quivering with indignation, she acceded.

29: A Good Kisser

Winnie retired to bed that night in a very disordered frame of mind. Such a big day in her life and yet she felt... odd. Very odd. She could not help remembering Hebe's betrothal day, when William had turned up in a brand new coat, looking very solemn. He and Hebe had stayed in the book room for a whole hour, and in the end Mama had had to go in and drag them out, looking slightly rumpled but grinning ecstatically and holding hands. *'Oh, Winnie, kissing is so wonderful!'* Hebe had said later.

She wished she could agree, but she had not enjoyed being kissed by Mr Lomax at all. Nor did she like being called Winifred. Then there was the odd conversation over the celebratory drinks. Someone, Mama perhaps, had asked where the present Mrs Lomax would live.

"She will retire to the dower house, ma'am," Mr Lomax had said. "In fact she has already put the arrangements in train, and will be settled there by the end of the month."

"That will be a great wrench for her, no doubt, to leave her marital home, no matter how pleasant the reason for it," Mama had said. "I hope she will not be too far away from you, for she will want to see you often."

"There is no difficulty in that direction," Mr Lomax had said smugly. "The dower house is connected to the main house... it is the west wing, in fact. It is all most conveniently arranged, for my mother will not need her own cook, and my wife will benefit by all my mother's experience of managing the household."

Even Mama had been taken aback by that. Winnie made another mental note, to remove Mrs Lomax to a greater distance than the west wing, and how that was to be done, she could not imagine.

So many little worries, to take the shine off her happiness. She *was* happy, was she not? She thought she was, and she certainly ought to be, but she was beginning to wonder just what it would be like to be married to this man. No, this was foolishness. He loved her, after all... did he not? He had an affection for her, so he would want to do everything in his power to make her happy... surely he would.

All would be well. Everyone was so pleased for her, imagining her happily settled at last. Papa had whispered to her, "If you are even one tenth as happy as your mother has made me, you will be very happy indeed, daughter." Even Walter had smiled and wished her joy, and said, "I hope he knows how lucky he is."

That had made her a little bit cross, because he could have had that luck himself, if he had wanted it. If he had thought she was any sort of prize worth winning, why did he not offer for her when he had the chance? But her reasonable side asserted itself, and told her that it was just a form of words, just one of those things one says to a betrothed couple.

Oddly, after all the drama of the day, she fell asleep instantly, but then woke very early, when it was barely light. Knowing she could not sleep again, she dressed in an old gown that could be fastened without Martha's aid, and sat down to write a long letter to Aunt Sofia, to tell her all that had happened.

Well, perhaps not quite all. Not that unpleasant kiss, for one thing. Not the dower house, either, nor her unsolicited change of name. She threw down her pen in disgust. This was not how it should be! She should be overflowing with joy, holding nothing back.

Perhaps a longer than usual walk would lift her spirits. She pulled on her half-boots, grabbed her cloak, and went downstairs. Outside, the air was still muggy, the threatened thunderstorm having come to nothing. She set off this time for a full circuit of the perimeter. It was only three miles but it would serve... no, if she went down the drive first, she could complete one and a half circuits before going to the tree house, a full five miles. That would blow away a few cobwebs.

It was invigorating, walking with a brisk stride again. She had got so used to walking at Mr Lomax's dawdling pace that she had almost forgotten how good it felt to stretch her legs. It was not much help to her mind, however. She was still faced with the same dispiriting problems.

She came to the tree house. To her surprise, Walter was there, slumped on one of the two swings.

He looked up, saw her, smiled rather wanly. "Could you not sleep, Mouse? Excitement kept you awake?"

"Nothing like that," she said rather glumly, sitting on the other swing. "Just... wondering if I am doing the right thing."

"Oh." He sat up a little straighter. "Nothing but nerves, I suppose. Perfectly natural, after so momentous a day."

"Perhaps."

"Although... you seemed very happy last night, when he finally proposed."

"Yes. I was. But then... we went for that walk in the garden."

"And... something happened?"

She nodded. Briefly, she wondered how much she should tell him, but she had never kept secrets from him, except the one Very Big Secret. He had always been her friend, her confidant, her dispenser of male wisdom. So she spoke the words.

"He kissed me, and it was horrid."

"That is not right. Kissing should never be horrid!"

"Well, that is what I thought, too," she said, pleased to have this suspicion confirmed. "Papa kisses Mama sometimes, when he thinks no one is looking, and she giggles and seems to like it very much. And Hebe said kissing is wonderful. So I think there must be something wrong with me, because I did *not* like it, not at all."

"Winnie! Have you never been kissed before?"

"No, never. A lady does not allow herself to be kissed until she is betrothed, so how could I be? I suppose I shall get used to it. I shall have to, because once we are married I imagine a certain amount of kissing will be involved. Perhaps I shall grow to like it. Do you think I might?"

"You might. Perhaps it was just the shock of it. Or perhaps he is just a bad kisser."

"Oh, are there good kissers and bad kissers? I did not know."

"There are. I do not like to boast, but I am accounted a good kisser, but then I was well taught."

"You were taught to kiss? By whom? Oh, your mistress, I suppose."

"Winnie! You are not supposed to know anything about such matters."

"Well, I do. Her name was Maria and she lived at Pickering. I heard Mama and Papa talking about it, rather loudly. They sounded upset, although I cannot imagine why. So what is the difference between good kissing and bad kissing?"

He chuckled. "Winnie, you are incorrigible!"

"Well, I want to know! Did Bea like it when you kissed her?"

"Hmm — how odd. I cannot remember ever kissing her at all."

"Why ever not, when you were betrothed for months?"

He gave a little shrug. "I never wanted to, particularly. And she never asked. There was nothing romantic between us, you know. She wanted the title and she was determined to get it, and in the end it was easier just to let her have her way. But I was quite relieved when it fell through. It was the only good thing about the whole business of Nicholson and the inheritance. You know what I think, Winnie? It seems to me very likely that Lomax botched the whole kissing affair. Probably he just grabbed you and set about it, without any warming up first, so no wonder you were startled."

"Warming up?"

"Kissing is not just the actual kiss, you see. There is far more to it."

"So what should he have done, instead of grabbing me?"

"It needs to be romantic," Walter said, jumping off the swing. "Let me show you, because then you will know how it should be done, and you will be able to give Lomax a little hint. Pretend that I am Mr Lomax." He minced towards her in a parody of Mr Lomax's manner of walking. "First, I should say something about how beautiful you are, and enchanting, and charming... that sort of nonsense. I would come a little closer..." He leaned nearer, his face inches from hers. "Then I should ask if I might kiss you, and of course you would say…” His voice became girlishly high. “Ooh, yes please, Mr Lomax!”

She giggled. “How absurd you are, Walter.”

“Mr Lomax, remember?” He grinned boyishly at her, relishing the game.

“How absurd you are, *Mr Lomax*. And then… you would kiss me?”

“Not yet. First… first I would just touch your hair… like this, and say… ah, so soft, like silk. Something trite of that nature. And then I would run one finger down your cheek, so lightly you can barely feel it. Can you feel it?”

“Barely,” she whispered.

“I might run one finger across your lips… like so.”

“Ohhh,” she breathed.

“I might tell you that your eyes look as clear and unfathomable as a mountain pool.” His voice was bewitchingly low. “Your cheeks… so soft, so perfectly soft and smooth, and your lips…” His eyes were focused there, his face no longer mischievous, but oddly intent. It was almost as if he meant it…

“Your lips…” he murmured again, his hands cupping her face, gazing at her as if he had never seen her before.

She could not breathe, could not move, transfixed by his face so close to hers, the intensity of his voice, his *touch*… the warmth of his hands against her skin, his ragged breathing, his eyes fixed on her mouth. He moved slowly nearer.

Her lips parted and she closed her eyes.

“Winifred! What do you think you are doing?”

Mr Lomax’s voice, blaring and harsh, broke the spell so abruptly that she jumped.

Walter shot away from her and spun round. There were voices, Mr Lomax's raised, angry, and Walter's more temperate. Winnie could not tell what they were saying, for she was still cocooned in the warmth of that moment. Their argument seemed to have nothing to do with her. Walter had almost kissed her, had held her face in his hands and looked at her with... with what? Not the playful friendliness of their normal dealings, that much was certain. It was almost as if... as if he *loved* her.

No, that was foolish. He was playing a part, that was all. He had always been talented in that way, taking the starring part in all their childish dramatic performances. He was a good actor, no more than that. But oh, how much it had told her of her own heart! If she had felt one tenth as much for Mr Lomax when he had kissed her, as when Walter had merely *touched* her, she would have gone to her wedding with the lightest of steps. But now...

"*Winifred!* You are not attending!" Mr Lomax's voice grated on her so much that she shuddered. "I *said,* I shall see you in your father's book room directly. This appalling behaviour cannot be kept from him. There must have been some great mismanagement in your upbringing to lead you to act in such a reprehensible way."

She gazed at him blankly. What was he talking about? It was all nonsense. If only he would go away and leave her alone to savour that glorious moment with Walter...

***

Lomax! Where had he come from? What was he doing there, so early in the day — before breakfast, and at the tree house, for surely he had never walked so far before.

Walter could make no sense of it. All he knew was that Lomax had to be appeased, had to be made to understand that he was safe, Winnie was his and Walter would not for the world jeopardise that.

Except that he had, of course. So stupid, so reckless, so *thoughtless!* When would he ever learn? A fine one he was, to talk to Winnie about growing up when he had just put her whole future in doubt — *again!*

"This is not what it might seem," he said to Lomax, raising his hands placatingly. "It is just... it is not... we are not..."

"It is fortunate that I learnt of these early morning walks of Winifred's... *'go to the tree house before breakfast and you will find her quite alone,'* Lady Strong told me. Well, she was quite wrong about that! At least now I am undeceived. *'A healthy walk before breakfast'*, indeed! Ha! An assignation, that is what this is."

"No, no, nothing of the sort," Walter cried. "Please believe me—"

"I have nothing to say to you, sir!" Lomax said. "You are the worst sort of scoundrel, but the blame here is not yours alone."

"You must not blame Winnie," Walter said desperately.

"Who else should I blame? She is a wicked, wicked woman. I am sorry I ever met her!" He was shouting now.

Walter again raised his hands. "No, no, I assure you. There is nothing amiss here. Do not act hastily, sir, I implore you."

"Step aside, sir! Winifred, your father's book room, immediately. *Winifred!* You are not attending!"

It was true. Winnie was standing as still as a statue, gazing into space with a shocked expression on her face. She appeared quite oblivious of him as he yelled at her, ordering her to be hauled before her father like a misbehaving child. Then he stomped away.

And still Winnie had not moved. Some part of Walter wanted only to take her in his arms, to hold her... so help him, to kiss her. He wanted so badly to kiss her, to feel her sweet lips under his, her body pressed against him, yielding to him... but he must not. If there was any chance of recovering the situation with Lomax, he must take it. He could not forgive himself if he had destroyed her one opportunity for happiness.

"Winnie?" he said gently. "We must follow him... try to make him understand. Your father will listen, I am sure. We can still salvage your betrothal, if we hurry. Will you come?"

She said nothing, merely gazing at him unseeingly, lost in some world of her own where he could not reach her.

"Winnie?"

She neither moved nor spoke, so he reached for her hand. The instant his fingers met hers, she jumped, as if stung, but he kept hold of her.

"We must go and talk to your father. Come now."

Unresisting, she let him lead her away, through the woods, past the orchard and lily pool, through the flower gardens and into the house. He heard voices at once, Lomax's angry and raised, together with the lower murmur of Sir Hubert. The book room door was open, and Walter drew Winnie inside, pushing her gently forward with one hand on her back.

"Ah, Atherton!" Sir Hubert said with obvious relief. "I am sure you can clear this up very quickly. Lomax thinks you and Winnie were kissing, but that cannot be right, I am sure."

"No, indeed. He is quite mistaken."

"I know what I saw," Lomax said, lifting his chin and glaring at Walter.

"There was no kiss," Walter said firmly. At least he could say so in absolute truth, even if they were only moments away from doing so. "We were... The thing is, Lomax, Winnie and I are old friends... like brother and sister, you might say, so she confides in me. She was... concerned about something that had happened between you, and I was reassuring her that... that everything would be fine once you are married. I was merely smoothing the way for you, if you like."

"Smoothing the way," Lomax spat. "What nonsense! You were seducing her... or she was seducing you, more likely. She is a harlot!"

"Now, I will not have my daughter spoken of in such terms," Sir Hubert said, frowning. "Whatever happened, I am sure there was nothing in it. I can vouch for what Atherton has said... they are exactly like brother and sister. There has never been anything at all romantic between them. I am sure you have nothing to worry about, Lomax."

"I heard raised voices. What has happened?" Lady Strong's soft, feminine tones were a welcome addition to the charged atmosphere in the book room.

"Your daughter has behaved with wanton impropriety," Lomax said, rounding on her. "I had hoped that she had been correctly raised to be a lady, but I see now that it is not so. She is a very wicked girl and I want nothing more to do with her."

He made at once for the door. Lady Strong cried out distressfully, and grabbed his arm.

"No, sir, no! I am sure there is some mistake. Sir Hubert, help me to convince him. You must not go, sir, indeed you must not! Do not leave poor Winnie broken-hearted. Pray let us talk about this."

He pushed roughly passed her into the hall, while she, still clinging to his arm, and Sir Hubert on his other side, followed. Walter heard Lomax order his carriage, and then the three voices rumbled on, the Strongs trying to urge him back into the book room and Lomax, in tones loud enough to be heard all over the house, insisting that Winnie was beyond redemption and how could he possibly marry such an evil woman?

"Winnie?" Walter said softly. She had not moved an inch, had not spoken, had not changed her expression. "I am sure he will come back. He will not leave. He loves you, so he will come back."

But she said nothing.

More voices were heard in the hall… Lily, he thought, and Hebe. Then the carriage crunching over the gravel and pulling up. More pleading voices and angry responses. The carriage door slammed, and the horses started forward. The sound of the carriage grew faint and then disappeared altogether.

Silence.

"Well, he has gone," Sir Hubert said tiredly, as they came back into the book room. "A little excessive before breakfast, if you ask me."

"How can you even think about breakfast!" Lady Strong wailed, on the edge of hysteria. "Winnie is ruined, and whatever is to become of her now?"

"Winnie?" Walter said again. He took her hand again, gently stroking the back of it with one thumb, and again she jolted into awareness.

"Has he gone?"

Walter nodded. "I am so, so sorry," he whispered. "I am the world's biggest fool. I never mean to hurt you, but it keeps happening anyway. This is the second time I have driven Lomax away, and this time there may be no way to bring him back. It is entirely my fault, and so it is for me to make things right, as far as that is possible. I cannot give you Lomax, I cannot give you anyone worthy of you, but I want nothing more than to give you the home and family you crave. Winnie, will you marry me? It is only second best, I know that but—"

"I will." She lifted her eyes to his. "Yes. I will marry you, Walter."

Joy raced through him so abruptly that he quivered where he stood. Yes! She would be his wife! He almost cried out with exhilaration.

"Wait a moment," Sir Hubert said. "You are not in a position to offer for anyone, Walter."

"It is entirely unsuitable," Lady Strong said firmly.

"No employment, no income, no prospects," Sir Hubert said. "I do *not* approve."

"Nor I," said Lady Strong. "Walter is not a fit person to marry my daughter."

Winnie ignored them. Her hand still resting in Walter's, her eyes fixed on his, she smiled. "Thank you, Walter."

He smiled back, then raised her hand to his lips. "My pleasure."

30: The Urn On The Stairs

Another Saturday, and another gathering in the old nursery to reflect on progress. Luce and Neate sipped Madeira, while Pettigrew Willerton-Forbes and Sandy worked their way through a plate of cakes. Michael was occupied in cleaning his array of pistols. Only Miss Peach was absent, still off on business of her own in Pickering.

"Pettigrew, who would you put money on at this point?"

Pettigrew brushed crumbs from his waistcoat. "John Whyte, the illegitimate son. He has only recently discovered his origins, and is bound to be resentful. And now he has disappeared, riding a valuable horse of Mr Bertram Atherton's. A clear sign of guilt, if you ask me."

"Very possible," Michael said. "Whyte has probably sold that horse of Mr Bertram's, changed his name and vanished beyond any finding. Then there is our other missing suspect. We know where Miss Tess Nicholson is, but she refuses to return home."

"You could go to her," Luce said.

"Yes, I could travel all that way and she might still refuse to see me," he said. "She is the niece of an earl, so I can hardly force the issue. Nor can I arrest her, despite my blustering to Shapman. Besides, she is surely too dainty a creature to have wielded that axe." He sighed. "Her lover is not at all dainty, but he seems genuinely honest, to me, unless I have completely lost my touch. Frankly, I think the answer lies at Pickering. This house of Nicholson's, occupied by a respectable widow or in use as a house of ill-repute, take your choice, and what was he doing owning a chandlery?"

"What about these quarrels Lady Alice mentioned?" Luce said. "Lord Farramont, Eustace, Kent..."

"And the problem with any member of the family," Michael said, "is why go to the bother of an axe? Far easier to add rat poison to the decanter in his room, which anyone who knew the chaplain well could have done. No one in the castle would need to kill him with an axe."

"Except one," Sandy said softly.

Michael exhaled sharply. "True. Despite all our efforts, we *still* cannot eliminate the Lady Alice. I cannot bring myself to believe it, yet she is such a capable lady, she could easily have murdered her husband."

"How would she have done it?" Luce said. "She simply leaves her bed, walks down the stairs, retrieves the axe, then goes back upstairs — is that it? A blind woman?"

"Why not? You have seen how competently she manages the stairs. She rests just one finger on the rail and glides up or down as swiftly as you or I. And she can do that at night just as easily."

"She wouldnae even need to do that on the night of the murder," Sandy put in. "No one saw the axe on the stairs, after all. She could have taken the axe earlier and hidden it somewhere. Or her maid could."

"Not the maid," Michael said. "She is a God-fearing woman who would have told us at once if her mistress had asked her to acquire an axe. No, the Lady Alice would have done it herself."

"Assuming she knew the axe was there," Luce said.

"True. But she knew there were displays of weapons on the stairs. She could easily have examined the display and found the axe."

"Do you think so?" Luce said. "I should like to see it. In fact, why not try it? You have tried everything else — the drainpipe, the scullery window, burning the nightgown. Let us put the axe in place, I will blindfold you and you can retrieve it."

Michael laughed in delight. "Very well, wife. I love an experiment! Sandy, bring the axe. Luce, do you have a scarf for a blindfold?"

It took them some time to secure the axe in place, for the belt which should have held it was broken. In the end, they borrowed a belt from one of the gardeners, by which time word of the plan had spread throughout the castle, and a little knot of servants stood in the great hall, watching.

"There!" Luce said, when all was ready. "Here is an axe, conveniently located for the use of any passing murderer, you would think. Now, Michael, where is Mr Nicholson's room?"

"At the top of the stairs, the right-hand ones."

"Then you must start there."

Taking the stairs two at a time, he raced ahead, while Luce followed more sedately. Then she bound his eyes securely.

"No peeking."

"Certainly not! That would be cheating."

"Now, you are Lady Alice," Luce said to him. "You have just come out of your room behind us, and you have your left hand on the rail to guide you down."

"Very well," he said, placing his hand on the rail.

"Now, you know exactly where the axe is, so go and retrieve it. Sandy, make sure he does not miss a step. I will not be pleased if my husband falls and breaks his neck."

He could hear a low murmur from the watching crowd below, but someone hushed them. Feeling for each step with his foot, and holding onto the rail, Michael slowly descended.

"Are you there, Sandy?"

"Right here, Captain," he said, the voice so close Michael stopped in surprise.

Then, relieved, he carried on until he reached the half-landing. "Now I have to let go of the rail and cross to the armour display."

"Exactly so. You are doing very well," Luce said kindly.

Cautiously, he felt his way across the open space, arms spread out before him, feet inching forward. "Ha! The vase," he said, his hands resting on its lacquered surface. "So, a little to the left." One of his hands touched a suit of armour, which swayed alarmingly. "Aha! I am there. Now what am I touching? I think this is the rightmost display, so the axe must be about—"

Someone gave a squeak of alarm. Then something hit Michael hard in the chest, bowling him over, while with a cacophony of metallic crashes and clatterings, objects bounced off him and all around him, falling with dull thuds down the stairs, followed by louder clinks and tinkles as a variety of metal objects bounced across the tiled floor of the great hall.

For a long, long time, Michael lay motionless, as the clatter gradually died away. Then he started to laugh. "Well, that was spectacular!"

The scarf was whisked from his eyes, and he gazed up into Luce's anxious face. "Are you injured, Michael?"

"Not in the slightest, and see, I have the axe!" He raised his hand, still firmly gripping the axe handle.

"Just as well, or it might have chopped off something vital as it fell. The mace missed you by a whisker, and Sandy was accosted by a flying helmet. I think you have some apologies to make."

She indicated the great hall below. Michael jumped up and stared down at the devastation he had caused. Bits of armour and weapons were scattered over the entire floor, as servants bustled about gathering up items.

One servant in particular glared at him balefully as he carefully descended, avoiding scattered debris. Lady Alice's maid, Malling, was breathing heavily, her posture rigid with anger.

"You thought *her ladyship* killed poor Mr Nicholson!" she spat at him as soon as he was within range. "How dare you! As if my mistress would ever demean herself to... to *murder*, and her own husband? Never! She adored him, that I'll swear to on the Holy Book."

"No, no, Miss Malling, I assure you," Michael said, hands raised placatingly. "My object was to prove that the Lady Alice could *not* have murdered her husband, for you can see what happens when a blind person attempts to take the axe. Disaster. She could not have done it. As soon as this mess is tidied up, I shall go directly to her ladyship and apologise for ever suspecting her. But first, I must apologise to everyone else for causing so much trouble."

"No trouble, Captain," the butler said, winking. "You are as good as a farce at the theatre, what with drainpipes and dogs, and now this. And no harm done, after all."

It took two hours for order to be restored, for Michael could not be satisfied until he had rebuilt the display exactly as it had been before, which, without Mr Eustace, was not as easy as it looked. But eventually, the last gauntlet and greave and breastplate was in place. Then he had to extract the axe again, without the blindfold this time, and without knocking over the display again.

"It is surprisingly awkward to do," he said, frowning. "At night, by the light of only a candle, it would be excessively difficult, and to pull it away sharply enough to break the belt — no, it could not be done without setting off the cascade. Interesting."

"Michael, there is someone in the great hall who I believe wishes to see you," Luce said.

He turned and saw Tom Shapman at the foot of the stairs, watching him expressionlessly.

"Mr Shapman, are you wanting me? Have you had word from Miss Nicholson... or some information for me?"

"No word," he said. "Information... in a way."

"Then come upstairs, Mr Shapman."

They all trailed up the staircase to the old nursery. Sandy sat down and reached for pen and ink to take notes. Luce took up her sewing and sat unobtrusively in a corner. Michael waved Shapman to a chair, but he shook his head.

"Very well, Mr Shapman. What is it you wish to tell me?"

"I've come to confess."

"I... beg your pardon?"

"I've come to confess," he said, loudly enough that Luce jumped in surprise. "I killed him. I killed Mr Nicholson."

The stunned silence lasted for several heartbeats before Michael recovered his wits.

"Why?" he said sharply.

"Because he wouldn't allow me and Tess to marry, that's why."

"She will be of age in a few months, and you could have married then."

"Aye, and he'd still make life difficult for us. He said he'd make sure I never got any more work round here. This way, Tess would be left some money, and we'd be free to marry."

"So she persuaded you to—?"

"No! She knew nowt about it. It were just me."

"Why the axe?"

"So it would look like a madman on the rampage. But you kept asking questions and getting nearer, and my conscience was troubling me."

"As it should!" Luce said in shocked tones.

"Aye, ma'am. I didn't want to sit through another of Mr Dewar's sermons with this burning inside me, so here I am."

His tone was level, as if he were describing a routine matter, and not a brutal murder.

"Very well," Michael said. "Describe what happened. How did you get in, for instance?"

"Through the scullery window with the broken latch. The back stairs are right by the scullery, but they're pitch black at night and I didn't want to light a candle, so I came out at the great hall where there was a bit of light, and up the main stairs."

"Where you picked up the axe?"

"Aye. Then up to Mr Nicholson's bedroom. I'd mended a window in Lady Alice's room just a few weeks earlier, so I knew she slept apart from him, so I... well, you know what I did. Then back the same way and out."

"Was there any blood on your clothes?"

"Aye, quite a bit, but I wore an old smock. Burnt it when I got home. There was blood on my shirt sleeve, too, but I was able to wash it well enough. I can't afford to burn a good shirt."

Michael watched him pensively. He had met quite a few murderers over the years, but he had never seen one as impassive as Tom Shapman.

"Show me," he said eventually. "Show me exactly what you did. Sandy, you will need to unlatch the scullery window, since the broken latch has been fixed. And bring the axe with you."

Michael led Shapman downstairs, and out of the castle's front door and down the steps to the kitchen level. "Now, Shapman, show me this window."

Unerringly, Shapman turned in the right direction and strode round the corner. "That's the one. There's a bit of stonework jutting out to put a foot on."

Michael knew that very well, having climbed in that way himself. "Up you go, then."

"Oh, you want me to go in that way?"

"Yes. Everything you did that night, I want to see."

"Right."

Shapman was a big man, but he was agile, and he hopped onto the stone and then up onto the sill very nimbly. Pulling open the window, he climbed inside. It was a bit of a squeeze, but he managed it without getting stuck or tearing any clothing. Michael followed him through and swiftly opened the door to the kitchen. The dogs rushed in, tongues lolling, sniffing suspiciously at Michael, Sandy and Luce. Shapman, however, laughed and knelt down to fondle their heads.

"How are you, you daft creatures? Yes, I'm pleased to see you, too."

"They know you well, then?" Michael said.

"Aye, I've fixed a lot of windows and doors here, and I often get a meal in the kitchen afterwards. I love dogs, don't you? Wish I had one of my own."

"Stairs, Mr Shapman," Michael said.

"This way."

He led the way to the service stairs, and up to the main floor, then out into the great hall. Pettigrew Willerton-Forbes was just passing through, but he stopped when he saw them.

"Mr Shapman is just describing how he murdered Mr Nicholson," Michael said blandly.

"How interesting," Pettigrew said, in the same conversational tone. "Pray continue, Mr Shapman."

For the first time, Shapman seemed disconcerted. "Oh... well... right. Stairs."

"Do lead the way, sir," Pettigrew said, smiling benignly at him.

With a nervous glance, Shapman crossed the tiled floor and took the stairs to the half-landing.

"Is this where you found the axe?" Michael said.

"Aye. So I took that, and—"

"Show me precisely how it was positioned."

"It was in the vase thing... that one."

"In... the *urn?*" Michael said, astonished. "How did you know it was there?"

"I put it there, of course. I'd been working on the attic door, came down the stairs, saw the axe and thought it might be useful. So I put it in the vase... urn."

"Sandy, put the axe in there." Michael reached in, but his arms were not long enough to reach for the handle. "Shapman, lift it out again. Hmm. Sandy, can you reach it, too? So, only a tall person. Luce, can you reach it? A very good hiding place, Mr Shapman. Would you be so good as to put the axe in its original position on the display? The place from where you removed it?"

Shapman frowned, gazing at the display. But then his face resumed its expressionless appearance. "I don't remember. I was in a rush."

"Do you remember if the belt here was broken?"

"Can't say that I do, sir."

"Very well. You have retrieved the axe, so now what?"

"Up the stairs to Mr Nicholson's room."

Again, he unerringly turned the right way and went directly to the door. He was able to describe the layout of the room, glossing over the actual murder with the laconic remark, "You know what I did in there," and then described how he left the castle by the same route.

"And did you see anyone? Hear anything?"

"No, nothing."

"You will hang for this, of course," Michael said.

"Aye, sir."

"Sandy, see him safely locked up in the basement somewhere — Simpson will know where to put him. I shall send word to Sir Hubert. It will be his duty as magistrate to get him to... York, I suppose, Pettigrew?"

"Yes. He has missed the Summer Assizes, so he will have to wait for Lent, now. You had better tell Lord Rennington, too."

It was late in the afternoon before Michael returned to the old nursery, where Luce, Sandy, Neate and Pettigrew were sitting around the table. All the papers had been cleared away, and only the axe lay in the middle of it, the last reminder of the murder.

Michael sat down with a sigh.

"Bad, was it?" Luce said sympathetically.

"Fairly bad. The earl is delighted the business is settled at last, but very cross that we have been here for almost ten weeks and in the end the murderer walked in and confessed of his own volition."

"He was one of your principal suspects," Pettigrew said. "You would have got there in the end."

"Perhaps."

"But you believe him... or do you?"

"Oh yes. There is too much detail there — the axe in the urn, for instance, which neatly accounts for why no one remembers the axe in the display. And the bloodstain on his shirt cuff — that is very convincing. He lives alone, so it would have been easy enough to burn the smock in his own kitchen."

"But everything else he could have known," Pettigrew said. "The scullery window, Nicholson's room... everything. His reason is the flimsiest in the world. You are not easily deceived, but you believed him innocent. And I note he arrived here to confess just days after you threatened to arrest Miss Nicholson."

"You think he is protecting her?" Luce said.

"It makes no difference," Michael said testily. "Shapman has confessed, his story is consistent with the facts, and unless he recants, he will hang for it. He is adamant that Tess had nothing to do with it, and we must accept that. There is nothing more for us to do here except to collect Miss Peach from Pickering and go home."

"You are just cross because you did not solve the mystery yourself," Luce said.

Michael smiled. "I am a little, yes. It feels… unsatisfactory, somehow. So much discovered about Nicholson's life, and so much yet to be discovered, and now… it all stops. If nothing else, I should like to have discovered this fortune that has been left to Miss Nicholson."

"The lawyers will find it," Pettigrew said. "Besides, Michael, it may feel unsatisfactory for us, but the earl and his family have enough to deal with just now. Nicholson's legacy has overturned all their lives. At least with the murder out of the way, they will be able to adjust to their new circumstances without that cloud hanging over them."

"Very true, and in a year or two, I might even be able to see it in that light myself," Michael said. "But at the moment, it looms in my mind as one of my more spectacular failures."

31: In The Rain

Breakfast was Winnie's favourite time of day. Dinner was too formal a meal, with everyone in their finery and very often guests as well. There was a rigidity to it that she disliked. But breakfast was just the family, the boys joking around, Lily being agitated about something or other, and Mama soothing her, with Papa smiling benignly on them all. And now there was Walter, too, who was as much family to her as anyone.

Her betrothed! Not that it was acknowledged by anyone. Papa disliked it because Walter had no money, and Mama disliked it because she had never quite forgiven him for having a mistress all those years ago, as if a man who had once transgressed could never be redeemed or forgiven. So they had insisted it be kept secret, and Walter was not even permitted to tell his own father. Even so, he had offered, and she had accepted, and in her heart, Walter was her betrothed.

One day he would be her husband if nothing prevented it. Every day she woke up wondering if this would be the day her father finally put his foot down, or Lord Rennington found some better prospect for Walter, or perhaps Walter himself would think better of it. And every night she retired to her room, still betrothed. It was like a miracle, some unexpected and quite undeserved grace. Nothing was said about a wedding, but she could be patient. She had waited ten years for Walter, after all. She could wait a little longer.

One breakfast brought a surprise, a letter for Papa.

"How is this, Maynard? The mail, so early? Ah, it is delivered by hand, I see. It must be— oh!"

The others all looked at him expectantly. "A matter of business, Sir Hubert?" Mama said.

"No..." He gave Winnie a searching look. "It is from Mr Lomax. He has reflected on matters, and now wishes to repair his position with Winnie. In short, he still wishes to marry her."

Walter gave an exclamation. "Oh, very fine behaviour! He walked away from her before, and now he thinks he can simply walk back into her life and resume his betrothal as if nothing ever happened."

"Walter..." Winnie began, but her mother laid a hand on her arm.

"That is for Winnie to say, Walter," she said. "She must be allowed to choose her own future. Winnie, we will discuss this after breakfast."

Walter rose and bowed stiffly. "Of course, ma'am. I should never wish to stand in the way of Winnie's happiness. Excuse me."

And with that, he turned and left the room.

Winnie's eyes followed him all the way, resting on the door long after it had closed behind him.

"You will be Mrs Lomax yet, Winnie," Lily said in a loud whisper.

"No, I shall not," she said sharply. "Papa, you must write to Mr Lomax and tell him I cannot marry him, not now."

"But Winnie—" her mother began.

"I *cannot* marry him!"

"Why, because of this odd betrothal to Walter?" she said sharply. "That is nothing at all. It can easily be set aside. It was never a real betrothal, you know. It is very gentlemanly of him to offer for you, but now that Mr Lomax—"

"Mr Lomax! Mr Lomax!" Winnie cried, jumping to her feet. "I shall *never* marry Mr Lomax! Papa, please write and tell him so."

"I am afraid you will have to tell him yourself, my dear," her father said ruefully. "He is in the village as we speak, and will be here in..." He glanced at the clock. "...about half an hour."

Winnie heaved a frustrated sigh. It was too bad of the man to come back after he had left so decisively. And now everything was uncertain again. Walter would nobly step aside, and her parents would push her towards Mr Lomax. Why could they not understand?

Slipping from the room, she found the butler hovering in the hall, wringing his hands anxiously.

"Oh, Miss Winnie! And it's raining so hard."

"Is it? Maynard, where did Mr Atherton go?"

"Out, Miss! In the rain, and not a proper coat or a hat or anything but his regular clothes. He'll catch his death of cold, Miss."

"I know where he will have gone. My cloak, Maynard — the old winter one."

"James has already gone for it, miss. We knew you would— Ah, here he is."

Hastily, she threw on the cloak and dashed out of the front door. It was indeed raining hard, the drops pelting down and bouncing off the lower steps, those not sheltered by the portico. Clutching the cloak tightly about her, Winnie ran down the drive, and onto the path through the shrubbery, a quicker way than through the flower gardens. There was some shelter there, and more under the trees of the home wood, but even so, she was soaked before she reached the oak tree, where the swings sat motionless and dripping.

Quickly, she climbed the steps to the tree house, her heart in her mouth. Surely he would be here? He must be!

He was sitting on the floor, his knees drawn up to his chest, his head lowered so that she could not see his face. He was soaked from head to toe, water puddling beneath him and little rivulets running from his hair. The rain drummed on the wooden roof just above Winnie's head.

"Walter?" she said uncertainly. He started at the sound of her voice, but kept his head lowered. "Are you ill?"

A shake of the head.

"Just upset, then," she said, sitting down on the floor beside him. Not touching... not presuming to touch him, no matter how much she longed to take him into her arms. "What is it about Mr Lomax that bothers you so much?"

He half lifted his head. "Jealous."

"Jealous?" That was a surprise. "What can you possibly be jealous about... unless... is it that he has his inheritance and you have lost yours?"

He lifted his head a little more, a tiny smile curving his lips. "Not that."

"Then what is it? What else can he possibly have that you do not?"

A long silence, then he said in a low voice, "He has you."

Now that was not funny, so very far from funny that she answered him sharply. "Why do you dislike him so much?"

He lifted his head fully, not looking at her, resting his head, still dripping, against the rough wooden wall of the tree house. With a sigh, he closed his eyes. "I do not dislike him... not much, anyway. Well, he is a coxcomb, of course, but I do not hold that against him. It is not Lomax himself I dislike, it is all that he represents."

"You are not making much sense, Walter."

The lips curled upwards again. "I suppose not."

He sat up a little straighter, stretching out his legs. Goodness, he was tall! His feet nearly touched the opposite wall. Winnie had a sudden memory of when they were children, and this tree house had seemed so large. They had all squeezed into it — herself and Walter, Eustace, Josie and Kent, Bertram and Lucas, even Hebe and Mabel. Not Izzy. Even then, she was too grand for tree houses. Not the younger ones, or at least she could not remember them at all. Mostly, what she remembered was Walter and Eustace. They were the leaders, the oldest, the biggest and strongest. Everything revolved around them, and later, for her, it was all about Walter.

He sighed again. "It never occurred to me that you would marry," he said, his voice low again. "You were a fixed part of my life, my good friend, my very *best* friend, and I stupidly thought you would always be there. And then along comes Lomax and steals you away from me... taking my friend far away, to... somewhere in the south."

"Oxfordshire."

"Yes. Far, far away. I am happy for you, Winnie, truly I am, and you deserve a man like him who can keep you in comfort for the rest of your life. For all I make fun of him, and despite his ditherings, he is a good man at heart. He will not throw away his fortune at the gambling table, or go chasing after other women. And the fact that he keeps coming back means that he truly loves you, so that shows commendable good sense. Once he is settled and married to you, he will be as steady as a rock. I am just miserable for me, that is all."

Winnie considered that with a sinking heart. His best friend. That was not a bad way to be considered, but it was a long way from what she had hoped. Still, she could set his mind at rest on one point.

"I am not going to marry Mr Lomax."

His head shot round to face her so quickly that she was showered with little drops from his wet hair. "Not? Truly?"

"Truly."

"But why ever not?"

"A dozen reasons, at least, but mainly because of the horrid kiss."

He gave a bark of laughter. "Winnie, that is the most ridiculous reason I ever heard."

"It is not the kiss itself, precisely, it is more what it tells me. Walter, I could perhaps live with Mr Lomax's other failings — perhaps — if I cared for him, but I cannot marry a man for whom I feel nothing."

"Nothing?" There was a strange look in his eyes that she could not interpret.

"You showed me that when you almost kissed me."

He gave a wry laugh. "That! I should not have done it, Winnie. It was quite wrong of me."

"No, no! It was the best thing you could have done, for you showed me what a kiss *ought* to be. Not horrid and rough and unpleasant, but gentle and... and *tender*. That is the word. You, who see me as nothing more than a friend, showed me more tenderness than Mr Lomax, who professes to love me. So you see, I cannot possibly marry him, not now I know the difference."

"You liked it?" he whispered. "When we did not even kiss?"

She wriggled herself round, so that she was kneeling, facing him. So close! If she reached out her hand, she could touch him...

"I liked it very much," she said softly. "I should like more of it... a great deal more, and none of Mr Lomax's rough ways. How can I possibly marry a man who cannot even kiss me lovingly? So I shall marry you, instead. Or no one. I know you only offered for me from guilt, so if ever you think better of it, I shall—"

"I shall not think better of it," he said in an oddly urgent tone, and now his eyes were alight with... something. Some fire that stopped the breath inside her and made her turn to jelly.

She could not say a word, transfixed with hope and longing and terror all at once. Was it possible? Did he feel something for her? Not love, not this overwhelming yearning that afflicted her, but *something?*

"Winnie," he said, his voice barely above a whisper. "I... I..."

He could not speak either! They stared at each other for a long moment, and Winnie could no longer restrain her hands. She reached out, first one hand and then the other, to cup his face, just as he had touched her on that unforgettable day. He gave a little groan and closed his eyes.

"Winnie..."

It was an invitation, but she did not dare, and after a moment his eyes opened again. He raised his hands to hers, his fingers touching her so delicately yet burning into her. Then he smiled.

"Dear Winnie! What a darling you are, but I never appreciated you until Lomax came along. I just thought of you as good old Winnie, game for anything, always there for me, ready to listen or offer me her pithy advice. *'Pull yourself together, Walter!'* How many times have you said that to me, and usually it was just the kick on the rear that I needed. But I never thought of you as anything more than my good friend until I saw the way Lomax looked at you. And then..." He closed his eyes again, with a deep sigh, then opened them to look straight into her eyes. "Dearest Winnie, I know I am not much of a catch, not beside someone like Lomax. I have no money, no title, no employment, no grand estate to offer you, as you deserve. All I have to give you is myself and a heart that is true to you, now and always. Do you think… is there any chance, do you suppose, that you could come to care for me as I care for you?"

She almost laughed in sheer exhilaration. How could he possibly not know? It was extraordinary! She had no words, not then, for her heart was too full. Everything she had ever wanted was here in her hands, was hers forever, and her joy was so overwhelming that she did not think she would ever be coherent again.

There was only one thing she could do, the one thing that needed no words, that even a brain turned to soup could manage.

So she leaned towards him and pressed her lips to his.

It was like coming home. All the long years of hopeless yearning, of smiling when he carelessly flicked her cheek and called her Mouse, of pretending not to mind when he looked admiringly at other women, of congratulating him when he betrothed himself to Bea Franklyn, all of that was behind her. For ten endless years she had waited for this moment, for a kiss steeped in warmth and affection and friendship and happiness and *love*. His arms were round her now, holding her tight against him, and she knew she had found a love that would sustain both of them through all the trials and joys of life together.

Eventually, sated for the moment, she lay snuggled against his chest, savouring the feel of his arm around her back, his other hand playing with her hair.

"I love the way this one curl always escapes from bondage," he said, twisting it loosely around one finger. "I love everything about you, but this one lost curl is especially lovable. You always look slightly disarranged."

"My mother despaired a long time ago of ever keeping me tidy," she said, not looking at him, suddenly shy. "I am afraid I have mangled your cravat."

He chuckled, rocking her slightly as his chest rose and fell with each breath. "It was ruined anyway. I got soaked, and now you are wet, too."

"It is a small price to pay," she said. She dared to look up at him, but the joy radiating from his face almost undid her. It was too much! She was not worthy of such affection.

"I think you have answered my question, anyway," he said.

"What question?"

"Whether you could ever care for me."

She tilted her head to look at him fully. "I cannot imagine how you can even ask me that, Walter Atherton. How can you not know that I have been head over ears in love with you for the past ten years?"

"What!" He moved sharply, rocking her violently, so that she clutched his cravat again. "*Ten years?* But you were only fourteen ten years ago."

"That is old enough to fall in love. You probably do not remember the occasion at all, but it was July, and I was here in the woods with Hebe and Mabel... not Lily, I think... no, it was just the three of us, and we were paddling in the stream, our skirts pulled up, and completely drenched, because Mabel thought it was funny to splash us. I must have looked an absolute fright. Then Hebe slipped over and twisted her ankle, and we did not know quite how to get her back to the house. But then, out of nowhere, you appeared to rescue her on that white horse you used to have. Do you remember its name?"

"White Knight."

"Exactly! White Knight, and so you were. You were up at Oxford then, so we had seen nothing of you for months, and you were the last person we could have expected, and yet there you were, riding up to rescue Hebe like a hero from one of those romantic novels. You never even dismounted, you simply swept her up onto White Knight and carried her off. It was the most astonishing thing, and I fell in love with you on the spot. I had never before wished that I had twisted my ankle, but I did then."

"I wished it too, as it happens, for at least you would not have cried. Hebe cried all the way back to the house, you know."

"Did she? Good gracious! But she always was a watering pot. The least thing would set her off. So you *do* remember!"

"Lord, yes! You looked like the veriest ragamuffin, I remember that well enough. I wondered who on earth would marry a hoyden like you. Little did I know it would be me. But I cannot say how soon it will be, my dearest Mouse. Ah... you dislike that name. But what am I to call you, otherwise?"

"Darling?"

"Beloved? Dearest one? Love of my life? Dear heart? I could run on like this all day. Sweetheart. My cherished love? Flower? My pet? Light of my heart? My angel?"

"Oh, not that. I have never been angelic."

"To me you are, my sweet, beloved Winnie. I am not sure why we are talking so much when we could be kissing. Can you think of any reason?"

"None at all."

After that, the only sound was the rain still thundering on the roof.

32: A List Of Transgressions

"Miss Winnie! Miss Winnie! Are you there?"

The distant voice, barely heard above the rain, broke into the euphoric bubble in which Winnie existed. Walter was there with her, the man she loved with all her heart, who by some miracle also loved her, and what need had they of the world beyond? But it seemed that the world beyond had need of them, for there it was again, that faint voice.

"Miss Winnie! You're wanted at the house right away."

Tearing herself with the utmost reluctance from Walter's arms, she went to the tree house door and peered down. There was an umbrella directly below. As she watched, it tilted, and the anxious face of James the footman appeared.

"There you are, Miss!"

"What is it, James?"

"You're wanted, Miss. We've been searching all over for you. Mr Lomax is here."

"Very well, James. Go back to the house and tell them we are on our way."

"Shall I leave the umbrella for you, Miss? It's still raining pretty hard."

"You keep it, James. I am already wet, and there is no point in you getting soaked through as well."

He went off, and Winnie turned to Walter. "We shall have to go, at least, I shall. If he is here, I must see him, I suppose."

"Yes, it cannot be avoided now, but..." He looked suddenly anxious. "You will not... take him back?"

"Heavens, no! I should not have done so, no matter what, but... everything is different now, is it not?" She blushed, for some reason overcome with shyness.

He chuckled and wrapped his arms around her. "Everything is different. The world is a fine place this morning, I find. Whatever your parents may think about it, we are engaged to be married, I have the woman I love in my arms and I could not be happier. If I were to cut myself, I think I should ooze happiness instead of blood. Oh, Winnie, to think I never realised what I was missing until Lomax came along. I shall be forever grateful to him for that."

"Then so shall I be, too. I suppose we cannot be married soon?"

"No. Your father is quite right about that. I still have an allowance from my father, and the house he made ready for me when I was betrothed to Bea, but it is not enough to support a wife in comfort. I should hate you to have to scrimp and go without anything, my dear one. Your uncle thinks he can arrange employment for me. He is very pleased with my progress, you know, so it seems I am not useless at everything, after all. In time, I shall be earning enough for us to marry. Can you wait, do you think?"

"Walter, I have waited ten years for you, so another year or two is neither here nor there. But I must go and face Mr Lomax. I cannot keep him waiting any longer. If we run all the way, perhaps we will not get so wet?"

They ran, holding hands and giggling like children, their joy so irrepressible that it could not be contained. They raced up the steps to the front door, which stood open, and burst into the hall, still laughing.

Maynard smiled paternally at them, but Mama stormed out of the book room on wings of wrath.

"Wherever have you been, Winnie? Mr Lomax has been here for nearly an hour. And look at the state of you! Quite disgraceful! Upstairs with you at once, and make yourself respectable."

By this time, Winnie had extricated herself from her dripping cloak and handed it to James. "Is Mr Lomax in the book room? I shall see him at once."

"You will not go near him in that disgusting state. I am quite ashamed of you. Go upstairs and change. Martha has laid out the green twill for you, and Harding will help you dry your hair. As for you, Walter, you are not wanted here. Kindly remove yourself from the hall. Go, Winnie, go! At o nce!"

"No, Mama. It would be unconscionable to keep Mr Lomax waiting any longer. What I have to say to him will not take long."

"Winnie, go upstairs this instant! I insist."

"I am very sorry to disobey you, Mama, but no."

And so saying, she marched, head high, straight past her appalled mother and into the book room. Her father jumped up, relief written plainly on his face. Mr Lomax leaned against the mantel, just as he had before he had proposed to her. Then she had thought his pose suggested eagerness or perhaps nerves. Now she thought it predatory. Still, she need not fear him, and his shock when he saw her, drenched from head to toe, was amusing.

Before she could speak, Mama rushed in. "I must apologise for my daughter, Mr Lomax. She is too eager to see you to take the time to make herself respectable."

"I can apologise for myself, Mama," Winnie snapped. "Mr Lomax, pray forgive my dishevelled appearance, but I would not for the world hold you here a moment longer than necessary."

"I should not mind waiting," he said faintly. "Whatever has happened to you, Winifred? You are normally as neat as a new pin."

"My name is Winnie, and no, this is very much my usual appearance. Perhaps not quite so unkempt, and definitely not so wet, but I am not as a rule a tidy person."

"But it was what first drew my notice to you," he said plaintively. "So neatly dressed, and stylish, too, yet that gown..."

"Has seen better days, yes. It is one of my old morning gowns. I usually change before you arrive. What does it matter? Clothes are not important."

"Clothes are not important?"

For a moment, she was in genuine fear that he might swoon away altogether, for he swayed alarmingly and his face was unnaturally pale. Where were the nearest smelling salts? Mama might have some... or Lily...

"Winnie," Mama said, tugging at her sleeve, "now that you have seen how your appearance distresses poor Mr Lomax, will you not consider his feelings and tidy yourself a little?"

"Yes, indeed. I shall be very happy to wait for you," Mr Lomax said, his voice a mere thread. "Pray go and change, my dear Winifred."

"*Winnie!* My name is Winnie, and I am not your dear. Have you forgotten that you broke off our betrothal and walked out of here in a fit of pique? After that, you really cannot expect to just carry on as though nothing has happened."

"Certainly not, but I forgive you, my dear."

Winnie gasped at the effrontery of it, but then she began to laugh. "*You* forgive *me?* How very, very entertaining. I do *not* forgive you, however."

"Forgive *me*?" he gasped. "What, pray, have I done that requires forgiveness, apart from offer you the consequence of my name?"

"Do you want me to list all your transgressions, Mr Lomax? Very well, on your own head be it. You believed foul rumours of me without making any effort to find out if they were true. You led me to expect an offer of marriage in London and then left town in haste, without telling me. Worst of all, you then *lied* about it. Did you imagine I would not know? That I would not care? As if all that were not bad enough, you have so little consideration for my feelings that you repeatedly call me by the wrong name when you know I dislike it, and you planned to let your mother continue to live in the marital home, without even consulting me. And perhaps I could have put up with all of that... *perhaps*... if you had not been such a terrible kisser."

Now he was red-faced with rage. "How dare you, madam!"

"How dare *you* inflict such an unpleasant experience on me, sir! I strongly suggest you practise a little before you attempt the manoeuvre on another young lady." Seeing him quite speechless, she began to feel almost sorry for him. "Mr Lomax, I am very sorry you have had a wasted journey. I am truly grateful to you for ending our betrothal, for I might never have had the courage to break it off myself, and our marriage would have been a great mistake. We should not have suited."

"You are not at all as I supposed," he said, glaring at her. "You deceived me into thinking you a demure and unworldly young lady who needed my protection. Now I see you are disobedient and wild, and possibly much worse than that. On one point only we agree — we should never have suited. I am very glad to be undeceived regarding your true character. My mother always had reservations, and now I see she was quite right. I bid you good day, madam."

"Good bye, Mr Lomax," she said calmly, making him only a small curtsy, for a bubble of anger still burned inside her.

"I am so sorry, Mr Lomax," Mama said, intercepting him as he headed for the door. "Such a pity to leave now, when your charming company would be so welcome. You add such distinction to our gatherings. I wonder if..."

Her voice faded to a murmur as they reached the hall, Lily following in her wake, shutting the door behind them.

Walter, who must have crept in unnoticed, chuckled gently. "Well done, Winnie!"

Hebe emerged from the corner where she had been lurking, watching the whole spectacle unfolding. Her eyes were wide with shock. "Oh, Winnie dear, what have you done? To say such things to him!"

"He deserved it," she said curtly.

"Burning all your bridges and no mistake, Winnie," her father said quietly. "I am still not minded to approve your marriage to Walter, you know."

"I know, Papa. We will wait until Walter is settled somewhere and has some employment."

"Yes, I suppose it is inevitable, whatever I may think about it. Walter and I need to have a long chat, and perhaps see what your Uncle Alfred has to say. And Walter, you need to talk to your father and explain your new situation. This betrothal of yours cannot stay a secret any longer, I fear. But before all of that, you both need to stop dripping all over my rugs and get yourselves into dry clothes before you are both carried off with chills on the lungs. You will want to survive long enough to get to the altar, I imagine."

***

Winnie passed the evening in a haze of delirious happiness. In the small corner of her brain that was still functioning, she noticed Papa was unusually serious, Mama was not speaking to her, Hebe glowered disapprovingly and Lily... there was something strange and excitable about Lily. Only Uncle Alfred beamed paternally at her and whispered his congratulations.

None of it mattered. Nothing at all mattered, for Walter loved her and her joy could not be punctured. She had the memory of his ardent kisses to warm her inside, and his words of love still ringing in her ears, and what more could she ask for? He came straight to her side in the drawing room that evening, sat beside her at dinner, lingered hardly at all with the gentlemen and then spent the rest of the evening playing backgammon with her in a corner, while music and conversation and the distribution of tea and cake swirled unnoticed around them. His eyes softened every time he looked at her, a little smile hovered permanently on his lips and from time to time his hand gently brushed against hers, almost as if by accident, sending a little jolt of fire through her. She was in paradise. Surely no one had ever been so happy as she was?

She had not been in her bedroom long that night, for Martha had only just left when Hebe came in and sat on the window seat beside her.

"You are in love with him." She sounded surprised.

"With Walter? Yes. I have been in love with him for years."

"I had no idea! How could I not know? How could you never show it, you unnatural creature? When he became engaged to the Franklyn girl, you should have had hysterics or gone into a decline, at the very least, but I never suspected a thing. I thought you were insane to throw over Mr Lomax and his four thousand a year for a man with nothing, but I understand it all now. And Walter loves you, too."

"*Yes!* Is it not wonderful? To love and be loved in return... it is the most amazing thing."

Hebe smiled. "It certainly is. I am so happy for you, Winnie, because no one deserves it more than you. And to hide your true feelings for so long... I could not have done so."

"I am not like you, Hebe."

"No. Is he really such a terrible kisser? Mr Lomax, I mean. I nearly died when you said he should practise! Was it horrid? I cannot imagine any kiss being horrid. William's kisses are... glorious." She gave a little wriggle of pleasure.

"And so are Walter's."

She smiled at the memory, and Hebe hugged her and wept a little, and told her how lucky she was to have found love, which she knew perfectly well. She was the luckiest girl alive.

***

Walter determined to take Winnie to see his father the very next day, but Lady Strong said stiffly that the carriage would not be available, nor could she chaperon Winnie that day.

"We can ride," Winnie said at once. "We can take a groom for propriety, and the rain has stopped."

"But everywhere will be a foot deep in mud," Walter said. "We will not be fit to be seen."

"Winnie would scarcely care about that," Lady Strong said sourly.

"Nor would my father, but I care," Walter said. "I hardly wish to present my future wife to my father liberally coated in mud. For a casual visit, perhaps, but this is a little different. We will go another day, when the carriage is available, and a lady is free to act the chaperon."

"I do not know when it will next be free," Lady Strong said. "With Hebe to leave us again before long, I have a number of outings planned."

"Then I shall despatch a groom to Corland, and ask them to send a carriage for us. Winnie's maid will have to keep us from scandal."

It was Uncle Alfred who settled the matter in the end. "You may take my carriage, Walter. With the roof stowed, even my dear sister-in-law cannot possibly object. You can hire a couple of horses from the inn, since Kitty obviously needs her own carriage horses."

Lady Strong sniffed, not mollified even by this consideration, but Walter merely smiled at her. He was smiling so much these days that his happiness spilled over even onto Lady Strong.

"Your mama disapproves of me, I think," he said to Winnie, as the carriage rolled away from Birchall House.

"She disapproves of me, too, at the moment," Winnie said easily. "Do you mind?"

"Not in the slightest. I do not mind anything very much just now." He took her hand in his, then methodically peeled off first her glove and then his. "Ah, that is better. Your hand is so soft and warm."

"My lips might be warm, too."

He chuckled, but took the hint, and for a while there was silence within the carriage. Only when a particularly sharp jolt threw them apart did she laugh and say, "Perhaps it is not the best idea to arrive flushed and dishevelled."

He sighed, but he could see the sense in it.

Simpson and Wellum met them in the entrance hall. "His lordship is in the drawing room, sir," Simpson said, as Walter handed his hat and gloves to Wellum.

"The drawing room! What is he doing in the drawing room? Visitors?"

"Mr and Mrs George Atherton are with him, sir, as well as Miss Emily Atherton and Miss Penelope Atherton, and Mrs Vaughn."

Mrs Vaughn? One of Mother's list of prospective wives for his father, he thought.

"Miss Olivia is there, too, sir," Simpson added.

Miss Olivia! Walter had almost got used to the loss of his own title, but it was still a sharp wrench to remember that his sister was no longer Lady Olivia and must now face the prospect of finding a husband without either title or legitimacy.

"Well, let us go and tell them our news, shall we?" Walter said.

Winnie smiled up at him, and the affection in her eyes filled him with contentment. This was how a betrothal was supposed to be, a joy that was bone-deep and all-encompassing, filling every corner of his life, every waking moment. This was how it would be for the rest of their lives.

He tucked Winnie's arm in his and turned to face his father.

33: A Betrothal Is Announced

It was not so easy, Winnie discovered, to announce that one is betrothed, not when the earl had guests, anyway. She and Walter were scooped up and led into the drawing room, glasses of something pushed into their hands, introductions made, chairs brought forward for them. Bemused, she obediently sat, and the group continued as if nothing had happened, effortlessly absorbing Winnie and Walter into the conversation. No one asked why they had turned up together, although curious glances were thrown their way. It was all very awkward, but Walter gave her a wry smile, which cheered her.

There was great interest in the recent visit to London, so for some minutes they both fielded questions about the journey, and then Walter's visits to the Treasury and his prospects of obtaining a position there. Winnie had very little to say on that subject, so she quickly lapsed into silence. The earl smiled at her once or twice, and if he had been closer, she was sure he would have spoken to her, but he was across the room, being polite to Mrs Vaughn. Who was she? Probably some relation of Mrs George Atherton's, whose house was filled every summer with relations from all over the north. The earl looked uncomfortable, and the lady not much more so, yet neither made any move to draw apart.

It was the strangest feeling to Winnie, sitting in the drawing room at Corland Castle as a guest, but knowing that one day in the future she would be a member of the family. The earl would be her father-in-law. Olivia, sulky and silent in a corner, would be her sister. Mr and Mrs George Atherton would be her aunt and uncle, and their daughters her cousins. It was so *odd*. She had been here many times over the years, and always as an outsider. Even in the early days of her love for Walter, when she had dreamed of marrying him and even imagined herself as the Countess of Rennington one day, it had never occurred to her that all these people would be her family, just as they were his.

And now she wondered just what they would think when they knew of their betrothal. They would say that he was marrying beneath him, probably, for even though he was not now to be a peer, he was still the son of an earl. They would say, too, that he should marry a woman of fortune, now that he had none of his own, and he was handsome enough and charming enough to be successful, if he would set his mind to it. He did not have to settle for Winnie Strong, daughter of a baronet of little wealth and no importance. Perhaps it would have been better if Walter had come here by himself.

And better yet if she could stop brooding and be conversable, as was expected of her, but her mind was blank. For some minutes she sat in silence, half listening to the swirl of conversations going on around her, and half occupied with her own thoughts. So she was startled when Mr George Atherton, who was sitting nearby, called across to her, "I believe congratulations are in order, Miss Strong. I wish you joy."

"You know?" Winnie said, startled.

"My dear, everyone knows of your good fortune."

"George, dear," his wife said, waving frantically at him from across the room.

Taken by surprise, Winnie burst out, "Well, I do not know how, for it has all been a great secret, and we only came here today to tell his father of it."

There was absolute silence in the room. Mr George looked panicked, then glanced across at his wife, who sighed and shook her head slightly.

"Oh, I see," Winnie said, laughing. "You are thinking perhaps of Mr Lomax. No, that is all off, and now..."

Her words trickled away into the silence. Everyone stared at her, astonished. Then, slowly working it out, they looked at Walter and back again at Winnie. Only the earl, not as quick on the uptake, still looked puzzled.

Olivia was shocked out of her torpor. "You are going to marry *her?*" she said, with as much disdain as if Winnie had been an opera dancer. "Whatever for?"

"For the usual reason," Walter said calmly, rising to his feet, "that she makes me very happy, and my life would be miserable without her. Father, I apologise for springing this on you. We had hoped to find you alone to tell you discreetly, but it is true — Winnie and I are engaged to be married."

"And how long has this been going on?" the earl said, frowning.

"I am not sure what you mean by *'going on',*" Walter said.

"When did you propose?"

"Oh... a little over a week ago."

"And she accepted you then?"

"She did, but—"

The earl rose from his chair and positioned himself directly in front of Walter. "So you have been engaged for more than a week... my eldest son is engaged for a full week and does not think to tell his own father? But I cannot discuss this now, not when I have guests. You will wait for me in my study, and I shall arrange for Miss Strong to be conveyed home."

"No, Father, we arrived together, and we will leave together. You talk to us both or not at all."

For an instant, the two men glared at each other, father and son, their eyes locked together. Walter was slightly the taller, with the broad shoulders and well-built figure of the habitual sportsman. The earl was armoured with the dignity of his rank, and centuries of haughty expectation of instant obedience. But he was not a belligerent man, so after a few moments, he nodded curtly.

"In my study, then."

Winnie wished she could curl into a tiny ball and hide under the furniture. Oh, to be a mouse in truth, and scuttle away to a safe hiding place! Instead, she had to accept the arm that Walter offered her and allow herself to be led from the room past the shocked faces of all of them.

They had only just left the room, and were still in the passage leading to the great hall, when they heard quick footsteps behind them. It was Mrs George, with a warm smile on her face.

"My dears, what wonderful news! I am so happy for you both. You must not let Rennington browbeat you, you know. He will come round to it soon enough. He is a bit lost at the moment and it makes him tetchy, but his tempers never last long. You must both come to Westwick for dinner very soon."

And then, with a quick wave, she was gone, dashing back to the drawing room.

"She is right, of course," Walter said. "You must not look as if the weight of the world has dropped on your shoulders, my darling. You were so happy on the way here."

"But I could not bear to be the cause of a rift between you and your father."

"Then you must give me up at once," he said, pulling her into his arms and kissing her gently. "Go on, jilt me." Another kiss. "I am waiting." Another longer kiss.

She pulled away from him, laughing delightedly. "Silly man! I waited ten years for you, and nothing in the world would induce me to give you up now. If you want to be rid of me, you will just have to jilt me yourself."

He answered that without a word being spoken, so it seemed to Winnie that they were in perfect accord on the subject, but he continued to reassure her for some time. Only when they heard voices emerging from the drawing room did they reluctantly break apart. Passing through the great hall, they came to the library and the study beyond. A little while later, the earl found them sitting decorously side by side on a sofa, not so much as holding hands.

"Well, now, Walter, what is all this about? Have we not had enough dramatic changes in our lives? Why hurtle to the altar in this harum-scarum manner? I do not like this sudden start, nor do I like being kept in the dark like this. Just because your circumstances have changed does not mean you can go off and do whatever you like."

"Actually, that is precisely what it means," Walter said with a slight chuckle. "There is still family affection between us, naturally, but *legally* I am not your son... I am the son of nobody. I could, if I wished, go off and do exactly as I like, without reference to you or anyone, but of course I would not do so. I still value your opinion."

"And my money, I dare say. I still pay your allowance."

"For which I am very grateful, but I hope one day to be independent of your charity."

"You will never do so by marrying a daughter of Strong's! There is no money there to keep you afloat. No offence, Winnie."

"None taken, my lord, and we have no intention of hurtling to the altar. Our marriage will have to wait until Walter is established in a career and can afford to support a family."

"Ah, you always were a sensible girl. Pour us all some wine, will you, for I need something to fortify me, after doing the pretty to guests and now this revelation." The earl passed a tired hand across his face. "And why not *tell* me what you are up to?"

"Sir Hubert insisted on secrecy just at first," Walter said. "He disapproves mightily of the entire business. I am not a fit husband for his daughter, you see."

"What, a baronet objecting to an earl's son? The man is getting above himself."

Walter laughed. "He is perfectly right, Father. I cannot possibly afford to marry, so I have no business offering for Winnie at all. But... it has happened, and astonishingly, she has accepted me, so there we are. I am sure you will be glad about it in the end. She is far too good for me, you know, and a considerably better match for me than Bea Franklyn, fortune or no fortune."

The earl's lips quirked into a half smile. "There, I will agree with you. Winnie is such a sensible girl, she will keep your feet on the ground. I never understood what you were thinking with Bea Franklyn."

"I was not thinking at all, to be honest. I never thought deeply about anything very much. What need had I to consider my future, when my whole life was mapped out for me from birth? I was destined for an idle life, waiting for you to die. A suitable wife was part of the plan, and Bea thrust herself under my nose. You had told me many times how Mother snatched you up when you were looking in quite another direction, and how happy that made you, so it seemed to me that I was merely following your example. I dare say we should have been contented enough, but there was no great affection between us. Not much on my side and none at all on hers. But now! Everything is different now. I cannot be glad that someone took an axe to Nicholson, but his death and the discovery that he was never ordained has shaken me out of my rut. It may have taken away my inheritance, but it has brought me something infinitely more precious to me — my darling Winnie, and the freedom to choose my own path in life. I am going to go back to town in October with Mr Alfred Strong and take up a position in the Treasury, and in time, I shall marry Winnie and be blissfully happy."

The earl nodded thoughtfully. "I thought perhaps you were snatching at the nearest female after Bea Franklyn rejected you, but now I see that is not so. But what about you, Winnie? Jane has been telling me all the ins and outs of this fellow you met in London. You were betrothed to him a matter of days ago, yet now you are to marry Walter."

Winnie crossed the room to kneel before his chair and take his hand. "Dear Lord Rennington, I have been in love with Walter for years and years. He never saw me as other than a friend for most of that time, but when his betrothal ended and we were to go to London together, I hoped that finally he might see me as something more than a friend. When Mr Lomax appeared and still Walter gave me no sign, I finally despaired of him and accepted Mr Lomax. Happily for me, my betrothal gave Walter the nudge he needed, and when Mr Lomax jilted me, Walter was there to step forward. I am sorry we were obliged to keep it from you for a while. I hope you can forgive us, and wish us well."

"I do wish you well… I wish you both joy. You will do very well together." He sighed. "I only wish my own marriage were so happily settled. I am not used to this business of courtship. What did you think of Mrs Vaughn?"

"Buck-toothed," Walter said at once.

"Walter!" Winnie cried. "She is not buck-toothed. She is a fine-looking woman, I thought."

"No, she is a little buck-toothed," the earl said, frowning. "Or at least, she seems to have too many teeth for her mouth. It is most disconcerting when she talks."

"Really, my lord," Winnie said. "It is character that counts, not teeth."

"No, no, teeth are very important," the earl said solemnly. "Hair and teeth and eyes and a good figure. And not weeping at every little thing. And not chewing with her mouth open, or slurping her soup, or—"

"Conversation," Winnie said firmly. "That is what truly matters."

"Ah, so you chose Walter for his powers of conversation, did you?" the earl said, his eyes twinkling merrily, and Winnie had the grace to blush. "There now, how pretty you are when you colour up like that. Walter, bring Winnie to dinner one day soon… Thursday, if that would suit. Then we can toast your future and plan a modest celebration of your betrothal. How lovely to have some good news for a change! Bring Alfred Strong with you, and he can tell me all about this Treasury position you seem so keen on. Now off you go and tell your Aunt Alice the news, and see if you can persuade her out of her room. It is time she rejoined the world."

***

Winnie was both excited and nervous about the dinner at Corland Castle. For the first time, she would take her place amongst the Athertons as a future member of the family, but she knew that Walter's choice would not receive universal approbation. However, she was received very cordially.

The company was small enough and intimate enough for complete informality at the dinner table, and with Mr Nicholson's murderer safely behind bars in York, the atmosphere was light. Even Lady Alice felt well enough to emerge from her seclusion and join the company. Captain Edgerton kept them all entertained with his improbable tales, sometimes of India and sometimes of his murders and other investigations. Kent and Uncle Alfred sat on either side of Lady Alice, describing the various dishes to her, and cutting larger portions into smaller pieces for her to manage more easily. The genial Scot, Mr Alexander, managed to amuse Olivia, no easy task, while also conducting an intense discussion with Eustace. They made a strange pair, Eustace so dark and slender, and the Scotsman big and blond. Winnie had Lord Rennington on one side of her and Walter on the other, with Mrs Edgerton across the table, which arrangement she felt could not be bettered.

"You will be leaving Corland very soon, I imagine, Mrs Edgerton, now that the captain's business here is concluded," Winnie said during a lull in the conversation.

"We leave tomorrow to collect Miss Peach."

"Your companion? She is not here?"

"She is at Pickering."

"Pickering?" Eustace said, in astonished tones. "What is she doing there?"

"Enjoying herself enormously," Mrs Edgerton said, with a merry laugh. "She has had a very dull life, poor thing, so finding herself involved in a murder is tremendously exciting for her. She has thrown herself into it with gusto."

"But what is there to discover at Pickering?" Eustace said. "A sleepy little place, I should have said."

"There is Mr Nicholson's house, for one thing," Captain Edgerton said eagerly. "Then there is the matter of the missing fortune, and—"

"Michael," Mrs Edgerton said gently. "It is over, remember?"

He subsided at once, with a rueful nod.

Lady Alice turned her sightless eyes towards him. "I am not convinced there is any fortune to find, Captain. You like chasing hares, I think, but not everything is complicated. Sometimes a murder is merely a sordid matter of a thwarted love affair, and perhaps a fortune is nothing but a few thousand pounds in the bank."

"I expect you are right, my lady," he said. "It is in the nature of my work to chase hares."

"And to believe the worst of everyone," Lady Alice said. "Of me, of my daughter... you even suspected Lord Farramont at one time, I believe."

"And Mr Eustace," the captain said. "I am happy to have been proved wrong on every point, and very happy that Shapman confessed."

"He also exonerated my daughter," she said. "I cannot forgive him for taking my husband from me, but at least he has not dragged Tess into his own disgrace. His actions may have been inspired by his passion for her, but she herself is entirely innocent."

"Indeed, she is," the captain said. "Tomorrow, I and my friends will be gone, Mr Eustace will rearrange the armoury display on the stairs, and you and all your family will be able to begin the long process of rebuilding your lives."

"Which process one of my sons has already begun," the earl said. "Walter and Winnie have found happiness and brought some sunshine into our current darkness. Let us drink a toast to their future together."

Winnie acknowledged the toast with blushes and smiles, and Walter gazed at her with such love in his eyes that she almost exploded with happiness.

When the ladies withdrew, Winnie played cribbage with Olivia while Mrs Edgerton good-naturedly read to Lady Alice. When the gentlemen began to drift through, Uncle Alfred took over the reading. Winnie wondered what would become of Lady Alice when Mrs Edgerton had left and Uncle Alfred had gone back to London in October. She would have neither husband nor friend, only her own family, busy with their own affairs.

As they drove home that night, Winnie and Walter side by side, and Uncle Alfred with his back to the horses, she ventured to say, "Uncle, how will Lady Alice manage? She will not always have you or Mrs Edgerton to read to her. She must miss Mr Nicholson terribly."

"Indeed," he said, "but Lord Rennington is already training a footman to assist her at meals, as she used to have before she married. As for reading to her... what she needs is a companion, someone of her own age to talk to and depend upon. She manages very well, despite her blindness, but she cannot do everything for herself."

"Ah... a companion. Yes, that would answer. A cousin, perhaps."

"Or, in time, another husband," Uncle Alfred said. "She is still a fine-looking woman, and the sister of an earl will always attract attention."

“Another husband!” Winnie said, shocked. “Surely she would not! How can anyone love two people in a lifetime?”

“You are a romantic, Winnie,” Uncle Alfred said with a little smile. “You are so much in love with Walter that you cannot imagine having room in your heart for another, but I can assure you the heart is infinitely large. Does not a mother love every child just as much, whether she has one or ten, or even more? The mother with one child does not love him ten times as much as the mother with ten. So it is with marriage. One may love again and again, and each love is different from every other. The first love is perhaps the most intense, and the most painful, but there is just as much joy in a second or third love as in the first.”

“You almost sound as if you speak from experience, Uncle,” Winnie said, suddenly suspicious.

“Perhaps I do, and perhaps I do not,” he said, and although it was pitch dark in the carriage, Winnie was certain he was smiling. “So do not despair for the Lady Alice. She may yet recover from her grief and learn to enjoy life again. So all her friends must hope, anyway.”

34: Settlements

Winnie went to bed in a haze of joy, her head full of Walter… his lazy smile, his imposing size, the warmth in his expression when he looked at her, but more than that, it was the very maleness of her beloved that set her shivering with delight. She could see now that Mr Lomax, with his obsession with his appearance, could never have made her a satisfactory husband. He could not set her aflame with one smouldering glance or a touch on her hand, or set her heart leaping just by entering a room. She was grateful for his affection, transient as it was, but love was surely a better foundation for marriage than gratitude.

She had not long finished her prayers, climbed into bed and blown out her candle, than there was a scratching on the door.

"Winnie? Are you awake?"

"Come in, Lily."

She crept in, the flickering candle making her face seem to dance about. "I am so glad you are still awake. May I ask you something? About… about Mr Lomax?"

"Of course," Winnie said, but her heart sank, all the same, for he was the last person she wished to talk about, or even think about, if she were honest.

"I have been wondering about something you said to him, and—"

"Oh, sister, I wish you would forget all of that. I was unspeakably rude to him."

Lily's face shifted, but in the dancing candlelight, Winnie could not work out what was in her mind. "So... you are regretting what you said? And jilting him?"

"I regret the *manner* of my speech to him, but not its import," Winnie said crisply. "And he jilted me, if you recall."

"Then you would not have him back?"

"Not for a king's treasure! Even if I were not engaged to Walter, I would not marry Mr Lomax now if he were the last man on earth." Her words resonated in her head, making her smile — was that not exactly what she had once said to Walter? Then she had not meant it, but now... "No, I would not have him back. Everything I said was true, Lily. He and I should not suit at all."

"I think you may be right," Lily said. "It seems to me that when he first encountered you at the Post Office, he saw you as a... a princess in need of a knight to rescue her. He has a very chivalrous nature, and wished only to protect you from the world, but I do not think you like to be protected, Winnie."

"No, indeed! There are occasions when a gentleman's greater strength is useful, but on the whole, I believe I am perfectly capable of protecting myself. As I had already done at the Post Office, in fact. Not that I was ungrateful for Mr Lomax's intervention, but neither I nor my reticule were in any further danger."

Lily lapsed into silence for some little while as the candle flickered. Then abruptly she said, "Was it truly terrible when he kissed you?"

Winnie laughed. "Why the interest in kissing?"

"I should like to be prepared, that is all. I very much hope to be kissed one day, and I should like to know what to expect… and what *not* to expect. Will you tell me what he did wrong?"

"He took me by surprise. He just… grabbed me, without warning."

"So… he should have warned you?"

"He should have asked. A gentleman should always ask, unless a lady makes it obvious that such attentions would be welcome. And then he should be very gentle and say sweet things and stroke her hair… that sort of thing. It should be romantic and tender and loving, not abrupt and harsh."

"Romantic and tender and loving… I see."

"Lily! What are you planning?"

"Heavens, how suspicious you are!" she said, laughing. "Goodness, my candle is almost out. I shall have to feel my way back to my room. Good night, sister… and thank you."

"Whatever for?" Winnie murmured, but her quicksilver sister had vanished, the door closing quietly behind her. "Hmm… now, what was that all about?"

At seventeen, it was not surprising that Lily's head was full of romance, and perhaps her questions were no more than idle curiosity, but Winnie thought she would mention the matter to Mama.

***

Winnie's days were so busy, she hardly had time to breathe. There were dinners held to celebrate their betrothal by several of the neighbouring families. There was a visit to Knaresborough to see Mabel, for she was too close to her confinement to travel. At Mama's suggestion, there were whole days at the castle, as Walter showed Winnie every corner of his home, and introduced her to everyone, even the secretaries, stewards, gamekeepers, poultry maids, bakers, brewers, dairymaids and woodsmen. And there was church, when she could walk in on Walter's arm and imagine the day she would walk out again as his wife.

The earl and several members of the family were at St Timothy's, obliged by the death of their chaplain to attend divine service at the parish church instead of the convenience of the chapel at Corland. They did not linger afterwards, for it was starting to rain, but the earl dashed across to speak to Papa.

"Tuesday," Papa said with satisfaction, as soon as the carriage was in motion. "His lordship and Mr George Atherton will call on Tuesday at noon to discuss settlements, and then we shall see, Winnie. Yes, then we shall see. But I am not optimistic that you will be able to marry soon, my dear. You must be prepared for a long engagement, I fear."

"I do not mind that, Papa," she said.

"No, but... who knows what may happen?" He threw a quick glance at Walter. "And you will be two hundred and fifty miles apart for much of the year, which is not at all ideal."

"I do not mind a long engagement, either, sir," Walter said. "Winnie is worth waiting for."

Winnie threw him a shy glance and was rewarded with a look of such fire in his eyes that she blushed and looked away.

"How romantic!" Lily sighed as Papa smiled benignly at them, and even Mama's disapproval lifted momentarily into a slight nod.

Tuesday came, and with it Lord Rennington and Mr George Atherton, together with an attorney. It was of no great interest to Winnie. She would have her five thousand, that much she knew, but how much the earl could do for his son now that he had lost his inheritance was another matter. It was one thing to make an allowance to the heir, for he had a claim on the estate, but an illegitimate son had no such right.

Walter's employment would pay him only two hundred pounds a year, and the interest on Winnie's dowry was only another two hundred or so. Although many families lived on a great deal less, Winnie had never been brought up in great economy. Her father's income was not large, but with the home farm and their own productive kitchen garden and orchard, they lived very well. How she would manage in London on only four hundred a year, buying everything in, was beyond her understanding.

So, they would wait until Walter was better established, and she would live at home until then, and there was no point at all in thinking about wedding clothes or a house or children. She could have had all of those, and lived in luxury for the rest of her life with Mr Lomax, but she had made her choice. She would be happy in poverty with Walter, rather than miserable in luxury.

With this settled in her mind, she went down to the stillroom and set to work. She was so engrossed that it was a surprise when Walter came in some time later. She was huddled over her little fire, stirring a mixture, so he came up behind her and wrapped his arms around her waist.

"Mmm, you taste good," he murmured, kissing her bare neck.

She shivered in delight. "Finished so soon? So, is it all settled?"

"It has been almost two hours, and yes, it is all settled." He kissed her again, more lingeringly.

"Stop that, silly boy. Can you stir this for me while I fetch some more water? It is getting a bit too thick."

With a sigh, he released her. "What evil potion are you brewing here? It smells revolting."

"It is a purgative. Do you want to try it?"

He shuddered. "Heavens, no! Do you not want to know what was agreed?"

"About the money? No, I leave that to the men to decide. It will not be enough, that is all I need to know."

He was silent for a moment, stirring the pot as she carefully added more water. When she reclaimed the spoon, he said, "I should have thought you would have wanted to know when we may be able to marry."

She looked up at him in sudden terror. "If it must be years and years away, I had sooner not know."

"What would you say to next month?"

She squeaked and almost dropped the spoon. "Are you teasing me? That would be unkind in you."

"No tease. We shall have an income of almost two thousand pounds a year and—"

"What?"

"—and somewhere to live in town. Father has said we may live in Grafton Street, if you should not dislike it."

"Two thousand a year! Walter, how is that possible?"

"Your Uncle Alfred is to put up twenty thousand for you. We will have over a thousand a year in interest from your money, and my father is to give me the same allowance he promised me if I had married Bea. He wanted to give me a sum of money rather than an allowance, but so much of his estate is entailed or tied up in some way, so Uncle George has concocted some ingenious scheme of an allowance and small sums spread over several years, and eventually the allowance will stop and I shall be independent."

She stared at him, almost uncomprehending. "Two thousand a year! That is as much as Papa has."

"It is not quite two thousand, and your father has two thousand five hundred, but it is a very good income, certainly. And it means we can be married in a month, and I can take you to town with me as my wife. Do you think you will mind living in Grafton Street? There is plenty of room, and Father keeps a full staff there, so it will suit us very well to start with. Then we can look for a property at our leisure, when we know better what we want. But if you dislike it—"

"I must talk to Uncle Alfred."

He laughed. "Of course. He is in his office. I shall be glad to get out of this room. That brew of yours stinks."

Leaving the mixture to cool down, she went upstairs with Walter to see Uncle Alfred, who greeted her effusive thanks with hands raised in defence.

"Now, now, you must not make more of this than it is, Winnie," he said, smiling at her. "Since I have no children of my own, you and your brothers and sisters are my family now. I have watched you all grow up, and I long ago set aside enough to do something for you girls when you marry. It was supposed to be five thousand apiece, but Hebe and Mabel had no need of it, and very likely Lily will not, either, so I am disposing of it where it will do some good. Walter should have been a very wealthy man, and it is not right that he should be left to count every penny now."

"But Uncle, I had no idea you were so rich! This will not leave you counting pennies yourself, will it?"

"Lord bless you, no! I have done very well over the years. I had a fortunate inheritance... no, I will tell you the truth, I think. I was married once, Winnie, many years ago."

"But she died."

"She died, yes, but it was expected. She had consumption, you see, but she wanted to experience matrimony before she died. It was my great privilege to allow her that experience. We had but six months together, but they were happy months for both of us. Her father settled a great sum on her, to be mine afterwards, although I would have done it for nothing. Still, it has been a useful cushion, and if ever I had married again... but that did not happen, and so my expenses were few. I lived here for a part of each year and in bachelor lodgings in town, before Sofia married and offered me a home. My investments have proved fruitful and so there we are. I am still very comfortably situated, should I ever be so fortunate as to marry again."

"Might you do so?" Winnie said curiously.

"Well... I am not averse to the idea. I can see how happy Kitty makes your father, so if I should ever find a love as strong as that, I should be very willing. One never knows what the future may bring. Shall we have a small glass of something to toast your future happiness? But you will have to see Dewar soon to call the banns, for we must be in town by the middle of October."

"So soon! But what about my wedding clothes?" Winnie said fretfully.

"I imagine your Aunt Sofia would be delighted to help out there," Walter said. "Yorkshire seamstresses are excellent in their way, but they cannot compete with a London modiste."

"My head is in a spin," Winnie said. "I had resigned myself to a long engagement, and now you are quite sweeping me off my feet, Walter."

He chuckled. "Perhaps I shall do so in earnest, then, and get a licence from York. We could be married before the end of the week."

"Oh, let me at least catch my breath! The banns will do very well. And now I must get back to the stillroom and see how my evil brew is getting on."

"Very well, child," her uncle said. "The post has arrived, so Walter and I have matters to attend to, but I shall not keep him for long. You will have much to discuss, I am sure."

She reached up to kiss him on one cheek, then demurely curtsied before leaving the room. Her head was so agreeably occupied with her changed circumstances that she entered the hall at a rush, only to stop short in outright horror at the figure standing there, making a delicate adjustment to his cravat in the mirror above the fireplace.

"Mr Lomax! What on earth are you doing here?"

He spun round, seemingly just as shocked to see her. "Winifred! Miss Strong... I did not... I thought..."

"Truly, you are wasting your time, sir," she said acidly. "I wish you would give up this idea and go home to Oxfordshire."

His face drooped. "Do you think so? But I thought... ah, Sir Hubert!" He turned to Papa in relief as he emerged from the book room with Maynard.

"Ah, yes, Lomax. I have been expecting you. Do come in. Not to worry, Winnie, this is not about you."

"Then what—?"

"Your mother will explain it all. This way, Lomax."

The two men disappeared into the book room, leaving Winnie bewildered and not a little angry. What was he doing here, after she had sent him away so decisively? And what would Mama explain?

Behind her, Maynard gave a discreet cough. "You will find Lady Strong in the drawing room, madam, together with Miss Lily, and Mr and Mrs Plaister."

The drawing room. Very well, then.

Maynard opened the door for her, and she swept in, quite prepared to do battle, but was disconcerted to see William Plaister stretched out on the floor in his shirt sleeves, rolling a ball back and forth to Prudence. On the sofa, Mama and Hebe sat side by side, poring over a newly arrived journal, while Lily worked on her tapestry. It was a scene of such domesticity that Winnie could not help smiling, her mood softening instantly. How could she be cross with Mr Lomax when she had her own lovely family about her, and a wonderful future in prospect?

So her tone was mild as she said, "Mama, why is Mr Lomax come—" But one glance at Lily's sudden change of expression told her the truth. "Oh, *Lily!* So that was what Papa meant."

"Is he here?" Lily said breathlessly. "You have seen him?"

"I met him in the hall. He is with Papa now. I suppose I can guess what is afoot."

Lily jumped up, thrusting her tapestry roughly into her workbox and rushed across the room to take Winnie's hands. "You do not mind, do you? You do not want him yourself, whereas I..." She blushed, and looked at her feet.

"You have always admired him, have you not?"

"Oh, *yes!* He is everything that a man ought to be, in my view. So handsome, so finely dressed, and so much elegance in his manner! He is wonderful, Winnie, and... and he seems to like me, too." Again, she blushed.

"You will not cast any rub in their way," Mama said, and it was not a question.

"No, not if you and Papa can overlook his previous behaviour. He called me... bad things, and insulted you, too."

"Mr Lomax was overwrought," Mama said firmly. "He has impressed me with his sincere repentance for his previous outburst. He was very shocked, that must be his excuse."

Winnie could not excuse him quite so readily, but there was no point in arguing. "Then if he is what Lily wants... but, dearest, do you not mind that his mother will live with you?"

"No, indeed, I shall be very glad to have the benefit of her greater experience. You know how I have always depended upon Mama for guidance, and now I shall have a source of wisdom even when I am married. *If* I am married! Oh, how long will it take? I cannot bear the waiting."

Maynard came in to summon Mama to the book room, and as the door closed behind her, Lily turned pleading eyes on Winnie.

"You will not upset everything, will you, Winnie? Please? I know it will be uncomfortable for you, and Mama has managed it all so far without you knowing anything about it — you did not know, did you? We drove out with him here and there, and he dined with us when you were out, for no one wanted to distress you. But now... if he offers, I mean to have him, and I will not give him up, not for you or for anyone."

"Lily, I would not for the world stand in your way. If he is what you want... and perhaps you will not mind the horrid kisses so much."

William gave a shout of laughter, and Hebe said gently, "Winnie, dear, you have no delicacy whatsoever."

Lily lifted her chin and said defiantly, "I do not find his kisses horrid, not in the slightest."

"Oh! Then you have... oh!" Winnie laughed. "How very forward of you, Lily."

"Well, you told him to practise, and it seemed to me that I should like to practise, too, and so we... practised together. And it was most agreeable. Oh Winnie, I do love him, and I know he was in love with you, but I think he is a little bit in love with me too, and I mean to make him very happy, truly I do. He is everything I could ever want in a man," she added with a sigh.

Maynard returned just then with a wide smile. "Miss Lily, you're wanted in the book room."

Lily gave a little squeal, her whole body wriggling in excitement, and Winnie gave her a quick hug. "Off you go, dearest, and may I be the first to wish you joy."

She ran out, and Winnie flopped on a chair, shaking her head. "She is seventeen, Hebe! Has she any idea what she is doing?"

"None at all," Hebe said equably, "but one never does when one marries. It is a great adventure, with surprises around every corner, as you will discover."

"Yes, but Mr Lomax! The man who abandoned me twice, and *lied* to me!"

"Lily will not mind that sort of lie, designed to shield her from unpleasantness. You never needed to be shielded. I think Mr Lomax wants a wife he can protect, and Lily wants to be protected. She is not like you, dearest, and she will do very well with Mr Lomax, who is a sensible man at heart."

"And I shall do very well with Walter," Winnie said with a sigh of pure delight.

"Indeed, you will, since you have the good fortune to marry a man of sense who also loves you to distraction."

Walter entered in time to overhear. "It is true that I love you to distraction," Walter said, lifting her hand and pressing a long kiss on it. "As for sense, however, I cannot in all conscience make any claim in that direction. A sensible man would have recognised your worth long ago. A sensible man would never have betrothed himself to Bea Franklyn when he could have had you. A sensible man would never have believed malicious tittle-tattle about you, or repeated it. I have been abominably slow to come to my senses, my love."

"Better late than never," she said.

"True. I had hoped to whisk you into the village to see about the banns, but Maynard has hinted that a celebration may be in the offing. Tomorrow, however, no matter what, and then we may be married a month from now, if that would suit you."

"That would suit me very well," Winnie said, smiling up at him. Then, unaccountably, tears spilled down her cheeks.

"Darling, whatever is the matter?" he said, enfolding her in his strong arms. "What have I done this time?"

"We are going to be married," she whispered through her tears.

"Is that a weeping matter?"

"Walter, I have waited so long for this... for you... and now all my impossible dreams are coming true. It is so hard to believe."

He hugged her tight, and for once he had no words to answer her.

Epilogue

The carriage splashed to a halt, as Winnie peered out of the window at the imposing building towering above her.

"Here we are — Grafton Street," Walter said cheerfully.

"Very grand," Uncle Alfred said, with an approving nod. "I shall enjoy staying here, I believe. Oh look, they are expecting us."

As Winnie watched, the front door opened and servants in the livery of the Earl of Rennington emerged, two to attend to the luggage, one to open their door and let down the steps and a fourth to hold an umbrella over them, although the rain had all but stopped. Behind them, the stately figure of the butler, and behind him, a familiar tall Negro. And behind *him*, a small, rather plump and not at all stately person, tearing down the steps at an alarming rate.

"Aunt Sofia!" Winnie cried. "How lovely, but what are you doing here?"

"Getting everything ready for you, of course, with the help of the indispensable Percival. The luggage, Percival."

The Negro nodded and went to the following carriage, where Martha and the valets were descending.

"Well, now, Winnie dear, let me look at you. Oh yes, marriage agrees with you. Such a bloom on those cheeks! Walter, you look well, too. And Alfred — ha! You look the same as ever, you old rogue. Come inside, out of this damp weather."

Aunt Sofia, it transpired, had spent three days at the Grafton Street house with Percival, arranging everything to her satisfaction. Most of the principal rooms were still under holland covers, but she had ordered one of the drawing rooms, the dining room and a small parlour uncovered, the latter to be used for breakfast.

"There is no one else in residence at the moment, for everyone is still in the country. Alfred, Mrs Mawbey will take you to your rooms. I reserve the right to show Mr and Mrs Atherton to their apartment myself. Lord, how charming that sounds! Mrs Atherton! This way... yes, we are going up the other staircase. But how is Lily? Is she getting nervous? The wedding is only a month away now, is it not?"

"I cannot tell you, for she and Mama have gone to Wallingham Manor to inspect it."

"Goodness! That was a sudden start. You wanted to do that, I know, but I did not think Lily one to care much about furnishings and so forth."

"It is not so much the furnishings, but it troubled Mama that Lily had never met Mr Lomax's mother. Since she is to play such a major part in their lives, she felt it was as well to get matters on a proper footing, so to speak."

"So when you say they have gone to inspect the Manor, you mean they are to inspect Mrs Lomax Senior."

Winnie laughed. "Something like that. They will only stay a week, but I think it will be good for Lily to see what she is taking on. Aunt, surely we have walked the length of the street by now."

"This house is enormous, is it not? But we are here at last. This is your apartment."

She threw open a door and ushered them into another world. Gone were the pale colours and delicate modern furnishings. Instead, they were back in the era of the Jacobeans, with dark wood panelling on the walls, ornately plastered ceilings and heavy oak furniture.

"I had no idea this place existed," Walter said. "Is this where the legendary Great-uncle Arbuthnot lived?"

"Was that his name?" Aunt Sofia said. "A very ancient gentleman, I was told, who moved here from a medieval manor house, and brought all the furniture with him, even the panelling. He shut himself away in here and never came out until he was carried out in his coffin. It has been untouched for years, and only used when the house is full to the rafters, but the countess said you may do as you please with it... new furniture, redecorate, whatever you want."

"The countess?" Walter said, startled. "My mother?"

"Yes. It was all her idea — she wrote to me, you know, and suggested I see that everything was made ready for you. I should never have dared otherwise. She thought this apartment would suit you, but I am not sure. It is so... old-fashioned. It will take a lot of work to improve it, but the countess said the earl would foot the bill."

Walter laughed. "He said the same thing. It will be a fine project for the two of you. So what do we have here? How many rooms?"

"Four — a drawing room, a small parlour which makes a very cosy dining room if you want to be private, a bedroom with dressing room, and something that was a book room, but I have converted it to a second dressing room, and it could be another bedroom if one of you gets crotchety. Great-uncle Arbuthnot was a single gentleman, I presume, and had no need for more than one bed."

"Nor have we," Winnie said, blushing.

"Well, you are both good-natured, so perhaps you will never need it, but Edmund and I married at an age when we were both set in our ways, and a bed in the dressing room has kept us from murdering each other more than once. There is a vast nursery on the top floor, when the time comes that you need it. Ah, yes, the service stairs are tucked away behind that panel there. Thank you, Percival, just put the tray on the table. Tea, if you want it, some cakes and suchlike. Walter, there are decanters in that sideboard there. Dinner at six. Shall I order baths for you, at five, say?"

"That would be wonderful," Winnie said.

"Very well. Then I shall leave you to rest and settle in and... well, make yourselves at home. Since you very kindly invited us to dine with you tonight, Edmund and I will see you later."

With a quick kiss for Winnie, and a nod to Walter, she was gone.

'*Make yourselves at home*'... how strange that was. A proper home of their own! After five days in the guest bedroom at Birchall House, and three days of travelling, they had finally come home. Hand in hand, they walked from room to room, saying little, merely looking. The arrival of their luggage, together with Martha and Rashleigh, drove them back to the drawing room.

"Tea?" Walter said.

"I would prefer wine... or Madeira."

Walter poured, but then set both glasses down and scooped her into his arms. "Well, Mouse, what do you think of our new home? It is a trifle… dark, is it not?"

"It is in the old style, that is all. It reminds me a little of Aunt Minna's house in York. They have some rooms with panelled walls and heavy furniture, the sort that needs four hefty men to shift. I do not dislike it. With a few colourful carpets and some paintings on the walls, it will be charming. Do you dislike it so much?"

"I cannot dislike any place that has you in it, Mouse." He hugged her tight as he spoke, and his smile was so warm that she blushed.

"Why do you call me Mouse?"

"Oh… I beg your pardon. You dislike it, I had forgot."

"I do not like to be compared to a rodent, Walter. Something small and insignificant."

"Oh… is that what you thought? But I did not mean it that way at all. Eustace and I were up a tree one day, when you came rushing past below us. We were not supposed to be there, so we kept quiet and just watched you as you went by, scurrying along, head down, off on some important business or other. You must have been… about twelve or so, for your hair was still down, and you wore a drab gown and that dreadful old cloak… all brown, from head to toe, but your hair was so shiny… glossy… I cannot describe it, but from where we sat, you looked just like a mouse following a trail, knowing exactly where you were going. You always knew where you were going, Winnie, and you have no idea how I envied you that certainty… of having a direction… you always seemed so sure of what you were doing. You were in control of your life, whereas I… I just drifted, allowing other people to direct my actions. Even my betrothal… I let Bea Franklyn push me around. The first time in my life I ever acted from my own wishes was when I tried to deter Lomax from marrying you, and even though I told myself I was acting in your best interests, it was really because I wanted you for myself. I just had not quite realised it then."

"A mouse who knows where she is going... that is not so bad," Winnie said.

"I always thought of it as an endearment... a term of affection," he said.

A knock on the door made them jump apart as Percival's head appeared.

"Is there anything else you require just now, madam? Sir?"

"No, no. We have everything we need," Walter said.

"Then I'll be off," he said.

The door closed behind him, and instantly Walter pulled her back into his embrace. "Ah, Mouse! This is where you belong."

She stretched up to kiss him, but he pulled back a little.

"Not yet. There is something I must say to you, something important that I want to get right."

"Could it wait until we will not be interrupted?" she said. "At bedtime, perhaps?"

"But I am liable to be distracted, then."

"I had noticed. In fact, I get distracted myself."

He chuckled. "I had noticed that. We are both easily distracted. So let me say this now, once and for all. Darling Winnie, I love you so much I can barely breathe when you are with me. I think, if I am being totally honest, that I have always loved you... at least, ever since I saw my lovely Mouse scurry past me for the first time, but I was too stupid to recognise it. Can you ever forgive me for making you wait and for making you *suffer* while I was betrothed to Bea? I cannot imagine what you must have thought of me. And now that I have you, I am terrified — absolutely terrified — of making a mess of things. The worst moment of my life was when I made you cry. I could not bear it if that ever happens again, and I am stupid enough that it might happen. Please, my dearest darling, please will you tell me if I do the least thing to make you unhappy? Or if you think I might? Help me, Winnie, because I want our marriage to be perfect."

"Oh, Walter, nothing is ever perfect. Every one of us is human and fallible and liable to make mistakes. You will and so will I, but we will get past that. So long as we talk to each other... as long as we are *honest* with each other, everything else will fall into place. Stop worrying! We are together, we have a roof over our heads and food to eat and enough money to live on without too many economies, and most of all, we have each other, and our love. I love you, Walter Atherton, imperfect as you are, and I always will. Now, may I kiss you? Because I cannot stay on tiptoe forever, and I should like some reward for the discomfort involved."

"I have a better idea," he said, scooping her off her feet and into his arms so suddenly that she gave a little squeal of surprise.

"Oh yes, much better," she murmured, realising her face was now most conveniently placed next to his. His lips hovered over hers—

The door burst open, and a footman appeared. "You called, madam?"

Winnie blushed scarlet to be caught in such a position, but Walter did not flinch.

"No one called. Your services are not required."

"Very good, sir," he said imperturbably, bowed and withdrew in good order.

Winnie buried her scarlet face in Walter's shoulder, but he said calmly, "That will teach the fellow to walk in on two people only recently married. Now where were we? Ah, yes, I recall."

A silence fell in the room. After several minutes, finding the activity excessively pleasant, they retreated to a comfortable chair beside the fire, of a size suitable to accommodate a large gentleman with a lady draped across his lap, and there they stayed in perfect contentment until the dressing bell sounded.

THE END

The next book in the series is *Determination*, wherein Miss Beatrice Franklyn is determined to betroth herself to Mr Bertram Atherton, while he is equally determined that she shall not. You can read a sneak preview after the acknowledgements. For more information, go to my website at https://marykingswood.co.uk

Thanks for reading!

If you have enjoyed reading this book, please consider writing a short review on Amazon. You can find out the latest news and sign up for the mailing list at my website at https://marykingswood.co.uk.

A note on historical accuracy: I have endeavoured to stay true to the spirit of Regency times, and have avoided taking too many liberties or imposing modern sensibilities on my characters. The book is not one of historical record, but I've tried to make it reasonably accurate. However, I'm not perfect! If you spot a historical error, I'd very much appreciate knowing about it so that I can correct it and learn from it. Thank you!

Isn't that what-his-name? Occasionally characters from an earlier series pop up, or are mentioned. Lady Esther Franklyn's father, the Duke of Camberley, approved the marriage of his daughter, the Lady Grace Bucknell, to George Skelton, the Earl of Brackenwood's heir, in *The Governess.* Lady Esther's brother, the Marquess of Ramsey, had a tumultuous romance in *The Betrothed*. Lady Harbottle, in *The Widow*, and the Duchess of Orrisdale, in *The Duke,* were also Bucknells before their marriages.

About the series:

Book 0: The Chaplain: a man adrift, dreaming of a home (a novella, free to mailing list subscribers).

Book 1: Disinheritance: a man freed, looking for a new purpose in life

Book 2: Determination: a man pursued, forced to outwit his adversary

Book 3: Anger: a woman alone, trying to choose a different path in life

Book 4: Secrecy: a woman neglected, scheming to secure her own happiness

Book 5: Loyalty: a man of dreams, torn between the past and the future

Book 6: Ambition: a woman thwarted, unswervingly set on making a brilliant debut in society

Any questions about the series? Email me at mary@marykingswood.co.uk - I'd love to hear from you!

About the author

I write traditional Regency romances under the pen name Mary Kingswood, and epic fantasy as Pauline M Ross. I live in the beautiful Highlands of Scotland with my husband. I like chocolate, whisky, my Kindle, massed pipe bands, long leisurely lunches, chocolate, going places in my campervan, eating pizza in Italy, summer nights that never get dark, wood fires in winter, chocolate, the view from the study window looking out over the Moray Firth and the Black Isle to the mountains beyond. And chocolate. I dislike driving on motorways, cooking, shopping, hospitals.

Acknowledgements

Thanks go to:

Allison Lane, whose course on English Architecture inspired me.

Shayne Rutherford of Darkmoon Graphics for the cover design.

My beta readers: Caroline Allenby, Carmel Beattie, Penny Bennett, Charles Crouter, Kelly Darpinian, Julie Desbrus, Sharon Flaherty, Melissa Forsythe, Erica Hague, Donna Sue Holly, Corinne Lehmann, Kathryn Marsh, Leann McKinley, Tina Miles, Pat Oen, Wanda Olson, Rosemary Paton, Kristen Pinto-Coelho, Melanie Savage, Jennifer Schellenberg, Helen Schneble, Laura Sporcic, Wendy Stubbs, Carol Sturz, Jeanne Thomas, A Usami

Last, but definitely not least, my first reader: Amy Ross.

Sneak preview: Determination: Chapter 1: A Meeting At Corland Castle

WESTWICK HEIGHTS: JUNE

'Ast ego, quae divom incedo regina, Iovisque et soror et coniunx, una cum gente tot annos bella gero! Et quisquam numen Iunonis adoret praeterea, aut supplex aris imponet honorem?'

The clock struck four. Mr Bertram Atherton emerged, blinking, from Carthage, and laid aside his book. It was time for his glass of Canary. He rose and crossed to the sideboard where resided the decanters, poured himself a modest amount, then took his customary tour of the library. *His* library, as he liked to think of it. Not literally, not yet, but one day all of

Westwick Heights would be his, and since no one else in the family was in the least bookish, the library had become his particular domain. There was something peculiarly satisfying about the shelves filled with volumes, the unique smell of musty paper and ancient leather bindings, and the exhilarating possibilities to be found within them. If ever he became crotchety or unsettled in any way, the library could always restore his equanimity.

With a sigh of pure pleasure, he settled back into his chair and set his glass down on a side table. Adjusting his spectacles more firmly on his nose, he picked up his book.

'Talia flammato secum dea corde volutans nimborum in patriam, loca feta furentibus austris, Aeoliam venit. Hic vasto rex Aeolus antro luctantes ventos ...'

And he was gone, lost in a world of long ago, the prosaic nineteenth century vanished in a burst of poetic Latin. There was nothing like Virgil to weave a magical tale. For an unknown length of time he was immersed, quite unaware of his surroundings.

A loud cough drew Bertram back into the modern world. "Oh... what is it, Carter?"

"Beg pardon for disturbing you, sir, but this has just arrived from Corland... from his lordship."

Bertram glanced at the letter on the salver. "It is addressed to my father."

"Yes, sir, but the master is not in his study, not in the house at all, and the groom who brought this insisted it was very urgent."

"Is an answer expected?"

"No, sir. The groom has already left, but it is very important, he was quite clear about that."

Bertram frowned, considering. "I think my father might be in the stables. Greatheart was heated in one fetlock yesterday, and Whyte was going to apply a poultice. Let me see if I can find him."

"Thank you, sir. I should be most grateful, sir. The groom was most insistent."

Bertram carefully marked his place in *The Aeneid*, took the letter and set off for the stables. It was just like his father to disappear there merely because one of the horses had a minor injury. To Bertram's mind, that was the purpose of grooms, to see to such matters, but to his father, every horse was treated as if it were a precious child, to be cosseted and fussed over. No, that was not even an appropriate comparison, for he had always been relaxed about his children's well-being. Bertram and his brother Lucas had had the freedom to do very much as they pleased, and although Mother flew into a panic at the least sniffle or sign of fever, no one minded their scrapes and tumbles and the mischief that all boys get into. Mother's health and Father's horses — these were the real causes of alarm at Westwick Heights.

As he had expected, his father was in the stables, together with Morton, the head groom, and Whyte, the youngest of the grooms. Whyte had grown up in the village smithy and farriery, so he had lived his whole life with horses and had a great skill, even though Morton still distrusted anyone so young. The three of them were leaning over the rail of Greatheart's stall, deep in discussion, looking up only when Bertram was almost within touching distance.

"Ah, Bertram," his father said, his expression vaguely puzzled. "Going somewhere?"

"Shall I saddle Catullus, sir?" Whyte said.

"No, I came in search of you, Father, not a horse. There is an urgent note for you from the castle."

"Urgent?" The frown deepened as he took the letter, turning it over and over in his hands, but he nodded, gave his final instructions to the grooms and followed Bertram out of the stables.

"Any idea what this is about?" he said as they walked back to the house.

"None, sir. The groom who brought it was most insistent that it is a matter of great importance."

"We had better know the worst at once, then."

They were close to the small summer house, so they went inside and sat. While his father broke the seal and read the letter, Bertram admired, as he always did, the fine view of the house. Westwick Heights was not a large building, but it was elegantly constructed from the local honey-coloured stone, and looked as if it had grown naturally on the small eminence which gave it its name. From where he sat, he could see down the hill to the village of Birchall, and the chimneys of the estate on the far side, half hidden by sheltering trees. If he craned his neck, he could see the road meandering down to the town of Helmsley. Bertram spent most of his life mentally travelling the Ancient World in Latin, or occasionally Greek, but if he had to be in the modern world, this was where he would always choose.

"What do you make of that?" his father said, passing him the letter.

'To Mr George Atherton, Westwick Heights, North Riding. George, A family matter has arisen which must be addressed. Pray be at the castle tomorrow at noon, and bring Jane and Bertram with you. This is very important, so do not fail me and do not be late! Rennington.'

"A family matter? Involving us?"

"Yes, it is odd, is it not? Yet my brother would not write in such terms unless it were so. He is not in the least fanciful. What do you think it can be about?"

"Surely it must be regarding Nicholson. It is three weeks since he was murdered, so perhaps the villain has been caught."

Bertram hardly liked to think about the murder. He read about death and war and unspeakable horrors every day, but they were safely in the past, distanced from real life by thousands of years, and most of what he read was mere fanciful mythology, not even real. It was another matter entirely when a man one had known well, an uncle by marriage, died by violence. Arthur Nicholson had been chaplain to the Earl of Rennington for many years, and was married to the earl's sister, Lady Alice — a genial, inoffensive man, Bertram would have said. Yet someone had taken an axe to the room where he slept and hacked him to death. It was too dreadful for words.

His father clicked his tongue. "But how can that affect the family... or us? Unless... surely it cannot be one of the family? No, that would be unthinkable. It cannot be anything to do with the murder."

"Well, scandal, perhaps? Money troubles? The castle is about to fall down and they all want to come and live here?"

His father laughed. "You are right, of course. It is futile to speculate. Most likely it is some legal matter. He went haring off to York last week, remember, so perhaps he saw the lawyers. Whatever it is, we shall learn of it soon enough. Let us go and tell your mother."

Futile as it might be to speculate, nevertheless that was all the family did for the rest of the day. First his parents invaded Bertram's library, then his brother Lucas, and then his sisters drifted in. It needed only his little brother Philip to arrive from the nursery, and there would be a veritable party in progress.

By the time they assembled in the drawing room before dinner, they each had their favoured theory. Lucas had settled on financial woes — Lord Rennington was in the basket and wanted their father's fortune to bail him out. Julia, with all the wisdom of her twenty years, thought it was some fresh scandal involving their cousin, the earl's heir.

"Birtwell has got himself into some mess or other, you may be sure. A girl, most likely, and Uncle Rennington is looking to us to help him patch it up. Or Bertram, perhaps."

"Nonsense," their father said tersely. "Birtwell has never been one to get into *that* sort of mess."

"George, please," Mother said. "This is hardly a fit topic of conversation in front of the girls."

"Julia started it," Lucas said.

"And she should not have done," Mother said, lips pursed. "Most unladylike. Depend upon it, this is to do with the Dowager Countess. She must be on her deathbed at last, and how she has lasted as long as she has is more than I can fathom."

"That would merely be a letter to inform us of her death, not this odd summons," Father said.

Penelope, who at sixteen thought everything related to marriage and romance, said, "Perhaps the earl wishes to arrange a match for Bertram."

"Ooh, good idea," Julia said. "But with whom? Not Olivia!"

The three girls collapsed in giggles.

"She will make a great match," Mother said. "An earl's daughter with a good dowry and as pretty a face as hers will marry into the nobility, you may be sure. She will certainly not marry her own cousin."

"Tess Nicholson, then," Penelope said. "Her father left her a fortune, so she is quite a catch now."

"She will be in mourning for her father for quite some time," Mother said. "Really, girls, you are too fanciful by half."

"We shall find out what this is all about soon enough," Father said.

***

The carriage was ordered in plenty of time, for it would never do to be late for such a meeting. Besides, Bertram and his parents were agog with curiosity by the time they arrived at Corland Castle, the principal seat of the Earl of Rennington. The castle was a monstrously ugly building, in Bertram's view, for although it was newly built, it was very much in the heavy style of the Normans, with four corner towers linked by uncompromisingly solid façades. The interior was austere, and festooned with collections of swords, pikes, maces and a multitude of other sharp, malevolent objects whose sole function was to kill in as unpleasant a manner as human ingenuity could contrive. The whole place made Bertram heartily glad he was born in a less warlike and more enlightened age. He liked his violence strictly between the pages of a book.

Simpson and Wellum, the butler and under-butler, greeted them in the echoing entrance hall, its stone floor and marble statuary chilling the air, despite the summer heat outside.

"Good day, sir, madam. Good day, sir. You are in excellent time."

"What is this all about, Simpson?" Father said, as Wellum collected hats and gloves and canes.

"I couldn't say, sir. His lordship has not taken me into his confidence. Lord Birtwell is already in the study with Lord Rennington, and the others are gathering in the library."

"The others? Who else is summoned?"

"Lady Rennington, the Lady Alice Nicholson and Miss Nicholson, Mr Kent and the Lady Olivia are already here. Mr Eustace has not yet arrived."

"That boy is always late," Father muttered.

Simpson showed them into the library, where the door to the earl's study was resolutely closed.

Mother went at once to Aunt Alice, who sat beside the countess, her back rigidly straight.

"How are you, dear?" Mother said, in the special voice she reserved for the sick or newly bereaved. "Bearing up bravely, I am sure. I hope you are taking a little beef tea every day. It is just the thing to stop you falling into a melancholy."

As they talked, Bertram was struck by Lady Rennington's face. His aunt was normally the most imperturbable person, but today her face was grey. That was a worry. This was serious, then.

Bertram and his father gravitated to the other side of the room, where Bertram's cousins, Kent and Olivia, sat. Kent was a slender, dark-haired young man of twenty-two with a perpetually cheerful countenance.

"Uncle George! Bertram! How are you? Is this not amusing of Father to summon us in this melodramatic way? Do you think someone else has been murdered? Or have the rats got into the grain stores again?"

"Your father is far too generous a man to trifle with us for rats, Kent," Bertram's father said. "There must be something major afoot. Olivia? Are you well, dear?"

Olivia was as dark as Kent, but had a more rounded figure which suited her striking beauty admirably. She was given to bursts of histrionics, however, and although she was nothing like so bad as Izzy, she was still trying company and Bertram avoided her as much as possible.

Today she had decided to be lachrymose, a handkerchief pressed to her face. "How can I be well, Uncle, with this... this *thing* hanging over me?"

"What thing is that?" he said kindly.

"Whatever it is Papa wishes to tell us. It is bound to be horrid, and if it means that my come-out has to be put off *again*, well... life will be insupportable. I want to be *out,* Uncle."

"You are already out, are you not? You attend the assemblies at York and Harrogate and —"

"That is not *out!*" she said scornfully. "Out is Almack's and being presented at court and everyone knowing who one is."

"We are called in," Kent said, nodding towards the door of the study, which now stood open.

Mother led Lady Alice in, then Father and Kent. Bertram hung back, waiting for Tess, the daughter of Lady Alice and the murdered chaplain. She was a dark, slight creature, always hiding in shadowy corners as if she did not want to be observed, but Bertram could not help feeling sorry for the girl.

"How are you, cousin?" he said gently.

"Quite well, thank you," she said in her soft voice, as if surprised he had asked. Without another word, she followed the others into the room.

The study was crowded, for it was not a large room, being situated in one of the circular tower rooms that sat at each corner of the castle. Chairs were found for the ladies and for a few minutes, as they settled themselves, all seemed perfectly normal. Just another family meeting. Only the grey faces of the earl and countess suggested something unusual. And had the countess been crying? That was a bad sign.

Bertram looked at his cousin Walter, Lord Birtwell, the heir to the earldom, and then he knew something terrible was afoot. Walter looked dazed... shocked, as if he had suffered a great loss. It must surely be another death, for what else could grieve the family so? Izzy, perhaps, or Josie. One of the Lochmaben family, maybe. Or something of import to the nation

— the King or Queen? The Prince of Wales? An invasion by the upstart Corsican?

"No Eustace, I see," Kent said, laughing. "I suppose he has lost his way on the ride over here." His light-heartedness grated on Bertram's nerves. How could he jest at a time like this?

"It is barely twelve miles, and he makes the journey often enough that he can scarcely lose his way," Olivia said. "How silly you are, Kent."

"Eustace has no sense of direction," Kent said, grinning. "He can lose his way in his own house."

But the countess silenced them. "Charles, must we wait for him? Can we not just get this over with?"

The earl would not start without Eustace, however, so they waited until, a full twenty minutes after the designated hour, Eustace strolled in.

"Well, whatever happened here?" he said. "Has someone else died?"

"How can we know?" Olivia said. "We have been waiting for you to arrive. Why are you always late, Eustace?"

"He is here now," the earl said tersely. "It is immaterial whether he is early or late, for the situation will not change, no matter how long we wait."

"For heaven's sake, Papa! Tell us what has happened," Olivia cried.

They turned to him in trepidation, even Kent reduced to solemnity for the moment.

"Something terrible has occurred... has been discovered. Nicholson..." He took a deep breath, then rushed on. "Nicholson was never ordained as a clergyman, so the marriages he conducted are not valid. The countess and I are not legally married, and all our children are illegitimate. Birtwell... Walter cannot inherit. None of my sons can inherit. George, you are my heir now, and Bertram after you."

Bertram felt as if someone had punched him in the stomach. Birtwell disinherited? The title, the estates... *everything*, passing to his own father, and then to him? He would be the Earl of Rennington one day!

And in that moment, his placid future of books and ancient kingdoms and long-dead warriors vanished like smoke. Even his home, lovely West-wick, would be lost to him, and he would have to live in this mausoleum of a castle. His life would be filled with stewards and attorneys and land management and government bills and the wretched Season every year, he would have to marry suitably and there would be no peace to be found anywhere.

Nothing would ever be the same again.

END OF SAMPLE CHAPTER of *Determination*; for more information or to buy, go to my website at https://marykingswood.co.uk

Printed in Great Britain
by Amazon

46889807R00239